Plague of Locusts

Vast Array, #1

Daniel G. Keohane

Other Road Press
www.otherroadpress.com

Plague of Locusts

ISBN: 978-0-9837329-7-6

Published in February 2022
by Other Road Press, Princeton MA
www.otherroadpress.com

Cover Design by the author

Printed in the United States of America

For **Andrew,**
Who knew what was in the ship before I did

And In Loving Memory of
Mark Lowell
You were here when this world was formed
And when others fell apart

Other Books by
Daniel G. Keohane

Margaret's Ark

Solomon's Grave

Plague of Darkness

Plague of Locusts

Daniel G. Keohane

Part One

The Serpent

Plague of Locusts

1 – Gendrick, 2J System, Third Planet

Father Gendrick Hellerton stood on the balcony and stared across the scrubby plain, watching the sun drop behind the western mountains. His thick black hair, wired with strands of early gray, curled against the back of his robes. The sky darkened from greenish blue to a rich burgundy, then to violet, slowly moving towards black. He watched in silence. Doneele had suggested he step outside, to witness his first Toojay sunset and its spectacular light show. He could have watched from the safety of the Union common room, but she told him to stand just beyond the open doorway. He wasn't disappointed.

The horizon exploded in flash-lightening jags of red and yellow, curling and uncurling in the distance like the auroras of Earth, a display meant only for him, welcoming the young priest to this world floating an unknowable distance from what had once been home. The lights of the auroras swayed like native dancers lost in a rhythm and language he suddenly yearned to understand. Gendrick thought there must be a pattern, a story told in the spoken flashes of color as they faded lower, then lower still as if the dancers were bowing to their audience. He could not move, nor did he want to, feeling his long black robes drift forward in the draft of warmer air racing outside from the

Union room behind him, merging with the cooling night beyond the railing. His hands remained buried in deep pockets, but he did not feel them, did not *want* to feel them, did not want to do anything but watch the lights dance farther and farther away, performing their silent song for others, perhaps, at other scientific outposts beyond the mountains. Were they as rapt as he in this moment with –

The robes tightened against his body. The astounding sky disappeared, replaced by the artificial glare of the Union's overhead lights. He stumbled back, only now noticing the screaming alarm but unconcerned by its meaning. Someone's arms curled around him as he fell away from the balcony doors. The arms did not have strength to hold him. Gendrick rolled sideways and landed face-first on the carpet. One of his hands splayed in front of him against the worn fabric. The other remained trapped in the robe's pocket.

The alarm abruptly cut off. Gendrick rolled over in time to see the reinforced glass doors slam shut. Outside was lost against the room's reflection in the glass.

"You all right?"

He looked up. Mother Doneele stood above him, her blue robes twisted around her thin frame. Her voice was muffled by a breathing filter, gray hair poking wildly from the straps.

Gendrick thought again about the colors, the dance on the horizon and felt a momentary pang of loss. Until he realized what he'd done.

"I don't ... " he whispered, looking at the doors. "How long was I standing out there?"

A small *ping!* sounded, and Doneele lifted the mask from her face. She smiled. "Long enough, I hope. A half hour, give or take." She was slightly out of breath from the exertion of pulling him inside. He thought there was a tone of humor in her voice.

A half hour? That wasn't possible. He slowly got to his feet, accepting the woman's proffered hand. Emergency doors on either side of the common room were now sliding open. How much danger had he been in, standing outside at dusk. What had he been thinking?

What had *she* been thinking?

The outside motion light snapped on, illuminating the balcony.

A shiny, black nightmare rose up from the spot where he'd been standing a moment earlier. Its wasp-like face turned clockwise as if sniffing the air and stared at him through the glass. Its eyes were more human than insect, forward-facing with large black pupils. They peered at him through armored slits. Gendrick could barely breathe. This was the first living Locust he'd seen in person. Even with the triple-thick conductive glass between them, he was frightened. Nearly three meters long from triangular face to the point of its scorpion tail, it filled half of the balcony. It danced-skittered in a frenzied, random pattern, tail rising and lowering and tapping against the tiled floor. The feet were pointed, segmented into tridents. The sound through the wall speakers was a constant, furious tapping and scraping.

Doneele stepped forward and laid a hand on Gendrick's shoulder. "Whatever it's saying, I'm guessing it's not *welcome to Toojay.*"

The Locust stopped its dance with a suddenness that made Gendrick step back. Beside him, the older priest did not move, but let her hand drop. The lower half of the monster's face split into four distinct mandibles. From the speakers on either side of the door it breathed a low, hollow hiss.

"It's a bit upset right now," she said. Doneele's calm

voice both relaxed him and furthered his embarrassment. Her attitude was wrong, considering that one of these monsters had killed her husband less than a year ago. "They see our compounds as they approach and sometimes one veers off, hoping for an easy kill." *Definitely not right*, he decided, but at least this time she did not smile. "They remember, or maybe heard stories from the others. Either way food is scarce and he was hoping . . . well, just hoping."

The Locust's face closed with an audible click, then it charged the door. Doneele stepped back reflexively. When it hit the glass the face reopened with a scream as the voltage coating the outer surface poured over its shell. The sound sent gooseflesh along Gendrick's back. Angry, perhaps frightened, almost like a human's but with a raw, scraping undertone. The massive, segmented body twisted, the cry reverting in spasms to the original hiss, though now in staccato gasps. Four long dragonfly wings unrolled like ferns from its back, blurred, then the creature was gone.

Gendrick stared through the door, willing his pulse to slow, watching the empty balcony. Two of the four chairs had been tipped on their sides. When the motion light clicked off, he stared at his own reflection, realizing the creature he *now* saw was the alien in this place. And the prey.

Doneele's hand returned to his shoulder. Gendrick twitched in surprise. She either didn't notice or ignored it.

"He'll be hard-pressed to catch up to the swarm in time to get much more than leavings at this point – if they manage to catch anything. I don't know how the swarm survives at its size with so little food."

Gendrick swallowed. "He?"

She held a sheet of Ep in front of him. The electronic paper showed a partially blurred image of a Locust in flight. Alongside, in a separate window, a series of categorized descriptions. The top-most identifier was in red. Doneele said, "Loki, god of mischief. We haven't managed to tag many of them, about sixteen in total, but he's one." She shrugged, folded the paper and returned it to an inner pocket of her robe. "Seems only the tagged ones wander close enough for System to register these days. The others stay clear. I use 'he' only because of the name they gave him. Could be a 'she' or some other gender yet to be learned."

Gendrick turned away from his reflection and faced the large common room, hands returning to his pockets. A small wooden cross played between the fingers of his right hand. "Is that significant? That only the tagged come near the compound?"

Doneele made a small noise which could have meant *maybe* or *what a stupid question*. They wandered to the far end of the room where she lifted the two mugs they'd put down before going to the doors. Gendrick took a sip. Cold now.

"Our xenologist, you'll meet her soon enough, treats everything as significant. These creatures learn. Maybe they decided tagged ones won't get re-tagged. Maybe they've appointed Loki as an ambassador."

An ambassador which would have eaten me if given the chance, Gendrick thought. It almost *had*. How could this woman have let him stay exposed for so long? Maybe she'd adjusted to the death of her husband better than the church leaders realized. In any case, Gendrick's arrival as her replacement meant she'd be going home soon. Maybe that was all she needed, that her time here was almost done.

He kept his back towards the outside doors. Doneele took a sip from her own mug – a year's worth of grounds, among other more urgent supplies, had accompanied him on the trip from his stopover at Eden. A lot of coffee would be drunk in the next few days. Cold or not, she seemed to relish it.

She raised the mug, clinked it lightly against his.

"Welcome to Toojay," she whispered.

2 – Peyton Kay, 3rd Jump Hole / 2J-Side

She enjoyed the waning hours of second shift, especially times like this when she woke too early and couldn't fall back to sleep. The *Washington*'s ring was big enough that privacy for its small crew was never an issue, but not like this. Aside from the two-person skeleton crew on duty, everyone else was asleep. Knowing this, Peyton Kay's solitude seemed more real, less artificial than everything else on the exploration vessel.

She hovered in the center of the narrow room, enjoying the feel of her body in zero-g as all around the curved, cushioned walls of the Hub rolled with the spine's perpetual rotation, giving the outer ring its gravity. She floated, no more free than an animal in a zoo, her world defined by the size of the ship's hull. Being here alone, in the quiet, offered her a chance to pretend. Crew did whatever it could to ignore the fact that the eternal vacuum of space waited outside.

Peyton stared out the spine's front window. Like everything else, it was in constant rotation, though less obvious since the window was round. What she saw outside was an enhanced image, given the glass was one and a half meters thick. *Everything* fore-facing was reinforced in the event the shielding failed, or something unexpected wandered towards them which they were not equipped to repel.

The stars were clear and bright, even the ones directly beside the massive gas giant floating just to port. No air in space to diffuse the planet's constant glow. Stars wedged between stars, piled on top of stars. Unlike the reality of massive distances between them, *out there* looked very crowded. An illusion, much like the illusion that there was nothing but empty, dark matter twelve and a half degrees from the starboard edge of the window.

She twisted into a seated position and managed to stop most of her momentum with the practiced swing of both arms. "System," she said aloud, "enhance external view, delineate Hole borders."

The view into space flashed with lines, adjusting as the onboard AI computer located the Hole in relation to Pey's physical position. A white circle settled over the edges of – nothing. Nothing visible, at least. The Hole *was* there, the newly discovered wormhole designated 3JH, or Third Jump Hole. It led to the next unexplored system and the reason the *Washington* was out here in the first place. The ship's official designation was ISO-SEV-3421, though every acting Captain was allowed to use a more colloquial name for the duration of his or her command. It was usually something personal, and often easier to remember. Ken Burlov had chosen the *Washington* for no other reason than it sounded stately. Most of the crew assumed it was also the first word that popped into his head, since Ken didn't usually bother wasting brain matter on anything not directly related to the mission.

The *Abad* (ISO-SEV-1620) lurked somewhere out there as well, supposedly on the opposite side of the Jupiter-like planet to see if the newest Law of Nature might have an exception, two Holes orbiting the system's gas giant instead of only one. Pey and the others noticed small probes from the *Abad* flitting past from time to time, zipping around the apex of the planet, always coming from different locations, keeping an eye on them. They had every right to snoop, as much as Pey's people had the right of first exploration, being the ones who located the Hole.

"Thank you, System," she said softly. "Normal view again."

The circle disappeared.

She floated, hungry but not wanting to head down for breakfast yet, wanting to enjoy the view one last time before everything changed. Tomorrow they would take a shuttle pod into the area of space previously demarcated by the white circle. Enough probes had come and gone that the Interplanetary Science Office's Command personnel had given the *Go* for the first human Jump. Peyton, Benny Solomon and Cannon White would become the first to "step," as it were, into the 3J, or *Third Jump*, system. Like the first two Holes, they would emerge at the orbital midpoint between the second and third planets. And, as they all expected, the third planet would be relatively Earth-like and eventually the next human outpost. Peyton and Crew would enter the history books, even if as nothing more than a footnote.

That had been the official plan. Being the first to find the Hole gave certain allowances for information suppression, provided ISO Command gave the OK. In this instance they did. Along with right of first exploration came its implied sister: right of first contact.

Unknown to all save the *Washington* crew and select individuals back on Eden, the probes found something unexpected beyond the Hole. Sitting less than five thousand kilometers from the exit point was a massive, oblong object three times the size of the *Washington*. After numerous photos and scans, the only conclusion anyone could agree on was that it was a spacecraft. Dark, silent on any known frequency, the ship orbited the Hole like an artificial moon.

3 – From Elisa Kay McDonald's third grade science quiz

November 19, 2193
Yvonne Chase, instructor.

All answers will be limited to 50 words. Please read all questions first. You will not be able to go back and change what you have entered.

Define the following terms:

1J3P – First Jump, Third Planet from the sun. We all call it Eden. This is where we live. The first official colony.

2J3P – Second Jump, Third Planet. Everyone calls it Toojay. Its [*] not a real colony yet. Scientists are still looking at it. It has real nasty bugs [*] called Locusts on it that eat the cows.

[*] *inserted notes:*

-2 points, "Its" is possessive. You meant "it is" hence "it's" would be the correct spelling.

-4 points, Locusts have not yet been categorized as "bugs" and a scientist should never presume without experimentation.

0J3P – I'm not sure how to say zero jump, Mrs. Chase. Can I just say it means Earth? Third planet in the original system.

[*] inserted note (no deduction): that's fine, Elisa, but thank you for asking.

3JH – Third Jump Hole. The new Hole my Auntie Pey discovered! They are going to fly inside today! We're so scared but were [*] also excited!!!!!

[*] inserted notes:
Yes, Ellie, you should be proud. We all are!
-2, you meant "we are" in both instances in your answer, so both should be spelled "we're" not "were" as in "You were typing too quickly on this answer."

Looking at the map in the frame below, which point would be considered 1JH/0JS, and why? – Point C, because it is talking about the first jump hole, but on the Earth side, beside Jupiter. Auntie Pey is at 3JH/2JS because she is still in the 2J system. But not for long!

[*] inserted note (+1 extra credit), for your bubbling and contagious excitement!

4 – Gendrick, 2J3P

It was late. Almost midnight on Toojay, measured by its twenty-nine and a half hour day. Most of the residents in the compound were in bed. Gendrick sat up, waiting for his body to figure out it should be sleeping. His personal Ep was folded open on his lap, the top half serving as screen, bottom as keyboard. He hesitated, staring at the words which equated, after all this time, to nothing more than pen-scratching. Since opening the file he'd typed four sentences and deleted them all.

A small circle appeared then disappeared in the lower corner of the screen. The auto-save. Ironic, he thought. Nothing saved still amounted to nothing. So much was already being written about what was going on, even in fiction. Science fiction was having a boom in light of 3JH's discovery. Writers and artists conjectured what would be on the other side of each Hole. Fodder for the imagination, until the *Washington* passed through its invisible gate and opened up the next Earth-like colony. Then, the race would be on for the next Hole. And the next.

And the next.

Gendrick typed, *Humanity reaching out, farther and faster, thinning, finally able to breathe.*

He liked that. Did not delete it this time.

So much change coming, he continued to write, *so many chances for people to reinvent themselves. Moving farther from broken Mother Earth and its constricted bubble of life. The Church, rather than falter under the continued discovery that their home planet was not the center of the universe, has experienced exponential growth.*

One hole per solar system, so far as anyone has yet to disprove, leading to a configuration much like Earth's system. Where these are located, which galaxy, which universe *for that matter, has grown into a unique scientific field. In each new system, the third planet, approximately the size of Earth, is capable of supporting human life, rest stops on God's Highway – once the various unique bacteria and other microscopic killers have been identified and immunizations developed. These latter speed bumps had been unexpected, since it was assumed any alien microbe could not infect humans, HG Wells' literary solution to his classic invasion story notwithstanding. They could, however, and the discovery that much of Eden was genetically compatible with Earth's species only added to the overall astonishment of its discovery.*

Unlike the Locusts sweeping along the twilight apex of Toojay, however, nothing else on the third planet of the 1J system, Eden, proved much of a challenge to colonization. Much of the wildlife was passive, unaware of the dangers of Man. There were predators, some still being discovered even now on that Utopian planet yet critical for maintaining balance. The planet seems to have been waiting patiently for centuries, or millennia, to be discovered by its eventual residents. As if every planet we uncover beyond the Holes will be copies of Earth and its neighbors, waiting for mankind to evolve enough to find them.

Secret rooms hidden behind false walls.

It felt good to type it all out, though it didn't read nearly as good as he thought it did when it was falling out of his head. Still, Gendrick touched the Save icon before losing his nerve.

Someone had built the Holes. Some*thing*, at least. Tunnels leading to the same relative spot inside the orbit of the next habitable world, using the gravitational flux of the previous system's largest gas giants and sun to open a wormhole, punching a path through space to the next perfect spot. Arrival near the third planet, departure beside the fifth. And so on . . . .

Had God been the architect of it all?

He typed, *Is God the architect of all that we now see, all that we watch and read every morning on our papers?*

This sentence and the few paragraphs before it were, so far, the entire body of work for which he'd been commissioned. To chronicle the continuing saga of humankind's discovery of *God's Vast Array*, an ongoing work-in-progress chronicling the exploration of the universe along His road. It would be distributed periodically by the Apostolic Christian Church's massive publishing arm. He was not the only author, though the original idea *had* been his. *God's Vast Array.* Gendrick had come up with the title before anything else. It probably had been one of its major selling points.

Two other people, both ordained ministers in the church, were contributing from their own unique perspectives – one from Eden, stationed at the Church's main offices, another on Earth chronicling the perspective of those living day to day on a world still recovering from the after effects of the Final War. Since he'd originated the concept, Gendrick was able to choose his own vantage from which to see the expanse. He chose as far away from Earth as possible.

He had plenty to run away from – the monastery with its restrictive, celibate lifestyle, his heart torn from his chest by the woman he thought would become his wife and for whom he'd eventually left the monastic order. He'd planned to follow the life of a regular married priest in some quiet parish. When things didn't work out that way, he was going to leave the planet one way or another.

The Lord must have decided not to argue the point. Since Mother Doneele was scheduled to return home, the

Church sent him here.

He touched the icon for word count. A few hundred words written of a volume he should have been building throughout his trip here. It wouldn't be much longer before they'd expect his first installment to be lifted from the veil of his Ep's personal repository and shown to a billion eager eyes. Father Hutchins and Mother Mannino had posted at least two of their own already. Gendrick hadn't read them yet; didn't want his point of view swayed.

He highlighted the last sentence he'd written, finger hovering over the delete icon.

No. It was a good sentence. Maybe he'd write more before Vernaine McCarthy, Prelate over the diocese on Eden and officially Gendrick's boss, discovered he was more a stowaway than correspondent, and dragged him back through 2JH to make room for someone more motivated to document the history of humankind in space.

On their call tonight, the small man seemed more concerned if Mother Doneele was showing him the ropes. Father McCarthy seemed preoccupied with the woman, asking about her mood, state of mind. She'd be leaving on the next transport in a month. Gendrick did not mention the bizarre initiation with the Locusts. The Council was worried enough about her without Gendrick adding to it. Everything at the compound was monitored and logged. They could scan the vids if they wanted to, and decide about her mental condition. He was no psychiatrist, seminary training aside. Gendrick would serve primarily as the new priest for the three scientific communities dotting Toojay's largest continent, at least until two more arrived. Most faiths, if they had the funding, tried for a presence at each outpost. Gendrick's secondary role, however, was that of journalist.

He bent the upper corner of the paper. High quality

Ep. He should try to earn it. He moved the cursor to the end of the sentence and entered, *Are we destined to go forth and multiply, populate every new Earth like modern Adams and Eves? Have we suffered through the fire and earned back the Garden?*

He wondered about this for a moment, then decided they had not.

There would always be serpents to make a mess of things. Always be sin to wedge itself between man and God.

A knock on his outer door. Gendrick pressed save and closed the file. He quickly opened it again, added *always be serpents* then closed it a second time.

"Yes?" The clock on the wall reminded him how late it was. He wished he was more tired. Doneele poked her head in, gray hair more wild than usual as if she'd just risen from sleep.

"System said you hadn't turned in yet, so I thought I'd see how you're doing." She stepped past the door, a far more humble rendition of the woman who'd almost let him die on the balcony a few hours ago to prove a point. Thirty years older than he, according to her System profile, Doneele showed the chiseled lines of her age around the eyes and mouth, but a handsome, angular face with a spatter of freckles along both sides of her nose. Possible Irish descent, long thinned over the generations. Her evening robe was white and loose-fitting and, as required for their profession, revealing nothing of her figure. Even so, he sensed an athletic physique, well-proportioned as hinted by subtle shifts in the cloth. Much of this was likely enhanced – the Church frowned on physical or genetic mods that were done for cosmetic reasons, especially among clergy – but everyone did it and their effect was no less impressive.

With one final check to make sure his file was closed,

Gendrick folded up the paper and laid it on the table beside his bed. He swung his legs to the floor. Doneele raised a hand.

"Don't get up, please." She moved quickly, keeping one hand held out as if to control him. She sat on the mattress and held her hands restlessly on her lap. "Can't sleep?"

He smiled, looked down at those hands. Smooth, too much so for her actual age. A mental warning bell chimed in the back of his mind. Subtle physical signals passing between them. *Careful*, he thought, then wondered why.

"No," he said, trying to sound casual. "It'll take a few days to get adjusted to the cycle here."

She laid one hand on his knee, ignoring the sudden tension in his body. "You should have been doing that on the flight."

Her palm radiated heat through his robe. He nodded, thinking of Helena suddenly, their last conversation, their last *fight*, her leaving in her new boyfriend's truck. Her new life was likely the polar opposite of being married to a priest. When Doneele's hand gave his knee a squeeze, he turned towards her, not realizing she'd been moving toward him then only mildly surprised when their faces met, her lips barely touching his. She did not move closer, but neither did he pull himself away, not at first. Then her other hand pressed against the back of his neck.

No, no, no.

He grabbed both her hands and leaned back. "Wait," he said, trying to mean it. Of course he meant it. What was he thinking?

She smiled and leaned back. "Sorry. It's been so long, and it's hard not to look at you without remembering how good – "

"Doneele, stop." He stood and put a hand lightly on her shoulder, knowing even this contact was a risk. A hurt, stupid part of him didn't want to stop, but he forced himself to remember why he was here. This woman was three decades older than him, and not well. That latter fact was still an assumption on his part – the Prelate was deliberately vague about the reasons for her removal. But she'd lost her husband in this place. It was enough.

And he'd lost a fiancé. All the more reason not to trust his own judgment.

Mother Doneele saved him any choice. She stood and touched his face, looking neither angry nor disappointed. That was good. Gendrick was suddenly embarrassed for both of them. And maybe a little relieved.

"Too soon?" She asked.

"Yes. I'm sorry." *Run from temptation. New world*, he thought, *new rules on the frontier.*

He made a mental note to write that one down. Once his pulse slowed.

She made a pretense of straightening her robes. She tapped the top of the small desk on her way towards the door. "Let's pretend I just left you a rain check," she said. "Either way, see you at breakfast?"

"Looking forward to it," he lied.

"Good." Another quick, genuine smile. "Good night, then!"

"Good night . . ."

The door closed.

Gendrick sat on the edge of the bed for a long time, trying to sort out what had just happened.

5 – Peyton, Orbit 3JH/2JS

PreOp took most of First Shift. Peyton knew she should have tried for a quick nap when they were done, but wasn't tired. She probably wouldn't be until this leg of the mission was behind them.

"Five kilometers," Cannon said, a bit redundantly since the number was spinning lower and lower on each of their screens. But the ISO insisted on constant verbal communication through the Hole. The relay orbiting from the other side was active functioning at one hundred percent. Crew's communication should not be affected save the sixteen seconds spent in transit.

"Four-point-two."

Once on the other side, they could talk again. *If* they came out. Not that anything passing through had ever been lost, but the fear was there, lingering like an ulcer each time. Mostly everyone maintained a mental image of moving through a doorway, from one side to the other. In truth, they traveled very, very far away. How far, no one had yet been able to determine. Nothing looked familiar in the systems; constellation, clusters, nebulae – *everything* was different.

"Three-point-nine."

Without System highlighting the growing circle of empty space, it would have seemed they weren't moving. Peyton focused on this circle. The stars beyond were unreachable with the pod's present course because something stood in their way.

"One-point-two."

She touched icons on her sleeve, checked her suit's internal and external systems, then those of Cannon and Benny, who were doing the same for hers and each other's. Always checking and rechecking, mostly to keep their minds occupied as their bodies were thrown a *gabillion* miles away from home in sixteen seconds.

"Point-three."

A hushed voice from Ken on the *Washington*'s bridge said, "Godspeed, folks."

"Contact."

The ship was squeezed like a tube of toothpaste. Peyton's head collapsed, brains liquefying. Her scream became solid, forming its own life as Cannon's body crushed into hers and Benny's. Their minds touched, merged, swirled together, all of their tears and cries and laughter forming butterflies and clouds and a bright sun over all. Then the darkness, always the darkness pouring over them in a vile, angry wave as it ripped into her chest with clawed hands and –

She blinked and gasped for air. Anticipating the reaction, the suit's oxygen intake had been opened more than usual before contact. It regulated itself back to normal levels, but Peyton struggled with a sudden wave of euphoric dizziness, slowly realizing things outside the faceplate of her helmet were as they had been.

Normal.

The viewport revealed stars no different than what she'd seen, though a nebula now colored the bottom port side of the window.

Her eyes were drawn to the center. She'd seen the probe's vids, every motion and still image and graph plotting all wavelengths visible and not. Even so, looking at what hovered in front of them, blocking a third of the stars though it loomed more than a thousand kilometers away, caused her to gasp and whisper, "My God."

Cannon laughed. It was a quiet sound with no humor. "Amen, sister. Will you look at that."

The pod continued its slow coast away from the Third Jump Hole, the proximity reading above the viewport now incrementing. They sailed towards a large, gray-brown shape dully reflecting the constant glare of a sun 128 million kilometers behind them. The derelict ship was rectangular, three times the size of the *Washington* with no indication of windows or decks. It hovered silent and dead, slowly rotating on its fore-to-aft axis, perhaps to prevent one side from being exposed sun-side too long. The rotation was too slow to simulate Earth gravity, at least not the standard g they were used to aboard the *Washington*'s ring. It was not a human vessel. *Could* not be.

Of course, though the term 'derelict' was already being used by the crew to refer to the vessel, it seemed fully intact and, of course, no one knew what, or who, was inside. It was just easier than saying 'unidentified and potentially non-terrestrial vessel.'

No one spoke, save Benny's whispered, "System, zoom image, twenty mag." The ship filled the viewport. They'd seen this before via the probes, from every angle, but the knowledge that it was now directly in front of them made its presence more ominous.

"OK, folks," said Ken's voice, clear as ever in the helmet's speaker but now traveling from the other side of the Hole, "you've had your few minutes of gawking. Begin scans, both of the ship and the third planet. Can't forget 3P's the original reason we're here, after all."

It took another minute before the three of them rose fully from their reveries and began instructing System –

using typed console commands to avoid a confusion of voices all vying for attention – to scan the derelict and begin longer-range probes of the Earth-like planet glowing like a massive blue star beyond. All information would be relayed to ISO Command without filter, and they would start the process of transmitting the planetary data to the *Abad* and more general information to the media, but only after filtering out anything related to the alien ship. For now.

Washington had the right to this initial contact, but as soon as Pey and the others returned 2Jside the cat would need to be let out of the bag. It was a fair rule – a law, in fact, strictly enforced by the World Senate and its space exploration branch, the ISO, rewarding discovery in the short term, but mandating open research by all organizations with a legitimate claim to the information. Information was a right of all humans since the Senate was formed thirty years after the Final War. Peyton assumed that the *Abad* was already curving around 2J5P, wondering why the *Washington* had sent only a small, manned shuttle rather than passing through the Hole itself.

Peyton smiled at the thought of how Captain Marlay would react when he learned the *Washington* crew was going to give the *Abad* first exploration rights of the new planet, and why.

"Nothing," Cannon said. "No change from prior scans. Just a big, scary phallic symbol floating in front of us."

Pey snickered. Ken said, "Keep it pro, Can, as much as possible."

At that, they all laughed.

Their pod was a bulky, ugly structure built to carry the maximum amount of first-hand equipment with no thought for aesthetics. It lumbered forward, disk and flat-panel cameras scanning ahead on all conceivable frequencies of both audio and video. As with the automated probes, nothing penetrated the other vessel's hull.

By the time they'd come within three hundred clicks and slowed to orbital speed, the vessel had turned what had been its underside toward them. There was no obvious "under" to the thing. The ship had details, long symmetrical sections protruding from points along the axis and at times running the full length of the hull. Storage tanks, perhaps, or propulsion systems. Nothing was open to space nor gave any clue as to the purpose of any protrusion or bump. More importantly, no obvious way *in* except for long, rectangular indentations which might be shuttered viewports or landing bays or something completely different.

Benny monitored the shuttle's pre-programmed course, adjusting it slightly – mostly to appease his need to play the part of the pilot he was supposed to be – until they faced what was mutually decided to be the ship's bow. He matched rotation. The ship's face filled the screen. Cannon reduced mag to fifty percent. Slowly, they shifted sideways, always facing the ship but drifting past the bow and along the starboard side. In this way they'd take in the entirety of the vessel over the course of the next three hours.

An occasional, long scuff marred the hull where a rock might have skimmed off, on its way towards the sun.

They passed along the largest of the indentations. It likely was *not* a viewport, but Pey found some comfort in thinking of it that way. It made the vessel's creators a little less alien.

Cannon said, more to himself than anyone else, "Knock, knock, you bugger."

"Who's there?" Pey answered reflexively. Benny snickered.

"Banana."

Pey smiled inside her helmet. "Banana who?"

"Banana bana—"

"Guys . . ." Ken again over the com.

Cannon cleared his throat. "Sorry, Captain, sir. So far, no one's home."

Pey checked her readings, infrared and x-ray at the moment, then looked up at the screen above the back of Benny's helmet. Stared at the long, shuttered "window." Part of her hoped Cannon was wrong.

Part of her prayed he was right.

6 – Doneele O'Coin, 2J3P

"Gendrick Hellerton, meet Arun Renault."

Doneele waved her hand absently over her bacon – the usual *faux*-meat strips the majority of the population ate, both from choice and necessity – and added, "Arun, meet Gendrick."

Arun's long-thinned Indian descent was discernable only by the slight brown tint to his skin and, of course, his first name. The senior linguist was a foot shorter than the new priest but with the chiseled, tough-hided features of someone who worked outside often, as was the case for most working in the colonies. Gendrick smiled. "Call me Gen, please."

Arun stood by their table, breakfast tray in hand and nodded before finding a seat across the table from him. "Gen it is. So big news in 3J. That should give you plenty of material for your writing project."

Doneele rolled her eyes. The discovery of the derelict was the only topic of conversation since she'd woken up and scanned the news release. Not that a group like this would be apathetic about such an enormous discovery but, to Doneele, it represented something else. What, she couldn't put her finger on, not quite. Except the dark world she was trapped in, at least for another month and six days before the next transport arrived to carry her home had suddenly grown larger.

She needed to fit in for a while longer, pretend to care

about these people as she'd already been doing for too long. Stay under the radar until it was time to go. Of course, next to nearly killing Hellerton, her first order of business had been to try and sleep with the man. An unexpected slip of the mask she'd maintained, but there *was* an attraction, even if he hadn't let it go too far. His hesitancy was a case of lingering social mores, a sense of what was appropriate and what was not this far from home. It wasn't from a lack of interest. After last night Doneele hadn't felt so *alive,* not since Zechariah died.

That might change in another month and six days.

After returning to her room last night, she'd checked the flight schedules, a recent and nightly routine, and gripped the front of her robes, felt her heart pounding. In fear, not excitement. She would not fool herself. Fear that she might not last this final month without tearing herself apart.

When she eventually did arrive back in the shaded paradise of Eden, everything would be better. Until then, God had provided her with a way to cope, as He always did. Love would cradle her in its arms, if not today, soon enough. Zechariah had been like that, early in their marriage. Before they came *here.* An anchor for her storms. Then he left her, long before he actually died. Left her alone to wander and drown on this arid rock.

Gendrick nodded. "I imagine so."

Doneele looked up at the overhead monitor. Something different had replaced the incessant talking heads. The men followed her gaze. Arun fingered the speaker icon in the center of the table.

" . . .inside," a woman said, "but we're not taking any chances. Scans continue, and the *Abad* is on its way for a rendezvous at Third Jump Hole. Since we'll be remaining at this location, they'll continue towards the third planet.

We've relinquished first right of exploration to them."

Gendrick's smile was sudden and wide. He let out a small laugh, before looking around the table, hoping no one noticed. Doneele pretended she hadn't, assuming the priest was impressed with the news of the derelict's discovery. Except for that smile. *That* meant something else. No, he wasn't the type to drop his jaw at some beautiful woman on a video. That was ridiculous. After taking another sip of coffee his gaze was drawn back to the overhead screen, still smiling like a little kid.

Granted, the woman speaking *was* beautiful with rich, almost black skin, a rare dark beauty in these days of mixed ethnicity. Even so, Doneele thought Gendrick's reaction – if she was the reason, of course – a little much. Below the image were the words, *Peyton Kay, Chief Scientist, ISS Washington,* beside a myriad of glowing dots representing media organizations vying for attention.

Standing beside her was a stocky blond man, face clean and handsomely chiseled (*Ken Burlov, Mission Captain, ISS Washington,*" the ever-present caption explained). He raised a hand, looking at something off-screen. He pointed and said, "Someone from Eden Central has a question?"

A box opened in the lower corner of the vid to reveal a woman in a white wraparound sari. She asked the usual question – one which would be asked all day, no doubt, with a hope for a different answer. "Captain Burlov and Chief Kay: what are the chances the vessel has a crew, that there are life forms aboard?"

Doneele noticed with amusement that Peyton Kay closed her eyes in exasperation. Burlov nodded seriously, as if this was a the most inspiring question of the morning. As acting captain for the mission, he was required to play the role of politician. When he turned to his crewmate and said, "Pey?" Doneele decided he also had a sense of humor.

The woman smiled uncomfortably as the image focused on her alone in order to set up for what everyone hoped would be the next big moment in News History. Peyton said, "Very likely."

Murmurs from everyone at the cafeteria almost drowned out her next sentence, "As likely as it being completely empty with nothing on board whatsoever." She shrugged.

Doneele looked at Gendrick. He was smirking. Her *husband* had been the type to gawk at beautiful women from time to time, but not this man. Gendrick's expression was almost . . . forlorn. *Love struck*? No, that was stupid. Arun had already turned his attention back to his plate.

Chief Kay added, "We just don't know, and until we do . . ."

Doneele pressed the speaker icon on the tabletop. Peyton Kay's voice cut out.

"Well, this'll be on all day, and we've got a full schedule."

Gendrick blinked himself out of the spell he'd been under. "You're right." He looked embarrassed, shoveled more cold eggs onto his spoon. "Interesting, though."

Arun nodded. "That's the understatement of the year." He nodded towards the monitor. "You know her?"

Gendrick blushed and nodded. "Actually, we grew up together. Best friends since we were little. I knew she was out this way, but still nice to see her again, especially with all this going on." He picked up a piece of bacon and waved it in her general direction. Doneele was surprised their table wasn't covered in food shards with so much gesturing towards that ridiculous screen.

"Nice," Arun said, between bites. "I have to admit, when I heard the news this morning I wondered if they'd found the *Jupiter* or the *Enterprise*." He shrugged. "No such luck. Doesn't look anything like them."

Eleven years prior to the first Hole's discovery, two ships had been launched to explore the universe outside Earth's solar system. *Generational Starships*, as they had been dubbed by the media, self-sustaining mini-ecosystems with elaborate hydroponics facilities, entertainment and living quarters. They were built for *very* long-range missions. Crew would consist of entire families, most conceived and born enroute – under strict controls. Generations would grow up never knowing what it was like to stand on Earth, feel the wind on their faces or rain down their backs. All to ensure the human race's expansion one day among the stars, and its survival as Earth continued to die. It was a one-way mission, funded by the Government as one attempt at finding somewhere habitable off-world, or at the very least preserving something of humanity. There had been no shortage of volunteers. A controversial and vastly expensive program, it was canceled after contact had been lost first with the *Jupiter*, then a year later the *Enterprise*, each having passed the Kuiper Belt into uncharted space. No message or signal of any kind had ever been received beyond that point. No one suggested a third mission, and the program was scrubbed after 1JH was discovered.

Doneele laid her right hand on Gendrick's left, feeling a stab of pain inside her chest when he twitched in response. *Surprise*, she decided, nothing more. She removed her hand. "We're going to head outside at nine hundred. I think you'll find it interesting."

Gendrick stopped eating. "Outside?"

Arun reached across the table and laid his own hand on Gendrick's right, just a tap of his fingers before pulling them back – an unspoken joke meant only for Doneele; he could be an ass that way. That was why she liked him so much.

He said, "Relax, Gen. The Locusts are long gone. Don't like the daytime. Our resident xenologist Ochi Miyoko is pretty sure the light doesn't really bother them. It's just that the hallucinogen Acclarin is made inactive in direct sunlight so they stick to sunset, giving it time to kick in. Toojay's version of vampires, I guess."

Gendrick nodded, glancing at Doneele then back to his food. Acclarin was a hallucinogen ever-present in the atmosphere, excreted by the Locust swarm in-flight and which became potent after sunset. It had almost killed Gendrick the other night, making him forget to step off the balcony to safety. Anything which breathed and was unfortunate enough to be caught outside after dark would become too disoriented to run for cover, or even want to. Sitting ducks for the creatures as they arrived along the edge of night.

Like Zechariah and, when the planet was first discovered, many other, less-deserving souls.

Gendrick looked at her, unsmiling. She leaned back in her chair and stared at him. "Remember one thing," she said. "Last night, its effect almost made you Loki's dinner. The next time, you'll have no one to blame but yourself." She pointed towards his face, grateful her finger was steady. "You've had your warning."

He smiled. "Noted," then looked around. "Bear with me if I keep looking at the sky now and then."

Arun smiled. "Trust me, you'll be far too fascinated writing down the wonders I'll show you for that little book of yours to worry what might be diving towards your back." He raised both hands and curled his fingers into talons.

Gen smiled uneasily and looked down. One thing Doneele already understood about the man – he was good at hiding his thoughts, and his work. His Ep was on a secure channel. Maybe it was simply an artist's need for privacy. Or maybe he had some skeletons hidden in those bits and bytes. Didn't matter. If she wanted to, she had ways of hacking in – criminal offense or not. She wouldn't unless it was necessary. What mattered, for some childish reason she hated herself for, was how Gendrick finished his meal in silence while surreptitiously watching the replay of the news conference and his beautiful, dark friend on the overhead screen. She wouldn't be jealous. He could pretend all he wanted. His attraction towards Doneele was there. She merely had to coax it out of him.

7 – Peyton, Orbit 3JH/2JS

ISO Command finally cut off media communication an hour ago with a promise of daily updates. They wanted more, always did, but Crew needed to do their job and that wasn't possible if they spent their time answering the same questions.

"Here it comes," announced Zhou Lihua's voice over the com.

Peyton swung her right arm in a half turn. Her body responded, floating and turning until she was in a rough approximation of sitting, then moved both arms to stop the rotation. She was careful not to touch Cannon floating a couple of meters beside her. Any contact meant unwanted momentum. He was on duty in the Hub this shift – so Peyton decided to join him for the big show before wrapping herself in the blanket she'd brought and catching some zero-g sleep. On the screen, 2J5P's steady red and orange glow reflected off a tiny star emerging from the gas giant's far side. Otherwise the sky was its usual star-filled emptiness. In a smaller box at the lower left hand corner, System cut to Li's console on the bridge, the side-image showing a small woman of mostly Chinese decent with close-cropped black hair. Pey had earlier instructed the computer to shift the window's bridge view towards whoever spoke, giving her the illusion of turning in the speaker's direction. Like her, almost everyone off-shift was still awake, waiting for the *Abad*'s arrival – to gloat, perhaps, but also curious what its still-silent crew had to say.

A separate box at the lower left-hand side of the screen showed only a blank white image. Tuned to the *Abad-Washington* frequency. Silent.

"Ten bucks says they go into the hole without a word," Cannon muttered. She turned her head slowly, careful not to send herself into a spin. He was smiling, always a mild look of amusement on his handsome face. She resisted the urge to reach out and touch the day's beard growth on his cheek. She knew her feelings were partly the need for companionship out here in the middle of nowhere, and partly – perhaps mostly – excitement and pride at what they'd uncovered. Cannon was married, a long-distance relationship but a happy one. She'd never lower herself to breaking that. Nor would he.

Besides, what better way to ruin their friendship?

"You're on," she said, and smiled back. He looked at her, his face becoming serious (though still in a mocking way, she could read him too well).

"Stop that," he said.

She laughed, let herself roll backwards in a flip. "I wasn't and you know it."

He grunted, smiling again. "You need a boyfriend."

She slowed her rotation again. "Oh, you *wish* I was thinking that."

This type of conversation was dangerous among Crew, since flirtation invariably led to the real thing. They were too far out, breathing in air filled with the stress of knowing death was as close as a bad decision. She and Cannon had had their own serious discussion about this a few months earlier, when something almost *did* happen. Now, these small comments and jibes were their way of venting some of the built-up steam. Neither wanted to break the fragile thread, but both *needed* it to hold them together.

They floated in silence for a few more minutes, watching the star grow and gain detail. The *Abad* was cruising at breakneck speed towards them.

Cannon said, "System, please estimate, vocally, the time of *Abad* arrival."

The calm, male voice of the computer responded, "*Abad* flight plan notes a shift in course at 21-365, estimated arrival at 3JH in twenty-nine minutes."

Ken's voice piped in. The bridge view shifted to the command chair in the center of the bridge deck. The acting Captain was pulling double duty today in anticipation of the other exploration vessel's arrival. "*Washington* to *Abad*, welcome Hole-side. Radish, are you folks planning on saying hello today or are you just going to pass by and give us the finger?"

Cannon howled at this, the act sending him rolling off towards the wall.

The *Abad*'s channel remained silent. The box an unblinking white square on the viewport.

After a few minutes, if only to break the silence, Cannon whispered, "I hope they turn when their plan says they will, otherwise we're going to be able to talk to them in person."

"They'll turn, but I think I'm going to be paying you those ten credits."

Finally, the ship, as ungainly and clunky as the *Washington* with its rotating ring circling a hub littered with antennae, changed course and aimed for the hole.

Ken's voice: "*Abad*, this is *Washington*. If you're seriously going to take the whole ship immediately into the hole I recommend slowing speed by half. The derelict isn't all that far from emergence."

"System," Pey said, "display Abad flight specifics."

As the starship moved sideways across the viewport, its gravitational ring turning languorously against the light of the planet, statistics poured across the page. The ship's *speed* was highlighted, System's AI assuming from Ken's statement this was the primary reason for Peyton's request. As usual, it was right.

The ship was turning again, its rear propulsion facing the Washington as if in insult. Its speed had decreased dramatically before the massive, three-hundred foot hull was compressed, crushed like a discarded drinking cup, and blinked from existence.

"Well," Cannon said, already preparing to push off the floor towards the maintenance hatch, "at least we know they're listening. Time to make my rounds. Did you have dinner?"

She leaned back and looked at the chron on the opposite wall, reading the numbers upside down. "Sorry, yes. I ate early because I've got a ten minute personal call slot coming up."

He was at the hatch now, preparing to climb down and, she assumed, allow her some privacy. "Say hi to little Ellie for me."

She smiled, working her toes toward the nearest wall for push-off into the opposite corner of the room. "Will do."

8 – Excerpted from the series, *God's Vast Array*

by Father Gendrick Hellerton, November 2193

*W*hereas *Eden is primarily forests and other woodlands, rivers and lakes with small oceans here and there to maintain enough salinity in the atmosphere – like the Canadian District, only planet-wide, Toojay seems custom-designed for those preferring the drier, desert life. Similar to the uncontaminated desert scrublands of Earth, only on a planetary scale. The other primary difference between the two planets is the amount of life. Eden teems with it. Some species are similar to Earth's, though most have evolved along other paths, unencumbered by human interference. The world's air is thick with the humid, living scent of growth and decay. In many ways this planet, Toojay, feels older and more basic, with a few thriving species of animals and insects, tough plant-life more spare than Eden but beautiful in its unique way. Because of this the air is thinner and dryer, less prone to bacteria. Toojay is harsher than its cousin, certainly more dangerous as the sun lowers to the horizon. But still, too deliberate to rule out as coincidence. It's as if these planets were prototypes of the final product where mankind finally settled, where life evolved and prospered and differentiated itself, where God finally put his stamp on one specific species, rebuilding them in His image then sending them out to populate the world under the pretense of expulsion from the Garden.*

I know I'm straying rom accepted Biblical dogma, but bear with me a moment.

Personally, I've always assumed God knew what would happen as soon as He said, Don't eat that fruit. *This view, one of my many personal theories on the Creation story that tends to antagonize more than enlighten people, has always seemed most . . . right, if not somewhat heretical to the fundamentalists of our ilk. But there's a question that commonly arises about the Creation story, if not spoken verbally, then as an unsettled feeling of Wait, but . . . Yahweh had used the Garden to build the perfect humans, the perfect image of life with Him, but what was happening outside the gates? Was there a race of other, Lesser Men, waiting for Adam and his family to become the final ingredients in mankind's recipe once they were outside the Garden? Unlike many of my predecessors I've always found myself drawn to the stickiest of Old Testament questions, one I've personally asked God with no forthcoming answer: Who was Mrs. Cain?*

I promise, there is a point to all this. A point, or another question: when Adam's first son murdered his brother and was sent away, was there a Mrs. Cain waiting for him in the wilderness, generations evolved from prehistoric man, reaching the pinnacle where God felt she and her kind were ready for the first infusion of Himself, of his Perfection. A slow, methodical process, if so, and quite deliberate. God is patient, if nothing else. All great chefs are.

Maybe not. Maybe Cain eventually settled down with a descendant of his parents (to put it nicely for those more sensitive among us) and began his own line. It's not infeasible. Diversity in genetics was not as critical at this early juncture of mankind, only propagation of the species. But maybe . . . What if . . . These words have been the seeds for wars and execution of heretics in our past, but also the seeds of a deeper understanding of the One whom we cannot fully understand.

What is God's plan? What was it then, and what is it now? I like to think it has never changed in thousands of years (or billions of years, depending on your scientific view). Maybe His plan is to use us to spread Himself, genetically and in Word, throughout creation. Initially the goal was to carefully cultivate from Eden's metaphoric womb an eventual race of modern humans who would become the

Israelites, who one day spawned God's own physical presence in the world. The history of this tribe is chronicled in the Old Testament, of course, but there were other branches, growing from the trunk but perhaps no less critical to His plans. These settled and grew in other corners, serving other purposes, themselves splintering in variant groups with more variant beliefs. Until at last, after many millennia, these systems of humanity's faith came together again, often violently but always necessary for the Plan. With Christ's arrival, everything imploded, everything changed. For the better, at least from my perspective as His follower. But no less bloody. Jewish and Roman and Greek and Arab; Jewish and Christian and Muslim and Hindu.

Violence was always the norm, Satan scrubbing the Earth to which he'd been banished with the blood of innocent and guilty alike. All the while, God preparing humanity for its final purification.

This theory doesn't necessarily reflect that of the Church. But find me ten people who agree completely on how such an issue of faith and science could possibly work together, and I'll call you a liar.

With every step I took away from the Union entrance on the morning of that first full day on Toojay, walking on dry, willowy dirt with Arun and Doneele, I couldn't help wonder if it had all been laid down billions of years ago as a place-setting for me and my modern brethren by the Almighty.

Everything was tinged with a subtle, orange-peel scent of the dormant chemical Acclarin. I imagined myself like Adam, leaving the safety of the green trees and warm embrace of God, stepping across a world that was wild and dangerous. I didn't want to, so conscious was I of the Locusts curving around the far side of the planet. That first morning I would have liked nothing better than observe from the relative security of the compound. But I had to move on, accept God's nudge out of my personal Garden. I had done so when I left Earth, then later from the aptly-named Eden.

Because Life moves on. I needed to participate in the Grand Experiment or waste away. Waste my purpose in this ever-expanding *universe.*

    Whatever that purpose might be.

9 – Gendrick, 2J3P

"OK," Arun said. "As we get to the first boulder, please follow my steps. We might have only an hour before the winds pick up and wipe the slate clean. Try not to stir anything up."

The *slate*, Gendrick understood, was the reason the linguist was so excited. The Locusts had a language, one that Arun planned to prove was a deliberate, logical mode of communication. Perhaps one day a dialogue could be had with the creatures. If they were, in fact, more than simple insects but intelligent with a complicated mode of communication, like bees dancing outside the hive.

Doneele walked between the two men in the procession, her long blue robes cinched up and wrapped around her sash, tucked into tall black boots to prevent brushing on the ground. Gendrick's black robes were done up the same way. The temperature was comfortable, nearing twenty-five Celsius. It was still early, though. Along with the ever-present vestiges of the dormant hallucinogen, the air carried a tang of dirt and a scent Gendrick could not place, minerals native to the region. The threesome rounded the first and largest of a clump of three boulders jutting from the scrub like warts. They climbed to the top of this and followed where Arun pointed. "There," he whispered, indicating a clearing nestled to their right.

At first glance Gendrick saw nothing but sand, disturbed in places around clumps of grass. Farther out, two small animals with striped markings chased each other around another clump of boulders. If he hadn't been told what to look for he wouldn't have noticed anything out of the ordinary. The sand rose and fell in crests like small brown waves frozen at the shore. Arun wore knee-high black boots like the others, pant legs tucked inside, a long-sleeved white shirt, looking more archeologist than linguist. Now and then the coolant wires woven through his clothes glimmered in the sun.

"See there," he said. "Only one *speaker* each time, like in the vid I showed you, dancing and spinning, never a flutter of wings. Drawing something in the sand. *Writing* something. All of that's been long flattened out, though. The wind here is nothing if not consistent. But they came back last night."

The vid they'd watched had been made from this very spot three and a half weeks ago. A common meeting of Locusts after the majority of the swarm passed on. A small camera mounted on the rocks, one of hundreds scattered over the plain, caught three Locusts huddled together, two motionless with their backs to the camera and facing the third as it skittered across the sand in an elaborate dance. The pattern created by its pointed toes and occasional jab of the scorpion-like tail were illuminated in false light by the lens filters. Gendrick had seen videos like it before on the ship, and before he'd left Earth, on a documentary specific to Toojay. The vid he'd seen this morning was still legally sealed within the colony's private repository. On it, after a few minutes of the dance, the Locust stopped. Eleven seconds ticked by on the chronometer. During this time nothing moved. Then the Locust wiggled, very slightly, and the impromptu wall formed by the other two parted. The creature clambered onto the rock, its wasp face closing in on the camera (it had been placed securely but unhidden atop the center rock). As it stared, slowly opening and closing its mandible mouth with a hiss through the vid's speakers, two other nightmare faces peered around it. Sudden movement flashed above the leader's head and the vid ended.

The next day Arun ran to this spot to find the camera crushed, a gaping hole torn ten centimeters above the lens. The Locust had swung its tail overhead and stabbed it. What struck Arun the most, he'd explained, was not that they had attacked the camera, but *where* the creature had chosen to jam its stinger. Dead center on the on/off switch. It had done it too forcefully. The machine was crushed, ending the transmission as effectively as if it had pressed the button correctly.

"What does it say?" Gendrick asked from his perch on top of the rock, trying his best to follow the man's pointing finger.

Arun smiled, "No idea. But last night was the first time they've come back to this spot since they wasted the original camera."

Gendrick glanced around but saw no sign of another. Maybe it had been hidden. He rose as high as he could on the topmost rock and stared at the patterns, momentarily seeing an image in the sand before losing any picture that might have formed. His imagination working overtime, nothing more, like seeing pictures in the clouds. In many ways looking at the patterns reminded him of the clouds off to the west last night while he was hallucinating. He looked at Doneele and asked, "Why do you think they came back last night?"

The woman smiled. "We took the new camera away. We caught them instead on a longer-range model mounted just that way," she gestured north towards a pair of similar boulders, "out of sight in the crevice between those two rocks."

He stared at her, knowing the statement's immense implication without having to ask anything else. The Locusts understood technology, at least enough to know when they were being watched. At that moment he was also bothered by an unrelated thought – was this woman planning to return to his room tonight? He hoped not.

The fallacy of human weakness and thought, Gendrick thought to himself. He'd just been told one of the most momentous secrets of this planet's scientific community, second only perhaps to the discovery of the ship beyond 3JH, and his first thought was whether this person was going to make a move on him later.

Gendrick wondered, not for the first time, why God bothered putting up with humans at all.

10 – Elisa, 1J3P

"**M**s. Chase let us watch you on the vid today at school."

Auntie Pey's image smiled from the large screen lining the wall of the living room. Elisa loved seeing her Aunt smile. She and her mother were the prettiest women she knew. They were the *same* pretty, since Auntie Pey and Mom were twins.

"I didn't have any food stuck between my teeth, did I?"

Elisa laughed. "You did! A big green piece of spinach was dangling out of your mouth, and nobody said anything!"

Auntie Pey covered her mouth. "Oh, my!" Her words were muffled. She smiled behind her hand, as the ship's walls rolled past behind her.

"I'm just kidding."

Pey's hand rose up and slapped her forehead. The sound was tinny through the speakers. Everything sounded that way when she talked to them from space. Mom said it was interference that the system had to fix.

Auntie Pey said, "Phew! That's a relief." She turned her head slightly to address Elisa's mother.

"Carroll, how bad are they?"

Mom sat between Elisa and Dad on the couch. "You mean the media? Not too bad. We did a press conference this morning. That appeased them for now. We're not as interesting as the rest of you."

Pey glanced at Elisa again. "You are to me." Her words, and the fact that she looked at Elisa when she said them, filled the ten-year old's chest with a tremulous warmth. Dad spoke up for the first time.

"Pey, you clear for us to send more books? They're being tight about allowing too many uploads to the *Washington*. I guess that's to be expected. I don't imagine you've got a lot of free time, anyway."

"Thanks, yea, you're probably right, but send them along. I'll get some bandwidth and let you know the ID. Send them whenever you can. Not another romance, is it?"

"Nope, promise. A nice, cozy horror story."

"Excellent."

Elisa looked worriedly at the chron counting down on the corner of the screen. Less than two minutes to go. She said, "Auntie Pey, are you going to be able to talk to our class soon?"

She nodded, taking on a serious expression. "Absolutely, Ellie. But they want me to talk to the whole school, now. Day after tomorrow. We need to play it by ear, though, since I might still be through the Hole. If I am, we'll do it as soon as I'm back on this side."

The counter was under a minute.

Mom tightened her arm around Elisa and said, "You be careful, Pey." This part was always the saddest, and Elisa closed her eyes at the sound of her mother's voice. It reminded her how dangerous things were up there.

"I will, C. I promise."

"You're not – " Mom began, then hesitated. The chron ticked lower.

No one spoke.

Ask her, Elisa thought. When her mother still hadn't spoken, and neither did her father, Elisa said, "Are you going inside the ship?"

Auntie Pey's smile did not drop, but when she answered, her mother's embrace tightened a little bit more.

"I sure hope so. If we can find a way in." Her eyes moved briefly to the corner of her own screen, then she looked up and said quickly. "I love you all. Bye."

"Bye." All three of them said in unison.

The screen turned white, small black letters spelled TRANSMISSION ENDED.

They sat without speaking on the couch for a few minutes, Elisa thinking about Auntie Pey being the Guest of Honor at her school, her parents thinking other, sadder thoughts.

Dad said, "Time for bed, Ellie," and got up from the couch. He stood in front of Mom and kissed her on top of her head. "She'll be fine."

Mom nodded, a small movement since his lips were still on her head. "I know."

Dad straightened. "Come on, kiddo. You promised to go right to bed if we let you stay up." He hunkered down in unspoken invitation and Elisa climbed onto his back. She wrapped her arms around his thick neck, resting her face against his warm, pale skin, rolling her much darker arm over his neck, enjoying the contrast as he moved like a jet through the house, arms out straight, except when he passed through the doorways.

The windows of every room were open, letting the outside breeze fill her bedroom with flower smells. As he tucked her under the covers a large insect bumped against the screen, wanting in. It would keep it up all night, drawn by the hall light outside the bedroom door. She would let the drone of its wings lull her to sleep. Elisa hoped she would dream about her Aunt, but not of the empty spaceship. The picture on the vid was too scary.

"Good night, Goof Head."

"Night, Daddy. I love you."

Kiss on her head. "Love you, too."

The room fell silent as her father's footsteps receded down the hall towards the living room, the silence broken only by the insistent scraping of the bug against her screen.

11 – Doneele, 2J3P

The chair was hard. No cushion, nothing to offer comfort. That was how she preferred it – for her back, which seized up if she sat with bad posture for very long, and because she did not want to be comfortable in this place. Not anymore.

She stared in silence. Stars filled the current window on the electronic paper, bright and teasing. No more rear glow of the shuttle's drive as it pushed away from Toojay towards the orbiting transport. There hadn't been anything but stars on this video for a full day. The transport was gone. When the *Ventura* had arrived, carrying supplies and Gendrick Hellerton, its orbit was close enough that Doneele could see its long, ringed spot of gray embedded among the billion stars through this particular satellite feed from high orbit.

Aside from the stars, the image was empty. Scrolling below it, a constant traffic update, such as it was.

Next transport arrival: ETS Horizon . . . *Departing 1J3P =1 day, 17 hours . . . Estimated Arrival 2J3P: 1 month, 3 days, LT . .*
.

Select here for inventory and itinerary . . .

She stared at the numbers. They did not change. If the transport's only stop was Toojay, it would arrive in just over a week and a half. But there were the two mining operations in the 1J system. Not until falling to within a week would System begin to report hours, then minutes.

She would be leaving on the *Horizon* when it arrived, *one month, three days* from now. Enough time, per Prelate McCarthy, to get Hellerton acclimated to his new assignment.

Gendrick had turned in early tonight, making an excuse of being tired. That was expected. Everyone was exhausted on the second night. That's all it was. What had she been thinking, making moves on him last night? A fellow priest, no less. They had no vow of celibacy holding them back, but they *had* vowed to uphold the standards of the Church in this terrible, terrible place.

A moment a weakness. That was an overused excuse out here on the fringe. Living on the frontier offered plenty of opportunities for weakness. An excuse no different than Gendrick's.

She tapped the Ep and brought up her associate's profile page. Gendrick was more handsome, more *present*, in person. She felt a renewed stirring of lust for the tall, dark, handsome man of God – that's what it was, lust. She would not hide from the truth, regardless of the comfort one's lies sometimes offered.

She laughed. She'd been a priest far too long, thinking like that. It was a short-lived and wild sound.

Then the room fell silent.

He really had been tired, and she was an old fool who thought . . .

Doneele closed her eyes. They ached. Bright flashes of light behind her lids. *Breathe* . . . she thought. *Breathe . . . There, keep breathing. Good. All is good. All is bright.*

She relaxed a little, opened her eyes.

Gendrick Hellerton's profile photo – *he wasn't tired he just doesn't want to be with you* – stared indifferently at her from the screen. She tapped the window closed, revealing the endless void of space from the previous window.

One Month, Three Days.

She closed that, too. Doneele's finger hesitated over the menu, then tapped-up Zechariah's album. His personal files, not the sterile, fact-laden System profile – she would never bring that up again. The last time she did her eyes invariably found the word "deceased" in the upper right corner. It was distracting and cruel. Always, it had been that lone word she focused on. She had better photos of her husband she could bring up, happier moments.

Zechariah smiled and leaned on a boulder. The vid was taken outside the compound not long after they'd arrived. He had no official role in this place, except as her husband. Still, wherever they were, he found a place for himself.

Just look, she thought.

She could tap the image and he would speak, his voice clear but the words no different than the last time and the time before that. Words repeated so often they were meaningless. Window dressing. She only wanted to see his face in this captured moment, before he changed.

He hadn't changed, a voice she'd come to despise whispered from its hiding place. *You did. This place changed you. The Locusts changed you. But not him. He was good, and loved you . . .*

Stop . . .

She closed the image and stared at the blank paper for a long time. Still seeing her husband in her mind, leaning on the rock, smiling at his wife from beyond death.

He and the new priest looked very much alike, despite the age difference. Maybe that was why she felt such a need to lay so much of her heart at his feet, so much hope in his ability to carry her through this final month. All of it was wrong. She should be relying on the Lord for that. She should, but she did not. The Lord was probably also tired, and wanted to turn in early.

Doneele was alone, and would stay alone for the next month and three days. Then she would walk willingly into the belly of the *Horizon* and let it carry her away, bring her home. After that, her fate depended entirely on McCarthy, and whether he chose to break the Church's most sacred tenant and reveal the truth of what she'd done.

12 – Gendrick, 2J3P

Doneele hadn't pressed Gendrick to invite her in, accepting his exhaustion as genuine, which it was. The longer days on Toojay would take some getting used to. Even so, her expression had momentarily darkened. She wasn't pleased. Different *world/rules* concept aside, she was moving too fast. Gendrick needed time to think, to decide what he wanted, *whom* he wanted. Last night's contact had lingered too long. Allowing it again, especially so soon, verged on sinful. If nothing else, the heart was a fragile thing, and rushing into any form of physical intimacy would risk more pain for both of them. She was lonely. So was he. There was a time for logic, and for restraint. Human history was nothing if not a constant lesson of how distance from home thinned the veil of morality and common sense.

He liked that thought, opened up *Vast Array* and typed it. Saved it. Closed the file. Opened it again. Leaning back on the bed pillows, Gendrick curled his legs and opened a new document, this time a letter, and typed.

Dear Helena, I've finished my second day on Toojay. I'm sure, given enough time, my daily life here will slowly smooth over the rips and tears in my soul. You know the ones — you made them. I hate you. I hate what you did. Yes, I suppose I'm still glad I left the monastery. It's archaic restrictions were not for me, even if on the surface my move into the regular priesthood was for you, so we could one day marry. I think God has a plan for me outside of those old, moldy walls on Earth. Here, maybe, on this alien planet. This unfinished Earth Prototype. *If not, maybe the next planet. Or the next.*

I'll keep going out, farther and farther into the galaxy, millions upon millions of kilometers away from you and the moron you married instead of me.

You can stay on Earth and live out your life in smiling happiness. Move to Eden. Have children, someday grandchildren. Not me. I've been cast out of paradise, into the wasteland. I'll find a place.

Without you.

I hate you.

Love, Gendrick.

He saved the file and, like the dozens of others he'd written since leaving Earth, did not send it. He never would.

He had to stop doing this.

Opening to the public web and the Central News Agency, Gendrick clicked on Peyton Kay's image and watched the broadcast again. He stared into her face, listened to her voice and relished the warmth which spread through his chest, seeing and hearing her again. He'd researched the *Washington* and *Abad* crews on his trip out here, knowing he would be the only official contact with the Church this side of the 2J Hole for the time being. Pey's appearance on the *Washington*'s roster hadn't been a shock, he knew she was here – but seeing her face, hearing words which she'd spoken only hours before – rather than those of his memory or older news videos – had been a pleasant surprise.

His best friend since childhood, out here billions of kilometers from their old neighborhood.

True, he worked hard to get this post. So he could escape and start over. But run a billion-billion miles away for an off-chance he may get to see Pey in person again? No. Well, not the *only* reason, but she was suddenly the best carrot anyone could have laid before him.

People on the three worlds knew everything they wanted to about the crews of *Washington* and *Abad*. They were adventurers, Lewis and Clarke for the twenty-second century, opening invisible doorways into new worlds and new futures. Even as he departed onboard the *Ventura* for Toojay the odds of getting to see Peyton Kay in person were low. She would keep moving forward, he was to remain here. But he hoped, and prayed often, that after all this time God was still a hopeless romantic.

Once upon a time, Peyton was the best friend any boy could want. She climbed trees better than him, but Gendrick could throw farther. She was graceful. He was awkward. He knew her better than his own brother Kevin. Not that there hadn't been other friends, some shared with Peyton, some not, kids from school who lived on the opposite end of the Manitou Beach township – one of the scores of grid-like, prefab *survivor towns* his great-grandparents had settled around Saskatchewan, after things post-War settled and the new Government finished rewriting borders. Gendrick was third generation, Peyton second. Manitou B was home to both, but each itched for their own *elsewhere* as they grew up.

Gendrick lowered the volume of the news recast, but let the video loop. He saw none of it, and was instead sitting beside her on the Kay's back porch. September of '74. He was seventeen. It was the night of her eighteenth birthday. Everyone had long left the impromptu party. Her twin sister Carroll was inside, making out with her boyfriend Tom in the living room (they eventually married). Warm air, lingering summer. He and Pey talked shoulder to shoulder on the steps outside, sharing future plans, even some memories. Just talking. They turned to each other in the same moment, after a silence, then smiled and kissed. They did not stop for hours. Nothing more than kissing but that night nothing else was needed. Eventually, both leaned their elbows back against the steps, too tired and sore-jawed to do anything expect smirk in the dim morning starlight, enjoying the weather. Neither was uncomfortable with what had happened. Neither talked of anything more to come.

More *did* come. For a couple of months, they gave it a shot. Perhaps they each privately understood it *would* end, and this knowledge fed the impetus for one brief period of intimacy before reality set in. Pey was heading to South America to pursue an aeronautics degree in Brazil, a path which would eventually bring her to Eden as it had become the main base for the ISO once the quarantine was lifted. Gendrick's trip would be shorter: western District of Indiana and barely forty kilometers from the restricted hot zone which bled from the old regions of Ohio, Pennsylvania and beyond. His goal was a Bachelor's in Theology and minor in History. Their lives, always connected and intertwined, would branch in opposite directions – Pey to the stars, Gendrick firmly rooted onto bruised and battered Earth. Or so he'd planned. Eden had become the destination for thousands of emigrants leaving their home world for paradise.

As graduation loomed beyond the New Year, their relationship reverted back to the foundation on which it was based, nothing more. Unless one of them canceled their dreams. Neither would, even after many silent moments when Gendrick fought the urge to ask her to marry him.

Sitting on his bed now, staring blankly at the Ep, he wondered what life would have been like . . . It didn't matter. She wouldn't have let him come with her even if he'd offered. In truth, though both swore their relationship was intact when they moved apart, Gendrick hadn't spoken or written to Peyton Kay after she left Earth four years later, having been accepted for advanced training within the Exploratory Space Program of the ISO.

That was eight years ago. He thought of her often, but never obsessively. More like a warm memory he clung to whenever present day seemed too dark. Gendrick hoped she thought of *him*. Maybe she did. No reason to doubt it.

The Pey of today looked much the same as the twelve year-old holo he'd brought with him to Toojay, tucked away in a bag waiting to be unpacked. Taken during their high school graduation party, six excited and exhausted seniors, Gendrick, Peyton, Carroll and Tom, Domini Lemonciello and Milline Casa. In many other ways – her posture, facial expressions and figure – she'd matured.

Gendrick was lonely, and one of his oldest friends was less than a week's travel away. She'd just made one of the biggest discoveries in the history of the humanity and wouldn't have any time to catch up with an old buddy.

Still . . . it was Pey.

Just do it.

He opened a new document.

"Hey, Pey. I saw the news this morning. Congratulations on the discovery. God's universe gets . . ."

He stopped. Considered. Considered what? Not mentioning God? He was a priest. If anyone in the universe knew him, it was her.

He highlighted the line, but instead of deleting the sentence he opened a new window on the Ep and accessed her profile. Still single. That fact has struck him as a good thing when he'd first read it. As before, that reaction bothered him. Why was it *good?* She deserved to be happy. Still, she was living her dream out here. *That* was very good.

Registered as Disciple of the Apostolic Christian Church, as were most Christians these days, it being the predominant sect of the Church for the last hundred years. She'd registered as *disciple*, not *congregant*. That showed some seriousness to her faith.

He leaned back on the pillow and sighed. This wasn't a personal ad. He was writing *Peyton*, for heaven's sake.

" . . .God's universe gets more interesting every day, doesn't it? I recently arrived in your neighborhood, stationed at Toojay under the pretense of writing a series of articles for the ACC on the expansion of mankind through the galaxy. Heading west *as it were.*

"To be honest, I haven't done a lot of writing on it. But things are picking up."

He should send the letter via private channel, but doing that for an inter-location email pretty much guaranteed someone would open it.

He erased that last two sentences. No sense worrying his employers. He continued,

"Maybe, if you have time, we could talk. Boy, I've missed you. We've both *been bad about staying in touch, but now that we find ourselves in the middle of the same nowhere, I've run out excuses. It's been too long. Keep discovering the universe, and when you can take a breath give me a shout back. I'd like your opinion on what you've uncovered. Not for a story, promise – I'm not the media. Mostly, I'd just love to hear your voice again. Now go be famous, and drop me a line when you have a second. Doesn't have to be any time soon, but when you can. I'll be down here for a while. Love to hear from you.*

"Gen. (PS: the pompous "Father Gendrick Hellerton, 2J3P" *that'll appear at the bottom is an automatic signature, the church insists on it.)"*

He mailed the letter before he could second guess himself, then opened *Vast Array*. He needed to type something clinical, professional. He needed to do his job. He began typing, *"Whereas Eden is primarily forests . . ."*

13 – Peyton, 3JH/3JS

Everyone understood the need for precaution but, with the helmet on, her breathing was a distraction, echoing back through the speakers of the suit. Peyton slowed her respiration in an effort to make as little noise as possible.

"You all right, Pey?" Sure enough, System had informed Ken on the *Washington* that her breathing pattern changed.

"I'm fine. Just hate hearing all this heavy breathing."

Cannon chuckled over the intercom, but said nothing. He didn't need to. She laughed back. "Shut up."

"I didn't say anything." A moment later, his tone changed. "*Abad*, this is *Washington* Survey One. Requesting green for approach."

Protocol. The *Abad* had parked two thousand kilometers on the opposite side of the derelict and had their own survey shuttle orbiting the ship. After returning 2Jside, basically to get out of the way as the *Abad* came through the Hole and to get as good a night's sleep as possible, Peyton, Cannon and Benny were back through the Hole for a second personal survey of the ship. This time, they had some company.

"Survey One, you are green. Thanks for the wave. Nothing so far."

The speaker was identified as Rourke O'Shannon, a geologist, and a fairly recent member of the *Abad* crew. Peyton was glad to hear his voice. They'd been, if not friends, friendly acquaintances since flight school days.

"Hey, Shan," she said. "Nice of you guys to start talking to us again."

They drifted under the massive ship. Peyton keyed System to scan infrared. No sense in wasting any chance when they were this close. They'd done this the other day, and before that with drones, but coming out here and repeating everything in person was better than sitting around the *Washington* waiting for something to happen.

Rourke's voice over the speakers, "Well, we're not having any luck ourselves. We figured we should start being nice to you again. Read any interesting books since we last talked?"

"Keep it professional, people. Save the niceties for personal time." That last comment was laced with a thin middle eastern accent. Radish Marlay, the *Abad*'s captain. A brilliant man, but not very friendly.

"Yes, sir," came Rourke's voice in reply.

They circled the ship, Benny keeping their shuttle on the opposite side of the derelict from the *Abad*'s to maximize coverage. Nothing.

Until a woman's voice (*Sarey Ramprakash*, per System's identifier) broke silence from the *Abad*, "Contact. Repeat, contact. Sun side, flank. An opening. Big, too."

Her voice was also accented. Indian descent, or Pakistani, though protocol required all official communication to be English.

And she sounded scared to death.

The ship on the viewport heaved suddenly away, not because it was moving, but because *they* were. Benny had changed course. A minute later, they hovered a dozen meters beside the *Abad* pod, both facing the alien vessel. Its hull partially reflected the nearby sun, though most of its sheen had dulled by passing dust.

Facing them was a massive door – or the place where a massive door once had been. It was now open, large enough to fit ten of their shuttles side-by-side . . . not that anyone suggested they try.

Most importantly, it had not been there before. Previous passes by this spot had shown only one of the indented *windows*. The assumption, or hope, being a long-shuttered viewport. Now they knew.

The interior was dark. Peyton turned the infrared camera in its direction.

"Pey, anything?" Ken's hushed voice.

She looked at the image, delineation of floor, a wall far in. "Something, yes. Empty space beyond, but it obviously leads inside. A hangar, maybe? No movement; no other details."

They waited, both crews scanning, everyone privately fearing that at any moment a fleet of ships would emerge with guns blazing. That was what Pey expected, at least.

More silence. More scanning. No further detail. No heat signature nor any sign of an atmosphere.

Eventually, the invitation couldn't be ignored.

Ken's voice broke in on the common channel. "Radish, this is Ken. I'd like to send in an IR probe, see what's inside. Agreed?"

"Agreed," came the answer.

"Pey, prepare the launch. We'll guide it from here. Do not approach any closer. Let me know when it's away."

"Acknowledged." She keyed in commands to System to release the latches holding the infrared scanner to the hull. Slowly, the probe drifted free. System took over and guided it forward with a short pulse of its booster.

Benny spoke aloud. "System, display probe view up front, half screen. Keep the other half showing the open door with normal view shipside."

Pey looked up. On the front-facing screen above Benny's seat (he'd slid his pilot's chair back a few notches in order to see it, himself), the upper half showed the interior in varying shades of red. The darkest corners were deep maroon. On the lower display, the rear of the probe drifted into the opening.

The maroon hatch grew larger on the screen, until it swallowed the image completely. The light adjusted. What had earlier been the darkest maroon lightened to bright red, System correcting the contrast. Peyton made a few minor manual adjustments, mostly to give her something to do.

They stared into a vast and empty chamber, large enough to fit most of the *Washington*, though the starship itself would never fit through the hatch. The probe moved to the center, stopped, began to rotate.

"Do you have UV on that one?" O'Shannon's voice from the *Abad's* pod.

"Affirmative," replied Cannon with uncharacteristic formality. "Recording in UV and actual light on separate feeds, lines two and three respectively, not that line three's going to show much without turning on the spotlight."

"Don't, it'll mess up the IR."

"Duh."

Pey smiled. That was better. Nothing made a situation more nerve-wracking than Cannon being serious.

Sarey Ramprakash saw it first. "Wait," she said over the common line. "Stop rotation. There! Near the right side of the screen."

The image stopped. Something had broken the monotonous lines of the massive room's edges. A blur, far in one corner. Cannon whispered, "System, rotate the probe three degrees starboard then stop."

The view shifted slightly, stopped again. The blur was now closer to the center of the image, verifying that it was not merely a smudge on the lens.

"System, zoom in on that blurry thing we're all looking at."

Rourke whispered, "Blurry thing?"

"Hush," came the equally quiet voice of the *Abad's* captain.

System adjusted the camera angle until the blur was centered, then zoomed in.

"Still hard to see," whispered Cannon. "Suggest natural light?"

Ken's voice. "Agreed. Radish?"

"Yes."

"System," Cannon said, "switch public view to natural, then activate floods and begin to move in on anomaly. Slowly, please."

The image went completely black, then exploded in white light. Pey blinked, unable to locate the blur. Then she saw it, realizing at the same time that System was moving the probe closer – zooming in wouldn't do much if the light wasn't fully upon it.

"Oh my God," muttered Rourke from the other shuttle.

"Watch your mouth," Radish barked, though with the awed hush everyone felt.

"Sorry, sir. But, is that what it looks like?"

Beside Peyton, Cannon turned in his seat until he faced her. She looked at his shocked expression behind the faceplate.

No one spoke. No one wanted to be accused of making a rash judgment.

Still . . .

Peyton looked away from her friend's face, with some effort, and back to the image on the top half of the screen. There was no question what it was. Obviously dead, *long* dead by the look of it. But a Locust, all the same.

14 – Gendrick, 2J3P

"Now, the odd thing is, a lot of these fossils aren't really fossils. Our best dating methods have them at only a couple hundred years. Here," Ochi Miyoko tapped the oversized Ep on the wall of her cubicle and brought to the fore a new image, "is a true fossil. Same animal, more or less." She brought the first image forward and tiled them. Now side by side, Gendrick could see the differences. The younger sample was a simple skeleton, its bones on the way to fossilization, perhaps, but no more than anything else buried in the ground for a long period of time. The true fossil beside it resembled a design fused in the slab of rock.

The xenologist looked up at Gendrick from her seat, waiting. Was she testing him? He looked at the images then asked the only thing he could think of.

"So, it's still around now?"

Miyoko shrugged. She was a tall, lean woman with long black hair dusted gray much like his, though she was fourteen years older than him according to her profile. "I don't know. We've found no traces of this species on the surface. This is the youngest sample we have." She pointed to the first image on the screen. "Whatever wiped them out, happened a couple hundred years ago. Best bet."

She turned in her seat. She had more to say, but again seemed to want Gendrick to keep the conversation going, prove himself worthy of hearing her sage words.

Across the room, which had been dubbed *Command*

Central by the residents since it had the most up-to-date equipment and was one place where all aspects of the scientific community – paleontology, known more colloquially (and accurately, Gendrick thought) as xenology, linguistics, biology – shared a common space, tossing theories and questions over cubical walls like paper airplanes. Arun was bent over his own Ep, lost in his world of sand scribbles and alien dances. He'd brought Gendrick here this morning after breakfast (Doneele was conspicuously absent for that meal) and introduced him to Miyoko with a brief, "Our xenologist has some interesting theories you might want to hear, especially considering what the folks up at the Hole discovered last night."

Gendrick looked at the pictures and decided Arun had been giving him a clue. He thought about the Locusts.

Locusts . . .

He looked down at Miyoko, suddenly excited, even if at the moment he wasn't exactly sure why. He said, "The Locusts. I assume you've found fossils of them, too?"

She smiled, a teacher proud of her student's ability to learn. She said with forced casualness, "No, not one. The oldest skeletons – if you can call them skeletons, not much left of them but the DNA matches – are . . . well, guess how old they are."

"A couple hundred years."

She swiveled in her seat, brought up an image of something that looked like chunks of rock. "Give that man a cigar," she said. "Now, popular theories, until last night, estimated that whatever traumatic event wiped out most of the species on the planet – forty-seven we've found so far, but we're a long way from cataloging all of them – seemed to have spared the Locust population. They had somehow . . . adapted."

He stared at the pieces of the excavated remains. A

dead Locust, he assumed. "Adapted? How?"

She shrugged. "Don't know. They seem fairly well entrenched in their pathology, perfectly designed to fly long distances, traveling the globe in a single day, mostly keeping within forty-five degrees north and south." At his blank stare she added, raising her hands flat with palms facing each other, as if holding a stack of papers, "They keep mostly to the middle two-thirds of the planet, probably because there'd once been the most food in this region. These days though," she made a noise, then raised her hands without finishing the thought. She didn't need to. *These days there isn't much on the menu.* "They eat quickly, when they find food, processing it while flying to the next. They even linger in specific regions throughout the night in some interesting social groups we're still working out. But the *cattle*," she brought up an image of a herd, perhaps the same which frequented the grasslands a kilometer or so beyond their window, "also seem to be one of the very few large species to have survived whatever happened. We have fossils of them going back thousands of years. Millions, maybe. We'll know more once we've excavated deep enough."

She closed the window then added, almost as an after-thought, "Like I said, that was the popular theory until last night."

Last night, he thought, *when they found a Locust on an alien spaceship on the other side of this system's wormhole.*

Gendrick leaned closer toward the screen. The position was starting to get uncomfortable, so he pulled up the extra chair and sat. "And the newest theory?" He took a sip from his cooled coffee, put it back on the desk.

Whatever theory she might share, he assumed, was her own since the woman was beaming with pleasure. "Ah, now, that would be telling. Let me give you a hint. Of the species for which we've found *true* fossils, as well as some more recent remains, guess which made up about a third of the total?"

"Were . . . you mean what kind of animals?"

She nodded.

He shrugged. "Snakes?"

She laughed and shook her head. "Birds," she said.

"Birds . . . I thought there *were* no birds on Toojay."

"Not anymore. Want to know what another third are consist of?"

"Snakes?"

"You have a thing for snakes, don't you?"

"Hate 'em."

"I like you, Father. You don't pretend to know things."

Gendrick smiled, uncertain if he'd been insulted.

She brought up another image, another fossil. This one he'd seen plenty of times in science classes over the years. Perfectly symmetrical leaves patterned along the stone. "Plants," he said. "I don't see the connection."

She twirled back and forth in her chair, looking down, deciding how to phrase what she said next. When she did, it took a few moments for the meaning to sink in. When *it* did, Gendrick's skin tightened.

"Plant life, everywhere. As abundant as Eden in some places. And lots more variety within the animal kingdom." She waited, watching him, then added, "My theory, one which has suddenly become quite popular with the media, is that the cattle out there," she nodded towards the room-spanning window, "did not survive some catastrophe that occurred a couple hundred years ago on this planet. They simply . . . adapted."

"To what?" He'd asked the question reflexively, but already, he was beginning to understand the answer.

"The Locust's sudden arrival on this planet."

15 – Peyton, 3JH/2JS

The large conference table on board the *Washington* filled only half the room. The other half existed – for the moment – aboard the *Abad*. The table on which Peyton laid her water bottle abutted the far wall, where the projected image of the *Abad* crew in their own conference room continued and gave the illusion of a single unit.

Peyton wiped her hands across her face. She was tired, but even when this meeting ended she still had plans. Gendrick Hellerton was on Toojay. After years of silence between them, her fault, mostly. She was a little surprised with herself to be so thrilled he was this close. Gen, the man she once loved, perhaps still did, even if he *still* didn't fit into her life's ultimate plan. Of course, *she* didn't fit into his life goals, either.

Their story sounded like a sad romantic tragedy. She'd told it to a few people, including Cannon. Always, people looked at her oddly. How could she cut Gendrick off from her life for so long if he meant that much to her? To parry this inevitable question, she'd remind herself that he'd done the same to her. Always, of course, the final judgment: *You shouldn't have started dating each other.*

They'd been wrong to do that, to try to start something at that point in their lives. She and Gen were never meant to be together beyond high school. But those few months were ones she remembered only with joy. No regret.

And now they were together again, relatively speaking.

The odds were . . . well, they were astronomical. There was a week's flight at top speed between them, but how many weeks had there been before? A lifetime's worth. Crazy odds, unless Gendrick decided to take up stalking as a hobby.

She smiled. If she was going to be stalked, who better by? He was one of the priests working on that new history for the church, a *history of the future* she'd heard it referenced as once. After reading his letter, Peyton looked up his installments, but so far he'd released nothing except the title, *God's Vast Array*. Nice title, though. A couple of others had begun to appear from the perspective of Eden and Earth. Nothing from Gen. With his letter, she longed to actually hear his voice. Yearned for it.

She sighed. No one noticed. Cannon was right. She needed a boyfriend.

" . . . send us updates twice a day, as will we." Radish Marlay was speaking.

Ken nodded to the *Abad*'s captain. "That's the plan."

Radish leaned forward onto his elbows. His dark face was always clean shaven and smooth, downturned, angry, mistrusting. According to Ken, during their one-on-one debriefing he hadn't been as much of a jerk as Ken had expected. Radish liked to act like the bully in public. It was a management style, in contrast to Ken's which was far more amiable – unless you screwed up. Radish Marlay preferred instilling fear in his crew ahead of time, even loathing. *If I'm like this now,* his demeanor suggested, *you don't want to end up on my bad side.*

Flanking him on the vid were Rourke O'Shannon, muscular with a shag of blond hair, and another member of the senior staff – a long wire of a man Peyton didn't recognize. They sat stiffly, without emotion. Neutrality aboard the *Abad* was a required defense mechanism.

Radish was leaning forward on his forearms, hands clasped. "I assume, though the assumption may be misplaced, that you will use extreme caution when you send any of your crew inside the hangar."

The "hangar" had become the term for the cavernous maw which had opened up to space this morning. No one could say with any certainty what its purpose was, but without a better option the word Benny had used over the com when they returned 2Jside had stuck.

Ken snorted, the sound more contempt than humor. "Well," he said, looking around this side of the table, "I'll at least let them wear their suits, what with the vacuum of space and – "

"Captain Burlov, may I remind you that what you are dealing with is not –"

"Captain Marlay," Ken interrupted, himself now leaning forward, "may I remind you that I know what the hell I'm doing?" Peyton had no doubt if he could have reached out and grabbed the man's shirt he would have. "Of *course* we'll be careful. Don't think for one minute I like the idea of sending anyone inside. None of us are fooled into thinking this machine is dead, *or* harmless. Nor do I consider that door opening at this moment in time a coincidence. Do you?"

Marlay leaned back, slowly, and shook his head. "No, I do not think so, either. None of us can afford any presumption." His face softened, just a little. "And I apologize for implying you do not have the best interests of your crew at heart." He actually smiled. "I'm entitled to a little professional jealousy."

Ken's subsequent laugh, false as it was, lowered the pressure in both rooms to a bearable level. "No problem, Rad. You – "

"Radish." He pronounced it *Ra – Deesh*.

" . . . Radish. You *should* be jealous. Still, you get to be first at 33P, since we'll be tied up here."

33P? Peyton nodded to herself. An obvious shortening of 3J3P, third planet in the new system. That one *could* stick. It was easy to say, at least. The media and scientific communities had already begun jockeying for naming rights. Something, eventually, would rise up as the planet's common name. Crew vied for the chance to toss out their personal favorites during interviews. Apparently, Ken had chosen *his*, since this conference was broadcast on public channels. Marlay would have his own by the next interview, and it sure wouldn't be *33P*. One more way these Y-chromosomes liked to compete.

The *Abad's* mission captain straightened in the chair and laid his hands flat on the tabletop. "Will you be arriving full-ship through the Hole soon?"

"Yes, but we'd rather wait for you folks to move far enough away before we come barreling out. Bad enough we'll have to hit the brakes as soon as we enter the 3J system to avoid the derelict. I'd hate to put a dent in your hull."

Marlay nodded curtly. "Good idea. Are we finished, then?" Nods all around. "Good luck, Captain. We'll be praying for your safety."

Peyton raised an eyebrow but otherwise tried not to show any emotion. People never failed to surprise her.

"Back at you," Ken said. "Good luck on the planet. I look forward to seeing what you find."

The first, detailed glimpse of 33P would come well before the *Abad* arrived. As soon as the *Washington* discovered the Hole an automated probe was sent towards the third planet. It would begin the process of scanning the surface, and the *Washington* could have normally claimed right of first exploration when it physically entered the system. This time around, however, a second probe had to be prepped and launched, since the first had been rerouted and was still preoccupied with the alien ship. Since the *Washington* chose to stay back, the *Abad* would hardly be a day and half out when the first good feeds from their probe arrived.

By then, Peyton and Cannon would be too busy sticking their heads into the proverbial lion's mouth to pay attention to anything else.

She glanced at Rourke's image from the *Abad*. As soon as he saw her looking his way he winked. The screen went blank a moment later.

Ken turned to face his crew. "What are you blushing about?"

Cannon, seated on the captain's right, broke his silence and laughed out loud. "How can you tell she's blushing?" He glanced back at the blank wall where the *Abad* had been. "Did O'Shannon just wink at you?"

Peyton got up and offered her friend a smoldering look, then half-smiled. "Doesn't everyone?"

Ken shook his head and walked to the door. "He probably had something in his eye. You guys get as much sleep as you can the next two days. Pill up if you have to. You need to be clear."

They didn't reply. In two days they would be the first humans to enter an alien spacecraft. Pill or no pill, there was no way they'd be sleeping much until then.

16 – Gendrick, 2J3P

Tomorrow was Sunday on Toojay. Gendrick had run through the profiles of the scientists and service workers manning this southern outpost. Sixteen were Christian, mostly Apostolic but a smattering of other, smaller denominations as well. Of the former, two were part of an unofficial offshoot of the ACC known as Marionists. Arun was one of these. The sect did not always mix well, theologically, with the general Christian population because of their reverence for Mary, the mother of Christ. In many ways they were spiritually, if not technically, a separate denomination, more closely tied to the Church's former Catholic roots. Gendrick was still their pastor. Of the remaining population in this corner of the continent, six claimed Islamic faith, three Jewish, one was an atheist, another a Wiccan and the four remaining had chosen "undecided." Though the numbers varied, the breakdown was much the same at the other two stations. Until other pastors arrived, he would need to work out a rotation schedule. Unless Doneele already had something worked out. It was likely.

Gendrick slowly paced the small chapel. Situated around the corner from Command Central, it was on the opposite end of the compound from the Mess and Living sections. He tapped his fingertips against the smooth plastic pews, only five rows but even *that* was too many. The cross had been lowered from a niche in the ceiling. He would have to raise it out of sight before he left, then recess the pews into the floor so Imam Kusher could have his morning Call to Prayer in an hour. Now, though, was how the room would look tomorrow when Gendrick addressed his congregation for the first time.

Last time they spoke, Doneele hinted all sixteen would attend his service, some merely to check out the 'new guy.' Half might return with any regularity. Less, she'd added, if he managed to bore them with his sermon.

No matter. All of this was temporary until a full colony could be established and a permanent church built. That might not be for years, especially with the Locust swarm circling the globe. There was time. Most of the people currently on Toojay would live out the rest of their lives asking questions and listening for answers, while a few were biding time until the next planet was found and opened for study. The latter would slowly move farther and farther away from their pasts. Gendrick could identify with them.

He blinked. He was writing *Vast Array* in his head again, something he'd been catching himself at all day since finding some momentum writing last night. He sighed, took out his Ep and tapped out a few notes before the musings faded from his mind.

Maybe Doneele's strange welcome had flipped the right switches in his brain. Near death experiences could do that. Maybe it was seeing Pey on the video. She was living her dream – maybe it was *his* time. Working on something an entire civilization would read almost as soon as he released it, chapter by chapter. This thought never frightened him. If anything, he found it funny. Here he was, an unknown priest assigned to a pre-colony planet, walking down an aisle with retractable benches, trying to work out what he wanted to say in his first sermon. And *oh, by the way,* the entirety of the human race could, theoretically, read whatever he was going to write tonight before going to bed.

And what *would* he write? Something about Ochi Miyoko's theories, of course. Nothing was as it seemed when he first arrived here. On Eden, one discovery led to the next, all fitting neatly into presumptions of planetary development, evolution of species, excavations of fossils dating back millennia. Here, very few of the fossils matched the planet as it was currently configured, save a few species of plant and animal.

What had he written last night in *Vast Array*? Adam and Even stepping from the Garden into the desolate wilderness. Like humanity of today, regaining paradise with a new Earth only to step from its gates of their own free will, into the desert of Toojay.

He wondered what the crew of –

"Father Gendrick?"

He looked up, startled. Doneele stood in the entryway, hands folded in front of her robes in the humble stance of their calling.

"Mother Doneele," he said, smiling in spite of a renewed discomfort being in her presence. Didn't matter if he liked her, however, he *needed* to be comfortable in her company. At least pretend to.

She remained in the doorway, face expressionless except for a slight twitch of her jaw muscles. "Working on your sermon?"

Gendrick risked stepping closer but stopped at the last pew to keep some space between them. He leaned against the back of the bench and casually crossed his arms. "Yep," he said, and tapped his temple. "It's in here for now. There's been so much to see and take in. Trying to sort it all out."

Keeping her hands folded, Doneele stepped towards him, then turned and leaned beside him against the pew.

"Sometimes," she said, quietly, "it feels like there's more new information coming at us every day. Too much truth to accept all at once. Hard to . . ." She trailed off, looked to the floor. Gendrick waited.

She didn't look up when she continued, "Father, I would like to take Confession with you, if that's all right."

The request did not surprise him. Though the formal Sacrament was not required within ACC Cannon it was urged, especially for the clergy. Confessing one's sins and shortcomings directly into the ear of God was every Christian's right, and requirement, really, but there was something healthy about speaking them aloud to another human.

Especially out here, where the world felt too empty, not enough people to notice what you've done. Not enough people to care.

"Sure. Do you want to sit down?"

She shook her head. "No. Here's fine." She looked towards the open door, then back down to her folded hands. Gendrick moved off the bench, closed the chapel door, returned to his earlier stance.

"OK."

She blessed herself using the old-style Catholic sign, finger moving from the center of her forehead, then her chest, crossing to the left then right shoulder. The gesture had long gone out of fashion in the church, as were her next words, recitations from another time. "Bless me, Father, for I have sinned. It has been a week since the last public confession."

A week? he thought, unable to shake the feeling the woman was mocking him with this formality. He cleared his throat, asked, "Who did you take confession with last time?"

She looked at him sharply for a moment, perhaps not

understanding his question. When she looked down again, she said, "Prelate McCarthy has been hearing my confession every week since my husband passed away, over a secured vid."

Gendrick remembered thinking only last night how *no* communication between planets was secure. He nodded, said, "Anything specific you'd like to talk about?"

She said nothing, only stared at the tips of her black shoes poking from under her robes. Gendrick began to wonder if this would be one of those *silent penances*, where the confessor pours out their sins privately to God but in the company of a priest.

Still looking down, Doneele said, "I miss Zech—my late husband, Zechariah. I miss feeling his arms move around me. He was a strong man, all of his strength completely natural. He liked to work outside, help the others when he could. He wasn't vain, didn't spend any time staring at his biceps in the mirror or anything like that. But he was proud of how he stayed in shape, with very little enhancements. He *liked* being in shape, even as we got along in years." She laughed at some private joke, continued, "I liked it, too. Liked how he held me, leaning against me . . ." She fell silent again. Gendrick waited.

"I made a mistake the other night, Father." She looked up at him, cocking her head and catching him with the hook of her one-eyed stare. "You remind me of him, when we were much younger . . ." She looked down at her shoes again. "I apologize for coming on so strongly. It was wrong. I should have remembered what it was like to come to a strange place and not know anyone. But," she smirked, caught herself and let her expression go blank again, "I was lonely. I felt your presence, so strongly drawing me to you." She was breathing deeper. At first Gendrick thought she might be crying, or fighting it, but soon sensed something else in the act, and her posture. Was she sending signals . . . *no. Just listen.*

"I have thoughts, Father. Debase ones. When they come it's hard to fight them, hard not to want to act on them. Even once, just to *try* it." She turned towards him. "Does that make any sense? To feel an attraction so heady and powerful you crave it while telling yourself it's wrong? This is not the first time. I've followed up on these desires before."

She was barely a half-arm's length away, breathing in that steady, rhythmic way. He needed to stay neutral, focused, and not let anything going on in this woman's head affect what was happening in his. She knew it, *had* to know. This needed to stop.

But she was making her confession.

She stepped closer, laid a hand lightly on his arm. "I only have a month left on this rock then my life is a blank window. I don't know what will happen." Their robes blended. "I'm afraid. Yet, over and over I lay in bed and think these thoughts and can't stop them. I don't *want* to stop them."

Gendrick was dizzy, trying to work out the right way to behave, to not lead her on, if he was somehow doing that. He was doing *nothing.* Maybe that was the problem. He closed his eyes and tried not to lean away. Her grip on his arm tightened, the unpleasant sensation of some attempted control over him. "I'm not *that* much older than you, Father. I can do so many —"

He opened his eyes. "Doneele," his voice was hoarse, but he couldn't pause to clear his throat, "what is your intention in making this confession?"

When she leaned against him, Gendrick put his hands on her shoulders and gently pushed her away. She'd asked for confession, but there was no question now it had been a bizarre attempt at seduction.

Her eyes, which had closed to slits, now widened, still heavy with emotion but with an added touch of desperation. "What are you doing," she whispered. "You want me, too. Some things you can't hide."

When she tried to press forward, Gendrick held her back, stepped sideways to allow himself an exit down the aisle if it became necessary.

"Doneele, you asked me to hear your confession. I don't remember sex being part of the Sacrament." He hadn't wanted it to come out that cold, but there was nothing to do about it now. The mood shattered.

Doneele's brows tightened over the bridge of her freckled nose. Her hands moved back to their earlier, prayerful rest in front of her. And she stared at him. Gendrick wished he was better at reading expressions. Hers was unreadable. Blank.

"I'm sorry, Father. That wasn't my best penance, to be sure." She tried to smile. It looked more like she was chewing on a piece of meat. She looked past him, up at something near the ceiling. She almost smiled, then looked down to the floor and the tips of her shoes.

"That's OK," he said. What else could he say, maybe another time? This woman was not well. Still, *was* it him? Something he was conveying, giving the wrong signals?

She looked up, hopeful for a moment, then the coldness returned. "Again, I'm sorry, Father. I don't think this should be considered a valid confession."

Doneele was gone a few seconds later. Gendrick remained where he was, listening to the rubber padding of her steps down the hall until finally moving to sit in the last pew, staring up at the cross hanging above the altar. Eventually it rose soundlessly into the ceiling. A young, bearded man stood by the switch.

"I'm sorry," the man said. "I didn't want to disturb your prayers. I'm afraid I'm going to need to use this room in a few minutes." He reached out a ringed hand. "You're the new priest?"

Gendrick nodded and stood, taking Imam Kushner's hand, and introduced himself.

He helped roll out seven prayer rugs as soon as the pews and altar were lowered into the floor, then excused himself. During the walk along the hall towards the cafeteria, he dreaded running into her. He'd messed up badly that first night, letting her into his room. But what could he have done differently this time?

He checked his watch. Arun had promised to take him outside again this morning. He had five minutes to get to the Mess to meet him. He picked up his pace as he pulled his Ep from the pocket of his robes. A message icon was flashing on the otherwise blank sheet. He tapped it.

Peyton Kay had replied to his letter.

He closed the window and refolded it back into his pocket. *Well*, he decided, *the day isn't a total wash*.

He hoped.

Arun waved to him from across the room. Gendrick managed to smile and wave back.

17 – Vernaine McCarthy, 1J3P

Prelate Vernaine McCarthy was a short, skinny man who moved slowly through life. He'd been named by his mother, partly as concession to his paternal grandfather, Vernon, partly in quiet rebellion. He thought often about many things, but spoke of them infrequently. The dappled green of the garden stretched a hundred yards from the back of the central office complex, blending into the forest beyond. Called *The Woods* by Silent Call residents, the wooded region stretched away for miles. He'd been told there was story behind the town's name, but never learned it, mostly from lack of interest on his part. He simply liked the name, enjoyed walking the length of the clipped lawn until reaching the curved, oddly proportioned trees lining the outskirts of the woods. The grass under his polished black shoes was the typical wide, soft blade native to the planet.

So much like Earth, yet in many ways, vastly alien.

He stopped near the edge of the trees and sat on a bench. Its marble radiated coolness through his robes. Everything on Eden was like that. Cool, relaxed, welcoming. Even at the peak of summer the days in this northern continent rarely reached past forty Celsius.

Eden was, truly, the garden regained.

He unfolded the Ep and fingered his personal access code, brought up the recording from Toojay. In silence, always aware of his surroundings lest someone wander his way and inadvertently see what he saw, he watched for the third time the interchange between Mother Doneele and Father Hellerton.

The first time he'd seen this, during breakfast, Vernaine had fingered the pause icon the moment Doneele looked up past Hellerton's shoulder and stared directly at *him*. He knew that wasn't entirely true. She was staring at the camera, supposedly concealed from human sight. When the complex was built, the Church had received a variance on the usually restrictive laws against hidden surveillance for the chapel only.

Doneele was smart – most *everyone* up there was or they wouldn't have been sent to Toojay in the first place. Unfortunately, the woman was also mad as a hatter. A dangerous combination, especially on the frontier. You needed to be clever in a place where every day could bring an unexpected and unwelcome surprise.

Everything was monitored, with few truly secure channels of communication. Secrets bred more secrets, after all. Still, there were ways around every locked door, no matter how well-hidden. The brightest minds living on the fringe found as many of these doors as possible, then pretended they did not exist. *Know your enemy, but to not let him* know *you know*.

Doneele's image stared at the camera and into Vernaine's eyes – she knew he would monitor all activity within the chapel, not to mention anywhere else she might go. She held the smallest hint of a smile on her face. Was it a challenge? A taunt?

You know my secret, the look said, *and there is nothing you can do about it. I may be insane, but* you *are a fool.*

No. He was no fool. The confessional was sacred ground. The words spoken in the Sacrament were for God's ears alone. The priest was merely a conduit. To break its sanctity would be to undermine God's judgment and grace. True, most people preferred to offer their sins up to God alone, with no human ear between. But many *needed* to speak the words, feel the full weight of their sin lifted. To know they've been *heard*.

Last year, Mother Doneele had done just that. The weight should have passed on, been laid at the foot of the cross to become no more tangible than wind. Somehow, it hadn't. The weight simply left her shoulders and fell heavily on his own. He felt its presence every day.

It was not his problem.

He looked at the half-smile casually drawn upon the woman's face. Had she chosen to come to Father Hellerton under the guise of Penance as a goad to Vernaine?

You can tell no one, that short look into the hidden camera said. *You can make me come home, but you can do nothing more.*

Of course he could. And he would. He would relegate this woman to some menial task here in the idyllic town of Silent Call, keep her close where he can watch her, wait to see if her behavior warranted more action. Somehow, he would find a way to lock her up, save her – and everyone else – from herself.

The prelate understood now that Gendrick Hellerton was not safe. It was midday on Toojay, with many more days to come before the next transport. Enough for Mother Doneele to gravitate towards him. She would do this, not as a rogue moon locking itself in orbit, but a shark circling prey. She may be mad, but she was moving in a deliberate direction. Goading Vernaine, challenging him to break his oath and report her.

Perhaps *wanting* him to. *Needing* him to.

Often, he wondered why she had not been arrested. Could her confession truly have been private? It was a good thought, or would be, in other circumstances. He did not fool himself into assuming she wouldn't be arrested the moment she stepped onto Eden's soil.

He tapped into the vid feed from her personal quarters, another concession since she was a direct representative of the Church. The room was empty. At least the video still worked. If she knew where the camera was in the chapel, finding this one should be a piece of cake. Of course, now and then he would pry into her life to find the signal interrupted, blank or rerouted to the mess hall or a group of rocks on the surface of the planet.

Could be a normal glitch in the system. He doubted it. She was very resourceful.

He folded the Ep back into his pocket and let his face drop into his hands. *Lord, help me to do the right thing. Help Father Hellerton. Keep him out of danger. Protect him from Doneele, and help her to keep it together. One month more, Lord. Please.*

He stayed that way for a few minutes more. Someone walked slowly past. He did not raise his head until he was sure they'd moved on. Whoever it was would assume the clergyman was deep in prayer. This was true, of course, but more than this he did not want conversation. Not now. Too much to think about. Too much to worry over.

Fear was a sin. He needed to trust God's plan in all this.

He finally looked up and around at the beauty of his home world. Such a blessing, like a gift left under the tree, now that the Lord's people had matured enough to receive it. Whatever would happen, it was in His hands. Not Vernaine's. All *he* could do was watch, and pray no one else died at the hands of Mother Doneele.

18 – Gendrick, 2J3P

"**Y**ou're sure we have enough daylight left to get back?"

Arun sighed, smiling. "Open your Ep, Gen. Connect to . . . ready?"

Gendrick fumbled open his paper then held it out to the linguist.

Arun nodded and looked down at his own sheet. The open window was being used to track their path. He thumbed an icon and it expanded to a photo image of Toojay from low orbit. He flicked the image with his finger. It duplicated itself on Gendrick's Ep.

In the picture, a vertical blinking began halfway from pole to equator, drawing across both hemispheres. The line was colored, white furthest south and north, bright red in the center.

"Red means a concentrated cluster, white means thin. Sometimes nonexistent. See, that's the western shore of WHU. They haven't even *begun* to cross the ocean to get to us. Not yet. Tap the red dot . . . there."

Gendrick did. The globe rotated away from the view labeled *Western Hemisphere / Upper Continent*, until their own continent rolled around, then continued rolling. The land was known only as EHC or *Eastern Hemisphere Continent* since it was a massive, contiguous land mass broken only by the occasional river and lake. The red dot he'd touched, far inland, expanded to highlight their location, dead center in the southern land mass.

Arun slapped him on the shoulder. "See? No worries, my friend." He gave Gendrick's arm a quick squeeze and before folding his Ep away and resuming his walk. Gendrick tapped the window to bookmark the application. He'd be checking this one often.

The two men were far enough from the compound that various clusters of boulders they'd passed now blocked any view of its buildings. They walked over a kilometer to reach the closest herd. The "cattle" were docile animals, but seemed to prefer keeping their distance from the scientific outposts. Likewise, the outposts had been built far enough away not to be a disruption yet close enough to approach by foot. The primary reason for this were the herds' underground burrows, where the cattle slept and waited out the treacherous, Toojay nights. One of the earliest laws passed for manned exploration of this planet was to keep as far from the entrance to the holes as possible. Every dusk the cattle wandered together into these sloping caverns. These *had* been explored surreptitiously, during the day when the animals were on the surface grazing. The trespass was accomplished using robotic cameras, but so far there had been only a couple of successful attempts. The cattle did not graze far from the entrances and managed to intercept the wheeled drones more than once. Finally, Miyoko had officially marked the underground burrows as the 'private land' of this largest remaining species on the planet. It was off-limits to humans. For the moment. Scientific curiosity would invariably bend this rule in some way.

Docile was putting it mildly when it came to them. Still, they were resourceful. Miyoko and her counterparts at the two other compounds had no reasonable explanation for how these four-legged, cloven-footed mammals could have built such tunnels (making the term "burrows" somewhat of a misnomer), let alone the elaborate niches and caves at their terminus sixty meters below the surface. Likely, they were remnants of another species, adding fuel to her growing certainty that this world had been a vastly different place a couple hundred years ago.

Arun gained ground a few paces ahead. He slowed, let Gendrick catch up, then continued walking the other man's pace. He was uncharacteristically silent.

"Father," he said at last, almost whispering.

Uh, oh. As soon as someone referred to Gendrick by his official title, he knew he'd be put to work. He resisted the temptation to spout *Yes, my son?* and simply said, "Hmm?"

They were approaching a large clump of boulders. Beyond, Gendrick thought he heard new sounds. Bleating. They were getting close.

Arun said, not sounding much like the goofy, relaxed soul who had waved at Gendrick earlier in the Mess with such flourish. He fell silent a moment longer, then looked sideways at him. "Did you sleep with Mother Doneele?"

Gendrick smiled, shook his head. "No, though not for lack of trying on her part."

Arun folded his Ep and tucked it into the front flap of the backpack he'd swung forward on one shoulder. Hefting the pack again, he shoved both hands into his jeans pockets. "Don't, if you can help it. As you've probably been learning for yourself, that might be harder than it sounds. Seriously, buddy, you want to be careful. I like Donny, but she's a little – " He fell quiet.

"Off-kilter?" Gendrick offered when the silence hung too long.

Arun laughed, nodded his head. "Yea. A bit. Since Zech died, she hasn't been right in the head. If you ask me, a few gears had started to slip before that. Just watch your back."

He smirked. "And your front."

Gendrick laughed and promised he would, wondering what Arun would think if he'd seen what happened this morning. Maybe someone *had* passed by and seen them.

Arun nodded. "OK. That's good." He said nothing more on the topic, but the silence felt a little forced. Gendrick wondered if there was more he wanted to say. One of his favorite teachers in seminary once said, *The sound of someone biting their tongue can be quite loud.*

They rounded the boulders. The ground sloped down from this point. Both men stopped. Gendrick stared. The herd filled the shallow valley below them. "How many—?"

Arun took a moment to survey the lower plain. "Three hundred, maybe. three-fifty?" His smile returned the man's face into its old light.

The animals were clustered into similarly-sized groups along the dry, grassy plain. Standing exposed to the valley below, the smell was a physical assault to Gendrick's senses. The linguist had become adapted to the smell as he gave no reaction. A heavy, sweaty odor, fleshy heat rising in the sun. The cattle – no official designation had yet been given them, though they were by far the most prominent species on the planet – were large and awkwardly built. Bodies the size of a North American quarter horse, their flanks were thin but wide, with short muscular legs. Their necks were longer than a horse's by half, flat and wide like their bodies, leading to a head with wet black eyes. Cheeks puffed out like a hippo's as if full of food. Long lines of drool dripped to the ground, a constant flow of saliva as they raised and lowered their heads to take small, conservative bits of grass to chew.

They moved languidly in the sun. Cows – the bovine terms had become common when discussing the females – occasionally bleated at smaller calves, though the younger animals seemed to be as slow-moving as the adults and not likely to wander too far and easily rounded up.

Arun walked fearlessly into their midst. Gendrick followed. The backs of the largest cattle were at eye level with the priest. Their feet were cloven, pig-like, but wide and flat and tapered at the end of both "toes" with a long, black claw. Used for digging, Gendrick assumed. The feet themselves were heavy and crushing.

"Hey, Johnny," Arun said to a large male. *Johnny* raised its head, chewed while taking in Arun's presence. Large eyes, black orbs which revealed no obvious intelligence, rolled shiny in the sunlight. It made a throaty noise, a subdued version of the bleating constantly sounding from the females. To Gendrick, the sound was akin to a human *harrumph*, as if the bull was more annoyed than nervous. It sniffed Arun's outstretched hands, held palm-down and fingers curled, then lowered its head to the ground.

"Johnny?" Gendrick was whispering. "I don't see a tag anywhere."

"Yea, I know. I make up names as I go along. No sense tagging these folks since they aren't migratory." He continued on, now and then running his fingertips along their flanks. A light, sandy fur coated them, not enough to cover their thick flesh but enough for some coloring, camouflage perhaps for living on the plains. The animals responded to his touch with quick flicks of muscles, as if shooing a fly.

Something Arun said finally registered. Gendrick spoke louder now that he was fairly certain the herd wouldn't stampede. "You call them folks. Have you seen any sign of intelligence? Cognitive ability?"

Arun shook his head. "No, not really, aside from herd reactions, and basic survival skills." He looked up. "They always know what time of day it is and give themselves enough slack to get underground before the air gets wacky."

"Most of them, at least. I assume some mustn't make it back in time. Otherwise what would the Locusts eat?"

Arun turned around, looked at him with more seriousness. "Ah, yup. True enough. Happens occasionally. Not often, though."

Gendrick risked a couple of fingers along a cow's fur. She looked up, smelled him, bleated and slowly stepped away. Not one for inter-species affection, this.

Arun scanned the herds, though his view of the plains was blocked by the large bodies milling around him. "There are quite a few herds. From what I've observed, it's rare for a slowpoke to linger for the flying monkeys at night. Most of the time, they all make it inside. I'm sure it happens, somewhere across the globe. The Locusts' metabolism is pretty slow, which is surprising considering they do pretty much nothing else besides fly all day. Most of their anatomy is guesswork, though. If one dies, there's not much left by the swarm for us to study."

"How many Locusts are there?"

Arun didn't need to flip open his Ep to answer. "Fifteen thousand, nine-hundred and twenty-two. Last count."

Gendrick found himself looking skyward again, fingered the Ep in his pocket. He wouldn't check on the swarm's location. Not yet. "Sounds like a lot."

Arun nodded then wandered around to the opposite side of a large male. He called over its back, "Yea, sounds like a lot, but not when you consider how freakin' huge the planet is. They travel in one line, north to south, the largest congregation close to the equator, but even so, fifteen thousand doesn't exactly blanket the landscape. There're plenty of gaps and at last count, we have over seven hundred thousand cattle just on this continent alone."

"And nothing else. No birds." Gendrick said, more to himself than Arun.

Arun came back around. "Not true, there are quite a few other species, much smaller than these guys," he patted its flank, "but –" he raised a finger for emphasis, "all of them are ground dwelling."

"So the birds . . .?"

Arun began walking with more purpose out of the herd towards the lip of the hole leading down into the burrow. Gendrick followed, hoping his new friend hadn't decided to go down into it.

"They got eaten a long time ago."

"The hallucinogenic chemicals activated in the evening are from the Locusts?"

"Not activated, as much as waking up. They fart the stuff pretty constantly, but sunlight makes the Acclarin dormant. It hits its potency almost as soon as the sun drops from direct view."

"So they brought this little trick along with them, whenever they arrived here?"

Arun shrugged. "Miyoko thinks so. We haven't been allowed to capture any living bugs, but studies of the pieces of bodies we found showed the sacks with high levels of the stuff. Like flying skunks, releasing it into the air as they fly."

Gendrick raised a hand to another animal, but it stepped casually sideways until he lowered his hand. "Kind of like terra-forming. They show up one day, *dropped off* if you buy into Miyoko's theory, then start to spray, and swarm."

Arun shrugged, stopped at the lip of the hole. The ground that sloped steeply down into darkness was smooth, well-worn. The far edges were crusted with loose sand occasionally breaking loose. "Well, they *are* locusts, after all."

"That's just what we call them."

When Arun looked at him, there was something new in his expression. Beyond serious, something darker. "It's what they are. Mindless eating machines. Swarming around the globe eating and farting out hallucinogenic drugs so they can keep on slowly destroying the planet." He smirked, offered an apologetic shrug of his shoulders. "Sorry. I may study them, but I don't have to like them." He looked back at the herd. "I like these folks more."

Gendrick glanced up. The sky was comfortingly bright. "I assume the Locusts must take a break now and then to make baby mindless eating machines?"

Arun shook his head. "Not that we've seen. Granted, we haven't been here very long, but you'd think after ten years one of our stations would have monitored something akin to the act of mating."

"That's not possible. How could they survive? Every species has to reproduce."

Arun nodded but said nothing. He circled the entrance to the hole but did not enter. Gendrick glanced behind him. Two of the larger cattle, males he assumed, had broken from the general herd and were watching them with wet, interested eyes.

Holes, Gendrick thought. Everyone's lives revolved around holes in one form or another out here. "Why are you studying the Locust's language if you think they're mindless, then?"

Arun kicked the ground, looking sullen. "Because they're not. I was just venting."

Gendrick waited. From the way Arun looked almost at random around the edge of the hole, he didn't think the man was finished talking. "They killed a good friend of mine."

"Zechariah O'Coin?"

"Yea, Mother Doneele's husband. *Late* husband."

"From what I gather he'd wandered out too far, didn't get back in time."

Arun shook his head, kicked the ground again. "They *ate* him, yea. Stupid, stupid way to die." He sighed. "I miss him."

A breeze picked up, slight but cool. Gendrick closed his eyes and breathed in the clean air. It felt good.

Too good. "What time is it?" He fumbled in his pocket for the Ep, shakily opened it up, tapped the bookmark.

The swarm was far off, currently crossing the eastern ocean.

"It's OK, Gen, we can head back." He gestured down into the hole. "I'd like to take you down there, but we're not allowed. Check out the vids from the robots, though. Some cool weirdness down there. But it's Xeno group's territory. They don't want us breaking anything." He gestured over Gendrick's shoulder. "Neither, apparently, do Moe and Curley."

Gendrick turned around again then took a sudden step backwards. The two males had come within a few meters of their location without making a sound. Arun didn't look very concerned. Gendrick pretended he wasn't either. The sun was halfway from its peak, and suddenly he didn't want to have any kind of discussion, not unless they were walking back. Arun tapped him on the shoulder, gave him a push. "Come on, let's go. I keep forgetting you haven't been here long enough to take your life for granted as much as the rest of us." He waved to the two cattle, who had settled themselves between the men and the hole. He was smiling again, a good sign. Everyone seemed happy here, enjoyed their work. Still, from what Gendrick had seen today with this man, there was a river of sadness running beneath it all.

An odd place, this planet. And in some unspoken way . . . *wrong*.

The sounds of the herds eventually fell away. It was good to see the compound between two massive, sandy stones. *Home*, for a long as they allowed him to stay. Even if it *was* broken.

19 – Cannon, 3JH/2JS

"The Kay's are sweet, and it helps to be able to talk with people going through the same thing." Leanne looked down, fiddled with something off-window on her lap.

Sometimes Cannon wished she would complain more, but they dealt with stresses in their own ways. He used humor, tried to see the universe as a set of rules meant to be broken. Leanne was the realist. No shouting at windmills for her. Her husband couldn't come home until his tour was up. She understood this and accepted it. She didn't like it, but what else was there to do?

Tomorrow he and Pey were stepping into the hangar of the derelict... the *alien* ship. They needed to start calling it what it was. This fact ratcheted up the tension a few notches. Leanne's shoulders were slightly hunched, and she had a hard time maintaining eye contact. All signs that she was scared to death.

"We'll be – " he stopped. *We'll be fine*, he was about to say, but what did he know? Saying that would be tantamount to lying. "We'll be careful."

She looked up. "I know. But I still don't understand why you need to go inside. Why take the chance? You said yourself that you've only seen part of the ship. You have no idea what's on the other side of those walls."

Though she intended that statement as cautionary, hearing it sent Cannon into a renewed fit of excitement. What *was* on the other side of the walls? *Who* was on the other side? The possibilities were only limited by his imagination. Leanne read him as easily as he did her. She said, trying not to smile, "That was supposed to be a bad thing, Can. Now you've got that look."

He smiled. "What look?"

Her trace of a smile faded. "The look you *all* get – the one that says *I want to stick my head inside something to see if it gets bitten off.* That look."

He laughed, feeling his cheeks turn red. "Yea, I guess. But I promise you one thing."

She leaned back in the chair. She was in the living room, in one of the two matching chairs they'd situated by the fireplace. "What's that?"

"I promise above all else to protect all of my parts for when I get back, just for you."

She narrowed her eyes in mock suspicion. "You promise, Can?"

Cannon looked her in the eyes and said, as seriously as possible, "Promise. You *know* that."

She did smile, then, though it was a tired expression. It was late on Eden, but it was the slot he'd been given for the call. "I know," she said.

He and Peyton Kay had been friends, close friends, for years. Not as long as he and Leanne had been together, but Pey had always been a part of their lives in some capacity. Leanne spent a lot of time with Peyton's sister and her family. They lived one street over at the base. It was a way to stay connected with loved ones too far away for anything but electronic conversation. She'd long accepted that he and Peyton loved each other dearly, and, more importantly, that it was a different kind of love than the two of them shared. But it *was* love. More than anything else, that far out in space, away from family and confined together for extended periods of time, he had to be careful that this friendship didn't drift too far, lose its perspective. It could, easily, but to let that happen he'd have to forget his commitment to the woman in front of him. He could never do that.

He prayed often that was true.

He thought about that wink Rourke O'Shannon sent through the screen to Peyton this morning. Maybe he should work on getting those two together. It wouldn't be for a long time, since the *Abad* was moving farther away every second. He should talk to Rourke at some point about it, if for no other reason than to lessen Leanne's lingering worry.

He leaned back in his desk chair, looked at his wife without speaking. She did the same. He missed sitting in the same room with her, but this was nice. They looked at each other, a quiet, soft smile unconsciously working on both their faces.

The Ep beeped. One minute warning.

"I love you," she said.

"I love you, too."

She straightened. Leaned towards the screen. "Be careful."

"I will."

As they did every call, both looked at each other in silence until the chronometer reached zero and the window blacked out with the words, "Communication Ended. Time Limit Reached," scrolled across the darkness.

It was the last conversation they would ever have.

20 – Peyton, 3JH/2JS

She leaned back against the pillows and sat cross-legged on the bunk with the Ep balanced on her ankles. The man looking at her through the maximized window was ruggedly handsome, long, curly black hair peppered with tendrils of gray, but still the same Gen from high school. Nothing artificial that she could tell. She didn't think the church was big on enhancements for their clergy. A line here and there was simply a reflection of one's life experiences, good and bad. He had nice lines. Peyton thought of Cannon's comment, of her needing a boyfriend.

Gendrick looked down a moment. The room behind him was dim. He was sitting at a desk in his quarters since there was a bed in the background. He seemed at a loss for words. Who had been the one to stop communication, and when? She tried not to think about it, because it didn't matter. She smiled, and it was genuine, like her smile with Cannon.

"So, Father, how do you like Toojay?"

He looked up and smiled. "Barren, my child, barren, but the people are friendly enough." He hesitated only a moment, then added, "You're not going to keep calling me Father, are you?" Trace of a smile. Sadness, she decided. Many of those lines were sad.

She shrugged, settled herself deeper against the pillow. "Technically this is an official call, so that doesn't breed familiarity. But it also means this doesn't eat into my personal com time." She sighed. "I missed you, Gen. I really did."

His smile was less sad this time. "Me, too. I'm sorry we stopped talking."

Ironically, both had no words to say. Gendrick finally broke the ice. "Going to enter the ship tomorrow, I hear. You sure that's needed, especially this early in the game?"

She rolled her eyes, absently waved a hand in front of her. "No, probably not. We don't have a lot of official protocol regarding first contact, but . . ."

He smiled again. "But, you're a scientist, an explorer, and there's no substitute for climbing down into the newly-discovered crypt to see for yourself what might be in there."

Seeing her friend flat on an Ep screen, Peyton felt the void of his absence so much more. It hurt. She wanted to grab him, hold him, just hold him, say she was sorry for her part in the separation, wrap her arms around her oldest and dearest friend because she needed to hold someone tonight, she was —

"You're scared, Pey." Not a question. He saw it in her face. She wrapped her arms around herself.

"Yea. I am. But I need to do this, Gen. To be honest, there aren't too many people who like the idea, but with no specific law or regulation to throw at us, the ISO can only recommend we wait. Ken — he's our captain for this jaunt — he thinks if we wait much longer they'll be able to actually make a decision — a legal 'no.' If that happens, we'll be waiting for years."

Gendrick reached off screen then pulled a coffee cup into view, took a sip. "I never said I didn't like the idea. I do, to be honest. Or my curiosity about the ship likes the idea. I'm worried about you going in there, but to have my . . ." he shrugged, decided to push through it, " . . . well, my best friend be the first human to step into an alien spacecraft in the history of the human race, that's pretty exciting."

His words sent the now-familiar mix of fear and overwhelming excitement through her, kicking up the already spent adrenaline, both equally-potent drugs fighting for control. "Gen, you've always had a good way with words."

He smiled wider, opened his arms. "Hey, I'm an author, now. Need to practice, practice, practice."

She leaned forward. "That's right. *God's Vast Array*, right?"

He nodded. "I hope they at least fix my grammar before shooting the first entry out for the universe to read."

"Gen, as soon as I heard about you writing that, and coming out here . . . don't you find it extremely odd that we don't talk for almost thirteen years and suddenly we're both in the same system with all of human civilization watching our every move? I'm doing the floaty thing out here in 3J orbit and you're writing a book that's published everywhere before you've even written the next chapter?"

He nodded again, and took another sip of coffee before answering. He licked the coffee from his lips. Peyton tried to ignore the gesture. Yep, she needed a boyfriend. He said, "God helps those who help themselves, I have to admit." He leaned forward a bit. "And I was very persistent."

She laughed. "Oh, come on, Gen, billions of people in the world – the worlds, I mean – and you're telling me you got the job because you wanted to hang out with me again?"

He just shrugged.

She laughed. What else could she do? That *couldn't* be true. To keep herself from completely turning to mush, she fanned her face with one hand and tried to sound as

Southern Belle-ish as possible. "My, my, I must say I'm very honored, kind sir."

He pursed his lips and waved his own hands in a dismissive gesture, helping her regain the moment. "'Twas nothing, my dear. Nothing at all."

After a silence which was far more comfortable this time, she said, "I'm glad you called, Gen."

"Me, too."

"Next time we talk, though, you should ask me some questions for your book, otherwise they might not let you use the official com."

"Deal."

A new window popped open, directly over Gendrick's face.

Jump –00:10:00

The chronometer began counting down.

Jump –00:09:59

She slid the window aside.

Gendrick had been waiting. Any alert taking priority would have appeared as a plain white box in his screen. "Everything OK?"

"Fine," she said. "But we're moving into the Hole in ten minutes."

He let his face slacken, fall into a more professional seriousness. "Please be careful, Pey. I know that's a stupid thing to say, but be careful. You and . . ." this time his eyes were distracted by a separate window. " . . .Cannon?"

She nodded. "Pray for us, Gen?"

"You bet. Do you want me to take your confession?"

She waved the suggestion away. "God and I are on good terms, I think. But throw us those prayers if you have them to spare."

"Always."

She sat straighter. "Maybe when I've got some leave, I

can drop by for a visit? Until this mission's over Toojay's going to be the only viable vacation destination without eating up our furlough on a transport ship."

His face — still such a beautiful face, she decided — glowed with warmth. He was blushing. Caucasians were so easy to read. "I'd like that."

Jump —00:06:14

"Gotta run. Or, well, *jump*."

He reached towards the corner of the window with one finger. "Have fun exploring the temple."

She laughed, and the window closed.

Jump —00:05:43

Peyton folded the Ep and tossed it onto the table beside her head. A few seconds later Ken's voice boomed from the speakers hidden in the walls. "Attention, *Washington* Crew. Five minutes until jump. If you're on the can, wipe and flush now . . ."

She fell back on the pillows and laughed, stretching her legs out on the bunk. And waited. After a minute, she reached back and grabbed one of the pillows, held it against her chest. Her head was farther back now. She stared at the ceiling, thinking of Gendrick Hellerton only for a few more seconds before his face changed in her mind to Cannon. For the first time in a long time, she couldn't decide whom she'd rather have here with her. Of course, neither was an option. Especially Cannon. That was their own rule. Neither was allowed in the other's room, both to avoid gossip and making any such gossip come true. But Gendrick . . . maybe someday . . . but she would not think like this now. Too much to do.

As the *Washington* bent and twisted through the Hole, she closed her eyes and thought of Cannon, not Gendrick, as she screamed. It helped.

21 – Doneele, 2J3P

Doneele thumbed the icon and the image of the two love birds blinked away. The only thing remaining on her Ep was a spinning rainbow, the icon for the spyware she'd used to monitor Gendrick's call without being seen. Technically illegal, but protection protocols were loose enough here to get around any sniffers.

For now.

And *for now* was enough to see how she'd been used. She sat at her desk, staring at the swirl of colors, hands loosely clasped in her lap, feeling the coals burning in her stomach. She knew those coals were dangerous. *Meditate.* She needed to meditate, let it go like they taught back on Eden, release the anger and ask God for strength. Who did he think he was, flirting with *her* one day and hitting on Susie Scientist the next?

She growled, the sound low and simmering but gaining strength, then knocked the Ep to the floor with a quick backhand and grabbed the edge of the desk. She screamed, then flipped the desk onto its side. The corner slammed onto the discarded paper. A warning beep signaled damage to the device. The colored, swirling rainbow was moving jaggedly across the screen, dancing around a physical rip on the surface of the paper.

Hissing a curse she reached down, lifting the desk enough to free the Ep and close out the icon before System detected it. Her room would always be under *some* kind of monitoring, now more than usual, after her stupid little –

She screamed again, a short, staccato sound, and kicked the fallen desk. Who cared *what* they found? The coals were growing, conflagrating into a full blown fire in her brain. She closed her eyes, silently screamed for calm.

Think! He means nothing, but other pain, other self-inflicted hurts fed the flames. *Remember it's all in your head, all of it, no one is out to hurt . . . shut up shut up shut up!* she silently screamed to the memory of a long-ago therapist. That woman was long distant and Earth-bound and always trying to claw her way inside her brain.

Doneele paced back and forth across the room, trying to calm the monster, back and forth, back and forth . . . slower, slower now. Finally, she stopped and sat on the edge of the bed. Hands on her forehead, breathing towards the floor.

Calm, be calm, you're fine.

You're fine.

She thought of how Gendrick's shape felt when she held him briefly that first night, remembered her own, casual discarding of the rules – both of the Church and common sense. She was too far away from any civilized place. She *wanted* to get hurt. Wanted to *be* hurt.

Eventually, when the red light on the System panel by the bed continued to be ignored, it beeped, once, quietly. She ignored it, breathing, calming herself.

System beeped again.

"System," she whispered. The subsequent beep was lighter, friendlier. Waiting on her command.

"Go to hell."

System beeped once, content with its verification that Mother Doneele was healthy enough to communicate, and extinguished the light from the panel.

But Mother Doneele was *not* healthy enough. She knew

it. Something was very wrong. Something bad was inside her, and it was getting stronger.

22 – Radish Marlay, Approaching 3J3P Orbit

U nlike on the *Washington*, where cleanliness was an afterthought and clutter standard equipment (battened down as it may be out of necessity), the bridge of the *Abad* was an example of spotless efficiency. Crew was expected to take shifts running a duster over every console, working every corner with portable vacuum units. The room, situated on the ring to allow for artificial gravity was, at least functionally the center of the ship, although it warranted less space than Mess or Recreation. Little room was available for the four-person Command crew to do more than rise up from their stations and squeeze past the person next to them, either to leave or simply turn around and talk.

Not that the captain welcomed idle chat on-shift. If you were on the bridge you did your job, limiting personal conversation to free time when you could do whatever you wanted. Provided they left *him* out of it.

Radish Marlay hated being Captain.

In many respects he was the loneliest person on Crew. This mission could become, if it hadn't already, the most joyous and exciting any of them had experienced. And they had the misfortune for *him* to be chosen as mission commander. His role, like most everyone's, varied with the assignment. Even one's assigned ship one could change. When Radish accepted leadership for the mission he knew how the *Abad* (contrary to everyone's whispered guesses, he'd used his long dead cat's name for the ship's call sign) would be run – like he did his family back home. At the moment they were on Eden but in past generations home was Earth, a large acreage in Colmar in northeastern France. His great-grandfather brought his children there from Turkey after the War, and Radish's father was eventually assigned a decent contract at an electronics plant, one of many which had recently opened. Everything back then was new, the world redrawing itself fifty years after the echoes of the Final War faded and humanity looked skyward for hope. Ancestrally, the Marlay tribe was Iranian, but those lines were thin at best, and where Iran once had been was uninhabitable.

Through all of this, the faith and traditions of his family never wavered. In fact, the war with the West had strengthened them, much as they had done to the Christians and Jews – the remnant of whom had been the architects of the global awakening which everyone prayed would hold for a thousand years.

One such tradition in his own faith was the absolute authority of the husband in the family. Gone was the nouveau-ancient insanity of forefathers who suppressed, often violently, their women. Such hard-edged views of the world led to resentment and, ironically, disrespect. It also led to wars, an excuse to seize power for oneself and lash out in anger at those closest to you.

Radish's father ruled with a hard eye and harder fists, and Radish was intelligent enough to learn from his misguided view of how a man should be and move in a new direction with his family. But the ingrained lessons remained – to lead, one must be distant, strict with those below you. Protect those for whom you are responsible and do not waver. Out here, for certain, it was the only way to stay alive.

He wished he could be like the *Washington*'s Burlov. The man was calm, outwardly at least, and familiar with his crewmates. Radish often wondered how the *Washington* hadn't yet drifted into an asteroid or some planet's atmosphere. But it hadn't. For all their bluster and humor, they were an efficient group.

For his part, Radish was always heightened, unable to let go of the constant . . . he should call it for what it was: *fear.* Fear for the crew, the mission and his reputation as commander. Even during *azan*, the call to prayers announced via his personal com five times a day by System, he could never fully let go the *Abad*'s reigns. He recited prayers and wondered if the next shift was getting to its post on time, if there would be too much of a break in focus to miss something on the long range scans or fore-deflector array (which aside from a heady magnetic field was nothing more than a battery of explosive weaponry meant to incinerate any stray matter in their path). Always, the ship first. *Allah* second. This did nothing but raise his mental angst, and his guilt.

The computer's AI was only a simulated *muadhin*, but out here there was no choice but to let it work out the schedule for him, tell him which direction to face though Radish knew that changed constantly as he prayed and the ring rotated on its axis. What he missed most out here was being able to sit and speak with his Imam. Even when he had the chance, through the com link with Toojay, Radish held back, aware of ears listening. His concern for personal image was a thorn he refused to pull.

Onboard, faith was yet another morsel fed to his loneliness. Radish was the only person of Islam on the ship. With a Crew of twelve, odds were the majority of Crew would be religious in profile only. Even Sarey Ramprakash had forsaken her ancestors' Hindu roots for Christianity. After the *Abad* reached the third planet (he was still pondering his own candidate for a name) and began a long-term study, the ISO would likely supplement their numbers. Paleontologists, xenologists, linguists, the whole gamut of scientific exploration with which they might set up the first of many research stations. It would be good to share his faith again with others.

He looked at the back of Sarey's head. Not for long. Women had an uncanny way of knowing when they were being watched. At the moment she was focused on the single-eye monitor mounted to her headset. Through it, early images flashed from the probe launched by the *Abad* as soon as they'd emerged from the Hole. She was single-focused on her monitor, fingers typing madly: details, figures, computations . . .

He'd noticed over the past hour this focus had become more intense on whatever was passing through the eyepiece. She rarely slowed in her typing (the fact she was using her fingers versus dictating to System hinted that she felt the need to be discreet about what she was seeing). Something was up. Whenever Man Johnson (his real name was Manfred but he stubbornly refused to use anything but that inane nickname) suggested she take a break, she only mumbled, "I'm fine, let me filter. I'll release what I've got in the morning. Promise."

At least, that was Radish's best guess at what she'd said.

He looked back down on his own screen – made of Ep but mounted permanently on the plastic console before him. It was blank, waiting for Sarey's initial report. Apparently that wouldn't be forthcoming for another few hours. All data was filtered through her console first, to validate its accuracy and avoid any miscues or useless details contaminating anyone's initial perceptions. It wasn't standard operating procedure, but Radish preferred this. Sarey's was a brilliant mind. He trusted her instincts. If any of her decisions came into question – and they did often, scientists made questioning each other a sport – all raw data was available to review.

He looked up, lingered again too long on the back of her head. Many of his prayers centered around this childish crush he'd been nurturing since leaving the 1J system. She was single, but not Muslim so that should be the end of it. *He* was married with five children. Even unwashed, her hair was so black it nearly shined a radiant blue. An illusion, but . . .

"Captain?"

Radish blinked, tried to hide the shock that he'd completely forgotten Man was sitting to his right. He glanced as casually as possible toward the large scientist. Man was big, all muscle which he sculpted down-ring in the gym as religiously as Radish went to his prayer rug. He sometimes wondered whether Johnson was driven in his regime because of, or to justify, the nickname. He never asked. Aside from being too familiar a question for a commanding officer to ask, it was often more interesting to wonder about such things than to waste time finding out the truth. Man was smart, however, and professional. He never complained about working these later, quieter shifts while most of his crewmates slept.

"Yes?"

"Permission to speak freely?"

Radish reflexively glanced at Sarey's blue-black hair, then returned his gaze to the communication's officer. That was the role Man had been assigned this shift. It would change tomorrow. He had a varied array of shipboard knowledge and to limit him to one function was wasteful.

After a long enough pause, to stare and project a

warning not to get too personal, he nodded.

Man never broke eye contact. He said, "You need to sleep, sir."

Sarey's head turned in Radish's peripheral vision, but was back over her console just as quickly. *She* needed to sleep as well, but would not, too intent on the data coming in and her frantic typing.

Radish shrugged. "The first feeds from the probes should be filtered soon. I prefer to be here when they are."

Man gave a half-nod Sarey's way. "That's why she's staying up late. By the time the information is compiled, you could have gotten some shut-eye."

Sarey stopped, leaned forward as if to bring herself closer to one particular image, typed a few sentences into her console, then raised the eyepiece and swiveled around in her chair. Radish forced himself to maintain eye contact.

"He's right, Captain," she said. "There's a lot of data coming in but the probe is still too far out for any detailed images or scans. Soon, but not quite yet. One of us being stretched too thin is acceptable. Not two. When I crash – and I will, I promise – I'd feel better knowing the captain was well-rested and Crew wasn't short-handed."

He was almost flattered by her candidness – though at the same time annoyed by Man's. Not much of a stretch to imagine why.

"Nothing striking coming in yet?"

Whatever answer crossed her mind lit up her face with such an intensity Radish almost insisted she share it, but his exhaustion was becoming palpable with the possibility that these two might convince him to leave. Whatever was held in check behind those large brown eyes would keep him awake if he heard.

Perhaps this thought also occurred to her. The light in her gaze dimmed. "All of it is striking in its own way, sir, but nothing worth handing out at this time, or losing sleep over. I should have the initial compilation prepared in . . ." she looked down at her console, " . . . about four hours or so. I'm going to begin caching the results in about three, then begin initial reports. You'll be the first to see them, I promise."

With that she turned around in her seat and flipped the eyepiece down. End of discussion, though from the tense way she held her shoulders she was worrying over his response. Man offered a quick nod in agreement. Radish would not win this argument.

"Very well." Always expressions like *Very Well*, never a simple *OK*. "I will turn in, but will be back next shift. I'd like the first prelim when I'm up."

Sarey only nodded in response. She may not have been listening. Still, her shoulders had visibly relaxed. For that, more than anything else, Radish rose and headed for the door.

"You have the conn, Mister Johnson."

Man laughed at that, and muttered, "Aye, Aye, sir."

Radish reluctantly smiled. It was safe to do so. His back was towards the others.

23 – Gendrick, 2J3P

"It was loosely written – and I mean that as a compliment, Gendrick. You write with a natural voice."

"Thank you, Father." Gendrick took another sip of his coffee. The Union room was mostly empty, since anyone who might be awake was in the cafeteria, fueling up for the day. On the muted video monitor above the balcony doors, the talking heads chittered over images of Peyton and fellow crewmen Cannon White and Benjamin Solomon. Their photos alternated with the derelict ship hovering beyond the third Hole. Gendrick had only time to grab a tray of food and a large mug of coffee before coming in here for his first talk with Prelate McCarthy since arriving.

The man seemed to be at his desk in his Eden office. Gendrick adjusted the Ep on his lap and leaned back. As if in response, McCarthy leaned forward on his elbows before continuing.

"Granted, some of the theology is a little, well, *loose.*" His smile unsuccessfully allayed any hope that he might be joking. Gendrick shrugged, trying to remain impassive. He was already here, what could they do? It never helped to act cocky, however. They were the Church and could do whatever they wanted, within the law.

He made a show of scratching the back of his neck in mock embarrassment. "I know, Father," he said, knowing McCarthy, unlike Gendrick, liked it when people used the title. "A couple of things got away from me."

McCarthy leaned back. "Look, I might be Prelate but I'd hardly call myself a literalist in some things. I like the way you're approaching this so far. Everything we've encountered since finding the first Hole only offers more questions. Questions are good, and I think it's healthy for the Church to tell people that. Just . . ." he waved a hand loosely above the desktop, " . . . try to stay a little closer to the middle of the road, dogma-wise?"

Gendrick nodded. He'd met with McCarthy a few times when stationed on Eden, waiting for the transport. The man was unassuming and, more importantly, open-minded. To a point. He ran a tight ship. The rope he was letting out in this conversation could very well wrap around Gendrick's neck if he pushed too far. "I will. I try to write in the Spirit, but there are times I worry whose spirit I'm letting be my muse."

The man laughed. "You see, that's the kind of line we'd probably take out before releasing. Just be yourself, and pray first before you write, for the *correct* Spirit's guidance. Then, speak the truth. It's all I ask. In fact, it's the only real way to *be* in this business."

They said nothing more for almost a full minute. The chronometer in the corner, faded so as not to prove a distraction, offered plenty of time. Gendrick took another sip, looked away towards the bright morning beyond the glass doors. He should say something. With a quick glance around the room, he lowered his voice.

"I'm getting along well enough with Mother Doneele. She seems eager for her departure, but also for company."

McCarthy visibly blushed. Did he know? Of course he knew, someone, somewhere, always knew what was going on.

"Yes, she has a hard time being alone for too long. I imagine she'll enjoy it back here where there are more people." Silence again. McCarthy's eyes darted to the side for a moment. Then he reached forward, tapping something out of sight on his monitor. Without leaning back, his face larger in the window, he lost any softness in gaze. *This* was the man who would tighten that rope someday.

"Father," he said, "I'm going to be as vague as possible, but you need to listen carefully. Mother Doneele is an intelligent, fiercely independent soul. But she has many qualities of which you should be wary. You need to be her friend, no, not her friend . . . her *associate*. Help her when you can, but don't get too close. She is leaving soon, and we can help her far better here."

Gendrick raised an eyebrow, try as he might to not show surprise. Not so much at the meaning behind the warning – and it *was* a warning – but the fact that this man knew more than he was saying.

"I understand, sir." What else could he say?

McCarthy loomed in the window and slowly shook his head. "No, Gendrick, though you are beginning to. Be there for her, professionally, but keep your distance in every other way."

Gendrick took a chance. "Try not to be alone with her, you mean." Not a question. This conversation was disturbingly like the one he'd had with Arun.

McCarthy nodded. "Yes. When possible. It's a large complex but with relatively few people, so that might be hard. But give it a shot. In a month she'll be gone."

Gendrick nodded. "Hmm. Yes, I get what you're saying."

"Don't be glib."

"I'm not, sir. Just . . ." something occurred to him, a thought which caught the edge of a fear he did not expect to feel towards another member of the clergy. "Father, are you being so roundabout with this because there's a reason you cannot tell me specifics?"

The other man finally leaned back, looking much smaller now. "A reason?"

"Do I need to say it?"

"I don't know what you mean." But his eyes pleaded with Gendrick to ask.

So he asked, "Was it heard during a confession, Father?"

McCarthy held his gaze without blinking long enough to answer the question, then said, in the same flat monotone. "I don't know what you mean."

Ok, this was getting a bit too much. Gendrick nodded his understanding that yes, indeed, it *was* because of something spoken during a confession. A hundred different options ran through his head, until he closed his eyes and took a long breath. When he let it out he looked back at his employer.

"So, big day in another hour over on 3J-side."

McCarthy nodded, his relief unmistakable. "Yes, indeed. Your friend Pey is going to make history."

Gendrick laughed. "No secrets in this new world, eh?"

He shook his head. "No secrets anywhere. That's the law." He shrugged. "Mostly."

"Mostly."

The chronometer beeped. One minute.

"Gendrick."

"Hmm?"

"Is she why you're there? Peyton Kay?"

"I suppose she was an incentive, but mostly it was a good place to run away to. Keep on going until the hurting stops."

McCarthy's smile was wide. "If we ever stop hurting, Father, we stop being human. The trick is to not let the hurt control you. Everyone who's running away is usually running *towards* something as well."

"Interesting idea. A bit too romance novel for my tastes, but I might twist that around and use it later."

The hand on the desk waved its fingers towards the screen. "It's yours, take it. Time's up, Father. Remember you're a priest first, scribe second. Even so, keep writing, and be careful."

"I will, Father. And I will."

McCarthy reached forward and disconnected with twelve seconds left on the chronometer. Gendrick sat there for fifteen minutes, first looking at the blank paper, then through the glass doors at the brightening day. He reached forward and laid his coffee cup down on the small table before pressing the mute icon on the tabletop. The voice of the announcer filled the otherwise silent room. He watched for a while, then folded the Ep into his pocket and wandered into the cafeteria to freshen his coffee. In a few more hours Peyton would be poking her head into the lion's mouth, and he wanted to be there with her, in spirit at least. Along with the rest of the human race.

24 – Doneele, 2J3P

Eels in her head.

It was an image that formed in her mind once, back when Zechariah was alive and she watched him move away from her, first emotionally then physically. Spending his free time hanging out with his new scientist friends. The eels had crawled into her mind then, wiggling, dancing -

"Stop it!"

When her intended whisper emerged as a shout, she tightened her shoulders and stared at the flat panel by the door. If System said one word to her, asking if she was OK in that passionless, pathetic voice, she'd throw everything in her tiny room at the screen until it was powder, then tear through the walls until she found every microphone and interface hidden within. Kill System for sticking its nose into her world too many times.

Too much. It was all too much.

System remained silent.

Eels in her head. Stupid, overly poetic metaphor that she wished she'd not thought of but there it was, the image *and* the feeling. She'd fought against it for years and years, even before it had a name, the wiggling brokenness, keeping it hidden it from Zechariah. Trying to, at least.

McCarthy knew about her struggle. Now, Gendrick as well. They'd taken everything away from her. Marooned her on this dead rock and expected her to hold it together, even with the only man who could keep her calm. Zechariah had been her lifeline. He kept her head above the waters, but the eels got in nevertheless.

The church sent her out of Eden, literally, for nothing. Nothing. She hadn't done anything wrong. Now she had a chance to grab hold of one small lifeline formerly offered by her dead husband. Gendrick Hellerton, and now they were poisoning him.

Looking down at her Ep, she resisted the temptation to crush it between her hands. The material was flexible and could take a lot of abuse, but not *that* much. She'd already requisitioned a new one. Doing it twice in two days would assure everyone in the compound would learn the truth about her.

There was nothing *to* know. She was fine. In a month she'd be on a ship heading home. Back to the Garden. To Vernaine McCarthy, yes, but she could handle him. And now he does this. Telling her confession to another was an unpardonable sin. So few of those left in the Church, but *this* – the sacred oath, the sanctity of the confessional. A Prelate, of all people, had broken it with less thought than tossing a piece of garbage on the ground.

Not that she'd actually heard what he said to Gendrick Hellerton – though she'd been monitoring their conversation, *and* recording it. If one risked arrest by breaking into someone's personal repository one always saved what was stolen. Just when McCarthy was getting to the garbage throwing, he'd switched channels, scrambling the signal so all she could see were pixels, all she heard were broken words. Some of them escaped, as her hack code tried to compensate. It managed a few morsels, enough to assume he'd told Gendrick, if not everything, enough.

She never looked forward to seeing McCarthy again more than now. She would see him again, and kill him. Somehow. Make it look like an accident. Doneele had become quite adept at doing that.

But she wanted to hurt him *now*. If Gendrick knew the truth . . .

The realization froze her from the inside.

If he told Gendrick what she had spoken before the ear of God, then the new priest was free to tell everyone else. *He* was not bound to silence, not like McCarthy.

Doneele's eyes were the first to break her body's paralysis. They looked left, then right, faster and faster, blurring the room. She did not see. Only thought, considered, weighed the possibilities.

She would find out soon enough if Gendrick knew the truth. He would tell someone, *had* to by law. Maybe McCarthy asked him to say nothing, wait until she was on the transport with nowhere to run. Not that running on this planet was much of an option.

Even so, they could lock her in a cell in the corner of the compound usually reserved for drunken brawlers. Keep her there like a cat in a box in a ship in a cargo . . .

Stop it, stop it!

Think.

She closed her eyes, tried to still the shaking in her arms.

Think.

If Gendrick knew even a little bit, she was at risk.

He was the risk.

But Gendrick did not *know* she knew.

She took in a slow breath, let it out slowly.

Gendrick did not know that she knew.

So, she had something he did not. *Knowledge* of his knowledge. He did not know that she knew, but she -

At the last breath, before she screamed, Doneele covered her mouth and lay back on the bed. She mustn't scream nor get any further heightened. System would detect it via her implanted biochip and the communication webs wired through every room. It was how the computer knew so much about everyone.

She needed to breathe. Calm herself.

Breathe, be at peace.

No eels. No fear.

No fear.

Think. Then do.

She'd read that somewhere. Some time, long ago when her life was real. Not the tight-chorded walk along a razor it was now.

Think.

She had a problem.

Take care of the problem.

It worked for Zechariah.

It would work for Gendrick.

He did not know that she knew that he knew. Doneele needed to remove the new priest before anyone else found out. Less than a month and she would be free. McCarthy would not prolong her stay here if something happened to her replacement. He would find someone else, quickly. The sad old man wanted her back under his wing.

Remove Gendrick. Deal with the other one later.

There. See? Simple.

The monitor on the wall was silent. System was not God. He could be fooled.

God.

No. One issue at a time. Gendrick first.

25 – First Excerpt from "Viewing The Apocalypse From a Theological and Historical Perspective"

Gendrick Hellerton's Senior Seminary Thesis,
Wesleyan University, April 28, 2185

Better minds than mine have looked back from where we'd come, to praise or mock God our Father for getting it wrong. If these latter thought much beyond their insatiable need to lower others, including the Creator Himself, to a station below their own, they may have understood it wasn't God's plans which had changed. Throughout time, everyone simply misunderstood what the Lord and His prophets had been trying to say in the first place.

There is a reason Jesus Himself said, But about that day or hour no one knows, not even the angels in heaven, nor the Son, but only the Father *[1]. The reason is simple: we humans, more often than not, get it wrong. If Jesus didn't know, why would we think we could?* Live as if you'll be dead by morning and you will have lived well *[2], said the poet Paul Musto a few decades ago, when there was a good chance you could be dead by morning.*

To understand the enormity of what is happening these days, one needs to look back at history and our near-extinction only a century and a half earlier. Radical Islamic factions in the East did their best to destroy the world with violence and hate. Radical Christian *factions in the West did their best to destroy the world with politics and fear. The purposes of one do not always cancel the other. Sometimes they feed off of each other. These did. There were, of course, other factors, but these were two of the biggest in my opinion.*

Read the book of Daniel, *or* The Revelation of John *and one would have surmised what was coming long before the first explosion. Many waited eagerly to be raptured into the air before the nukes came crashing down on top of them. Some who might have had the power to do so did* not *stop it. They didn't want to. It was foretold. That was the favored viewpoint, at least. Christians taken up into heaven, the Church removed from this world, the anti-Christ rising to power, the persecution of those "left behind" and the destruction and ruin of Earth. Finally, Christ's triumphant return and the restoration of the world to its pre-Adam splendor.*

It was a popular interpretation of Daniel's and John's (among others') writings. When the Final War *began, some of it taking place not far from the area once assumed to be* Armageddon, *near the border of Syria and Jordan – the Middle East, as the region was called – burned. Russia and much of Europe were crushed under multiple detonations of nuclear warheads smuggled into small, unsuspecting towns and cities. The eastern half of the old United States became the radioactive* Hot Zone *it's now referred to. No one was taken away to heaven beforehand; no pre-tribulation Rapture. Not that anyone noticed. Perhaps it* did *happen, since many millions disappeared, burned off the planet in the Five Days of Hell as that week in history came to be known [3]. A third of humanity was lost either then, or later under the mindless swarm of violence and panic as the fallout drifted across the world.*

Panic is like gasoline poured on a fire in order to douse the flames. [4]

God did not do this. We did this to ourselves, with a lot of help *from the Enemy.*

26 – Ken Burlov, *Washington*

"Ok, what haven't we checked yet?"

Cannon let out a frustrated sigh and said, "Shoot. I think I forgot to put on underwear."

Ken pressed his lips together, his way of stifling a laugh, nervous as it might be if given voice. "Aside from that. No one wants to look inside your suit, Can."

Cannon began to say, "Well, I can -" but Ken raised his hand.

"Focus, buddy, please."

Oliver Holman raised his Ep. "We've gone through the checklist three times, sir." The lanky man was referred by most of Crew as "physician," though his official designation was astronautical hygienist, a specialist in the health and hygiene of the crew required on every long range mission. Aside from dealing with illness or injury arising on missions, his was a role critical before any extra-vehicular activities. Outside the physical protection of the ship, risk management became gospel. Oliver ran through his pre-set checklist, including a final, cursory examination of every person involved – mostly via their hands and face since the rest of them were cocooned in the bulky suits.

Once in the shuttle Benny, Cannon and Peyton would go through the checklist for each other again, before anyone would be allowed outside the pod's hatch. Through it all, System monitored the critical details: pulse, respiration, output.

Oliver tapped a few icons on the paper and lowered it. He shrugged. "We're good."

Ken looked at the other three, in turn, then down at his feet, which were hooked under the nearest floor anchor. The anchors were cushioned, upside-down U's peppered throughout the inside of the center hub, used as foot- or hand-holds in the zero-g environment. When held this way, he could allow himself the illusion that the room wasn't spinning. Oliver and the three-person pod crew stood along the narrow steel pathway, the only exception to the cushioned interior. The path ran from the spine entrance to just below the ladder leading to the pod's sealed airlock above them. Everyone but Ken were held to the path via their mag boots, Oliver's set looking awkward on the short man considering he was not wearing an actual EVA suit. Without looking up Ken said, "Benny, how's the ship?"

Benny Solomon tapped the left breast pocket of his suit with his right hand, out of which his electronic paper was poking. With his left he waved his gloves toward the hatch above him. "System diagnostics green. I did a camera scan around the outside of the pod. No anomalies except that ding in Dish Three, and we already knew about that. It's working fine. Tethers fine. Door seals fine. Captain . . ."

Ken looked up.

Benny's face was scruffy, his black beard having become more unruly since they first traveled through the Hole. Superstition, no different than when a favorite sports team was on a winning streak. Ken let them have these quirks, as long as they didn't affect decision-making. Benny's expression was tight, confident.

" . . . everything's fine. We're good. I'll do another check of everything when we get inside the pod."

Ken glanced at Peyton. Her nervousness was obvious, at least to him. She'd normally be egging Cannon's humor into high gear by now. She nodded, gave him a wary half smile. "All set, sir."

All he wanted was give each of them a hug, tell them something profound as their captain. But he knew better. "Go do science stuff and come back safe."

It was better than a hug, at least.

Cannon's face practically glowed with amusement. "*Go do science stuff?*" He actually giggled. "That's awesome. We will!"

Ken felt heat on his face but knew, if nothing else, he'd made *someone*'s day.

"Well, that's good, Cannon. That's good." He gestured toward the airlock door. "Then go do it."

At least the mood in the room was lighter. Benny tapped an icon on his sleeve and pushed off with his toes, lightly holding the ladder with one hand to steer himself up, into the pod's open hatch. When he was in, Peyton did the same after taking a step closer to the ladder. At least she used both hands to guide herself up and in.

As expected, Cannon, after de-activating his mags, attempted a somersault towards the hatch. He missed, landing feet-first beside the shuttle entrance. "One of these days I'll do this first try." He turned himself around and grabbed the edge of the hatch.

Ken gave no reaction, not even the hoped-for eye roll. He couldn't hold back the smirk, however.

That was enough for Cannon. He called into the hatch as he pulled himself in, "Ok, folks, let's do science stuff for Captain Ken."

Once inside, his head reappeared, looking down. "See you soon."

Ken nodded. "Be careful."

Cannon said, "Close the door, System," then backed away as the pod's hatch closed. Oliver had already reached the entrance to the spine and was lowering himself down, feet first since the gravity would increase as they near the outer ring. Ken pulled himself along the handholds and followed.

27 – Gendrick, 2J3P

He didn't want to be out here again, not so soon. The sun was a little too far west for his liking. Not that he wasn't curious as to what Mother Doneele was so eager to show him among the cattle herd. His curiosity was not as robust as the scientists at the station, who wanted to study, touch and breath in any new discovery. They yearned to understand the patterns in the dirt and the curve of the wind, learn how their new home ticked.

The concept of this being yet another *third planet* on which men and women from Earth could stand and live and *be* had a heart-ramping awesomeness that appealed to him. Gendrick was commissioned to see the worlds beyond the first and share them with everyone who would listen. He was a step or two closer than most to seeing what His plan was. He should lighten up a little and stop looking for monsters sneaking up behind him.

He sighed and checked the time again, covertly looking at the map indicating their current position so as not to show impatience with the trip. Whatever it was Mother Doneele wanted to show him: she would, in her time. They'd be back inside soon enough. In the meantime his fellow priest seemed content with their silence as he wrote another *Vast Array* entry in his head. It was his default mindset now, inner thoughts composing and reframing what was laid out before him into words to be jotted down later. He assumed this was a good thing. His commission was becoming, if not a passion, at least a habit.

They passed beyond the unofficial border of the first herd's grazing land. Beyond this the plain stretched out, its horizon a deep blue-green broken by rising hills and more of those broken, seemingly abandoned boulders. He should ask about these soon, track down the geologist. No face came to mind. Had there been some ancient eruption that cast all these massive rocks across the landscape?

"Obviously, Arun already brought you through that herd the other day," Doneele said, gesturing casually over her shoulder with one hand. "That's his favorite think next to the bug's little sand scribbles."

Gendrick nodded, wondering what Doneele could possibly show him in the next herd that Arun hadn't in the one they were now past. He said, "To a linguist, the sand drawings are akin to finding the Dead Sea scrolls."

"He can try to read something in them if he wants. He might even find something. I doubt it'll be any more real than the *twelve monkeys on a keyboard* theory. Look hard enough, study enough samples, and your mind will make its own patterns. For no other reason than to give yourself permission to stop looking." She laughed at that, the sound a little too high and tense.

Ever since this morning's conversation with the Prelate, every word spoken by this woman sounded on the verge of hysteria. His opinion of her had become tainted. She may have issues, but she was a person, loved by God and to whom he should offer as much respect as possible. Caution, too. He needed to be careful, but everyone deserved some benefit of doubt.

Pey and her team were stepping into the vacuum of space and *into* an alien spacecraft. It was an insane and unnecessary risk, and it was what humans did – stepping into holes no one else had entered simply because no one had yet entered them.

He smiled. The expression was short-lived. He wanted to go back, didn't want to miss a moment of it. The fact that he could care less about his duties as priest or his responsibility to write *Vast Array* so he could watch a video should bother him.

No, it was more than that. What they were doing 3Jside was directly related to what he was writing. He needed to experience it. Toojay would still be here tomorrow, and these cattle.

"How far to the next herd? I mean, however far we go, we still have to walk back."

"Actually not far," she said. "When we built the compound, there was only the one herd for twenty kilometers. The one we're visiting *had* been here, initially, but they were more skittish and left their holes to join another beyond those distant hills." She made no gesture to indicate *which* hills. "It was a dangerous move – they barely made it before nightfall.

"This past year they came back, again a major risk for such a massive group of cattle to travel in one day. They're about half the size of the first herd but that's still a sizeable group. Talk to Miyoko about it someday, if you'd like. She'll probably tell you about it anyway. She was ecstatic over the whole event. Observing some form of migratory behavior, all that. Why they came back is anyone's guess. Maybe they stayed away long enough to decide we weren't a threat. Or maybe they were told to leave. There's limited food to go around. These creatures are communal, but neighborliness only goes so far."

Gratefully, she stopped talking. They walked in silence for a few more minutes, Doneele keeping two paces ahead, her blue robes wafting around her whenever the wind picked up. Occasionally, her boots showed from beneath, nearly silent on the hard-packed earth.

Though Gendrick was glad she kept a pace ahead of him, this trip had the uncomfortable feel of someone making an effort to be alone with another. He looked behind him. The compound was well out of sight. The smells and sounds of the second herd was beginning to carry on the breeze. He checked his Ep. Almost there, and less than two and a half hours until Peyton's rendezvous with the derelict.

He'd mentioned this to Doneele when she'd come into the Union room where he was working on his newest entry. The dark rage that seemed to play across her face when he'd tried to object had the look of jealousy. She didn't know his and Pey's history, however, and he was fairly certain he'd kept a decent poker face whenever the subject of the *Washington* came up. Nevertheless, she promised with a bright smile he'd be back in plenty of time for the big event. There was something in the next herd that had always fascinated her, and though she could show him via System, it was something – especially the first time – one needed to experience in person.

Trust me, she'd said. *You'll thank me later.*

He hoped so, as long as whatever it was had no resemblance to her first lesson in dealing with the Locusts.

They were too far out. *Relax*, he told himself. *You'll be heading back soon.*

Fifteen minutes later they crested a small hill and paused, looking down at the herd. The cattle enjoyed valleys for grazing. Perhaps the shallow-bowl layout was most conducive to the scrubby, wild grass prevalent in and around the grazing land. More questions for folks back at the station.

Doneele descended the hill. As she did, she pulled out a canteen and awkwardly took a swig while she walked, twisted the cap back on. Something was wrong with how she did that. Either because her back was to him – and so everything would seem backward – or the fact that she turned farther away from him as she did, but . . .

He was getting paranoid.

Still, he looked around. This herd was smaller than the first – maybe they'd lost some of their numbers during the migrations. Even so, an impressive number of animals. Farther out, and to the right, the main entrance leading underground, into their burrow.

They reached the herd's outer edge. Doneele stopped and held out the canteen.

He had his own, but she was offering. He did not want to drink anything from her canteen. He was being an idiot. And rude.

He wanted to go back.

Gendrick took the proffered canteen and tilted it to his mouth. It was cool and delicious. He hadn't realized how thirsty he was, but they'd walked all this way without stopping. This was a dry world – dry air, dry ground.

He forced the canteen away from his mouth. He'd drunk more than half its contents. "I'm sorry," he said, handing it back. A strange smile had worked itself across the woman's face. Had she been offended? "I didn't realize how thirsty I was."

She screwed on the cap, never breaking eye contact. The smile remained, though it was a fixed expression on her face, not matching the intense stare in her eyes or her neutral, flaccid tone of voice.

"It's to be expected," she said as she finished screwing the cap and pulling the strap over her shoulder. "There's an additive in the water usually reserved for feeding plants. In humans, it makes the water sweeter, almost *addictive* as soon as you taste it. They once added it to alcohol back on Earth, until the powers-that-be deemed it illegal."

Gendrick's scalp itched. What was she talking about. "It's alcohol?"

Doneele sneered, her laugh a hiss that sounded more mocking than amused. "No. It's water. I just said the *other* ingredient is . . . never mind. Your thinking is already getting muddled so what's the point?"

"Muddled?" The word slurred. The light around them dimmed. They'd stayed out too late! Night was falling. He looked up to the sky and stumbled backwards. "Locusts."

"Are coming, yes," she said from far away. "But not for a few hours."

He was on the ground, knowing that he'd fallen hard, but felt none of it. His head lolled to the right, watched impassively as Doneele bent down and removed his Ep, stuck it in the pocket of her own robes as she turned and walked away. He tried to call her name, but his voice was liquid thick. It poured loosely from his mouth and soaked into the ground.

She stopped at the crest of the hill then turned around. Her words were clear, but he had difficulty lining them up.

"Can't say . . . Zecharia . . . sorry . . . time to . . . sleep, Gendrick . . . wake up too late . . . Locusts . . ."

Locusts. The dark was falling, they were coming. Not right.

She had drugged him. Drugged the canteen. Poisoned him. Dying. Sleep, wanted to sleep. *No!* He couldn't sleep, had to get back. He rolled onto his side. Doneele was gone. Reaching out, fingers grabbed the dirt. Heavy. He was too heavy.

Then Gendrick closed his eyes, falling into unconsciousness at the base of the hill. Now and then one of the males in the herd would approach, sniff the air, only to return to its kind. One continued eyeing him, however, bleating in confusion. Gendrick did not notice it, too deeply was he asleep.

28 – Peyton, 3Jside

The sensation should not have been any different from being inside the center hub of the *Washington*, or for that matter in the shuttle pod after decompression, but it was. In the first, there were eight meters of hull between her and the outside vacuum, in the second only one meter but it was still *something*. Protection.

Now, letting herself drift away from the pod, careful to prevent slack in the tether from whipping too close to Cannon and his own line, Peyton sensed – not to mention *saw* through her expansive visor – that there was nothing between her and the nothingness of space but her bulky EVA suit. At least the suit was less cumbersome, with no cushion of air pressing against it from outside. She moved the tether a little to the left and flexed her fingers in the glove. It responded with the agility it was designed for, electronic fibers in the material enhancing the gestures of her fingers. She knew that any tear or weakness in the gloves would mean those fingers would freeze a half second before the rest of her body.

Nothing below or above but an infinity of space, one which destroyed all life.

"Benny, slow the tether a bit, I'm getting slack."

She continued to drift at her original rate towards the hangar, but now the tether was more taught between them.

"Better?" He said over the com channel.

"Yea," she replied. "It wasn't too bad, but the squirrel

was annoying me and I needed to say something to scare it away." She laughed, as did Cannon floating two meters beside her.

"Squirrel" was their private word for nerves. Not so private any longer, as every transmission was broadcast over public channels. It didn't matter. Everyone had a squirrel. The trick was never to be ashamed of it. The worst possible sin, for oneself and Crew, was to pretend it didn't exist. Keep it in the light so it can't sneak up on you and trigger panic, especially outside the ship.

Cannon's voice, all business, brought her head into a more professional level. It was one of many things about the man she admired – he knew when to be a clown and when to be serious.

"Turning one eighty to the right in five."

The number '5' appeared on the lower portion of her visor, System anticipating what they needed. The AI was reliable like that, and a little unnerving.

Cannon counted down in time with the number.

Four.

Three.

Two.

One.

Peyton was too focused on watching the numbers she was a second late in firing the mini-thruster on her left hip. She rotated to her right. Cannon's turn was complete by the time he came back into full view. She saw his right thruster fire an equally-short burst a moment before she felt her own rotation slow. Peyton did not, in fact, feel anything, simply noticed her sideways motion had stopped.

The massive, open door of the derelict hangar was less than ten meters in front of them. Benny had parked the shuttle as close as possible to its center, occasionally firing the pod's thrusters to stay in relative position as the ship turned on its slow, invisible axis.

Everyone assumed the name *hangar* was accurate. However the Locusts had traveled to Toojay in this thing, it needed to be large enough to carry their entire population. Could they survive outside the atmosphere? If they were migratory on a planet-wide scale, they needed the ability to adapt to vastly varying environments and atmospheres.

Maybe. Maybe not. Everything was conjecture at this point.

The Locusts had become a far more interesting species since the discovery of the dead creature inside this ship. Conversations on the *Washington* and *Abad* and across the human population had been going full throttle.

After another announcement from Cannon, and a similar five second countdown, both thrusters fired for one second. This time Peyton was more focused and she, and her friend, moved in unison past the threshold.

The hangar had been pre-lighted via two dozen glow balls strategically positioned around the room by drones. The lights were bright enough to erase most of the shadows, but not enough to be distracting. At each corner hovered small camera units, allowing full view of anything that might happen inside. Ken insisted on monitoring from every angle – not just from the EVA suits' cameras and those mounted on the shuttle pod.

Everything was done just in case. The media was delighted, of course, and would have insisted on this, anyway. Ken could have refused if there was no functional reason for them. But there were many, and the main viewport on the bridge glowed with a patchwork of windows.

"Not too far in," Ken's whispered voice announced. "Not yet."

Cannon said, "Five meters in, ten. Benny how's the

tether?"

"Keeping up, not to worry. Minimal slack."

Peyton turned her head to the right, slowly, careful not to go into a spin, and looked for the dead Locust. It was there, far across the chamber. She gasped, seeing this creature in person – as *in person* as was possible – instead of on the monitor. Even in death, it looked dangerous. Like dead wasps on her windowsill back home.

"Twenty."

"Far enough," Ken said.

"Stopping unwind," Benny announced, talking about the spool which had been letting out the tethers. Peyton and Cannon tensed in expectation of the tug from behind. It came, and for a moment their controlled free fall into the hangar became wild and erratic. The suits' internal AI Systems compensated with bursts from the jets, then the two astronauts were floating calmly, twenty meters inside an alien spaceship.

She'd been debating what their first words would be in this moment, what could live up to the *One Small Step* of two hundred and thirty years earlier. Cannon beat her to it.

"Hello! Anyone home?"

Peyton laughed. As did Benny and Ken on the open line.

Ken's voice. "So much for history, Can."

"You kidding?" He replied. "It was perfect." He floated a couple meters in front and to Peyton's left, but was turned enough she could see his face through the visor. He was looking at her with a soft smile. "I suppose you had worked out something more newsworthy to say, Pey?"

She shrugged in her suit, the act unseen through its bulk. "Nothing nearly as profound as that."

He looked up. "There, see? It was -"

The light that draped across his suit came from the

upper right corner of the chamber. The camera stationed there spun wildly away towards the far wall. Cannon had stopped talking, bathed in alternating blue and white light. His mouth was open, eyes wide in shock or paralysis.

"Cannon, what is that?" Peyton shouted through her viewport. He stared, in pain or terror she couldn't tell, the expression was the same. "Can you hear me? System forward thrust, I need to reach him."

"Belay that," Ken's voice, as loud as she assumed hers was, and almost as panicked. "Benny, pull them out. Out, now!"

Peyton moved forward, knowing that doing so risked falling into a spin, but the computer compensated with brief bursts from the thrusters, keeping her stable and preventing her from getting closer.

Benny's voice from the pod was detached, calm. "Trying sir, but they're not moving. Or Cannon isn't at least, same pulley. Retraction is only dragging the pod closer to -"

"Hold off, keep your ship outside the hangar until we know -"

That was all Peyton heard. In the next few seconds so much happened she had time only to acknowledge one terror before the next.

Cannon's body spasmed inside the suit, his legs flailing. The motion should have sent *him* to a spin, except the intensifying light held him in place. There was no sound from his suit com, no labored breathing or groaning. The look of terror on his face expanded, expanded more – then exploded. Through the speaker the sound of his skull tearing apart tore through Peyton's entire body. The inside of his EVA suit's visor was coated in blood and bone.

Peyton screamed. No words, only one tight, prolonged scream of horror.

The light flickered, lessened in intensity, then went out altogether.

"Ben . . ." Ken's voice was hoarse, "pull her out, pull *them* out, quickly."

The sudden tug on the tether and sense of motion was immediate, until the light shone again, this time directly into Peyton's helmet.

Her backwards motion stopped. Words from Ken, probably telling Benny to stop, but they were background noise. The light was all she could see, its massive silence all she could hear. It dimmed a moment as System lowered her solar visor, an attempt to defend her from what seemed to only be light. But she saw it. It reached her, filled her mind.

Images flooded her thoughts, of Toojay, from the vids and her single stop there on the way to the Third Jump Hole, its barren wastelands, the Locusts as she watched the swarm through the window one night. Other images from classrooms and news vids. Her life raced through and around her like a river freed of its dam. The flight from Eden, then Eden itself, image after image, every second of every minute lived there, training, prepping for the mission, playing with Ellie, laughing with Carroll, walks and walks and more walks and quiet moments standing in the sun, the rain, the trees and plants, minute after minute and she could only watch as some details were more focused upon than others. Insects, leaves, patterns of clouds, lessons in textbooks, Ep pages flashing by, English lessons from Earth, first grade, second grade, third grade. She wanted to scream, to thrash but she was nothing, did not exist, only her mind, her memories, her worlds. Earth, the broken beauty of it dimmed against Eden's perfection but no less majestic. The burnt, ruined hot zones, history lessons, scientific papers, star charts and navigation . . .

She watched the light drain her mind and waited to die,

hoped it would not be painful, looked forward to seeing Can again so they could talk about what just happened.

The images stopped, the light faded. All was dark. She was dead.

29 – Benny Solomon, 3Jside

"Now, Benny, now!"

"Do it," he whispered to System then the retraction resumed at full speed. If he risked breaking a few of Pey's bones to get her out before the next attack it was worth the risk. Icons flashed, System compensating for momentum by firing thrusters to maintain the pod's position.

Benny realized a better option too late. Fire the side thrusters to move the pod away from the hangar as he retracted the tethers. He was about to order this when Li's voice over the open com shouted, "The hangar door is closing!"

"System," he said, "fire all port thrusters maximum thrust now."

It did, but in the viewport he knew it was too late. The massive and thick doors should not have closed so quickly, but whatever track system the aliens used was efficient and frictionless – it had opened without anyone immediately noticing, after all.

The inflated but unresponsive EVA suits of Peyton and Cannon raced towards the entrance, began to spin as the door pressed down on the tethers.

In that last second, not knowing how far into the door's recessed frame the lines might be drawn, he reached out and pressed the icon on the panel before him to sever the tethers. An emergency protocol action in the event they needed to be detached immediately from the pod.

Ken shouted, "Benny, what are you doing?"

The door was already closed when he looked up, the derelict becoming smaller in the window as the pod continued moving away. "System," he tried to say, but couldn't talk. What had he done? Were they both dead, anyway? "System . . ." he licked his lips, "Stop."

It was all he could manage, but the computer understood. Thrusters on the starboard side fired. The pod stopped.

"Bring me back now," he said, his voice stronger. "Same distance as original EVA."

"Negative," Ken said. "Benny . . . why . . ." another voice interrupted him, fainter, speaking in hushed tones. Apparently someone was explaining Benny's spontaneous decision. When Ken spoke again it was a statement, not a question. "Li says if you'd kept pulling them the doors would have either crushed them or ripped their suits apart as the tethers were drawn into the hull."

Benny swallowed, then cleared his throat before whispering, "Yes, sir."

Deep breath on the com. A long sigh. "We've lost communication with her, but you probably just saved her life, Ben."

He blinked. "What do you mean? She's alive?"

Li's voice was louder this time when she said, "Yes, at least she was before the door closed. We lost every signal from inside when it did, but from preliminary – hold on." Silence. No one spoke. Benny imagined she was typing furiously or arguing with someone else offline.

Eventually, "OK, initial analysis shows the light that hit Pey was less intense. At least less focused of a wavelength. The readings are still off the chart, though. So many spectrums. I don't think the light itself was the signal, only a method of directing it. Most were . . ." She sobbed, then gagged. Her voice cut out from the com.

Ken's voice. "It's OK, Li. Raylene report to the bridge to take the console. Benny, maintain current position, until next steps are decided. We're trying to communicate with Peyton. She was alive when the door closed, vitals normal but heightened. Cannon's gone. I don't want to sound cold but if we have a chance with Pey we need to stay focused."

Benny nodded, knowing no one would see but assuming the stupid computer would send the word "acknowledged" to Ken's monitor.

He'd seen what everyone else saw in those final seconds. Saw his best friend's head explode. Saw it again now, closed his eyes and saw it again. And again. He wanted to pass out or simply die. Anything to not see it.

Pey needed him to focus. Still, he kept seeing it. Over and over.

Com channels had fallen quiet. The alien vessel was a small, grey stick in the center of his monitor. He should zoom in, look for a sign the door might be opening again. Not yet. He needed to breathe. He looked down and checked the atmosphere inside his shuttle. Clean. He reached up and unlatched his helmet, ignoring System's warning that he was breaking protocol not being in full gear during EVA.

He didn't care, took in a breath. The stale air of the shuttle was still better than the suit's. He gasped it in, wanted to cry out loud but would not. He was only coming to the surface for some air. He took a few more long breaths, then a few more, and slowly calmed. He had to help his friend. That was his focus. Peyton was alive. He prayed she was alive. She needed him to be ready to pull her out.

He'd made the right choice, didn't he? Would she have been out now if he hadn't done it?

He didn't know. Someone would tell him soon enough.

"Benny." Ken's voice. "You OK?"

He sniffed, tapped and icon on his screen to display current atmospheric conditions in the pod, for no reason other to do something with his hands.

"Yea. Yes, Captain. I'm OK. Status?"

"No change, not yet. Pull to three quarters current distance and hold."

Benny looked randomly at the controls and said only, "Do it."

System did.

Ken continued, "We instructed System to plot a flight path through the Hole if there is any indication the ship is preparing to scan you. Any flicker and your ship is on its way 2Jside, no questions."

"No questions."

"We're repositioning the *Washington* for the same thing. And, Ben . . ."

"Yes?" His voice was barely a whisper. He was so tired.

"System confirms if you hadn't released the tethers Peyton would have been crushed under the doors. You saved her life."

He looked at the monitor, said nothing at first. She was in there, and God knew what was happening. He finally said, "Not yet, sir, but I will."

30 – Gendrick, 2J3P

The cow bleated again, then nudged the human with her wet nose. Gendrick moved slowly, as if asleep, and tried to raise his arm to wipe the animal's snot from his face. His arm flopped back onto the ground, then he moved no more. The animal bleated again, partly from fear, trying again to wake this strange creature. Behind her, the herd was moving calmly toward the hole at the far end of the clearing.

She moved away to join them, her large eyes gazing skyward at the approaching dusk. It was late afternoon and the shadows from the stones were growing longer. She hesitated, then took a tentative step back towards Gendrick before fear won out and she turned around, trotted with the others moving in deliberate unison towards the entrance to the underground burrow.

Again, though, the cow slowed then stepped out of the flow of cattle and looked back. Another approached, craned his neck and bleated towards the one that had stopped. The first, shorter than the other by a head, turned towards her mate and did likewise, stretching out her neck towards the unmoving man at the edge of the clearing before letting out a long, anguished cry. The male glanced only briefly back at the alien before nudging the cow with his large head, trying to goad her into motion. She did not move, but instead stepped closer to the man and cried out again.

With a wet grunt, the male turned, raised his head to the sky and almost abandoned her to her fate. Instead, he grunted in resignation and moved as quickly as its bulk would allow towards the unconscious man. He nudged him with his snout, tried to flip him over, wake him up, but Gendrick only muttered incoherently in the hazy fugue into which he'd been drugged.

The female offered quiet, encouraging mewls. The male raised its fat lips, bared long yellowed teeth and bit into Gendrick's robes just above his right shoulder. The teeth pinched skin but neither the bull nor the man seemed to notice. It pulled, sidestepping towards the herd which had all but disappeared into the hole. A small section of skin pulled free from his teeth and this time Gendrick moaned in a barely-acknowledged show of pain. The robe remained firmly gripped between the creature's teeth. The female stepped slowly alongside him, encouraging her mate with more mewls and an occasional bump of her nose against his side. In this way the bull pulled Gendrick along the ground, making slow but steady progress towards the entrance. He occasionally looked skyward, searching for signs of color or the impending aurora. It would drop the man if anything untoward appeared above them, but the only things passing overhead were thin bands of clouds traveling far above in the upper atmosphere.

They reached the hole. Rather than enter first, the female followed behind, occasionally nudging Gendrick's black shoes in a vain attempt at helping. The male had no need of help, only encouragement.

Still moving in that near-sideways gate, the male dragged Gendrick's body down the steep, curving slope and into the cavern. Lit only by whatever ambient daylight found its way into the hole, the world became darker the farther they moved.

A new light crept around the final turn. At the same time the angle of descent lessened. The glow was subtle, but bright enough to illuminate the narrow cave stretching out of sight, filled with a hundred-plus cattle finding their usual places amid calves and mates to sleep and wait out the coming night.

Hours more would pass before Gendrick awoke in this new place. When he did, one more person would have died in the world he'd left behind.

Part Two

The Belly of the Whale

Plague of Locusts

31 – Peyton, 3Jside

She was not dead. The realization dawned slowly, followed by a calliope of memories of the past few minutes. The attack on Cannon, then herself. When it stopped, her body had been pressed against the suit with a fierce yank. Benny must have tried to pull her out. He hadn't succeeded.

She glanced around. The hangar door was closed. They were still inside.

Her com was silent.

"Ken?"

No response from anyone on the other side of the wall. She tried again. Waited. No one could hear her. At the very least *she* couldn't hear *them*. Everything inside the hangar was deathly quiet, compared to the confusion which had swarmed about her during the attack, or the *scan*. What the ship had done might not in and of itself have been hostile, but merely a method of identifying what she was. Where she'd come from. No indication there'd been devices within the walls from earlier scans or probes. The lamps still shone at full power, illuminating the vast chamber from every corner save one which had been tossed aside. It had collided with the wall to her left and was now dark, probably smashed. Any fragments were thankfully contained within its housing. It rolled and bounced around the chamber, far enough away for the moment she gave it no more thought.

She and Cannon had likely been the first alien life forms to enter the hangar, and their presence . . .

She sobbed, bit her lower lip, tried to refocus. *Stay professional.* She couldn't think about what was floating beside her, still tethered with her to the hangar door, maybe even to Benny's pod waiting on the other side. Benny might still be out there. Communication was simply down or blocked. They couldn't ask anyone to find out . . . . *she* couldn't ask anyone.

"No, Can, no, please." She reached for her face, forgetting she was in an EVA suit until her gloved hands covered the visor. At some point the solar shielding had been raised. There'd been no further scans. No more blinding blue light.

Peyton cried inside her suit, her vision blurring through the tears. She needed to cry, to mourn for her friend a little while longer. No one was talking, no one could hear.

She reached to her left, felt the electro-simulated sensation of the glove closing around Cannon's suit. Peyton kept her eyes closed, not wanting to see the madness coating the inside of his visor, or worse, what lay beyond it, needing only to hold her friend and cry and say his name over and over again. Why hadn't System lowered his solar shielding? Would it have done any good?

After a few minutes, her training insisted that she stop crying and move on.

Peyton opened her eyes and wiped her face on a spongy pad situated beside her head, then focused on the suit's display running along the lower portion of the visor. At the edge of her peripheral vision Cannon's lifeless suit hovered. She sniffed, tilted her head to wipe the rest of the tears and snot away.

Both would be absorbed and reprocessed.

Same with the spike in carbon dioxide she'd set loose with her crying.

Everything conserved. Reused.

She was marooned inside the hangar. She might be protected from drifting debris and solar radiation, but the latter was only a guess. Regardless, she was in no less dire a circumstance than if she'd been cast adrift in empty space.

She sniffed one more time, cleared her throat. "System," she said, taking some comfort in the control of her voice, "display current O2 and food levels."

No response. Nothing displayed.

She was cut off from the AI, too. They'd become accustomed to having the computer always at their beck and call. *Too much* so, many thought. Accessing the suit's internal system was a manual process.

Peyton raised her left arm and used her right glove to flip up a panel mounted to a hard plastic base between her elbow and wrist. An unmarked, flat rectangle was exposed. Using one finger, she wrote commands a letter at a time, grateful that their weekly drills in suit protocol occasionally included these overrides.

Most of her commands, spelled along the front of her visor, were gibberish. She flicked her finger across the pad and the nonsense disappeared.

One letter at a time, she practiced. A. B. E . . . no, slower this time, gently . . . C. O. Try again. O.

"Come on!"

D. E. F.

Over the next twenty minutes, Peyton practiced until she was able to spell the entire alphabet without error. She then spelled out the command to display air and food levels, hoping the suit's System understood that "food" included water. It did.

Across her visor, the answers came.

O2 level: 83.9 %.

Rations (liquid form): 100 %.

That would last her for a few days, at least.

H2O level: 94.4 %.

Three days, maybe more. If she was careful. The designers of the suit had accounted for everything. There were procedures to follow, risky as they might be, if there was a need to prolong it.

The oxygen level worried her. Eighty-three percent was taking into account any recycling of CO_2 back into O_2, breaking out the carbon and expelling it. The reconstituted oxygen could be used in emergencies. People tended to get sick if they breathed that stuff too long.

The sudden realization that there was one additional source of fresh O_2 nearby set off a deep burn in her belly.

Air and water.

Only if absolutely necessary.

Assuming no one was able to open the hangar, it could very well become so.

Communication status still showed *open*. "Benny, are you out there?"

No response, not even static.

She reached out, could almost touch the hangar door. The tether angled around her suit's right hip and into a tight wedge where the door joined with the hull, likely *into* the hull for some distance. They'd come this close to being crushed as Benny pulled them out.

She wondered why they hadn't. Maybe he'd cut the line, even if it meant trapping them here.

Saving *her*, trapping *her* inside.

Peyton bit her lip again and growled, fighting another wave of tears. She needed to focus, stay alive for as long as she could. For Cannon's sake, if not her own.

32 – Zhou Lihua, *Washington*

Li wrapped her arms around herself in a self-hug, held them against her chest while staring intently at the monitor. Dozens of readings flashed across the tick-drawing representation of the alien vessel. She watched for any change. After her initial breakdown and expulsion from the bridge, she'd given herself five minutes of melt-down in the bathroom next door before requesting a return to duty. Ken agreed and gave Raylene a nod. The woman returned to Internal Systems next door with a quick hand on her shoulder. Someone had also cleaned up the vomit Li had spewed onto the floor beside the console. She hoped it hadn't been Raylene, bad enough she had to cover her station while she blubbered and threw up again in the bathroom.

All shifts had been called to duty as soon as the attack happened. She assumed Internal Systems was as crowded as the bridge. The ship's com was cluttered with voices, stations talking to each other or to ISO personnel on Eden and Earth. Some people merely studied their appointed monitors in silence. No one spoke to her after she'd returned. She was pretty sure no one blamed her, either.

Li tried to remember the last time she and Cannon had been together – a quick snack last night in Mess, talking about the EVA. For a few minutes he'd gone off track and explained how his childhood dog would leap three meters off the ground (an exaggeration, she assumed) to catch a

Frisbee. It would do this over and over again, he said wistfully, never getting tired. This memory from his early teenaged years came without warning or purpose during a debate on the merits of the spacewalk. She was for it, but tried to take an opposing stance like many in the media had been doing. Ferreting out any misgivings on Cannon's part. Not because she wanted to psychoanalyze him. Li simply enjoyed talking to the man, watch the myriad of expressions on his face whenever he got passionate about something. She admitted to herself, more than once, that she had a crush on him. So did everyone else.

He reminisced about playing Frisbee with his dog the night before he was going to risk his life for no true scientific purpose except to be the first to set foot inside an alien spacecraft.

That was Cannon. So many places at once.

A real scientist.

She blinked her thoughts away and focused on the display. Now that she was back, she couldn't risk looking distracted, lest someone notice and send her away again. She wouldn't leave. They couldn't make –

Her console beeped.

Li opened her eyes, not realizing that she'd closed them. Red numbers beside the icon of the other ship. Thinking of it as a derelict any longer, even in name, made little sense. Let the others call it what they wanted, that thing was alive.

"Captain," she said, tapping the red numbers twice. A new window opened with a breakdown of the reading . . . readings, as two other red-colored figures joined the first. The information flowed in, on various spectrums, by a dozen probes circling the craft – the *Washington's* full contingent. "We're getting new readings from the ship."

His reply was hushed, and Li felt a twinge of anger at the fear in his voice. "Another scan?"

She looked up, caught and held his gaze for a prolonged second before answering, "No, sir. Something new, a charge skipping across the outer hull." She tapped the simulation of the alien ship on her monitor. It expanded into a full window on the main screen beside the actual video image. "Lateral charges, fore to aft."

Quivering green lines like jags of lightening skipped along the ship's outline from front to back on her view. On the true video, these were not visible. But they were *there*, as if both ends of the craft were polarizing, discharging electricity. It wasn't electricity, not in the sense anyone might understand. The alien craft *looked* no different, dark and lifeless, no visible sign anything new was going on.

Ken leaned forward in his chair, his head beside hers, his voice stronger. No more fear. That was good. "Some kind of defense?"

"No idea. Not yet, anyway."

"Best guess?" His trademark question, one which invariably drew out what his crew was thinking but hesitant to say – in most cases, she knew without humility, the guess was correct.

"It's . . . powering up, sir."

Ken looked towards the main screen and said nothing for a moment. Finally he sat back in the captain's chair and said, "Navigation."

The voice of the chief pilot, Randall Mbutu, answered from the Nav room – like Internals it was located elsewhere along the ring to avoid too many people in a single location. Nav was, in many ways, the true "bridge."

"Ready, sir, no change in position of the derelict, but our engine's powered to fifty-percent. We have mobility if we need it."

"Good. Let's keep the line open until further notice."

"Agreed."

"We have movement," came a voice over Randall's line, Ven Taragon according to Ken's monitor. As he continued speaking, System brought his voice to the forefront. "Or . . . to be precise, a *lack* of movement. Its rotation is slowing."

Ken watched the monitor. It wasn't obvious anything was different. "Slowing or stopping?"

Taragon said nothing at first, but the sound of him tapping his screen was carried across the com. "Slowing, but at a regular rate. Best guess is rotation will stop completely in forty-one seconds."

"Meaning? Anyone?"

Li looked at the increasing lines of green flashing across the false image of the ship in front of her. Before she consciously decided to speak she said, "It's leaving."

33 – Benny, 3Jside

Less than a minute later a half dozen voices flooded from the shuttle pod's speakers: Li's report of the increasing power surge across the derelict hull; Ven Taragon's confirmation from Nav that the ship was no longer in rotation and was, in fact, moving from its fixed location and towards the Third Jump Hole; Randall announcing the *Washington* was ready to move at Ken's command; and more which System did its best to filter. The fact that the alien ship was moving came as no surprise to Benny. System was already flashing its projected destination and suggested course corrections to the pod's navigation system in order to maintain current distance.

"Confirmed," he said into his microphone, to no one in particular. He spoke into the mouthpiece at the end of the wire looped around his ear, normally used while fully suited. The suit's helmet was still off and sitting on the floor beside him. Regulations called for it to be secured to its base on the left side of his pilot's chair, but he'd laid it down to his right without thinking, wedging it between his seat and the bank of monitors flashing the frenetic readings from probes scurrying to maintain their own position as the massive ship slid forward. He could afford a few seconds to move it to the other side of his seat, but he had other things to worry about.

Ken's voice came over the speaker, the computer relegating others to lower background noise.

"Nav, move us away from the Hole. Keep same distance from that ship at all times, location -" he paused, apparently consulting a chart of the region. Normally, Randall or Ven would have jumped in and made a suggestion, out of the usual impatience flight crew had with waiting for orders from *any* acting Captain. They were uncharacteristically silent this time. He finished, "four-five-one-one-seven. Confirm?"

Randall muttered his confirmation.

Benny turned off his microphone and said to the empty cabin, "System, bring me closer to the alien ship, enough to accompany it through the Hole but no closer."

System beeped without speaking, and the thrusters fired. No sensation of movement inside the cabin, but the readings showed that his orders had been followed, icons indicating the distance between the derelict and his pod shrinking while, on the largest of the screens in the center viewport, more lines showing their route towards the Hole.

He leaned forward in order to see the real thing through the thick glass. The ship was barely in sight on his port side but growing noticeably closer. A few seconds later, more of the alien ship lumbered into view through the window.

He sighed, kept the microphone turned off but the speakers still echoed the myriad of half-spoken conversations from the *Washington*. Li mentioned Benny's name. It had taken them longer than he'd expected to notice.

"Solomon, what the hell are you doing?"

Ken's break from professionalism would haunt him later, Benny guessed, if any of them survived. If nothing else it would add to the drama unfolding across humanity via the media feeds.

He reached up with ungloved hands and tapped the

side of his mouthpiece.

"It's heading for the Hole, sir. Peyton's still inside. I need proximity to maintain visual of the hangar door, in case it reopens."

"You're not following it, not that closely."

Benny started to reply, pressed his lips to subdue a response spoken out of anger rather than logic. Doing so would have ruined any chance of convincing them — not that he would obey if Ken refused. Besides, the Captain could override pod navigation systems anytime he wanted and drag Benny back onboard.

Ken said, "We have no idea what's going to happen or where it's going. I'm not losing another crewmember. Benny, get back here, we'll decide together from the *Washington*."

Benny waited a few seconds, to emphasize what he said next.

"Peyton's onboard, Ken. You all said she's likely still alive, and —" he had no "and" to offer at first, then a realization struck him. "And," he continued, "I think we're all starting to get a pretty good idea where it might be going."

The icons — his and the derelict's — remained unchanged on his monitor, closing in on a representation of the Hole. Another icon, larger than the pod's but dwarfed by the alien ship and tagged as *Washington* was moving quickly out of their flight path. At Benny's words System added a new image: a simple dot in the far corner of the two-dimensional representation of space on the other side of the Hole. Creepy how a computer was so good at reading his mind.

Ken said, "We don't know it's heading for Toojay."

Benny ignored him, knowing the chances his career would survive this moment were fading, and said, "Does anyone have another theory? Where else would it be going?"

As if enjoying their collusion, System flashed an written message, situated to the right of the main console. *Alien craft destination 2J3P, compute 90.2 percent likelihood.*

"Thanks," he whispered.

"I heard that," Ken said, though his tone had softened. "System just flashed the same thing on my screen."

Silence for a moment. Benny leaned forward and glanced to his left. The derelict was close enough now that he could make out where the hangar door had been – *still* was – but too far to see the tethers dangling from its hull. Peyton and Cannon were still attached to the other ends. At the very least *she'd* better be.

"System," he said, assuming there was a debate going on aboard the *Washington* and not wanting to say anything that might ruin his chances. "Visual view of the hangar door on Four, nine-fifty magnification."

On his left, Monitor Four $$$flickered into a camera image of the side of the derelict ship. The hangar was closed tight, the tethers drifting like two tiny whiskers from its bottom center. They were joined at their ends by the connector which Benny had released from the main line and which was probably still drifting outside his own pod.

"Thanks."

Still no response from the *Washington*. The two icons on the main monitor were closing in on the hole. The *Washington*'s had moved to a safer distance. The derelict continued forward, ignoring or oblivious to (which he doubted) the other ships.

"Maintain course," Ken said at last. "As soon as you're on the other side move back to the distance you'd held before going rogue on me." Normally Benny would have laughed at that. Not this time, though the light remark was appreciated.

"Will do, sir. Entering Hole in three minutes, twenty-one seconds."

"We'll be right behind you."

"Counting on it."

Conversation after that was merely a constant murmur over the open channel, stopping only during the few moments the universe collapsed into his brain as Benny passed through the Hole. He struggled to connect with Peyton mentally in this moment as both ships crossed the uncountable distance together, but could not, too intent was he on keeping sane.

Then they were 2Jside beside that system's fifth planet.

Once through, the derelict began to accelerate.

34 – Oscar Capino, INS *Martelo*, 0J4P Orbit

His paper was unfolded to its full size as he tapped the fan-shaped stylus into bushes along the bottom of the landscape. No actual *paint* was allowed ship-side. Too high of a risk clogging up, well, everything if the ring and its artificial gravity stopped. Instead, Frigate Captain Oscar Capino had to settle for pixels and a beloved set of stylus brushes, a gift from his sister three Christmases ago. They were frighteningly accurate and, best of all, never needed cleaning.

Painting served as a distraction from wondering when *the call* would come. When it did arrive he was touching up the rightmost shrub with some extra berries. They might be botanically inaccurate but looked nice in contrast to the abundance of green.

System displayed Rear Admiral Sehrish Raad's name in the upper corner of the painting. Below that, *Saving image...* since the AI knew a call from anyone outranking him would be answered. He tapped the name. A tall, unsmiling woman in plain blue hijab dominated the page.

"Admiral," Oscar said, casually putting his brushes aside. The long standing practice of saluting had been set aside for video communication, though the first words had better be the superior's rank. The Navy always had a way of reminding which rung you clung to. Oscar sat at attention, and left the organization of the brushes for later.

"The official orders are coming through now, Captain. Full speed to 2J3P after an orbital stop at Eden for passenger pickup. That's the plan for the moment, at least."

"Based on current reports, sir, that ship is going to beat us there."

She nodded, leaned forward as if about to impart some hitherto unknown detail but just as quickly she leaned back in her seat. "The general consensus is that the alien vessel will not stay long at Toojay."

Oscar blinked, then said, "Why not, sir?"

"Think about it, Captain. The planet is picked over. They understand the use of the Holes, and the ship seems designed to carry Locusts."

He hadn't realized he'd slumped in his chair until he suddenly straightened. "It's heading for Eden."

She nodded. "After picking up its burden, yes. Of course, everything is an assumption."

He looked away a moment, thinking. "Sir, even so, shouldn't we try to evacuate personal on Toojay?"

"Negative. All transports through the 2J Hole have been called back to the Eden System. All other traffic has been stopped until we can assess better what we're dealing with. There are shelter-in-place protocols. They'll follow those for the time being."

No they won't, he thought. *They'll run up to it with their scopes, tap the hull and try to figure out how it works.* "How many of our ships are mobilizing?"

"At the moment you and the *Far Darrig*. The *Yamato* is currently stationed at Stain, but given the climate there they ask it not be removed." Stain was the derogatory name for the Eden system's fourth planet, mirror to Mars. No one used its official name *Dressel* except politicians. It had grown into a profitable but highly volatile mining operation. While Mars itself had dozens of litigations on the books to protect it from industrialization beyond a few single-location mines, on Stain three separate corporations had begun digging before the lawyers and environmentalists could catch up. Some controls were in place, legally, but fill three dozen camps with people leaving home for a better life, only to become chained to drills in subterranean caves and breathing canned oxygen ... it made for a few unpleasantries which required more than the companies' usual, half-cocked security forces.

Too much money and lives at risk to let a military presence disappear for long.

At Oscar's raised eyebrow a look of exasperation crossed the Admiral's face. "We've agreed for the moment, but the *Yamato* will be ready should the alien vessel make it past you and the *Darrig*."

The statement should have filled Oscar with dread, but instead his pulse rose in excitement. This was, after all, exactly what most in the fleet had signed up for, when they were younger and stupid. "And the *Burlington*?"

"Staying in orbit around Earth. Let's hope it sees no action, Captain."

Here, a trickle of dread crept in. "Yes, sir. We've already begun prep for departure. Should be en route in two hours."

"Note the time of this conversation, Captain. I want daily status meetings in this slot. We haven't decided anything yet but knowing you and the *Far Darrig* are converging on 2J should keep the public uproar at a manageable level. For now."

He nodded, wanting to add that the presence of two Navy frigates was more than a symbolic assurance. His people would deal with whatever was flying that thing. He also knew most of the Crew on the *Far Darrig* and was glad to have their company.

She said, "We'll talk more soon. You are dismissed, Captain"

The window closed. His landscape reappeared. Oscar waved his hand and that window closed, too. The paper was blank.

"System, open channel to Second Bridge." Soft beep. "Mister Hatt, have we received our official marching orders from Command yet?"

"Yes, sir," the Lieutenant said. There was no visual, only voice. Oscar preferred this to too many windows open during ship communications.

He said, "Nav." A pause, then the senior Navigator said, "Mahone here." System dutifully displayed *Warrant Officer Daniel Mahone* below Len Hatt's name in the lower corner.

"Time to departure?"

"Breaking orbit in one hour, thirty-six minutes, sir. Destination Toojay."

"Eden first. Low orbit. I think we'll be picking up a passenger or two. As always, be ready for last minute changes."

"Yes, sir."

"Out."

Both names faded.

He folded the Ep slowly, stood and grabbed his uniform jacket from its hanger in the closet. They were moving out. He needed to be on deck when they did. Jacket on, he slipped the paper into the inside pocket and faced the wall.

"System, show outside view." The room darkened and the wall illuminated with a wash of stars. In the lower right corner a skiff moved towards them from Phobos. "Adjust to show Mars."

He was suddenly staring at the canals running along the region of Xanthe. The planet spun like a ball on a string as the *Martelo*'s ring rotated. They'd be in position soon enough to break orbit and head for Jupiter.

Oscar watched the beautiful, desolate landscape rising to his left then passing overhead, until he finally nodded and turned away, sensing more than seeing the image fade while he moved to the door. A moment later he was in the corridor, heading for First Bridge. Their ring's center hub was actually a smaller Corvette and served not only as the central, zero-G center of the ship, but also the primary weapons mount. If necessary it could detach from the spokes and act as a ship in its own right with better maneuverability than the larger, ringed frigate.

He needed talk with the SWO about weapons readiness but he'd do that on an open com. Something about having the Senior Weapons Officer broadcasting that the big guns were ready for action should put some of Crew's apprehension to bed. Nothing gave solace to a soldier more than knowing they could blow something up with a moment's notice.

35 – Doneele, 2J3P

Doneele O'Coin expected Security to be waiting at the main entrance when she stepped into the Union building, but no one stopped her. For the southern compound, Security meant only two men. Sherriff and Deputy, some called them, though their ranks were equal. Michael Broeger was the assertive one and seemed to enjoy the role more than his partner Dwell. Dwell didn't have a last name. Perhaps after winning this post he'd managed to have his profile legally altered. Fresh start and all that. Anyone could have found out his former name, but no one cared.

Broeger and Dwell would only know she'd left with Gendrick through System's logs, since she'd made it a point to bring him out through the southernmost door, ostensibly for an easier trek to the second herd. In truth, the camera above that door was on the fritz – there would be no visual record of them leaving, nor of her returning alone.

System knew they had gone, and where. Keeping your Ep always on hand was mandatory, and only one of two ways System could track them away from video surveillance. It was the reason she'd taken Gendrick's paper back with her. She'd been tempted to dig out the bio chip from the back of the priest's neck as an added precaution. She didn't know if a chip still worked without any biology to read. It might have looked to System as if Doneele was returning with his corpse. Thankfully the chips had minimal ranges and supposedly System didn't monitor them for anything but screening health. The point was moot, since she hadn't done it.

She glanced quickly around the corridor beyond the entrance. No one nearby. She tossed the priest's Ep under a chair a few meters from the doorway. If people were primarily tracked via their papers, it would look as if he'd returned with her then stopped, perhaps to remove his boots or rest, and the paper fell out of his pocket. A reasonable story.

Last year, no one knew her late husband was outside when the sun fell. Maybe she'd be lucky twice with the same trick.

It was almost dark. System would begin monitoring everyone's location. It might begin to wonder – if AI's were capable of wondering – why the new priest was hanging out so long next to the exit.

Nothing to do about it now. If she'd gone into his room to leave it, that might look suspicious. She passed by the entrance to the common Union room. Several people, Arun included, were facing away from her, heads riveted to the largest of the monitors. Something on the news.

The spacewalk, of course. Gendrick's girlfriend skipping around an alien ship for no decent reason except to make history for herself. All of them out there were taking risks when none were needed. Even *these* people to a lesser degree, laying their necks on the bloody chopping block hoping something interesting might happen. Zechariah had been fascinated with it all. Look where that got him.

She almost laughed.

No one noticed her walk past. She moved quickly through the compound to her room. No one accosted her. Still, Doneele could not escape forever. During the walk back from the herd her mind screamed to turn back, get

Gendrick, find some way to wake him. There *was* no way. The drug was four times the maximum dose. He wouldn't wake up for hours. Doneele doubted she'd have the strength to drag him the entire way back. They would never have made it. Her course was set the moment she gave him the water.

He needed to die. She'd worked out a dozen excuses why he might have gone back outside, if anyone asked: he wanted to return to the herd one more time; wanted to see their burrow again; wanted to be alone in the wilderness to pray. None felt believable enough, especially considering his paranoia about the Locusts. The thought of leaving his Ep near the door was a last minute consideration, and a better option. He'd stepped outside quickly to find his lost paper, planning to take a quick look then run back inside. It was too late, however, as the Acclarin took hold of his mind. He'd wandered away in a daze.

A hard excuse to disprove. Most of them were. If someone tried to contact him, he would never have heard since he did not have his Ep. Tomorrow, there would be little, if anything, left of his body to prove anything.

Everyone was so fascinated by the *Washington*'s little adventure, they might not know for some time.

Maybe she'd be all right.

Time. More time was all she needed to work things out.

Her door beeped, a gentle chime like an ancient, lone bell in a lost cathedral. It was calming. Someone at her door.

Doneele imagined her and Gendrick crossing through the Union room when he realized his Ep was missing. They'd parted company while he ran back the way he'd come to find his Ep.

That was what happened. If anyone asked her.

Her heart rate sped up. Fear, rising to terror but she

needed to breathe, keep it down.

Doneele hesitated. "Yes?"

"It's me," Arun's voice.

Doneele tossed her hair with her fingers, convinced herself she was tired, had just lain down for a nap and immediately fallen asleep.

She tapped the panel beside the door. It slid open. Arun's expression was light, no suspicion. The short man's face was easy to read. One reason she found herself drawn to him. Paranoia makes one choose friends who didn't keep many secrets themselves.

"Hello, Arun. I'm sorry, laid down for a nap after our trip and went right out." She made a show of smoothing her hair. "What's up?"

No invitation to come in. He seemed to understand, though he tried to be subtle as possible as he glanced over her shoulder to see if someone might be in her bed. "Gendrick here?"

She laughed, the spite in her reply genuine. "Hardly, you should know that. He's made himself clear in that regard." She raised a hand in a mock salute.

He no longer tried to hide how often he glanced over her shoulder, but his dark face had fallen. Concern took dominance over curiosity, brows knitted together. "Oh. Well, he's not in his room either. At least not answering. Figured he'd be watching the news. It's been insane up there."

She couldn't care less. "Oh yes, the alien ship. Big day." She yawned. "I would have thought he'd be watching with all of you. He seemed so fascinated by it all."

Arun nodded innocently. "He's friends with Peyton Kay. Maybe he's not answering because he's praying for her. The whole thing is pretty scary. He must be worried." When she did not react, his smile returned. "You have no idea what's going on, Doneele, do you?" She shook her head. "Well, it's bad and I'll let you go back to bed." He gave her an affectionate tap on the arm. "If you're hiding Gendrick please send him out soon. I mean, it's *really* bad."

"I'll double check, but no promises." The relief to not have to bear an inquisition almost made her laugh aloud. She hadn't felt such a wash of joy in a long, long time. She could not show it, however. She was supposed to be tired. "Good night, Arun."

"Night, Mother Doneele."

She backed up and tapped the door closed.

The lightness in her chest collapsed with the solitude. His visit had bought her *some* time. They would ask again, and discover what had happened, and remember Zechariah. He'd wandered outside and lost track of time, never answered *his* com calls either. His death was attributed to Acclarin disorientation before being overcome by the Locusts. There was nothing left but some DNA traces and blood splashed across a couple rocks. Nothing to show he'd been drugged, the same dosage she'd given Gendrick.

Two deaths under the same situation, both related to her in some way. Both having left with her prior to his death. Was she insane to think this would end the same way?

She considered the question. Of course she was insane, no reason to deny it. She was simply trying to manage it, handle the impulses, keep herself from coming apart. Waiting to go home. Just *go home*. Everyone wanted that.

She'd be fine. That also was a lie but she understood that, too. So it was all right.

Vernaine McCarthy would know. She'd confessed to her part in Zechariah's death in the sacred confessional. He was bound to a higher power than law, even if the law stated that *nothing*, especially religious doctrine, was higher than the statutes which had maintained the remnant of human civilization for nearly a century.

He would know, and be honor-bound to report it when news of Gendrick's death reached him. She could contact him now, give another confession. *No.* He hadn't taken her confession since that final time, contrary to what she'd told Hellerton. *Fool me once, shame on you. Fool me twice, shame on me.* A good motto to live by. McCarthy apparently did.

Doneele sat on the bed, leg bopping up and down on the ball of her foot. Nervous energy. A brief, overpowering wave of sorrow for what she'd done crashed around her. By now the sun had set. The lights would be dancing. If Gendrick woke up he'd stare at them in wonder. He'd be dead in ten minutes, fifteen max. The flock was concentrated heavily in this region, focused above the human settlements and of course common herd regions. He would watch them come, laugh at them, maybe sing as they tore him -

Stop stop stop stop stop stop stop . . .

Think.

Think.

But she must not think. Only do.

She would say the right words when the time came, and needed only to be clear-minded. It was how she'd survived this long.

36 – Arun, 2J3P

Normally, he'd enjoy the show outside. Now, however, he stared through the glass, hardly noticing the dancing ribbons of light rising from the horizon.

Where was Gendrick?

He'd checked with System for the priest's location. Its response, since the hour fell under the man's designated personal time was, "Is this an emergency?" Arun had said no, and opted to leave Gendrick a message. On personal shifts people had the right to privacy. System gave physical locations of others only if the requestor said 'yes' to the question. Courtesy dictated one rarely did, if it was not true.

That was earlier, when it had still been light out. He'd assumed Gendrick would be hanging around near one of the monitors, or watching the events unfolding in the 3J system on his personal Ep in his room. Then why wasn't he answering? If he was sleeping, he'd want to be woken for this.

Now, the sky was dark, the air alive with hallucinogens. If he was outside, wouldn't System . . .?

"OK, fine," he muttered, then tapped the panel beside the glass doors, keeping his back to the people sitting in chairs and eating meals they'd brought in from the Mess in order to watch the news together.

"System."

The panel beeped. Arun pulled out his Ep and unfolded it, deciding to move a little farther away from the crowd. As he did so a dispassionate male voice responded, "System," quietly, assuming Arun opened his Ep for privacy.

One of these days he'd love to find out how these things were programmed.

"Hey, yea. Listen, locate Gendrick Hellerton, this is an emergency."

"What is the nature of the emergency?"

"He's missing. I can't find him and it's dark – "

The paper beeped. Apparently mentioning someone was missing after sunset was enough. System said, "Gendrick Hellerton is currently located in Hallway B near the southern exit, three-point-seven-seven meters inside the compound."

Arun was walking in that direction before the computer finished speaking. Two minutes later he was standing beside the lone chair, staring down at a folded Ep laying cockeyed on the floor behind it.

System asked, having likely monitored Arun's progress, "Have you located Father Hellerton?"

Even in his growing terror Arun wondered why the AI suddenly decided to use Gendrick's formal title.

He said, "No. His Ep is here. Pretty sure it's his. One sec."

He reached down, lifted the other paper and unfolded it. Nothing on the screen except the name. *Father Gendrick Hellerton, Toojay Station South*. No one would be able to see more without the man himself swiping it. Arun held up his own with his other hand.

"It's his. He doesn't have his Ep."

The panel by the door beeped once, a small blue light flashing in the upper right corner. Arun had never seen a blue light on any exit panels before. A second later another panel at the end of the hall beeped. Another blue light.

He began walking in that direction. In the distance he

thought he heard another beep. If he was close enough would probably have seen another blue light. System was doing something . . . scanning? For Gendrick?

Less than ten seconds had passed as Arun stepped through the corridor's inner doors into the foyer outside the Union room, when System's voice broadcast throughout the compound. Even the vid screens had gone silent.

"Attention all personnel. Anyone with visual confirmation of Father Gendrick Hellerton's location, please announce so immediately. System is unable to locate him anywhere within the compound, nor within fifteen meters outside. This is not a drill. Repeat, anyone with visual confirmation of Father Gendrick . . ."

It repeated the statement before spouting protocols and the risks for anyone attempting to go outside during the primary swarm period. Said period would not end for another tree and a half hours.

Arun passed the glass doors and saw only his own reflection, and that of the bewildered people in the Union room. They were glancing about themselves, as if Gendrick had just been beside each of them the entire time. He passed through the room, ignoring the occasional question from the crowd. Most others scattered in various directions, each moving to a predetermined place they'd been assigned to look for a missing person, and forced to practice during the random drills. Arun was supposed to search the main scientific hub in the center of the compound. But a single thought drew him towards the residential wing, along the same hallway from where he'd returned less than an hour earlier.

He stopped outside Doneele's room and rapped loudly on the door. His leg was twitching. This was insane. She'd already said she had no idea where he was. She might have been lying. He could have been in there all this time.

Arun's stomach tightened because he did not believe that. Another, darker consideration was beginning to surface. He knocked a second time, with more force.

If Gendrick was here – anywhere – he would be watching and worrying over his friend from the *Washington*, not hiding under the sheets of a woman whom he'd already been warned was unstable.

No answer. She was in there. Probably asleep. She could be out, looking for Gendrick. Arun doubted it. Why he thought that, he wasn't sure. But the idea sent his leg into renewed twitching.

"Doneele!" He called, then knocked again.

The door slid open. The woman's earlier, sleepy appearance was gone. She seemed very awake. For the first time since this weirdness began, first with the alien ship attacking the *Washington* crew then Gendrick going missing, Arun was suddenly afraid for himself.

37 – Doneele, 2J3P

A few minutes earlier Doneele paced her room, trying to calm the eels in her head, although now they felt more like snakes. Time was running out. Too many holes in her story. If Gendrick had gone back to retrieve his Ep and stepped outside, there would be a record of the door opening. She wasn't certain of this, how much System tracked egress points during the daylight hours. Had she been unaware of another camera around the perimeter, a new one mounted on some random boulders? Would it show her returning alone?

She paused at the window – in actuality a mounted Ep programmed to show the outside landscape relative to her location, but which could be modified to show the view from any angle where there was an available camera. If one desired, thousands of other public views could be opened, from Eden or Earth. Everything visible to everyone else. Everything public. She flipped rapidly through the local options – nothing showing the path from the southern exit. The current image faced northeast. Night had fallen, drawing the swarm of Locusts overhead. They scattered and bickered for the best vantage as they prepared to swoop towards the first grazing grounds beyond the compound.

Closing in on Gendrick.

She wanted to change the angle to reveal southwest, the direction where he was either already dead or staring at the approaching monsters with the same stupid grin he wore on the his first night standing on the balcony. She did not change the angle, however; kept it facing in the opposite direction. She watched the shadows of the Locusts passing overhead, and remained silent.

It didn't help.

System beeped once. She didn't respond. The computer was still being civil, making its presence known (was it ever *not* present, she wondered?).

System beeped again.

She would deny. Deny, unless they *had* fixed the camera. If so why hadn't it shown on this monitor when she switched views? Without it, there was no visual proof.

He wanted to stay outside a little while longer. No, that had been Zechariah. Gendrick only wanted to run back to find his Ep. She couldn't mix up her stories.

System's voice broke into the silence, emotionless. "Mother Doneele."

She took in a breath, let it out slowly. "Yes."

"Did Father Hellerton return with you?"

In that moment, with that question, an odd sense of peace fell over her shoulders. A warm blanket. *Lie to it. It's a machine.* It could do nothing without provocation or proof. Would it have asked her if it had contrary evidence?

"Yes, he did. He seemed quite happy to be back, in fact."

"You are aware of the emergency announcement." Not a question. "Per emergency protocol, please report to Chapel to verify whether the missing person is or is not present in that location."

She sighed. The last thing she wanted was to leave her room. Not yet. Too keyed up. Then she realized, if the entire compound was searching for him, *everyone's* mood would be heightened.

And they'll start asking you *questions.* No, too soon for that.

"I'll check in a few minutes and let you know."

"Protocol requires th-"

She hit the panel by the bed, shutting System up. Not dismissing the AI completely. It could, and would, do whatever it wanted. But it was a way to simulate choice in dealing with the it. People didn't resent something as much if they could shut it up whenever they wanted.

That had been a mistake, however. She needed to play along.

She should go. *Now.* Look for Gendrick in Chapel. Doneele was cold under her robes, so she rubbed her hands along her arms. She wanted to sit on her bed, curl up in the corner, wait for it all to go away. She was tired of pretending.

System might not be fooled. It was likely monitoring her vitals, lie detecting in its own way. She was *not* lying, in her mind she remembered coming back with him, having a nice conversation. Remembered him lying motionless on the sand. Helpless. She smiled. The image calmed her.

She stared at the dark landscape through her pretend window, the sky black with demons. Too dark to see beyond the stark delineation where the external lights washed the darkness away fifteen meters all around the complex.

Three hard knocks outside her door. Doneele jerked her head around to stare. "What . . ." she began, heart racing, then closed her eyes, breathed, felt the snakes riling up, coiling for a strike.

System mentioned, without being asked. "Arun Renault has come to your door." It sounded petulant, smug, speaking when she'd clearly smacked him into silence earlier.

She offered a slight laugh, relishing in how her pulse seemed to already be slowing. Arun was back. That was not good. Still, her body was slowing. Calm. A gift from God, the peace of the Spirit.

Don't go there, she warned herself.

"Why, thank you, System. However, I didn't ask you."

It said nothing.

She turned fully towards the door but did not move closer. "Please let me know the moment you locate Gendrick Hellerton. I will check the chapel as soon as I am able."

System beeped once. Ostensibly, the sound indicated it had "left" the room. Ostensibly, but likely not the truth.

Doneele stared at the door, ready this time as the three hard knocks repeated themselves. It was beginning. No, it was ending. Arun had been here only an hour ago. Facts and suspicions must be clicking together in that genius mind of his. There was nowhere for her to go, but she would try. Somehow. Some corner of the compound must still be dark to Security's eyes. Perhaps it was still possible to play hide-and-seek in this universe.

She walked towards the door, imagining various possible moves and counter-moves for the moment when she tapped the wall and the door opened.

Slam into him, perhaps. Run past.

No. All is calm. All is bright.

A clear picture formed in her mind, reaching up through the coiling serpents. Brushed metal, ornate. A gift.

No. Yes. Just in case.

She turned and after two long steps towards the desk opened the center drawer. Single-blade scissors. Self-sharpening, it had fallen towards the back of the drawer from months of non-use. The blade issued a short-range static charge to make most materials stiffen enough to receive the cut. A gift more than anything truly functional, from her long dead sister twenty years ago. She always kept it, a reminder of that long ago nightmare living with her. The only possible weapon they would allow her to have in this place.

She'd held onto it all these years, mostly forgotten. In case. Just in case.

Three more knocks then Arun's tight voice called her name from the hall.

She gripped the handle, palm damp but not *too* bad. Two long steps later she tapped the wall beside the door, the blade of the scissors turned up into the sleeve of her robe.

Arun looked very angry. Doneele was calm.

He said nothing at first. If the security twins had been standing behind him it might have been harder to show confidence. But little Arun was alone. What did he plan to do?

She needed to go. Now.

His expression changed. Was that fear?

Good. She smiled, felt the corners of her mouth turning up. "Arun." More a statement than a greeting. "Come in."

He blinked, leaned forward then back on the balls of his feet. His entire body was suddenly alive with energy. He stayed on the threshold.

"Doneele, listen to me. Gendrick's not in the compound. He's out there." He gestured wildly toward the far wall. "System's got security and everyone riled up looking for him. Trying to work out why he didn't come back, or why he left again. I don't know. He left his Ep here." He held up the folded paper. "Normally I'd not worry about him getting lost, but if he didn't have this, well . . ." He tucked the paper into his back pocket then rubbed two fingers together along the bridge of his nose. "I've been trying to figure out his thought process since he got back. Did he see the news?" He didn't wait for her to answer. Arun looked down, side to side along the threshold. Doneele watched him, calmly, keeping a loose grip on the blade to prevent it from getting slick with sweat.

Arun looked up suddenly, "It's just like . . ." He looked at her with a fixed gaze. A deliberate look hardened his features. The way his eyes narrowed, face tightened.

She finished the statement in her mind. *It's just like what happened with Zechariah.*

She gently, very gently, put her fingertips on the back of his right arm. "It's OK. I know. Come in, calm down. There's a search. Have you gone to your location yet? I still need to look at Chapel but let's bring it up on the monitor, see if he's there first."

Her throat was hollow. She couldn't swallow, but the calm lingered, and her thoughts were clear. For some reason, her body wasn't playing along. Her stomach lurched. *Fear.* This was fear, rising like a volcano. Doneele's legs were cold. Everything pulling in, centering in her chest. She was panicking. Arun — stupid, trusting man — was letting her guide him inside.

Everyone would soon come to the same conclusion. *Just like Zechariah.* What had she been thinking? Behind him, the door remained open to the hall. No one passed by.

The snakes were jumping out of her, scrambling for cover. She could see them, there, and there, and there. She was coming apart. They flailed about the room, bending as if in pain, pressed down by the foot of a God she didn't believe in anymore and who was going to make her pay for what she'd done. What *had* she done to Gendrick? Why?

By now, he was dead. Dead. No reason for it. He'd done nothing. He was kind.

She bent down, doubled over.

"Doneele what's wrong?"

What's wrong? Guilt? Horror at suddenly facing the end of her life. No. Horror at what she'd done to a nice man, the man that she loved, that had married her and took care of her and never did anything wrong except put up with her, trusted her as she led him to slaughter like Abraham did Isaac, only an angel had not stayed her hand.

"Ooooooooohhh . . ." she said.

"Doneele, breathe, calm down."

Calm down. System. System knows by now. Or would know soon. Signs of guilt. *Everyone will know.*

In that final second it occurred to her that Arun may not have suspected her of doing anything wrong. Maybe *no one* had. But she'd already fallen into the abyss.

She straightened and, with her free hand, grabbed the desk chair and tossed it toward the open door. It toppled sideways, straddling the threshold.

"What are you doing? System," he began and if she never heard that word again she would be content for eternity, even in hell. Doneele flipped the blade down so it faced the floor then swung the arm upward, blade extended – a talon that lashed across Arun's throat.

His flesh opened and blood sprayed out in three distinct streams. Not enough. She grabbed him with her other hand and pushed him against the wall beside the false window and thrust the blade forward into his stomach, pulled it out, shoved it into his chest. It hit bone. Out then in again, until it passed through a gap. He was screaming, the sound cut off in a drowning gurgle as his lungs and throat filled with blood.

A few more ins and outs with the blade before she let him drop. Bright, bright blood sprayed over the floor and wall, her face and blue robes. Doneele's hands were red and slick.

Time to go. As soon as she moved toward the entrance System closed the door to prevent her escape. Its voice filled the hall outside, calling for security. The chair prevented the door from closing all the way. It opened then closed more forcefully. The chair held.

She leapt through the gap. An alarm filled the world around her. *Outside.* She needed to take her chances with the night and the monsters beyond. If she stayed, they would find her, put her in a box until she was old or until the powers-that-be passed sentence. *Death.*

Death regardless.

Death on her own terms, then.

Two turns. Overhead, System announced verbally that she was to be apprehended, had murdered Arun Renault, was armed and should be considered dangerous.

She laughed at the truth finally spoken aloud, then turned another corner. Joe Conn from maintenance was standing there. She didn't care. Doneele raised her bloody arm with the blade and made a noise like a growl. Joe sidestepped and threw himself against the bulkhead. She ran past. He did not stop her, but instead ran in the direction from which she'd come. Doneele hardly missed a step. One final left turn, down a narrow hall. Like a ship, two sets of airtight doors were situated at both ends of all hallways leading outside. In space, this was to avoid the risk of decompression. Here, the configuration was primarily if a Locust found its way inside.

The first door closed silently behind her with a soft *click*. There was no way back. System (maybe Michael Broeger or Dwell had managed to think for themselves this time) had sealed her in the corridor. No place to go but outside, and that way led to Locusts.

She never slowed, couldn't hesitate lest the computer figure out what she planned and lock the outer door. Could it? The door could not be opened from the outside without a swipe of one's Ep after sunset, but would it work for anyone stupid enough to go outside?

Who in their right mind would try?

She almost laughed at the thought, and the exhilaration of escape. A cloud of heavy sorrow rolled along behind her, ready to smother if she slowed.

Doneele slammed against the door latch, hitting it with her hip. It opened to the frantic screams of alarms filling the compound. She ran straight, away from the building and into the night. She'd gone no more than a half dozen strides before realizing she hadn't grabbed an oxygen mask. That could have bought her more time. No turning back now. System wouldn't be fooled twice. She tried to breathe shallowly, but kept on running.

38 – Ken Burlov, *Washington*

"I can't push it much faster," Benny said over the com. "This thing is still accelerating. If I don't do something *now* there's no way I can keep up, let alone maintain enough juice to maneuver. As it is, I've been pushing the fuel cells."

Ken stopped pacing, knowing his agitation was only stirring the same in everyone else. Not that he had much room to pace, but he felt the need to physically be doing something. He stopped, willed himself to be calm. Things were stressful enough already in the cramped bridge.

They'd come through the Hole, trying to accelerate to match the alien ship. Benny was right. Whatever was propelling it had a lot more horsepower. They were in a vacuum; all a ship needed was to reach peak speed then kill propulsion. It would continue at the same velocity. According to Li the sudden burst of ions from the back of the alien vessel – no apparent ejection ports, the ions were streaming from the hull itself – had not abated.

It was either a well-fueled ship or in a big hurry to get to its destination.

Before his own fuel expired Benny wanted to attach himself remora-like to the hull along one of the various strips where it did not appear to be charged up. He'd then kill the engines and be carried along for the ride, conserve what charge remained in his cells for when – *not if* – the hangar opened and Peyton could escape.

Even now, Ken saw it was a doomed plan.

Aside from the possibility that whoever was piloting that ship may decide it didn't want more passengers and turn its scanner towards Benny's pod, it (*he, she, some other gender,* God only knew) probably knew the man's small skiff was no match for it.

In a way Ken was relieved – he couldn't lose another crewmember, another *friend,* so soon.

"Li, any chance he can make it?" He was stalling, even as the image of the pod on the main monitor changed course to intercept the derelict. Benny wasn't waiting for a green light from him. Ken didn't have to say anything. Even without System's calculations scrolling below, it was obvious the derelict was pulling away faster than Benny could close in.

He was going to try, however, whether Ken approved or not.

Li shook her head, then realized Benny wouldn't see it. "No, sir. Benny, it'll be past intercept before you can catch it."

"Fifteen seconds left before I'm forced to shut down," Benny said, not hearing or not *accepting* her statement. In fifteen seconds System would kill his engines to allow enough reserves for the pod to re-dock with the *Washington*'s hub. His voice was breathy, like he'd been running and not sitting nearly motionless in the pod's seat.

Adrenaline.

Ken could acknowledge over the public channel that Benny was disobeying orders and let the ramifications fall on the man's shoulders later, but what he was doing was no less than he probably would have done himself had their positions been reversed – even *with* a family back home waiting for him to return alive.

"Do the best you can," he said, letting his practical side debate the possible repercussions coming *his* way now, since those five words made whatever might happen point back to the captain. A part of him felt a renewed excitement that Benny might just succeed. "If you miss it, we'll be at your position in . . ." he consulted his monitor. System, like the good information butler it was, scrolled the time across the screen. " . . .thirty-seven minutes."

Bridge Crew was silent, watching the main screen as it showed symbolic representations of the pod closing on the derelict. Li whispered, "He's beyond the stern now and still falling back."

Ken nodded. The larger bulk continued forward. Still accelerating. The small circle representing the pod had been left behind.

"Stay off the line of the stern, Benny, or you might fry."

"Yea, yea," came the whispered reply, "I know. Crap!"

With that one word, he'd acknowledged what everyone else knew.

System did not speak, but offered what statistics it thought they wanted to see across the bottom of the image. Distance between vessels, one hundred five meters, one hundred-twenty-five. Rising every second. He'd come close enough that Ken wondered if the alien pilot – if there was one and not some System-like automaton – had been accelerating only enough to give Benny a fighting chance. Seconds-to-fuel threshold also rolled quickly towards zero, but Benny did not cut the engines. Now, however, he was curving into a trajectory which was parallel with the derelict's path to avoid swinging into its ion *exhaust*.

The heavy, burning hole in Ken's chest blossomed. Fear, not for himself, not at the moment, but Peyton. For a short time there'd been hope, since at least Benny had been outside the hangar door, waiting for whatever happened next. Now, the rectangular icon was far beyond him, enough for System to recalibrate the perspective in order to keep its image and Benny's in the same window.

The fuel level for the pod's cells changed to yellow. The engines shut down.

"Out of gas," came Benny's hushed, sorrowful voice.

The words were followed by a sobbing that he seemed to be trying to suppress but could no longer hold in, sorrow for his friend and frustration at not being able to help her. She was being carried away, maybe forever.

"Nav, maintain current position and trajectory," Ken said, feeling the silence in the bridge and over the open ship's com, a communal mourning for another lost Crew.

She wasn't lost. Not yet. *Stolen.* They might still get her back, because he knew where the vessel was going, and assumed everyone else did, too, including the folks on Toojay.

Benny sniffled over the speaker.

Ken took in a breath, held it a moment, then let it out. Knowing the com was still open, not only to the ship but to the rest of the known universe, he said, "Randall, track the ship but assume its destination is Toojay. System, determine most likely landing or orbit for the derelict upon arriving. Obviously if its course changes let us know immediately. ISO command, I'll be setting up a conference at the top of the hour, Eden-time, with everyone involved – Toojay leadership especially. I want to know theories on its purpose. Is it sending reinforcements, or picking up? I'm guessing it's picking up.

"Eden Central command," he continued, "I want to discuss the possibility that it might not stay long at 2J3P. Please have ready who you think should attend."

He most likely just triggered a panic on Eden with that statement. He should follow protocol, but there *was* no protocol for this. His gut told him whoever was driving that ship knew where the next Hole would be after Toojay, and was simply picking up its critters before moving into the 1J system. Then, when it was done with Eden, perhaps move on to Earth.

They were locusts in the truest sense. If someone didn't think of something fast, their perfect new home would suffer the same fate as Toojay. Stripped clean of plants, animals, and maybe people.

His priority would be to get the right people talking, then let them handle it. He had more important matters to focus on.

"Li, Peyton's air and supplies?"

She flipped an image aside on her console and brought up an estimate System had worked out for Peyton's EVA suit. "If she follows protocol and lowers the suit temp, practices slow breathing, she should have seventy-one hours of air in her tanks without going into low hibernation."

Low hibernation was more theory than fact. Instruct the EVA's system to lower the suit to near freezing temperatures, and do so quickly, leaving the lesser AI in the suit's computer to electronically stimulate the heart and force breathing via an emergency oxygen tube inside the helmet. Everything maintained with slow, measured intakes of breath and heartbeat. Keep the blood oxygenated and the brain healthy, but always on the verge of death.

Historically, outside of simulation, it had only been attempted once. Unsuccessfully. But there'd been plenty of successful – and controlled – training exercises in the lab for it to become an official last-ditch maneuver for astronauts finding themselves adrift for extended periods.

"She may also have use of Cannon's supplies," Li added, looking down and biting her lower lip. To Ken's pride she stayed professional. "Readings prior to the door closing showed his EVA's system was still functional."

Just not needed, he thought, but did not say.

He nodded to her, but said nothing. "Captain Marlay, give me a shout in twenty minutes."

The *Abad* captain did not reply, no surprise there. But Radish would call him on his personal channel. Ken stepped past Li's chair and headed for the hall. "I'll be in my quarters, setting up the calls. Interrupt me if anything changes. Navigation, after you rendezvous with Benny keep along the derelict's path. Try to avoid ion trails that may linger. I know you know all this, but humor me. Go as fast as we can manage without endangering the ship. I'm guessing the derelict will be easing up its acceleration now that it's lost us, but that's just a guess."

"Yes, sir," came Randall's succinct reply. Ken wondered, vaguely, if he'd even been listening. Randall knew what to do. They all did, but someone narrating the plan for the folks back home was becoming second nature.

Ken walked quickly down the curved hall to his room, trying to show a confidence he felt slipping away with each step. He wasn't a very religious man, but in the silence Ken did his best to pray.

39 – Second Excerpt from "Viewing The Apocalypse From a Theological and Historical Perspective"

Gendrick Hellerton's Senior Seminary Thesis,
Wesleyan University, April 28, 2185

*A*fter all this, so much of it foretold in Scripture, Jesus still had not returned. At least, not in person. Much has been said on this topic, angles such as God's timing versus our own to, again, a misinterpretation of ancient prophecy. For a grounded, well-thought-out discussion I'd recommend Yves Stephanopoulos' examination [10] since this paper will be going in a different direction than that.

Over the next ten years the New Enlightenment [11] blossomed. And here is proof, this writer feels, that the Spirit of God had not forsaken the remnant of humanity. On the contrary. Mason Sanford, Shabaz Hague and Rebecca St Jerrold came together, rose to power together and offered calm in the chaos. They spoke of love and an ability to take control of the terror and the hate shredding their generation apart and, eventually, stop it. Some of human remnant knew who these people must be, or thought they did.

Sanford was labeled The Beast, St Jerrod the Harlot and Hague became Anti-Christ himself. Maybe they were, but no one ever forced my great, great grandfather to wear the mark of the Beast on his forehead. Not that I've heard.

Maybe our ancestors did sell out to Satan and simply forgot to *tell us.*

With near-supernatural speed and efficiency, communications were re-established with whatever satellites hadn't been fried from the electromagnetic pulses echoing from our atmosphere. Transportation was rebuilt, first on land, then the sea then, finally, the air. [12] The world quieted, and listened, and came together. Mostly. Whenever I look back on the writings of this time, it appeared that the devil had moved out of the neighborhood. Perhaps he had truly been cast into the pit. If not forever, maybe the next thousand years.

Until the assassination of Mason Sanford. [13] Rather than shatter whatever authority had been given from the masses to these three, it polarized the world around the surviving two. Islam blamed Christianity. Unbelievers blamed the religious. The Christians blamed both the unbelievers and Muslims. [14][15] For some reason (and this is, indeed, another fascinating observation), for the first time in known history, no one blamed the Jews. Even so, everyone else blamed whoever they disliked at the moment. In my mind, looking back, it was insane. Reactionary. Human.

I could go on. The Global Community took form, not with talking and diplomacy, but with action. Armies rallied behind the Remnant, the name for the surviving faction of humanity. "Faction" was the word used [16], not surprising since the tendency for man to use drama for gain has, even now, yet to fade from our collective psyche. Four billion survived the war and its aftermath. Billions more did not. As people continued to die in the fallout the most dangerous regions where radiation still carried through the atmospheric current were segregated and quarantined. The population moved together into safer climes, the New Continents. New laws, simpler ones, were drafted. Primary of these was — and is — open communication. Secrets bred deceit. Lies pushed us from the Garden originally then nearly wiped the human race from existence.

Acceptance of your brother's faith was mandatory, as was his acceptance of yours. The Christian may debate with the Muslim and the Jew and the Hindu on concepts and practice, but any violence shown to another for their faith was extinguished with far greater and faster violence.

There would be no more warring over God.

Any individual or group refusing to participate in the reconstruction of Earth under what they might deem Satan's rule, basing their decision not on God's scripture but man's flawed interpretation of it, did not follow these tenants. Try as they might to survive on their own, outside of the new society, they all but died off (if not physically, at least in power and voice). Perhaps even now they are the martyrs wailing below the altar of heaven, pleading for vengeance.

Perhaps. I don't think so.

History will show where the Prophets were pointing, but never before. *[17]*

There were the words of Father Palazzo in the Final Synod of Bishops before the remnant of the Catholic Church disbanded and merged with the Protestant Apostolic movement, bringing most of Christianity together.

I've always liked this quote from Palazzo, though would presume to add to it, if I might. Some *answers will come through history, but* new *questions will inevitably arise. History today shows that God had so much more planned after we'd finished slaughtering ourselves.*

He did not come down from heaven on a cloud to punish the unbelievers. Instead, He opened the doors of heaven and gave the survivors another chance. A new Earth.

I have not a single doubt in my mind that the sudden focus on technology and rapid building of the early space program – with the single-minded goal of finding somewhere else to live other than this infected, dying planet – was God's Spirit at work. Since a mere sixty-one years after the Five Days of Hell ended, as part of the government-funded push to find more habitable breathing room, the first Hole was discovered. A road had been opened for humanity, leading directly to Eden.

Doomsday came and went, and although the descendants of Isaac and Ishmael did their best to destroy each other, man was given a new

Earth, under newly re-discovered Heavens.
All of it, under the same God. All of it, part of His plan.

40 – Peyton, 2Jside

It was cold, but Peyton reminded herself it was far colder outside the suit. She'd lowered its internal temperature to ten Celsius, still a Spring day but, relative to the usual eighteen degrees, the difference was obvious. It would be getting colder soon, another notch in a few more hours. Not enough to hurt herself, or *potentially* hurt herself, not yet, but conserving air and food was the only goal in her life until that door opened again.

She finished peeing, knowing the urine would soak efficiently into the pad lining her jumpsuit and be processed and separated, the water eventually finding its way into the drinking tube a few centimeters to the left of her lips.

Still, if she had any pleasures left, quirky as this one was, peeing in her suit was one. Where else could someone stand – or float – at work and simply let go? Everyone would know if you did, anyway (if they bothered to check). Every bodily function was monitored during an EVA. Important to know if the person floating beside you was starting to freak out. Elevated urine output, among others, was an indicator that you might want to pull them back in.

The initial fear had settled to a slow burn in her stomach and back, like a shallow pool of heat. But the cold, and her requisite slow breathing, also worked to numb her emotions a little. Numb the fear and the sorrow which swarmed around her like wasps.

The ship was moving. She understood that now. Any

hope that dozens of folks might be outside the door forcing their way inside had been erased in the chaotic, psychic crush she'd endured as the ship passed through the Hole an hour ago. If they did *that*, then they were inside the 2J system. More often than she knew was healthy, Peyton found herself staring through the visor at the dead Locust in the far corner of the hangar.

They were going to Toojay. It had scanned her, sucked every bit of information it could from her brain. Such an immense technology . . . and for what?

Feed the Locusts by finding new grazing land? It made no sense. Why was this ship here, hiding on the other side of the Hole instead of orbiting Toojay or off looking for the next planet like she and her people were doing?

There was a reason, and she imagined the human race watching all of this unfold was asking a thousand questions she hadn't yet thought of. Maybe answering some, too.

A new itch gnawed at her brain, but she tried to ignore it. Had the derelict moved through the Hole with no resistance, or had it scanned the rest of the *Washington* Crew? Worse, had it used some new weapon to cut it to ribbons. . . *stop it! Stop it! They're fine. They* have *to be.*

Cannon's suit hovered close enough to touch. In fact, a half hour ago she did just that, needing to make contact, to reach out and touch the suit's arm. Not too hard, afraid of what she might feel, or not feel if she closed her hand too tightly around the sleeve.

He was facing away from her now. For that she was grateful.

But he was gone.

She looked quickly around the room. Most of the balls still worked to light the interior. In another ten or eleven hours that could change, depending on how long their charges lasted.

A renewed urge to unlatch from the tether and explore her surroundings took hold again. This consideration would likely happen more often the longer she remained in this spot, unable to maneuver more than a couple of meters in any direction while tethered to the hangar door. Eventually, she would need to unclip it and do *something*. Just to keep her sanity.

Peyton breathed in, slowly, felt the cool air enter her nostrils and fill her lungs. She held it for as long as possible, longer by another two seconds this time. Slowly, resisting the urge to blow out the CO_2 and gasp for more oxygen, she exhaled, until there was nothing left in her lungs. Then a pause, and she did it over again.

To explore would waste oxygen, use energy that might burn her scarce food faster, not to mention the bursts of air needed to move about the room, minor as they would be, could be better used to stay alive a little bit longer. Peyton had to believe there was a chance of rescue. She needed to stay calm. And wait.

Another breath. Hold. Release.

She'd fallen asleep before the third breath was complete.

41 – Doneele, 2J3P

Doneele ran into darkness, though the clear night air magnified the starlight and highlighted the shapes of the landscape ahead of her. With exertion, shallow breaths were no longer possible. She breathed in night air she hadn't tasted in so long. A tangy, orange flavor washed over her tongue. Just for a moment, then it was gone. Stumbling around a waist-high boulder, she worked her way towards another copse of rocks. Distance was needed between her and the rest of the compound. The air pouring through her nostrils was cool and pleasant, far different from her expectations on this poisoned planet.

Somehow, the now-active chemicals in the atmosphere didn't affect her.

She remembered nights on Eden with Zechariah, sitting on the back porch, talking softly, enjoying every moment God gave them in Paradise after they'd left the burnt-air taste of Earth.

Doneele slowed, stopped, leaned forward with hands on knees hidden behind her robes. She looked up to evaluate her surroundings. A clearing, nestled between the smaller copse of stones she'd just passed and a larger, more imposing construct of boulders and dirt. An altar laid out before her. Doneele thought of her husband and the quiet peace of Eden, the stars rolling above them which eventually sucked them up and away, into the endless cold nothing that was space – that was Toojay.

She stared at the altar, thinking of sanctification, of grace and judgment. Sacrifices throughout history and the requirement for blood. She'd led Zechariah up the mountain and laid him on the altar. His blood poured out, then was lapped up by the false idols of this planet. No offering towards God. The Lord no longer demanded blood sacrifices, having become one Himself.

Doneele fell to her knees and stared at this odd sanctuary, dark and foreboding in front of her. It was draped in the darkness of eternal night into which she'd run. She was dead, Doneele understood this now. She was merely waiting, prostrate before the judgment seat of the demon to whom she had given away her soul. For what seemed all of eternity, she waited.

At last there came movement from behind the closest boulder.

Lucifer ascended the black dais, taking his throne and standing tall within his black rotting shell of a soul. He rose high over the clearing and considered the prostrate woman below him.

Then, Satan laughed and spread his wings.

42 – Loki, 2J3P

At first, the three Locusts were too intent on the story to notice the human stumbling towards their gathering. Loki's Mate and the Follower, as it referred often to the third, were the receivers of the tale. Loki, as was most often the case, the giver.

It twisted and jittered in the sand, measuring out the distance in time from this night and the one in which the story's event had taken place. Many travels past. Other lines, measuring distance. The Locust danced and tapped along the sand with its pointed tail, narrating how it caught a full-grown cow which had lingered too long in the growing dusk, pulling it farther away from the entrance to its warren where it had hesitated a mere three paces away. It was a feast Loki pondered often, one which it shared with many others in that ensuing frenzy, and which had not come again. A curving sweep of its tail in a half circle. Both the Mate and Follower hissed quietly in commiseration for this detail. Follower, itself, was mate-less and rarely flew far from the other two during their travels. It never offered reasons for this, nor did Loki concern itself with why. Follower watched and read the story with rapt fascination.

Loki did not know the name the humans had given it. To its mate, it was also known as Mate. Follower called it, in the rare moments when it spoke to others about their travels together, Teller.

The Locusts did not feel hunger in the manner of the

outsiders which had settled here. To them, food was a daily exercise, at least from what Loki could see during the many times it observed them from a distance through the protected holes in their warren. Loki's kind did *crave* nourishment. Their internal systems, however, were the epitome of conservation, able to survive extreme periods with nothing to eat. Eventually, they required *something*, or they would die. None in the Swarm had bred young in so long, the stories of them – especially training of newborns in the art of hunting – had become more legend than memory.

Stories like the one drawn in the loose soil beside the copse of boulders were becoming just as scarce. Small moments reminiscent of these old tales, feasts uncountable, motivated the others. Soon, there will be another meal. Soon. If not, more of the Swarm would fall from the cool currents above and never rise again.

Until then, they flew, followed the dark, and watched for that moment.

A sound, hardly a hiss of something along the dirt, drew Loki's attention. If it hadn't paused in its dance it would never have heard. But it *had* paused.

Images of its only other kill since the story it was now telling, a small reptilian morsel running disoriented between boulders, came to mind as Loki quickly ascended the dirt slope between the larger of the two stones. A momentary thought that it might simply be a new human device hidden among the rocks was cast off at the scent of prey.

Loki rose onto the highest boulder, not wanting to fly and risk scaring off what might be waiting. Its mind reeled at the sight of the human crouched on the ground, two leaps' distant from where it stood. The Locust spread all four of its wings.

So unexpected was this moment, Loki hesitated. There

had been many stories of the last human prey, some only second- or third-hand, but no remnant of it had been left when Loki and its two companions managed to push their way through the frenzy, nor when they returned to the spot the following night.

They were the only three here, the others having already passed by the human warren after an initial, hopeful fly-by. Few of its kind dared risk contact with the walls, the pain they promised, nor wanted to be marked, as Loki had. To some, it seemed a shameful badge to carry. Loki found it amusing. The tag was small, embedded into its shell too far back to remove. Mate or Follower could have helped with this, but Loki refused. The humans tracked it with this device, it was certain. So be it. Loki saw it as an honor. He'd been chosen by these otherwise docile creatures. Perhaps, one night, they would make the mistake of attempting contact. The idea of feasting on their soft flesh was far worth the mark, shameful to some or not.

Now, perhaps, the moment had come. Loki fluttered its wings enough to lower itself beyond the stones onto the ground. The Mate and Follower moved along the ground, hardly stirring the soft sand, rounding the boulders to its left. The three Locusts stepped quickly towards the human, then suddenly stopped. Two other humans appeared, running directly towards them. All three Locusts bent forward, mandibles open, hissing in alarm and excitement at this new challenge.

Then the arm of one newcomer exploded in a bright flash of light. The Mate curled in pain and rolled away, screaming and thrashing in a sudden agony that tore open the night around them. The sound of Mate's pain was so intense and vocal Loki and Follower stepped backwards. The two newcomers ran directly for Loki's prey.

43 – Broeger and Dwell, 2J3P

Michael Broeger had ventured outside at night only three times in the two years he'd been stationed here. He'd been terrified every moment, even with System's assurances no Locusts were nearby. Most recently he'd been commissioned along with Joe Conn to repair two cracks in the glass doors of the Union room, to mitigate risk of Acclarin finding its way inside.

Tonight, the fear was made worse by a mad rush of adrenaline. If Doneele had really come out here, she'd be dead in a matter of moments, given she was heading directly toward Loki (being the only tagged Locust he had the honor of getting a more definitive label on the video) and two other Locusts. As he and his partner stood just inside the final door, donning the breathers and checking weapons, Broeger wondered why they didn't just relax and watch her die.

She'd killed Arun. For some reason most of the six people behind them in the outer hallway screamed for them to get her back. Why they wanted this was beyond him, but he and Dwell were already in motion towards the hatch before they gave themselves much time to consider what they were heading into. System, for its part, spouted protocol that the lives of all colonists must be valued and if a crime had been committed they would be tried for such actions, punished if found guilty. Something like that. Broeger couldn't focus on the AI's emotionless words, and

Dwell tried to drown out the legalese by repeating, "Yeah, yeah, we know, we know," over and over until System shut up.

Only with masks tight against their faces and com units in their ears did some of the voices on the open channel tell them to hold off, why take the risk? It was too late for second guessing, however. They each had a weapon, a duty and most of all: momentum.

Not until they were returning with Mother Doneele did Michael ever consider that the people who wanted her rescued might be a lynch mob, wanting her blood on their own hands rather than waste it on the monsters. Arun was well-loved, and she had slaughtered him. Most, he imagined, had already seen the carnage sprayed across her walls. If not, it was only a matter of time.

The guns were gas-powered with incendiary-tipped bullets. The suckers would, at a minimum, sting the bugs real bad. At best, fry up their insides. If they didn't explode in the barrels. It had been a long time since either of them had done any target practice with these. Or cleaned them.

They held the rifles before them like medieval jousters and ran towards the crop of boulders to the west. The herd (*flock* was the more accurate term according to local minds) had already passed. Only three monsters to deal with. Michael hoped he and Dwell had some element of surprise.

He was pretty sure no one had fired upon these creatures since the very early days of the settlements. That may work to their advantage. Michael had no illusions they might get of this without a firefight.

"Watch our backs, people," Dwell huffed as he ran a half step ahead. He was a short man, leaner than Broeger but not nearly in as good of shape. Still, Michael let his partner take the lead. What he lacked in physical prowess he more than made up for with enthusiasm. And sheer bravery.

"Skies are clear," someone said over the com. It sounded like Joe Conn. "But Loki's making his move. If you're going to do something . . ."

We'd better hurry, Michael finished in his head.

"Stay close, Dwell. It'll make us look bigger."

"I'd laugh if I wasn't so scared." His struggle to continue the pace was apparent in his breathing, labored even through his mic's white-noise filters.

They passed a small cluster of rocks on the right and ran directly into a scene Michael had hoped never to find himself in. Standing face to face with one Locust would be bad enough, especially at night. Now, there were three. All were flapping their wings excitedly, scorpion tails raised as they scurried on their waspy legs towards Doneele. For her part, the priest was kneeling on the ground with arms stretched out before her as if on a prayer rug. She stared up at the Locusts with an expression lost in the gloom. Michael had time only to note she wore no breather before he and Dwell were noticed. The larger of the three (Loki, he assumed, though with no prompts from System he couldn't be sure) practically split in two as it hissed through its multi-faceted mandibles and reared back, ready for a fight.

Dwell moved to the right. Broeger kept his weapon trained on the larger one. Ironically, the smallest of the three either hadn't noticed them or simply didn't care. It continued towards Doneele.

Everything after that happened fast. Dwell fired four quick bursts. One missed, sending a small cloud of dirt cascading against the base of rocks. The rest hit dead-center into the smaller Locust's chest. It folded in on itself and rolled backwards from the force, smoke rising from its wounds. It screamed, loudly and horribly, though for only a few seconds. Michael had moved his gaze away from the big one for just a moment, then caught himself and looked back. He hoped Dwell was focused on the third.

It wouldn't have mattered. As the smaller one fell silent, continuing to twist and buck across the sand like an Earth wasp sprayed with a can of insecticide, the others stepped back, their hiss-growls so fierce Michael felt the breeze of them above his mask. The smaller of the living Locusts scurried quickly behind the rocks. The larger – definitely Loki as it turned away to reveal the white plastic tag jutting between its upper wings – clambered along the rock face. It reached the top, turned back and hissed again. The sound did not seem directed to the humans, however. It had bent itself in the direction of its fallen companion. The latter's thrashing had slowed, but had not stopped completely. At least it wasn't screaming anymore.

"Let's just grab Mother Doneele and go now," he whispered.

"Yep." They each stepped sideways, converging on the woman, and grabbed her robes at the shoulders. It was a move they were required to rehearse once a month, the Toojay equivalent of life guard training. They turned sideways, leaving their barrels trained towards the rocks, and sidestepped in the direction of the compound.

"I can't see the third one anymore," he whispered as they dragged Doneele backwards along the sand. She did not resist, but neither was she helping. Dead weight. Loki had crested the highest rock. It was watching them. "Someone keep an eye on them, in case one or the other comes around behind us."

Loki was doing something bizarre at this point. Standing atop the rock, completely exposed should they fire again, it let out a long, protracted hiss. The sound was different than before, a smoother keening ran beneath the sound. Almost an actual voice – a slowed, tamer version of the other's scream. All four dragon-fly wings spread wide and vibrated. The scene could have been mistaken for fists shaken at them in rage as they dragged Doneele away. It could mean something completely different, but the expert in this kind of thing was a bloody corpse still curled in the corner of this deranged woman's room.

In unison, the two security men turned completely away from the boulders, needing to see what was in front of them.

"Watch the Locusts," Michael spoke into the com.

He left the rifle aimed toward the ground so it wasn't pointed towards Dwell, and his partner did the same. Then they ran as fast as they could, dragging their hundred and something pound prisoner between them. They passed the smaller group of boulders. Dwell's breath was labored over the com, much as Michael assumed his own was. The compound was well-lighted, every outside spotlight a beacon that nevertheless still looked too far away.

At the next announcement over the com, they both understood what true fear was.

"Move it! Move it!"

Dwell began shouting incoherently, yelling only to give himself a burst of speed. Gripping Doneele's robes tighter, they ran, using her weight as ballast so neither could stumble forward. Their backs were to the monsters which that last announcement implied were coming for them.

Michael Broeger forced himself to say, "How close?"

No reply. A woman, possibly Ochi Miyoko, spoke with a surprisingly calm voice. "Less than twenty meters. Leave her. She's not worth it. Leave her and run, you idiots."

Dwell showed no sign of letting go. Because of this, neither did Michael, much as he agreed with the xenologist.

They gave each other a brief glance and tried very hard

to run faster. They managed a little more speed. The priest was still dead weight. Michael was about to verbally agree with the suggestion and drop her, take the heat off of Dwell by doing it first, when Miyoko's voice returned. She sounded pissed off, considering she was giving them what both considered good news. "They turned away. Not following anymore. Loki's back with its mate, doing some kind of dance. The other one flew off in the other direction, probably catching up with the flock."

They both slowed a little, *needed* to.

Dwell said, "Its mate?"

"We think so. The way they interact and – "

"Oh, you're kidding me," Michael spat, grabbing Doneele's robes tighter. "Dwell, don't slow down. Move it!"

They did. Time blurred for the last minute of their travel. As they reached the entrance voices began buzzing over the com, System's included, but they were too exhausted to note the words. Only the tone: *Don't stop!* Joe Conn opened the door, mask across his face. The two security men stumbled inside, dragging Mother Doneele with them as the maintenance man closed the outer door then actually ran past them down the hall.

Michel threw off his mask and pulled the com from his ear both in relief and frustration. *Forget the residual Acclarin,* he thought. They could let their arms and legs go numb, dream happy dreams now. As long as they were inside.

"System, is the outer door charged?" He managed the question only as a whisper. System's voice had begun to reply when the monster outside slammed into the door from outside. No expected screech of pain from the Locust. System must have killed the hull's charge when they'd gone out.

Dwell cursed and clambered backwards, farther

towards door at the end of the hall. Michael joined him, only in that moment remembering they'd both been armed and could as easily have turned around and blasted the thing rather than run like madmen. Four people, including Miyoko, ran into the short hall, two helping the men to their feet, two others grabbing Doneele by the hands (*By the hands, duh, that would have been easier*, he thought absently) and pulled her towards the inner door. Everyone but Michael, Dwell and the catatonic priest were wearing breathers.

"Exterior is now fully charged," answered System, when the noise of their exodus quieted. Dwell actually laughed between heavy breaths.

The next impact against the door was followed by Loki's expected shriek of pain. At least it couldn't bust up the door any more than it already had. Even so, there was another impact after that, and another shriek of pain.

Its mate, Broeger remembered.

The next collision with the door was not as severe, but the resulting scream was no less intense. *Suicide by electrified door.*

The thought had no humor to it.

44 – Gendrick, 2J3P

Though he'd been awake for a few minutes, he didn't dare yet open his eyes. Gendrick felt the cool stone floor below his cheek and palm. He was near the herd. The smell assaulting him was more overpowering than when he'd wandered among them outside.

Wherever he was, it was not dark. A faint, green glow drifted beyond his closed lids. He had not been rescued by anyone at the compound. At least, he didn't think so. He'd awoken earlier, fighting against the grip of sleep, and noted the smell and the sounds of heavy shuffling footsteps, before drifting back into unconsciousness.

This time everything felt different. The heavy blanket of exhaustion, or the effects of the drug, had faded. He needed to open his eyes. Mostly because he *could*. Because he was alive and needed to find out why.

The left eye, closest to the floor and thus more concealed to whomever, or whatever, might be near, opened first. Mostly he saw his cheek and nose, then something moved across a thin slit of vision beyond. Its owner snorted and moved farther away, towards a distant, darker corner. Sudden splashing of water against rock.

A cow, relieving itself away from the others.

He'd been to enough farming communities on Earth to know cattle back home didn't do that. They defecated wherever they happened to be standing.

But he wasn't home.

At least not *his* home.

He understood, before opening his other eye, where he was. How he'd gotten here was another matter.

With both eyes open now, he took a short breath and let it out quickly. It was like breathing inside a bag of old mothballs. He coughed, curled up a little and pulled his legs under himself. He moved slowly, not wanting to appear threatening. But the sooner he faced his hosts – or captors – the sooner he could can deal with whatever was going on. He sat upright.

Higher off the floor, the smell was nearly impossible to take in. Ammonia, defecation, sour milk. He put a hand to his mouth and nose. The hand was covered in clinging dirt from outside. Its neutral odor was a relief.

A half-dozen bulls stood in a semi-circle around him, equally distant from each other. The stone wall behind them was seamed with green minerals which emitted a constant glow throughout the cave. This was the light he'd noticed through his lids. If he survived, maybe he would ask what that stuff was. Someone might know.

Maybe not. It was an alien planet, after all.

Worried his covered face might be an insult, Gendrick took one final breath of the dirt-lined palm and lowered his hand.

The bull standing directly before him in the center of the line of (*sentries?* he wondered) stretched its neck towards him and bleated. The sound was not nearly the volume he'd heard outside. What was the term his mother always used? *Inside voice.*

He nodded once and cleared his throat.

"Hi," he said, his voice also hushed.

The bull, easily Gendrick's own height, more so since he was crouched on the floor, raised its head, either confused or perhaps Gendrick's own odor was offensive. It lowered its head and snorted once, but did nothing else. None of the other bulls moved away. The animal in the center seemed to be in charge. It aimed its head towards the farther recesses of the cave, one eye always riveted towards the human. Each of its compatriots had the same one-eye stare while aiming their faces towards various corners of the cave.

If Gendrick tried to stand or move closer to them, he might have a problem with these boys.

Ten minutes or so later, after some time spent adjusting his robes, spreading the bottom out over his legs which were now folded cross-legged before him in a more comfortable position, Gendrick pulled the collar away from his right shoulder to inspect the throbbing ache he'd felt as soon as he'd begun to straighten. Bruised, painful to touch. There were tears in the fabric.

He'd been bitten.

The bull in front faced him full-on now, long nose pointed and dripping. Gendrick stared back, then turned and looked at the bruise again. One side of his robes was covered in dirt. He pulled the hem of the robe up to examine his boot. As he expected, a scuff along one side.

He took in a breath, the reactive cough less severe this time as the stench slowly worked its way into the back of his awareness, then looked in wonder at the animal.

"You did this, didn't you? You dragged me down here before the Locusts came."

A tongue darted out of the animal's mouth and ran across its nose. Its stare was unwavering. Gendrick straightened some more, moving slowly, not wanting to frighten him, and ran his hands along his own chest, his arms, patted them, then reached out towards the other. The bull was too far to reach, but that was not his intent. Hands turned, palm open, he said louder, "Thank you for saving my life."

It snorted, turned its head back towards the rest of the herd gathered farther in the back the cavern. Between the legs of one of his guards Gendrick was able to make out shapes in the recesses. Most stared his way. The sound of a human had likely never been heard in this place before. Let alone the *sight* of one.

He lowered his arms, wondering what these creatures called themselves. *Cattle* was such a condescending term. Cattle was food, had limited sentience. They were prey.

He looked at each of his "guards" and understood: they were not cattle. They were survivors, and likely far more intelligent than anyone gave them credit for; not as helpless as their physical bodies suggested.

Would they stop him if he tried to stand, walk around? They were big and heavy. Their legs didn't seem designed for kicking, but cows and bulls back on earth could break your neck if you weren't careful.

He didn't get up. Not yet. Perhaps he could sing, an ancient missionary technique used to intrigue indigenous people and appear less intimidating. Gendrick didn't think he needed any such presentation. If they were afraid of him, why drag him down here?

They wanted to help.

"What's your name?" he asked the one in front, assuming this had been his rescuer. It was the closest and most interested in making some kind of connection. Not that Gendrick expected the creature to answer, but he needed to talk, to *try* communicating.

Its watery eyes narrowed as if annoyed with the noise this human was making. Gendrick said, "My name is Gendrick Hellerton." He patted his chest. "Gendrick." He repeated the action and the name.

This was stupid. He was assuming it would

spontaneously alter the physical makeup of its vocal chords and speak some tribal name like, "Gork" or "Moon Watcher."

It *did* reply, however. The cow twisted its lips in a way Gendrick didn't remember it doing before, and let out a low, *almost-moo* noise. It sounded like "Moon."

Maybe his name *was* Moon-Watcher.

Don't be naive, he thought. It just mooed at him, nothing more.

Arun would be laughing if he were here, then whisper for him to leave this to the professionals.

"Gendrick," he said again.

It repeated the lip movement, and the semi-word, "Moon." Obviously it did not know the word *moon*.

Likely not its name, then, but Gendrick needed a verbal anchor.

"Moon." He said. "A pleasure to meet you."

He leaned back, supported himself with his arms stretched behind him, and straightened his legs. They felt tight, leaden. Maybe the drug hadn't worn off completely. How long had he been out? Was it the middle of the night or only evening?

He'd been sleeping for a while, that much he could assume. Whether real sleep or drug-induced he had no idea. Trying to get up too quickly might not be a good idea.

But he wanted to know how they'd react.

That was when clearer memories began to rise in his mind.

She'd drugged him and left him to die. Gendrick patted his pockets, looking for the Ep. Nothing. She'd taken it. Out of contact with the compound. Everyone might think he was dead, unless System could track him via the bio-chip in his neck. He doubted its signal reached this far without an Ep.

Mother Doneele had left him to die.

What had he done to drive her towards something this unthinkable? For a brief, overpowering moment he wanted to cry, curl up like a child bullied on the playground. But he didn't; he needed to stay rational, logical.

Was this what *really* happened to her late husband?

Too many questions, no solid answers. His leg began to twitch, body responding to an increase in stress. If he wasn't going to start blubbering like an idiot, he needed to move.

Slowly, Gendrick curled his legs under himself until he was twisted into a kneeling position. He waited. Moon watched him with wider-eyed interest, as did his five friends.

Softly, as gently as possible, Gendrick said, "I'm going to stand. I need to stretch, move around. I have no intention of getting closer to your herd, nor have I any intention of hurting you."

Moon watched him, saying nothing. Hardly blinking.

Gendrick said, "You brought me down here. You know I'm no threat."

He took in a deep breath, acknowledging the acrid staleness in the air but no longer bothered by it, then slowly let it out. He stood, leaning one hand on the wall behind him. It was damp but warm. Gendrick rose shakily.

His head bumped against the wall of the cavern as it curved towards the ceiling. He bent a little, slowly reaching up and touching the top of his head, wondering if any of the phosphorescent minerals in the wall had fallen into his hair.

Nothing on his fingertips. In the corner of his eye, Moon turned its bulk towards him. Not stepping closer, but it had pivoted so its flank faced Gendrick. The others hadn't moved, were, in fact, still as stone.

Everyone waited for the weird human to do something stupid so they could stomp him to death.

No, he thought, *don't think that way. No fear. Nothing negative.*

"Moon," he said.

Moon said nothing, only looked at him. Gendrick extended his left arm, fingers slightly curled in the same manner in which he'd approach a strange dog, and walked forward until his fingers barely brushed the long whiskers along its snout.

It sniffed, pulled the loose skin of its mouth back in an apparent gesture of repulsion. Gendrick probably smelled as bad, as *alien*, as they to him.

The good news was it did not bite his hand off.

"Thank you," Gendrick said again, meaning the two words more than he ever had in his life.

It snorted once, and licked the snot from its nose.

Gendrick felt his body relax, not realizing how tight his muscles had become.

"Well," he said, hoping his tone was keeping them calm, "I guess we hang out until morning, right?"

No response, only those large, wet eyes staring. Now that he was standing, the bull's head was even with his own.

Gendrick slowly rotated, trying to get his bearings. He spied a flattened swath of dirt where perhaps he'd been dragged, leading away between the two large bodies of Moon's compatriots and towards a darkened section of the cave. None of the minerals lining the wall in that section.

The way out.

Why didn't the Locusts simply come down here and have a feast?

Claustrophobic carnivores? More questions . . .

He sniffed. The smell, maybe? Wait. If it was night, why wasn't he tripping on the Acclarin in the air? He was conscious, and clear-headed. At least he thought so. All of this could be one big hallucination.

Assuming no Acclarin, the pickings here wouldn't be placated. Prey would fight back, try to survive. Maybe Locusts were like jackals, only taking what was easiest.

If he made it back to the compound, he'd have much to discuss with Miyoko.

Doneele had left him to die.

Why had she done that?

The thought kept rising and falling into his consciousness. When it did, he would look around and distract himself with his current predicament. This wasn't the time to wonder about *why* he was here. He had other pressing matters. Gendrick was *here*, and he needed to accept it as God's will. This was where he was supposed to be in this moment, and he needed to give it attention.

The missionary, finding himself in a strange land amid its natives.

Hundreds of years ago, his predecessors would work to convert the population to Christianity. Someday. Maybe. Right now, keeping their trust was the priority, and not getting martyred.

And find out what was on the other side of the two cattle barring the way from where he'd been dragged.

He needed to see.

Finally, Gendrick walked toward the two, leaving Moon behind.

In the corner of his eye he saw his host slowly keep pace. Waiting to see if his guest would embarrass him.

Gendrick approached the two guards and did the only thing his brain could come up with. He reached out to the closest and gently stroked its flank. It twitched and turned its head towards him. Nothing more.

Gendrick stepped past. It moved aside, not in

acquiescence, but to make room for Moon who was trying to get in front of him. Gendrick stopped and turned towards the animal.

"It's OK, my friend," he said, reaching out to touch its neck. "I'm not going out. Just," he gestured towards a spot beyond where the deeper shadows began, "over there. Come with me, if you want. Just don't stop me."

He stepped forward, watching the bull. Moon stepped with him, but did not intercept. It would know when Gendrick was getting into dangerous territory. When he did, hopefully it *would* stop him.

Just as possible it would turn back and let the crazy man kill himself. Either way, its actions would tell Gendrick what he needed to know.

Together they stepped into the shadows. He was surprised how well he could see from the ambient light behind them. Their shadows preceded them.

The room narrowed, then curved to the left and sloped upward. He stepped towards this darker area, but Moon leaned into him, almost knocking him down with its bulk.

Gendrick stumbled, and walked no farther.

"End of the line?" he asked. Moon said nothing.

Gendrick closed his eyes and listened. Behind him came the constant shuffle of cows moving in the far recesses of the cave, heavy wet breathing. Were they sleeping? He assumed all living things slept in some way. If so, Moon must be exhausted.

There was another sound, in front but distant. Wind, an occasional rustling.

Wings?

Was something up there, at the top of the ramp, waiting for a calf to drift from its mother and wander to the surface? Did the monsters actually wait by the entrance, hoping for a morsel? Even one, alone, falling back from the flock at the off chance of scoring more food . . . .

He stared up the ramp, into its menacing blackness. No sign of stars, so the ramp likely curved away. He couldn't imagine the entrance would be a straight line to the burrow, no sense of security in that, nor a deterrent to predators.

No movement. No more sound. Probably the wind.

What time was it? What might be going on back at the compound? All of this would have to wait until tomorrow.

He looked at Moon, whose head now rose a little past his own as it craned its neck, a gesture either of assertion, or unease. It sniffed the air.

Gendrick reached out and gave a quick rub along that neck before turning back towards the others. From this vantage, he could see how much wider the rest of the cave was beyond the place where he'd woken. The entirety of the flock rested comfortably in its recesses. Mothers, a smattering of younger calves, males: all of whom stared back along the distance towards him.

For no other reason than having something to do, he gave them a wave before slowly walking back to his earlier spot. Moon followed.

Now was not the time to push their hospitality.

Three of the five other bulls guarding him had moved on, probably to join their families for a night's sleep. The others waited. Gendrick looked to Moon and said, "Thank you again," before finding as comfortable a spot as possible against the wall of the cave.

Moon did not leave. Instead, he waited in front of Gendrick with one eye on him, until eventually settling into an awkward position laying on the stone floor. Its head lowered, eyes never quite closing. The other two took that as a dismissal, for they stepped quietly away.

At some point, sleep *did* come for the alien in their midst, and Gendrick did not wake until morning.

45 – Radish Marlay, *Abad*, 3JSide

Marlay swiped closed the window on his Ep. Captain Burlov's face disappeared. Their conversation had been short but civil, and private. Nothing said would have caused any stir in the community, but they needed to talk without concern for political correctness. The primary question needing to be worked out was whether or not the *Abad* would continue to the new planet or turn back. In the end, he could see in the other man's eyes he needed to know Radish's crew wasn't far away as he followed the Locust ship towards Toojay, or beyond. Covering his back. Neither of their ships had more than the barest defense abilities. Even so, two would be better than one if something happened.

The *Washington* had already lost two of its crew to these creatures.

The conversation both worried and angered him. The mission had gone awry with the attack by the derelict, and no one had woken him. Not even System. Protocol for any emergency situation required the captain to be on Bridge. He wondered if Man or Sarey told System to leave him alone, for a little while at least. Whatever the reason, System had woken him for the call from the *Washington*. Radish *had* needed sleep, no question, and physically felt better even having slept only two of his planned four hours. A nap, more than anything.

They were so close. But the third planet in this system was not going anywhere and the *Abad* still retained right of first exploration. There was no question of agreeing with Burlov's request, and the relief on the captain's face said as much before they offered perfunctory goodbyes and swiped off.

He leaned back in his small desk chair. He could go back to sleep, but that chance was gone for now. He'd dressed before receiving Burlov's call, in loose pants and shirt. He now tucked his feet into slippers and decided to forgo his usual protocol of proper dress on the bridge. Third shift was quiet. He passed no one in the curving hall on his way to Command. When the door opened the scene was much as he'd left it only two and a half hours earlier – except when Sarey looked up from her screen her eyes were swollen and red. At first Radish assumed this was from staring at data all shift, then realized she'd been crying.

"Captain," Man Johnson said. His face was neutral. Radish stepped into the small room and returned the gaze. He waited, trying to read Johnson's face.

Finally, he said, "You did not wake me."

"No, sir, but I'd planned to after you'd gotten at least three hours' sleep. When Captain Burlov said he'd be calling you, I allowed System to put it through."

Radish felt the muscles in his arms and shoulders tighten. The anger was a surprise and it must have registered on his face.

Johnson quickly added, his face still set. "I made a call. You'll likely not get much more sleep in the next couple of days, neither will the rest of the crew, so while we waited for direction, *I* waited. We all need to be fresh, you most of all."

Still no reply, but Radish felt the tension easing. He looked away, played the man's rationale over in his mind, trying to find issue.

Johnson relaxed a little in his chair at the Com station. "When the call from the *Washington* came through I called up first shift early. They'll be on duty in . . ." he glanced at his console, " . . .fifteen."

Radish let the breath he'd been holding out but allowed himself a muted growl. He moved to his chair and sat. "To be honest, I do not think I would have made the same call. But you made the right one. Thank you."

It irked him to give compliments, but under the circumstances the man acted correctly.

"Thanks."

Thank you, sir, he wished the man would stay. But formality was not in Johnson's nature. "Open a channel to Crew for me, please."

"All set."

"This is Captain Marlay. As most of you by now know, there has been an incident with the derelict ship. The *Washington* has lost one crew member and we are all praying for a safe recovery of a second. I will not go into the details here. I'm certain it is all over the news. However, given that the alien ship is currently heading towards 2J3P at a very high rate of speed, we have agreed to return to the 2J system to assist the *Washington* in whatever form that might take. Our probes will continue to scan the surface of 3J3P for now and we are analyzing results as they come in. The *Abad* will return to its original mission as soon as we are able.

"First shift please report to your stations. Third shift will remain until Second reports for duty, which will be two hours early. We will follow this double shift protocol until further notice. Refer to your personal schedules for specifics.

"Nav, set a course for the Hole. Issue a warning as we

approach, but do not slow speed unless necessary. When we pass through, hook onto the *Washington's* course and follow. I want forty-five percent reserves of fuel on arrival at Toojay in the event we need to get out of there quickly. If we need to slow to refuel then do so."

The hydrogen cells were generally refueled enroute, using large, sail-like catchers which expanded around the ring, catching the flow of hydrogen in constant motion away from the nearest sun. It was a slow process, and risky considering the additional surface area would be exposed to whatever small (or large) debris might pass through their space. Radish imagined it akin to a massive whale swimming through the ocean, devouring krill. A ship's "refueling" was normally done in orbit, or in close enough proximity to a sun to take advantage of concentrated levels.

"There will be a meeting with ISO Command, myself, Captain Burlov and other authorities from Toojay, Eden and Earth in a few minutes. As more information is known we will communicate it to you. Out."

He nodded towards Johnson but the man had already disconnected the ship-wide channel.

"When First arrives for duty, try not to get in each other's way." He rose and headed for the door.

"Captain."

Sarey Ramprakash was standing and facing him. He raised an eyebrow in response.

"May I walk with you to the conference room to discuss something?"

She looked down briefly at her console. Across the room Man watched the interchange with unsubtle interest. Before Radish could respond she pointed at the ceiling and made a twirling motion with one finger – he assumed the gesture indicated the entire room.

No conversation on the bridge was private. Every word

spoken, every action was public. His pulse picked up a notch. Though a darker part of him wondered if this was personal, he knew it was not. She had some information on the planet. Whatever it was, it had shaken her. Even so, much of her downcast expression and demeanor was likely due to Cannon White's death. They'd been crewmates on a prior mission, and he knew them to still be friends.

"I should not be late for this meeting, but walk with me."

She followed him out of the room, a half step behind and not speaking until the door closed. What she told him on the curving walk along the corridor to the conference room filled him with immense excitement, *and* dread. Mostly dread, though he did not understand why.

46 – Ken Burlov, *Washington*, 2JSide

"Do we have an estimate of its arrival?"

"Eight days at its present speed." Before Ken had given the answer System displayed the same answer (including hours, minutes and seconds) at the bottom of his screen. He imagined the same was shown to everyone.

The conference room at ISO headquarters on Eden was filled to capacity. Most significant bases of operation had moved to the new planet since Earth's resources were limited, though there were three faces along the edge of the screen belonging to the smaller, Earth-based leadership team. The screen on Ken's app was dotted along the edges with smaller windows of those at other physical locations, some three windows deep. Conference Systems had a way of organizing remote attendees by affiliation. Radish's face was in the upper right corner, prominent, since he and Ken belonged to the same group. He was grateful to see the man even after having spoken so recently. Especially at Radish's report a moment earlier that the *Abad* was already heading back towards the 2J Hole.

Comforting to know they weren't the only ones out here having to deal with this thing, whatever or whoever they were.

The woman running the meeting was of primarily South African descent, a tall, rounded face but with an angled, prominent nose, revealing more than a little European blood in her ancestry. Whenever she spoke, the camera would close up on her face with the caption *Margaret Onai, Chief Operations Officer 3J Mission.*

Ken liked Margaret. She was an office type, ran things by the book more often than not and enjoyed criticizing Ken for his frequent lack of protocol. Her verbal and written lashings were (mostly) for show. In person she smiled more, laughed at his jokes, and could drink like a sailor. On screen, as now, she was attentive to others' opinions and made decisions with little data that invariably proved to be the right ones.

"Ken and Radish, continue at your present rate but no more. The derelict is moving at a much faster pace than your vessels can manage safely, anyway, so you won't catch it. At this point the safety of both crews are your highest priority. Even so, we don't know what to expect when they arrive at Toojay and you may be needed as backup."

"I think we know what to expect when they arrive at Toojay."

The speaker was a heavy, double-chinned man in his mid- to late-forties. He was in the same room as Margaret, three seats down. The image cut to a full view of the room mid-sentence and held there. Before he'd finished the sentence the words, *Mason Dancy, Operations, 3J Mission* appeared on the lower right corner. No title, Ken noticed, or not enough to merit display.

"We don't know for sure either way," Margaret said. "For all we know there's yet another hangar full of more Locusts. Or something else."

"Doubtful," Ken, said. "Based on the overall mass of the object, and the size of the hangar, if there *are* more Locusts onboard there couldn't be many of them." He shrugged. "As for something else, something smaller but no less intimidating, we don't know. Nothing gets through their hull."

An image of Peyton floating helpless inside the hangar flashed in his mind, and he looked quickly down, losing any motivation to speak. Others must have thought similarly because for a moment, everyone was silent.

"I would have to disagree with Mister Dancy's assumption as well, though with no more specific reasons than what Captain Burlov has stated," Ochi Miyoko said (*Senior Xenologist, 2J3P*). "Only a gut feel on my part, but I don't think the ship is coming here to add more of a burden, but to remove it. Toojay is no longer capable of supporting the Locusts. What animal and plant life remains has adapted well to survival. The arrival of humans on the derelict ship triggered something, and our best guess – based on what happened to Officers White and Kay in the hangar – is that it now knows the location of the next Hole and is going to continue on to Eden. After it collects the Locusts."

Ken didn't say anything, not yet. More than one person was speaking now. The image cut back to the main conference room on Eden. Margaret rapped her knuckles on the table to try and garner some order. Ken whispered, "How could what hap-" But knew his words would be muted at this point. Only Margaret's voice was coming through. Selective filtering.

How could what happened to Cannon and Pey reveal where the Hole was located, he had been about to say?

Because they'd scanned Cannon's mind. Or tried to. Somehow, it had killed him.

Blew him up.

But not Peyton. If they had some elaborate, highly advanced . . . *mind-reading* capability, they would have failed with Cannon, then gotten it more gently from Peyton.

That was insane.

No less magical than their own scanning technology, or

his traveling through space in this giant, flying ring.

He looked at Radish's window. Sensing where he was looking System enlarged the other captain's image. Radish was looking back at him, face tight with concentration. Ken imagined his own face looked the same. Radish had been looking at the primary window, but his eyes suddenly scanned to the right. System probably enlarged Ken's window on his screen.

Radish mouthed one word, silently, but Ken understood. His chest filled with ice.

Hangar, he'd not said.

If the Locusts were to be taken away, that was where they were going to settle in for the ride, the massive chamber where Ken's crew found the dead one. That single word had a far bigger implication: Peyton was trapped in there.

Ken whispered, "System, let me interrupt." Then, louder, not knowing if the AI did what he'd asked, "I have an officer trapped in that ship."

There had been a somewhat more orderly conversation going on, which stopped when Ken spoke.

"Excuse me, Captain?"

He cleared his throat and sat straighter in his chair. "I said, Peyton Kay is in there. She's alive, or *was* at the time the door shut. If this theory – " he opened one hand, palm up, "and it is a theory at this point – is true, and if she is still alive, she'll find herself in the middle of the Locust swarm, if and when they enter the ship."

No response.

"Margaret," he continued, "any preparations we make, a *major* part if it needs to be the emergency extraction of Peyton from the hangar when it opens."

She nodded, but the gesture was half-hearted. "It's a valid point. If we knew she was alive we would consider—"

She didn't finish, seemed at a loss for words.

At this point, a woman in full naval garb and hijab spoke up for the first time from her own window (*Rear Admiral Sehrish Raad, ISM Command*). "Captain, we have two ships at the moment rerouting to the 2J system, but neither will reach the planet before the alien craft. I am sorry about Chief Kay but planning a rescue, let alone carrying one out, is not feasible."

They've already given up on her, he thought. Ken leaned forward on his elbows and said, "Ms. Ochi." The Toojay xenologist's window widened. "How many pilots are there on your planet? Assuming the ship remains in orbit for a time – it seems too massive to enter the atmosphere, so let's call it a safe assumption for the moment – we'd need someone within range if an opportunity presents itself."

The xenologist turned her head and the image shifted to allow a view of her own, much smaller conference room. "I don't know. Michael?" The tired-looking man sitting beside her (*Michael Broeger, Chief Security Officer, Toojay, Southern Complex*) reached up and ran the fingers of one hand through his messy red hair.

"Not sure. Most outer atmosphere flights are handled by shuttles belonging to whatever transport is in orbit. Last count we had a couple of licensed . . . oh wait." He reached over and pulled an Ep towards himself. "Thank you, System." He shook his head, looking irritated while reading through something on his sheet. "System tells me that, in total between the three stations, five are officially licensed to fly in true space. From my compound, Fayaaz Kusher . . . . he's the Imam for the Islamic community but apparently has a pretty high pilot certification . . . and Dwell." His eyes rose up a moment, then realized no one else thought this name was eyebrow-worthy and clarified, "Just Dwell. One name. He's in security with me." As he pointed to his Ep he continued, though System had already scrolled the names across every screen. "From the northeast, Nader Roman and Fawn Noble. And a single pilot out west." He glanced at the main window and sighed, with a slight grin. "I see you already know the name. Daniel Shaw."

Representatives from the other Toojay compounds began to talk, but Broeger waved a hand in front of him and interrupted, "Why are you asking who can fly, Captain Burlov? We're not exactly equipped to have a dogfight with that monstrosity up there."

"No," Ken said, "but we need someone to be able to get Peyton – *and* Cannon if at all possible – out of the hangar when it opens, before those things show any sign of going inside. And since we don't know where this will happen, we need to have –"

Margaret interrupted, "Ken, I don't know if it's wise to order anyone close to that ship. It's killed one of your Crew already and we do not know the status of the other."

He was ready for the argument. "It ignored Ben Solomon, who was as close as anyone for an extended period of time."

"Yes, but – "

"Dwell says he'll do it," Broeger muttered, pointing to his screen. System obligingly subtitled the words below his window in case anyone missed it. What had Radish said, *There are no secrets anymore.*

Margaret's face hardened. "It could come into orbit or enter the atmosphere at any point in the globe. I'm not saying we completely rule out a rescue attempt, but Mason, please provide the full list of qualified pilots and their flight history, the types of vessels we have available, configurations, etcetera, from each location. We need to be prepared, regardless of what is decided about Chief Kay's situation. But we also have to discuss a possible evacuation plan of all three compounds."

Multiple voices rose up again, mostly from the scientific outposts. The admiral who'd spoken earlier remained quiet, taking everything in with an intense, but otherwise neutral stare. Ken would hate to play poker with that one. The others' comments were finally muted. Margaret stared at the primary screen in her conference room, waiting. Finally, in response to the xenologist at the largest of the sites raising her hand, she said, "Ms. Ochi."

Miyoko nodded in thanks and leaned forward. "Every location is equipped with underground retreat centers, designed for this kind of situation — well, nothing specifically like *this* but severe weather, Locust breach, that sort of thing. Bunkers, basically. They're not too big, and some personnel *might* wish to evacuate but I'm guessing most would prefer to stay. Regardless of their intentions, the first space craft we have ever encountered from a non-human source is racing towards us. For good or bad, I personally do not wish to go anywhere when that happens."

Margaret leaned forward. No one else gave any other gesture to speak, though Ken noticed a couple of silently moving mouths in other windows. The CMO said, "You could die."

Miyoko smiled. "If I had to choose how I'd die, Ms. Onai, this would be it."

47 – Oscar Capino, OJ System

"**I** need to make this quick, Captain." Sehrish's expression had not changed since they'd both signed out of the conference call with ISO Command. The Rear Admiral outranked him twice over, but she'd lied to Captain Burlov and he wanted to know why. Based on her current, guarded expression, she'd probably guessed the reason for this new meeting.

"I will, sir, thank you." He glanced at the top corner of the paper's window. An X within a circle, all yellow. The conversation was secured within the Navy's protocol. No one in the public would have access. He continued, "You told them we would not reach Toojay in time yet the *Yamato* is no more than two days from their Hole. I understand it's tied up babysitting the situation on Stain …" she raised one eyebrow at that. He'd gotten too flip, but pressed on, "… but they could intercept the alien ship a day before it reached the planet."

She waited before replying. Oscar fell silent. He'd said his peace. The Admiral said, "And then what, Captain?"

He began to answer, hesitated. *Then what?* Shoot at them? Would that even do anything?

"I don't know."

"No, you do not. None of us do." Her eyes narrowed, dark face flushed. "We have no data except what the *Washington*'s scans have provided and though they were helpful in some respects, we do not yet understand its drive, whether there is a crew or other weapons."

He'd known Sehrish Raad a long time, and respected her talent for a number of reasons, not the least of which her habit of thinking outside of the box when she needed to. Like himself, though, she hadn't seen true combat outside of civilian skirmishes. Things on Earth were heating up lately but outright war? Nothing like that. He didn't like to think she'd fail this first test. He clenched his hand outside the camera's eye, but wasn't hiding his anger well.

"Captain Capino, do not make the mistake of assuming anything. Understand we are working how best to deal with the vessel should it continue beyond Toojay. Saving one scientist isn't worth the cost of undermining any course of action we might choose, especially considering how badly the populations of two planets will be affected should we screw this up."

"No, sir. I apologize." He was pushing the limits of her good graces but added, "Is there a plan?" Something changed in her expression, briefly, before the earlier guarded face returned. Had that been fear he'd seen?

"Need to know, Mister Capino. We will talk again in the morning."

She waved her window closed. Oscar had stepped in it more than once on the call. Nothing had any real precedent. No one knew what would happen next, but the military succeeded by everyone playing out their roles as ordered. Oscar wiped a hand across his face and settled himself. He was a Frigate Captain. He would get this ship to Eden then the 2J Hole, and do what he was ordered.

Not for the first time, he closed his eyes and prayed for guidance. When he was done, the only answer he could sense was the same. *Do your job.* His superiors would have a plan when he got there, or they would not. As he pulled his stylus brushes out of the desk drawer, Oscar thought again about the brief look of fear on the Admiral's face. That, more than anything, would keep him awake for some time.

48 – Gendrick, 2J3P

During the night the cave had been cool but not uncomfortable. When he woke, Gendrick reached out and ran fingertips along the rough surface of the wall, still threaded with the same dim green phosphorescence. They came away damp. Even his clothes felt as if dew had settled. Not dew, however. More likely the scores of cattle, and one human, breathing steadily in sleep with no efficient ventilation.

Gendrick was stiff from the damp settling into his bones and from lying on a hard cavern floor all night. He *had* slept, for what felt like a few hours. Without his Ep he couldn't be sure. The fact that he'd fallen back asleep, with Moon watching over him, was an accomplishment. The smell assaulted him anew when he'd woken, but as before, his brain understood there was no danger in it and eventually closed whatever receptors it needed to.

The motion of the herd had woken him. Not long after, Moon nuzzled his wet face into Gendrick's hair. He rolled into a sitting position, wincing in pain from his shoulder. The animal had saved his life, but depending on what kinds of bacteria he might have picked up, may also have killed him. The skin didn't seem broken, though, so he was probably going to be fine. Miyoko and the others likely knew what was inside these creatures' mouths and how to deal with it. He hoped they did.

The bull huffed once, its face only inches from his own. "Yea, I'm up. I'm up."

Gendrick waved his new friend away with one hand. Moon snorted, lingered a few seconds as it considered the gesture with wet eyes. The priest smiled and added, "Thank you again, my friend."

He got to his feet. Only then did Moon step into the flowing traffic, effectively blocking the others so his human guest could enter the throng. Irritated mewling rose in the chamber behind them, so Gendrick stepped quickly into line and walked towards the ramp.

Morning light painted the inside of the tunnel wall. The round path sloped up and to the right, curving nearly one hundred eighty degrees. When he emerged into dry, clear air, still tinged with the passive but lingering orange taste of Acclarin, the morning sun slapped him in the face with such joyous violence Gendrick squinted and cried out in relief.

He was alive. If he'd been hallucinating his rescue, the dream would not have gone on this long before a Locust ate his brain and shut the camera down. He wanted to fall and give the Lord thanks, but Moon was pushing gently against the small of his back to keep him moving. The herd was in motion. Stopping was not a wise idea.

As soon as he was able, he sidestepped from the path the others had worn away from years of travel into the clearing, then fell to his knees. Moon followed, watching him in curious silence. As he prayed, Gendrick raised his right hand and stroked the animal's side and asked what he should do now.

Back to compound, of course. But he'd made a serious connection with this . . . *creature, person*. This *life*. Moon was not a mindless, reflexive animal. It thought, and made a logical decision to bring a stranger into his home, maybe even risking its own life to do so.

"Father Gendrick?"

A woman's voice behind him. Moon mewled in surprise and trotted away towards the herd. Gendrick thought the voice might have been the xenologist's but he did not turn around. Instead he stared at Moon as he wandered down the hill, doing his best to memorize one or two markings to make his rescuer stand out. For next time, so he wouldn't embarrass himself and forget which one of these creatures had saved his life.

A hand, gentle on his shoulder.

"Father Gendrick?"

He finally turned around. Sure enough, it was the xenologist. Mi-something. He was useless with names without his Ep.

"Hi," he said, and rose to his feet. "I lost my Ep."

"Right here, Father." A short, skinny man with a narrow face emerged from around a boulder a short distance away. Dwell – he remembered *that* name – held up a folded Ep, while adjusting a short-barreled rifle around his shoulder. It was the first weapon he'd seen since arriving. "She tossed it under a chair so it would look like you'd dropped it." He smiled, but something about his eyes denied the expression. The reason was likely the same as why he felt the need to be armed. "To be honest, we didn't expect to find you." Dwell shrugged. "Not much of you, at least."

Gendrick sighed, the dust which already found its way onto his tongue actually tasted fresher than the damp air belowground.

The xenologist stared past his shoulder. "You went into their burrow last night, to avoid the Locusts?"

Gendrick could not remember ever being so excited to

relay a story. He put a hand on her shoulder and turned her around. "I'll tell you as we walk. You're probably going to pee your pants."

"Is that good or bad?" she asked, falling into step. He let his hand drop. Dwell handed Gendrick his lost Ep then followed a couple of steps behind, one hand resting on the top of his slung rifle. The man tapped something on his own paper and quietly relayed the news that the priest had been found alive.

Gendrick was too busy telling the woman beside him how the cattle had pulled his unconscious body into the hole to hear someone's voice respond, *Did you tell him yet?* from Dwell's paper. "No, I'll let him know before we get back inside." A minute later he seemed too enraptured in Gendrick's story to do much but listen and ask his own questions.

When they eventually passed the pile of boulders where Arun had shown him the Locust's sand drawings, the complex came into view. They also came upon three people bent over a ribboned area. The trio were hunched down, picking at the ground with tweezers or raking small pieces of something from the sand. The sand itself was dark and looked wet.

Gendrick paused. "What's going on?" He was mostly done with the highlights of his story. Miyoko (he'd asked her name finally, a couple of minutes into their walk) was taking notes on her Ep, using her finger like a stylus. She looked up and blinked.

"Oh, right. Loki's mate." She nodded towards the other man. "Quick Draw Dwell here killed it last night to save your murderer, Mother Doneele."

Dwell actually growled and took a step past them. "Don't start up, again, Miyoko. I was saving my *own* life, not hers."

Gendrick looked back and forth between them. "You arrested Doneele then?" he hesitated, as the woman's words registered. "She came out *here*, at *night*? She's alive?"

Dwell shook his head and raised a hand as if to ward off the interrogation. "She's locked up, not to worry. But . . ." He didn't complete the thought.

Gendrick looked down. "Well, technically I suppose she didn't actually kill me, but – "

"Father." Dwell's single word shut him up. Miyoko cleared her throat beside him but said nothing. She sniffed and looked away.

Gendrick felt a cold creep into his arms and legs. The security man said, "A lot happened yesterday while you were gone." He looked down. "Mother Doneele murdered . . ." The man's face curled in on itself. He seemed about to cry. He fought it, but not well.

Gendrick looked to Miyoko. There was a tear at the edge of one eye but otherwise her expression was hard. Not emotionless. Angry.

She said, "Arun is dead. He was trying to find you and confronted Doneele because she seemed to have had returned without you. So, she killed him," four words which froze Gendrick's world. Every other detail she spat out, as if needing the words out of her forever, were probably important, but only added to the vertigo he was falling under. " . . . slashed his throat and stabbed him over and over with some antique blade."

Arun was dead. The three people working the ground within the ribbons had stopped what they were doing and listened, their own faces set. Everyone liked Arun. Even Gendrick saw him as a friend in the short time they'd known each other.

Doneele murdered him, because he was trying to find *him*.

Dwell continued on towards the compound without them, hands clenching and unclenching at his sides as he walked. Miyoko's sudden silence beside him drove Gendrick on to follow. He didn't know what else to do. Her words had become a blade sinking deep into his stomach. Part of him wanted to blame himself, but he shook his head, not allowing it. He wouldn't let Mother Doneele do that. She'd drugged him, left him to be slaughtered by the Locusts. She was a murderer. A sick woman, no doubt, who had likely killed her husband the same way.

He almost stumbled, caught himself and continued on, Miyoko silent beside him. McCarthy knew it, too. He'd tried to warn him during their last conversation.

"Come on," the xenologist said, taking him gently by the arm and steering him towards the main entrance. Gendrick had slowed down again, lost in thought. She added, "All this going on, and we hardly have time to mourn, considering what's coming."

He followed her for a few steps, mostly ignoring what she was saying, thinking of Arun stabbed to death by the priest he'd come here to replace. Doneele was set to go home on the next transport, why then . . .

McCarthy knew the truth, that she was unstable and dangerous. But he didn't say anything. The *confession*. The oath they'd all taken, so sacred it never failed to bring a tinge of apprehension every time Gendrick was on the receiving end. People – those who actually believed their words would never leave the Sacrament – felt safe saying anything, laying out between themselves and the priest the darkest deeds done by their hearts and hands. Repentance brought forgiveness, after all. Jesus' promise.

There were laws, carefully crafted, protecting these vows. The church walked a fine line with it, clashing often with the community and not always winning. Secrets of such magnitude were illegal. Granted, they were illegal before the Final War and the rise of the new government, but the thread woven through all was the protection of religious practice, providing the practice was done in harmony with others. What would have happened had Doneele kept it together long enough to return to Eden?

And why was he obsessing over any of this now? His thoughts couldn't focus on what to do next.

"Father?"

They stopped in front of the main doors. Dwell had already disappeared inside.

"Hmm?"

"I just remembered you didn't have your Ep with you."

He shook his head and patted the right side of his robes where he'd replaced the paper. "No. No, in fact I haven't opened it since you gave it to me."

She took a breath, reached out and palmed the access panel beside the doors. They slid open and the two entered the level below the balcony where Gendrick had first encountered Loki. Where Doneele had let him stand until the last possible moment.

"There have been some crazy developments out on 3Jside with the alien ship in the last twenty-four hours."

"That's right, Pey's spacewalk. How did it go?"

Miyoko looked at him in a funny way, but said nothing. He smiled and said, "Sorry. She and I are old friends. We grew up together, in fact."

She actually moaned and leaned against a round pillar just inside the main entrance. "You've *got* to be kidding me." Her face was a raw mask of misery, more so than when she'd relayed the news of her own friend's murder.

Gendrick could only shake his head and whisper, "What . . . happened?" He didn't want to know.

She closed her eyes, stayed that way for a few seconds before straightening and grabbing his arm much like she'd done earlier. "Let's get some coffee and I'll try to give you as many details as I can before we run into too many more people."

They walked up the short flight of stairs, passing the Union common room then lingered at the entrance of the mess hall. Gendrick's heart was beating fast. He wanted to shake her, scream at her to tell him if Peyton was OK!

There were others milling about in Mess, so she guided him to a less crowded corner, forgoing coffee for the time being. Then told him. With the same dispassionate voice as before, relaying one terrible fact after another.

Gendrick said nothing, breathing deeper and heavier, fighting off the monstrous wave of emotion that threatened to send him screaming out to . . . somewhere. Nowhere. There *was* nowhere to go. Cannon White was dead. Peyton might be dead, too. Gendrick would know soon enough because although there was no way to get to her, it didn't seem to matter. She was being carried to their front door inside the alien ship. He gripped the edge of his chair, eyes closed, as the xenologist finished her summary of the meeting she'd been forced to attend last night, less than an hour after the incident with Arun and Mother Doneele.

One day, and all of this happens. *One day*. She was no longer talking. He sensed others around them now. People had spotted him, probably already heard he'd been found alive.

Arun was dead. Doneele in custody. After trying to kill him. Peyton . . .

He did not cry, did not let loose the scream which insisted be freed. Neither did he raise his eyes from the single spot on the floor in front of his chair. His right leg bounced up and down on the ball of his foot, trying to escape and pull the rest of him with it. In this moment he did not know what to do. He tried to pray, but nothing came. He only sat there and waited for it all to pass, for something to switch back on inside his brain to allow him the ability to move again.

49 – Leanne White, 1J3P

She lifted the tea bag by its string then let it drop again, watching the amber color spread through the water. *Seep*, she thought. *It's seeping.* She wasn't a tea drinker, preferred coffee. There was plenty of it back on Earth, as the southern hemisphere still thrived since the war. Mostly from necessity, as there hadn't been much left at the top of the globe. She missed her home, the kinetic, crowded *Brejo de Meio* just outside of Maraba. It had been built out, and up, after the war by refugees relocated around Brazil and its neighbors. It was a wonderful place to grow up. Because of this, when the young couple had boarded the ship for Eden, she'd been alive with youthful, hopeful enthusiasm. She and Cannon had grown up in *Brejo*, infected with its optimism, carrying it with them when they moved out to the stars together. Earth itself was still groaning through its pains, but not *Brejo de Maio*. It jutted its chin with scorn to millions who'd written off the planet and flocked to the new world. God had given the new planet to them, after all. A new Earth.

Now Eden was her home. As much as she missed the land of her birth, she'd decided that the taste of *this* place would be a hard thing to ever leave. That was before, assuming the days would be spent with Cannon. God promised a new world for humanity, but never promised anything for her, specifically.

Dangerous waters, these thoughts. Her faith was more crucial than ever, carrying her for as long as she needed to be carried. Leanne needed distraction, something other than thinking about the childhood home they'd both left behind. As soon as the news hit, her supervisor at the OAA messaged her to take as long as she needed before coming back to work. Until now, she hadn't thought much about it, but maybe studying Eden's unique weather patterns, jumping into the data of the southeastern storms which had begun to roll up from the pole, could be that needed distraction. Sitting here and playing with tea bags wasn't going to cut it for long.

Leanne took a sip and wished for coffee. She only needed to go into the kitchen and make some. Maybe Steve already had a carafe going. Carroll only drank water, so she'd likely not made any, herself. Besides, she was no more functional, mentally or emotionally, than Leanne at the moment.

At least Carroll had *some* hope to cling to. Her twin sister was trapped inside the alien ship but might yet survive. Cannon would not. Definitely not. *Confirmed dead*, she supposed the official description would read when they dragged his decimated body out of the hangar. She'd watched it happen, along with the rest of the human race.

She reached down and touched the paper, wanting to unfold it and replay their last conversation. *Last.* Her heart exploded inside her; a lonely crying silence. So many times this happened since last night. Her mind could dance around thoughts of home, or work, or fly among the clouds gently puffing around the paradise where she lived. But Can was never coming back.

She died with him now, again, in that horrifying, lonely moment, as she had before falling asleep a few hours ago, and early afternoon when her eyes opened and the memory returned. Still less than a day since it happened. How many times could one person die in that time?

She fell sideways on the couch and hoped no one saw her. She did not want comfort, not now, not while she was dying with her husband again. Later, they could try, when her heart began pumping again and filled her with heat. For whatever scant moments it might do so, before exploding and dying all over again.

Stupid little girl, she scolded herself. *You knew this was going to happen. Eventually.* Like a soldier's wife, she was married to someone who poked Death with a stick every minute of his life. Out there, in the vacuum of space, going farther and farther into a geographical, astronomical, *not-yet-worded*-ical universe where monsters devoured planets. Her husband had found their city-sized hive and decided to stick his head in and shout, "Hello!"

She would have smiled if she wasn't as dead as he was.

He made her laugh. Oh, how he could make her *laugh*. Cannon made everyone happy, sometimes at the stupidest times but always at the right time.

Someone was running a hand along her head. Small hand. *Ellie.* Such a good girl. Someone always seemed to be sitting with her, rubbing her back or her head. Probably because Leanne was perpetually curled up on someone's lap, usually Carroll's, like a child whose best friend moved away, not knowing who she'd play with for the rest of her life.

She felt heat working its way through her veins again. Life returning. For a while. Cannon was her best friend, and he'd moved away. She'd see him again. For all his humor and sharp wit and sharper seriousness (a side of him few saw, hidden away behind those walls of jokes), he was a man of God. At home he loved his wife, spent all his time with her and never bewailed Leanne's list of To-Do's waiting for him on the wall. Never a sidelong look of frustration for their lack of children nor her insatiable need to have sex every day they were together (not that he'd ever have considered complaining about *that*). They danced and twirled and celebrated each other as if every day was their last. No irony in that. Because every day could very well have been. And, now, it was.

He went to work at the ISO every day, after the requisite post-mission time off, but came back to her each evening. They'd pray together before going to sleep. She loved praying with him, covertly watching as he spoke to the Lord to see how *real* he became in those moments, how full of joy. On Sundays, sometimes Saturdays depending on their schedule, they'd attend church. He'd sing to Jesus, raise his hands, worship God with the same exuberance he gave everything else. He meant it, all of it. And she found that *incredibly* attractive.

She would see him again. They wouldn't be husband and wife. What was the verse? She couldn't remember, but someone had asked Jesus about that, and in his cryptic way he explained marriage was a human thing, something for *this* world, not the next. She *would* see him, and they'd talk. Maybe she could hold him again, laugh at his jokes, see him worship as never before.

The hand stopped stroking her hair, but lingered. Leanne opened her eyes, stared at the wall. The screen mounted across from the couch was off. Ellie had the habit of turning it on the moment she entered the room. It was her right to do so. This was her house. Leanne was a guest.

Neither Carroll nor Steve let her go home after the broadcast last night. She loved them for that. They were family. The only family she had, now, but she was blessed to have them.

"Thank you, Ellie," she whispered.

Ellie was sitting on the arm of the couch, just out of sight. She gently patted Leanne's head again. "You're welcome. Do you feel better?"

"A little." Her words were followed by a quiet smile. "Thank you. Did you want to watch something?"

A hesitation. For a ten year-old girl, that was all the answer Leanne needed.

"No," she said. "Mommy won't let me watch the news, and I don't want to watch anything else. Not yet."

Leanne sat up and pulled Ellie into her arms. How easy it was to lose yourself in hurt, and forget the pain of others is just as sharp. She pulled the girl close. She loved grabbing and holding her even before this new sadness demanded it. *Auntie Leanne*, she called her. That was fine.

"She's going to be OK," she said, turning and kissing Ellie on the head.

"You don't know that," came the whispered response. Leanne almost replied with one of the usual adult responses. *I do. Everyone's praying for her. They're going to pull her out of there as soon as the ship arrives at Toojay.* What did she know?

"No," she said, speaking gently into the girl's hair. "No, I don't. But we can hope, right?"

Ellie nodded, then called for the screen to activate, waving her hands in the air and swiping various windows closed which had remained active before Leanne turned it off. One window was a constant news feed with commentary of the events between 3JH and Toojay, side windows with interviews and talking heads and . . .

"Close those," Leanne said as she got up from the couch. "Mommy's orders."

She heard Ellie sigh, but noticed the media windows closing, leaving a single screen with some generic kids' show. A cartoon about a brother and sister and their adventures on Earth. Leanne walked into the empty kitchen, head stuffy with exhaustion.

Still early. The MacDonald's were upstairs sleeping. They'd likely sleep late today, as they'd been up with her watching the news until well after four o'clock this morning. The kitchen windows were open, cool, early afternoon air drifting through the screens. Next door, Declan Chin was already cutting his lawn. She loved summers here, especially *here*, ten kilometers outside the capitol – *the suburbs*. Farther east, things were cooler, even in summer.

The smell of Chin's cut grass filled the room with the tang of mint and rosemary. That was the picture her mind drew the first time she sat on the porch while Cannon mowed the lawn of the government-issued home they'd moved into, four and a half years ago that was. Mint and rosemary, alien in its source but a wonderful sensory experience. She would have greatly missed cut grass on Earth if not for this planet's wonderful new twist on the experience.

God's wonderful new twists on everything. Maybe there had been lessons learned at the creation of Earth, so He refined them over the millions of years this planet sat waiting for their arrival.

She wondered if Eden might not have existed at all even a *hundred* years ago, before they discovered the Hole. If God really did make worlds like this in seven days, then anything was possible. She preferred to think of this world as the original Eden. Some did, actually.

She made coffee and sat on the raised stool, leaned on the breakfast bar and waited. She should eat, but for now she closed her eyes and smelled mint and rosemary, and now coffee, vaguely listening to Ellie's show playing in the other room. She would eat, in time. Ellie would get hungry before then, and might cook something for both of them.

Leanne leaned on her arms, breathing in the morning, and thought of her husband. Death would come, again and again, and she would embrace it, die, come back to life. Each moment would come and go with more time to breathe between.

Until, some day, she could live again.

50 – Gendrick, 2J3P

He allowed himself a full day of ignoring the fact that Doneele was in a holding cell across the compound. There'd been plenty of distractions ranked higher in the day's priorities. When Gendrick had regained his equilibrium after learning about Pey, he'd forced himself to get juice and a small breakfast – toast and fried potatoes. During their first breakfast together Arun had warned him the food, and the coffee, would taste "thinner" in the final week before the next transport arrived. Not yet, though.

Miyoko had excused herself after he'd sat back down with his food. She had a lot to discuss with the team, to prepare for the arrival of the derelict, not to mention make plans to drag Gendrick in front of the others to go over again what happened in the cave. He'd asked for a couple of days' peace. She'd reluctantly agreed, with his promise that he would spend time writing down everything he could remember, no detail too small.

He promised, not meaning it, but later that night he eventually did what she asked. It would likely end up, in some form, in *Vast Array*, but not yet. Before that happened, he found a spot after breakfast in a corner of the Union room and opened his Ep.

Eighteen messages, four from System itself. Three from Prelate McCarthy, whom Gendrick was sure had already gotten the news of Doneele's rampage. Two messages were reporters asking for an interview about Peyton Kay. They'd done their homework and discovered the connection, but obviously hadn't yet heard of his own troubles. Maybe they didn't care. He whispered to System to send all calls from the media to his message queue until further notice.

For the next few hours Gendrick watched every recap of the events of the past twenty four hours. Images of the derelict – though he supposed "derelict" was a misnomer at this point since *someone* was flying it – were all the more nightmarish knowing Peyton was trapped inside. Every now and then he'd fold the paper and bend forward, praying as fervently as he could for her safety. Then he leaned back and returned to the news like a junkie craving his next hit.

Someone approached him mid-afternoon. Her eyes were wide with some personal terror (the approaching alien spacecraft, he learned soon enough). He did not recognize her, and forgot her name as soon as she'd said it, knowing System would tell him later if he asked. She wanted to talk about what was happening, what might happen, and give her confession. Mostly, she needed to know the *why*'s of it all. This moment, more than any other, reminded him that he had a job to do. Yes, he'd be distracted while doing it, always seeing the final image from Ben Solomon's external pod cameras of Peyton dwarfed within the hangar as the door closed. But, he did his best to focus on the woman.

Trillia Ferman was her name – he'd decided to simply ask rather than pretend to know. When she'd told him, Gendrick gently tapped the outside of his folded Ep, hoping System would understand that bit of information should be logged. It probably would. The computer was frighteningly intuitive, not to mention always listening to what went on outside of open connections.

He spent the next hour with Trillia, a petite blond who'd emigrated to Eden from Peru, Earth, in her early childhood and jumped at the first opportunity to work on Toojay when she'd come of age. To "throw her future away" (her mother's words – her father having never been in the picture as far as he could tell from the rushed overview of her life). She had an open face, eager to know the Church's take on what was obviously intelligent life outside of Earth. She'd actually phrased it as the first "openly cognitive species." The idea both fascinated and terrified her.

So many questions which Gendrick would need to write down later for *God's Vast Array*, when he had time to consider far more eloquent answers than he was offering young Trillia.

"The Locusts have been considered an intelligent species for quite some time," he'd offered, "even before this development. But I suppose until recently most of us still pegged them as insects, with an instinctive hive mind more than anything."

"Not anymore."

He nodded. "I suppose not." Gendrick considered this, then added, "I mean," he leaned forward, "they *may* have built that ship up there." He gestured weakly with his folded hands towards the ceiling. "Or merely came along for the ride."

Trillia leaned back in her chair. "You mean, someone else built it. Another species?"

He shrugged. "Who knows? We'll find out soon enough."

The girl wrapped her arms around herself as she glanced about the room, where a few people loitered about. No one moved to join them. The sight of a priest, as obviously unkempt and worn as he imagined he must look (not to mention how badly he probably smelled), with someone who may be taking confession, at the very least having a serious, personal discussion, tended to build an invisible barrier to others.

He almost smirked when he thought Arun wouldn't have had such qualms. The smile died before being born. Funny how someone he'd known less than a week could have gotten so insinuated into his thoughts. Renewed pangs of guilt over his new friend's death rose in his chest. Arun died trying to find him.

"Father?""

He blinked and looked up.

"Sorry?"

"Are you feeling OK?" She seemed to finally notice his appearance. "If you don't mind me saying, you look like you haven't slept in a while."

He tried to smile. "I guess you haven't heard about everything that happened here last night?"

"Oh, the murder?" Another tight self-hug. "Yes, it was terrible. I didn't know Arun too well, though."

Gendrick nodded, decided to go farther, if for no other reason than spare the woman the embarrassment of finding out later. "She tried to kill me, as well." He spent the next few minutes giving her a brief recap of what happened outside.

When he was done, Gendrick was surprised he didn't feel better for having shared what happened with someone besides the folks from this morning. Only now did he remember the hard stone in his gut which had been keeping his pulse up, a constant, thrumming fear. Adrenaline should have dissipated by now – he should be asleep. But he wasn't tired. Likely, he was *beyond* tired. If he lay down would probably sleep for hours. But he wasn't ready for that.

Trillia was staring at him, now and then looking down, then around the room. He was beginning to understand this random gazing of hers meant she was thinking hard about something. When she looked up again, her eyes had a renewed shine.

"The cows are intelligent, then? I mean, more than simply cattle. They found a way to survive, not by accident. They must have known what was going on."

Another shrug was all Gendrick could offer. "God's people might not all be human, or humanoid." *God's people.* The thought of going back to the cattle, play the role of old-time missionary was fascinating *and* ridiculous. But it was something he should consider. If nothing else, he *would* like to return, find Moon, thank him again.

He was tired. Gendrick leaned forward, and in a whisper asked if she would like to make confession. She nodded, and began to speak in a quieter voice. Her "sins" were nothing more than the usual actions and temptations everyone went through. When she was done, he reminded her that he was not forgiving her of anything, that God already did that by His death and resurrection and her acceptance of that gift. To him, this truth was important for people to understand. She nodded and he prayed over her. Before the old church collapsed and merged into its current incarnation, a priest would order acts of contrition. Rote prayers, or some physical act of repentance. No longer. People weren't forgiven by what they did, anyway. They were simply forgiven, as long as they asked for it. A surprising number of people refused to do that. Human nature was loathe to trust anything given for free.

He prayed quietly, his hands on her head, and her demeanor was far lighter when she stood and thanked him.

"Get some sleep, Father."

He nodded. That was beginning to sound like a good idea. Shower first, then bed.

He'd folded his Ep into the inside pocket of his filthy

robes and moved to stand up.

"Father?" A man stood before him, wearing an unkempt uniform of security. He thought there were only two security men stationed here, and this wasn't the one who'd found him. This man was larger, solidly built with a wild mane of curly red hair.

Gendrick settled in his chair, gestured to the now unoccupied seat across from him. "I'm sorry," he said. "I forgot your name."

Michael Broeger told him, then sat. He added, "I should mention that I'm an atheist." He looked around. "Not sure if I'm supposed to give up my spot for one of the Chosen if they come by."

Gendrick smiled, would have laughed if he wasn't so tired. "No," he said. "I'm here for everyone, Michael. Relax. We can talk."

Shower and sleep would not come just yet, he guessed. He could deal with Mother Doneele tomorrow. Gendrick realized he hadn't thought of Peyton for almost an hour, even with the overhead monitor across the room silently showing nothing but the incident.

There was nothing he could do for her anyway, except pray, which was significant enough. He needed to do his job for these people.

He settled in and spoke for a long time with Officer Broeger.

51 – Radish Marlay, *Abad*, 2JSide

They'd passed through the Hole twenty-five minutes ago, not long after the most recent conference call ended. More to the point, the meeting had been recessed for three hours until such time as they could reconvene with more personnel who would (though not necessarily *should*, in Radish's opinion) be involved in the pending situation on Toojay. There had also been a serious incident at the southern Toojay compound on the same night – practically at the same moment – that the derelict came to life.

Allah's timing was interesting, Radish had thought, if at times incomprehensible.

Sarey Ramprakash was seated at a small table in Radish's office, three doors down from Bridge. On the screen in front of them Ken Burlov had just signed in to the *Abad*'s private channel. The conversation would be logged and viewable by only a select few back in the ISO offices. Radish made the designation that any discussion on the third planet be considered non-public until such time he, or ISO leadership, deemed otherwise. Until facts could be recorded and verified, letting media in on the details of a discovery would add unwanted speculation and rumor to what was not yet a comprehensible collection of facts. They would be released soon enough, and that anvil hanging over every expedition's head allowed for focused, and expedited, work. That was the intention.

Radish appreciated that the human race – including the

overarching and increasingly influential scientific community across the planets – deserved to know, well before any single *interest* could grab hold of the information for its own gain (an action technically illegal, though that hadn't stopped people from trying many times over).

As such, this conversation fell under secure protocol. Ken was speaking from an equally private room, Radish hoped, on the *Washington*. At the moment he seemed to be alone.

"Judging from how you classified this conversation, I assume you managed some initial findings on your planet?"

Radish smirked. "I'm surprised you didn't call it 33P, since you came up with that name and it hasn't yet been dethroned."

Ken's smile was broader, though short-lived. "Personally, I think that one stinks. We can't keep making up names around a planet's designation. I'm hoping you'd have a more poetic take on it, something that'll sing."

Radish said nothing, only glanced briefly at Sarey. She leaned back. "Don't look at me. I hate poetry."

This meeting would degrade too much into casualness if allowed, so Radish said, "To business. Yes. This is about our findings so far. Sarey has put together a brief overview so I will defer to her. Some of this even *I* haven't heard outside of a brief conversation prior to the conference call."

He reached out to rotate the desk's Ep towards her but System had already moved her image to the center of the screen. Sarey had a few windows already open. She reached out and carried one to the side of the screen with Ken's face. His image reduced. The one displaying the third planet, the day/night demarcation dead-center, took precedence.

"We're still receiving data from the probes and building

a detailed picture of the atmosphere, which I won't bother with now. Nothing surprising, though no less stunning as before. Similar composition to Toojay, Eden and Earth. Breathable air, etcetera. We do not have bacterial or virology information yet but that will come."

She pointed to the demarcation between day and night. Dragged a box over the night land so it zoomed in. "No significant artificial lighting in the night sky, again as expected."

Ken interrupted. "Significant? Meaning . . . what, there *was* some?"

She nodded, then flipped to another image of the night-side planet in close-up. "Yes, though nothing like electricity, or any sort of artificial illumination, but fires. Clustered together here . . . and here. Small fires, in groups."

"Could they be naturally occurring?"

"No, though I did look into that. Later discoveries confirmed these are man-made."

Silence.

Sarey looked up, Ken was looking back, though slightly to the left, studying the image. He finally said, "OK, let's jump to the big news. I assume there's more than a cluster of fires." He glanced straight ahead. "And I assume *man-made* was a deliberate choice of words on your part?"

"It was." She flipped past three images and enlarged an expanse of land. "These are the best of the images so far at low altitude, well under cloud cover." The pictures revealed a scattering of plants and scrubs, patches of striking green dotting the landscape as if someone had flicked a handful of paint across the surface of the planet.

"A lot of it looks remarkably like Toojay, in particular a striking lack of diversity among animal populations. There are some, for example here," she enlarged a pack of five tri-pedal animals scurrying towards one of the green splashes.

Each had two strong-looking front legs, and only one smaller in back. Their bodies were bulky and fur-lined, the size of large wolves on Earth. What must have been heads were mostly retracted into folds of flesh around their shoulders, the fur thicker there and reminiscent of lion manes.

Sarey left the image on the screen for a moment and said nothing.

Radish had not spoken during her presentation, and continued this silence. Now was the first moment he'd seen the actual images since hearing about them in the hallway before the conference. Though his heart was already racing from excitement at what Sarey had not yet told Ken, seeing *these* creatures grabbed his attention enough that he would have been content to stare and study them for hours. A new species. Were they violent or passive? Carnivorous or herbivorous? From their appearance, he assumed the former, but would not express that out loud. Premature assumptions made for bad research.

Ken finally broke the silence. " . . .and?"

Sarey sighed and flipped a few more images aside. "Fine. Let's open the big box first, shall we?"

As if in apology, Ken muttered, "I'd very much like to return to these other images, but if there's something shocking ahead let's just get that out of the way first."

Radish said, "Patience had never been one of your virtues, Captain Marlay."

"What would you know?" He sounded petulant.

Radish shrugged, focusing on the window and deliberately kept his expression neutral. "I apologize. I am not good at levity." Even to his own ears the statement sounded robotic, but he was pleased to see Ken chuckle in response.

The new window was up. It was a video. Radish leaned

forward.

Before playing, Sarey said, "The photos you've seen so far, and this video, are taken directly from probes which entered the atmosphere and, if they didn't burn up on entry, remain at a constant height of sixty meters above whatever terrain they are flying over, at least until their fuel cells die."

"Mmm hmm," Ken said, his image leaning forward slightly. He already knew this but was showing more patience with her. "Fuel cells standard life?"

She opened her hand, palm out. "Seven years, best guess? We still have two originals following the Locust herd on Toojay. Granted, their usefulness diminishes once the human expeditions arrive and we get satellites in orbit, and many are lost in unexpected storms, such as the one that washed across upper Toojay a couple of years back."

"So," Radish said, staring at the window, "this video is from sixty meters. Not very high up. Any creatures shot by the camera can, in turn, see the craft quite clearly."

"Yes, and that's a significant point for later. Ready?"

"Please," Ken said, a hint of renewed irritation in his voice.

She tapped the window.

The landscape of the planet rolled past. It truly was like Toojay in many ways, mostly scrub planes, though with wooded clusters here and there. Around those, bright green patches of plant life spilled out.

A quick flash of something moving to the left. Sarey paused the video. "Lower left," she said, "we see more of those hyenas."

Ken said, "Hyenas?"

"They're extinct on Earth now, but look it up. Even with three legs these creatures remind me of them. May as well reuse the name until the xenologists come up something better." The video resumed. The new world rolled beneath them. Over a hill, down into a valley.

Radish and Ken both audibly gasped. Here, the bright green was more than simple splashes. The world was covered in it. A valley of nearly incandescent green, with smatterings of violet and red. Flowers, likely, or flowering ground cover. Along the edges of the valley, the forests of color were thicker, stretching back well out of scope of the scene.

Sarey paused the vid again, to allow this new landscape to sink in.

She said, "Early scans of the forests indicate relatively new growth. No more than two or three hundred years at best. Much more recent along the outer edges. One would think they would have promulgated more aggressively across the planet, with so much time and so little wildlife, as far as we've detected. I have to assume it took a while for them to re-seed enough to grow in any sense of volume."

Radish wondered if she had forgotten Ken did not know who "they" were yet. Or, she was simply dragging this out to annoy him. She was also making a significant point. From what had been happening lately, a larger-scale picture was beginning to form in many peoples' minds. Sarey was saying, "I'm quite excited to see closer images of these plants, especially the green. My guess it's more than simple grass."

Radish gestured towards the image. "Can one of the probes land amid some?"

"Yes, but I wouldn't recommend it. "

Ken said, "Why not?"

She said nothing but flicked a finger at the screen and the video commenced. More lush green blurred below them. The valley stretched out for kilometers. The grass suddenly parted in a wide swath.

The image rolled below them, out of frame for a

moment, then only blue sky was visible.

"What happened?"

"They are programmed to respond to any anomalies in naturally-occurring patterns."

"And this one saw – "

"Shh."

The world came back into view. The probe had risen in an arch and was now traveling at a forty-two degree variance from its original course, according to the words streaming along the bottom. It had, in effect, turned right, to follow what looked like a sudden river cutting through the valley.

Only there was no water. Sarey paused the image again.

It looked like a road.

Along this road, three or four people were running.

When he finally spoke, Ken's voice was a whisper. "Humanoid?"

Three creatures seemed to be running towards the side of the road, and looking up. Another stood in the middle, hands on hips, looking directly at the camera sixty meters above him.

Him, for it was obviously a man.

The image resumed, the probe dropped lower, or perhaps (and more likely) it was zooming in on the humanoids who, aside from the single man standing defiantly, were running in terror towards the tall, grassy plant growth.

The probe flew past them. Sarey paused again, brought the image back to a still containing all of the people in one frame.

"Mostly male here, but we have seen others with female characteristics.

"As you can see here," she zoomed in on the defiant one, though closer up he seemed more curious than anything else, looking up at the strange creature flying above him, "they resemble us. A lot. I've already found significant differences, like their noses, and no ear lobes to speak of. But -"

After a few seconds to collect her words, she continued, "They wear some kind of manufactured clothing. Nothing elaborate, but this one has what we'd consider shorts, and sandals, and a kind of shirt." As she talked the image zoomed in and out focusing on the various articles the man wore. "There's a greenish tint to all of their clothing, and some brown."

Ken said, "Woven from that grass. It's at least a significant ingredient."

"Exactly. From ongoing scans, there are many animals here, but they belong to only a few species. I would venture the *grass* – for lack of a better word at this point – is used quite extensively."

Radish leaned forward more, knowing such an act did nothing to clarify the images. "Are they human?"

"Obviously, or at least a . . ." She did not finish.

Ken broke the subsequent silence to finish her sentence. " . . .distant ancestor?"

Another shrug.

Radish's mind was racing. Were they native to the planet? If not, how long ago did they arrive? A hundred years? Not long enough to have evolved physical attributes too varied from Earth, but . . .

He said, "Could these be descendants from the earlier expeditions, the ones which lost contact outside the 0J system prior to the discovery of the Holes?"

Sarey's answer was immediate. "No. I thought of that myself. I simply cannot justify such varied physical attributes."

"Noses and ears," he began, but Sarey interrupted.

"Noses and ears are very significant evolutionary traits which could not have adapted over a mere three generations. I assume there are many other differences we've not yet seen."

Radish wasn't convinced, but that debate would be for another time.

"No," she said. "Better to continue with the assumption these people are aboriginal."

The image zoomed out.

Radish said, "Most appear frightened. They're running away from the probe."

"I don't blame them," Ken said. "I'd run away myself if a three meter-long bee suddenly began diving towards me."

Sarey looked at Radish, then at Ken's image. Both men's expressions had darkened as soon as Ken made that statement.

Radish finally said, "They think it's a Locust."

She nodded. "Most recent timelines estimate the Locusts arrived at Toojay approximately one-hundred and seventy-two years ago. They must have been somewhere else before that."

Radish looked at her face, then Ken's. Unless their life span was exceptionally longer than his own, the people on the video would never have seen a Locust themselves. But their grandparents might have. These were the remnant left behind after the swarm destroyed their planet. The swarm which then hitched a ride on that massive ship and moved on to the next planet.

"The Locusts have been here."

"I would assume. Swarmed the planet until there was nothing left, then moved on."

Ken said, "*Almost* nothing left. Some species survived long enough to begin spreading across the planet again. Those that did, probably still wonder if they might return."

Radish nodded. They would not return. Locusts seemed to be a species in perpetual forward motion. Toojay was all but stripped bare. Time to move on, to Eden.

52 – Gendrick, 2J3P

It was late. He should be asleep, after a day spent being a priest in the fullest sense. It was probably the first time since arriving he'd felt completely comfortable in his role here. Until now, he'd been mostly ignored by the community save the novelty of being the newcomer. To Doneele, well, he was something else. A projection of her late husband, maybe, a target for her rage or sociopathic tendencies. Whatever.

Now, the monsters were coming, and the people who called this place home needed him. Tired as he was, still numb from his "adventure" (as one person put it), Gendrick felt he was living the life God intended for him, being a shepherd. After the security chief left, Gendrick managed a half hour to take notes, check on the news and finally go to the bathroom before someone else came along. The Union became his adhoc chapel and confessional.

Fayaaz Kusher managed to drag him from his chair and into the mess hall for a late dinner. The Imam had been dealing with a similar day with his four constituents and a couple of former atheists considering a second look at Islam. This, on top of his duties in leading every Call to Prayer. Dinner was a comparison of notes and thoughts, minute details surrounding the attack inside the derelict and the ship's obvious destination, to speculation of what might have been discovered on 3J3P. They even prayed together for Pey's safety.

Eventually, their conversation moved to the grander

concepts of God's plan in all this. Kusher actually used the term "Vast Array" without irony. Gendrick hoped the term would catch on. It had a ring to it that might stick in people's heads. He allowed himself a brief moment of pride, before reminding himself that things didn't resonate into the core of a population, or its language, unless it originated from God, *or* the other guy. True or not, Gendrick had actually paused the conversation long enough to jot that thought down.

Later, after circumventing the Union common area, he spent some alone time in his room, hunched uncomfortably over the desk and praying again for Pey. When his words felt thin, he typed. So many thoughts, so much stress and revelation swirling around him, all Gendrick could do was write it out. He opened *God's Vast Array* and – making sure to lock it in draft mode to avoid spilling his unedited psyche to the universe – wrote in a disjointed but fevered stream of consciousness. Four hours later he woke up, having fallen asleep on top of his Ep. System, of course, had closed every window to protect the data. He'd woken, a small line of spittle running from his lip to the paper, and eyeballed the bed.

Distracted and productive, he'd managed to spend most of the day only thinking about Doneele once, sitting in her cell across the compound. He wouldn't allow himself the self-deceptive luxury of calling this lack of concern anything but spite. She'd tried to kill him, left him to be gutted, torn apart with nothing left but the scraps of his boots and robe. Now, though, he needed to begin that steep road towards forgiveness. For his own sake, if not hers. It was a requirement, if he wanted to believe he'd been forgiven himself for all the mistakes he'd done, even if none of it came close to attempted murder.

He should go to bed, back to sleep.

That wasn't going to happen, now that he'd given himself such a scathing self-sermon. Gendrick sighed and pocketed his Ep. He left his room without thinking about anything else. No more excuses. The walk was short, but during the trip he prayed for peace, and that ever-evasive forgiveness.

The security wing was a short hallway ending in a wide alcove housing a single long desk and three lockers. It widened to a bathroom on one side and kitchenette on the other. He did not make it that far. On each side of the hall leading to the unmanned desk was a door. Holding cells with reinforced glass windows at the top. Both were dark.

Gendrick picked the one on the left, looked inside. The room was not completely dark. A string of filament lights ran in a line where wall met floor along the perimeter of the room. It offered enough light to show he'd guessed wrong. He closed his eyes, took in a deep breath. *Lord, guide me. I don't necessarily need to speak with her but I need to face this, face* her. *Someday, maybe, I'll even understand it.*

He opened his eyes and turned around to face the other holding cell.

Doneele's face filled the window, staring back at him. Her hair was wildly unkempt, as if she'd been tugging and pulling at it since her rescue. Michael Broeger had relayed more details on her escape attempt, the killing of Loki's mate and its incessant raging against the compound walls throughout the night. In fact, part of Broeger's ad-hoc confession was his wish they hadn't taken such a risk for a crazy woman who'd killed two good people (the first being her late husband, he reminded Gendrick when he began to protest that he, himself, was alive). Mostly, though, he meant Arun.

He stared across the hallway. Doneele stared back. Neither spoke. By now, System would have opened a communication link for them. They only watched each other. Had she wanted to die out there, or merely run blindly from punishment?

You can never escape the consequences of your actions, he thought toward her.

Doneele's eyes narrowed, as if hearing. He was held in that gaze, a grip that wanted to pull him closer, show him the darkness behind her eyes and make the reasons for her actions logical and sensible.

He needed to get some sleep, soon. He also needed to break this silence.

"You killed Zechariah."

She blinked. "That's not a question."

System could have allowed her voice through the panel to be as clear as if she'd been in the hall with him, but it – or whatever long ago programmer had first written life into its operating system – decided to add a tinny fuzz, slight as it was, to emphasize that she was on the other side of a door.

Effect. Everything the AI did was centered around building an effect for its human users.

"No. What you tried to do with me, you'd succeeded with your husband."

She only shrugged, her left shoulder rising into view of the window. Mad as she might be, Doneele was careful. She would have had to be, to get away for so long with murder.

Why hadn't Moon and his friends saved Zechariah? Maybe the guilt at not doing so drove the animal to save Gendrick. Maybe he needed to focus more on this moment and stop dallying with *maybe's*.

He said, knowing she would not respond. "Vernaine knew, didn't he? That's why he wanted you back at Eden."

She smiled, slight as it was. The expression was more resigned than amused. "I am not admitting anything, but our superior must know that the sanctity of the confessional would only go so far. The laws of illegal secrets outweigh most everything else."

He had nothing to say to that. McCarthy might have thought they could handle her crime within the Church, but the Church would never be allowed to hide such discretions which, after millennia of abuses, nearly tore it to the ground. They might be stewards of Christ's Church, but the *government* was steward of mankind. God would win in the end – though *the end* seemed much farther away these days, if it hadn't already happened back in the War. For today, at least, the government had final say. McCarthy knew this, and was likely waiting for Doneele to return to Eden before turning her in to the authorities.

Fine line between the confessional and the law.

"Excuse me a moment," he said, and pulled the Ep from his pocket. Quickly noted with his fingertip *God wins in the end, though the end seems so much farther away these days,* then *Fine line, between the confessional and the law.*

He folded the Ep back and returned it to his robe pocket. Doneele watched him, eyes narrowing in confusion. She looked directly at him, let it linger before turning and moving away from the window. Gendrick followed her, watched through the glass as she sat, then lay down on the cot.

Her robes had been confiscated, too much of a risk of hanging herself, though Gendrick doubted there was anywhere in the small room from which she could hang anything. She wore a loose fitting jumpsuit, socks, no shoes.

She did not look at him, but lay one arm over her eyes when she said, "Go away, Father Hellerton. I'm tired."

"Why did you . . ." he was going to ask why she killed Arun, but he knew. Survival instincts gone haywire. Arun had been the first unfortunate soul to confront her. "Why did you try to kill me?"

No reaction, not at first, then slowly Doneele removed her arm and turned her head his way. The arm remained raised, ready to lower back over her eyes. "You –" she began, then looked away a moment, gathering her thoughts. Finally she sighed, and put the arm back over herself. With a slight shout, as if the inability to see stretched the distance between them, "I don't know, Father. I truly don't. I'm a sick woman."

Yes, you are.

"Please forgive me, as my husband never had a chance to." Her mouth pursed and he saw, and heard, the whispered curse. That was almost a confession, and System was recording every conversation in this place.

"Go away, please. Leave me to my fate."

He was about to offer to take her confession, but he imagined her reply. *I believe I already have given it.* Or something to that effect.

He turned and walked from the security wing, not trusting himself to say anything more. He was shaking, not understanding why and felt the urge to run, perhaps go outside, himself, and stare at the million stars and odd auroras dancing above them. That would be a stupid idea, so he returned to his room, trying his best to think no more about Doneele. Instead he pictured Peyton, alive, waiting for rescue. The news covered and analyzed her situation *ad-nauseum.* Every possible scenario was played out, then played out again. How she could survive the expected week-plus voyage from the Hole to Toojay, how might she conserve air, water, food, tap into Cannon's supplies, provided they hadn't been compromised in the attack.

In his bunk, Ep abandoned with his robes on the floor, Gendrick fell into a long and deep sleep, Peyton's face the only thing in his mind as he did so.

53 – Peyton, 2Jside

Peyton opened her eyes, lids struggling against the gunk which had built up and nearly glued her lashes shut. She glanced at the chronometer to her right, where the suit's System displayed how much time had passed since they'd been trapped. Three days, thirteen hours, twenty-seven minutes. Seconds were no longer displayed.

She'd recently begun to think of her and the AI as "they." Pey and Baby System, trapped together inside an alien ship. It made her feel less alone, especially on the increasingly rare occasions she moved the wrong way and bumped into Cannon's suit.

She was so cold, even with her body snug in an inner jumpsuit that trapped and conserved what heat was available. The EVA suit's temp was chilly, deliberately so. Gooseflesh ran along her legs and arms, up her back, threatening to drive her insane if she paid too much attention to it.

Relax. Let it go.

These words had become her best mantra for relaxation, for keeping her squirrel at bay. Nothing to do, not until she was rescued or died. Two options. Only two. Panic would simply make the decision for her.

Peyton's mouth was arid and pasty. She tilted her head to the left and drew a mouthful of water from the straw.

System beeped. It may have beeped a moment ago and that was what woke her. The readout on the lower portion of her visor told her why.

O2 level: 1.9 %

Rations (liquid form): 11.6 %

H2O level: 2.1 %

The cupboards were almost bare.

She'd apparently done well remembering her training, lowering the suit temp, meditating or outright sleeping. Three days. It would not last another, though.

Solid waste: 49.7 %

Not everything coming out of her could be recycled. At some point, poop was poop. She'd been moving her bowels less since she'd all but stopped eating solids unless absolutely necessary. Still, the waste bin was less than half full. That was good. She wouldn't need to dump the solids and have to watch them float around the hangar or bounce back against her. The situation was humbling enough.

It was time.

Do it, or die.

"System," she tried to say, needing to talk but feeling the dehydration clawing at the words. *Forget it*, she thought instead. *You'll figure it out. You always do.*

But it didn't. No response.

Then she remembered. No voice access. She needed to scrawl out the commands on her sleeve.

She needed to connect Cannon's air and water supply to her auxiliary ports. There might have been a way to transfer the solid food to her suit, but she could not remember. When she slowly swiped out the command – *Schematic for auxiliary transfer* – on her sleeve to begin the process, she also added *including solid food transfer*. System didn't offer the instructions for this, but schematics for the other two danced across her visor, realigning themselves in the order she needed to follow. Water and air only, from now on, once her remaining solids were gone.

It would need to be enough.

She flexed her fingers, watched the suit gloves respond. Most of the time her arms were aimed straight out in front of her. Her body was weakening, too long in zero gravity, even with the regular, if minimal (to reduce O2 usage) exercise regimen System reminded her to do every three hours – four if she was sleeping.

She turned her body slowly to the left. The suit fired miniscule amounts of air from her thrusters to help the motion and limit unwanted drift. She faced the right side of Cannon's suit. What she first assumed had been the sun visor finally lowered in his faceplate had been blood coating the inside. Same effect, even now. She could not see his face, but neither did she try. There likely was no longer a face . . .

His suit . . . *it's his* suit, *nothing more.*

He had long ago moved on, to a good place. Peyton often reminded herself if no rescue came, she would see him soon. Of all the moments in her life, to lose that faith would be like letting go of a rope while hanging from a cliff. It gave her peace, enough to dull the fear a little bit. If she died, well, what came next was always a little fuzzy. The concept of heaven was alien, undefined. Jesus deliberately avoided details, describing it mostly in high terms and parables. More and more, as humanity moved out into the universe, she wondered if heaven truly *was* like what she'd imagined as a child: a New Earth, with clean air and clear water, no more sickness, no more tears.

Really, that was Eden, minus the sickness and tears part. As her own, personal universe stretched out before her, she understood whatever lay beyond this physical realm could very well be *too* different for any of them to handle from this side of the fence. Maybe that was the reason for all the similes and metaphors. Eventually, Peyton stopped wondering. It served no purpose.

Until now. What was going to happen if that door did not open? Where would she go?

She should talk about this to Gen. Let him steal these musings for his writing project.

Peyton reached out, touched her glove to a coiled fiber tube stretching from the bulky backpack on Cannon's suit. The tube snaked from the pack, under his right arm then reconnected to the chest panel. As she worked, her visor lit with pictures and words from System, overlaying what was in front of her with a description of each tube's function. These connections could have easily been incorporated *inside* the suits to avoid exposure to the vacuum, but there were reasons for everything.

This was the reason. If one suit's oxygen failed, another could share, like scuba divers passing a single oxygen line back and forth as they worked their way to the surface. Her gloved fingers closed over the water hose where it joined the front of Cannon's suit. She felt the ridged contours along the skin of her own hand, minor electrical vibrations simulating touch. An arrow appeared across the visor, instructing her to turn the connector clockwise. She did, then waited. Mostly because the word *WAIT* flashed in red. The other suit's internal system was pulling air and stray water droplets back into itself to prevent escaping particles from acting as thrust. Even the smallest bits could send either, or both of them drifting away.

Not a concern now, considering they were both tethered to the closed door. But this was not the time to skip instructions.

In green, REMOVE HOSE replaced the red word.

She did, and pulled it to her own chest panel, feeling with her other hand for the connection. There was already a hose connected. Of course, her own empty tank. She whispered, "This one?" Last thing she wanted was to hook the water to the air or vice versa. No response. Holding Cannon's feeder with her left, she tapped the hose she believed was her current water intake then drew a question mark on the other sleeve.

YES appeared on her visor, then another arrow reminding her which way to turn the connector, from her perspective. She did so, waited when System said to wait, removing it when it gave her the OK. She let her hose drift in front of her and guided Cannon's feed to her chest again. She turned in the opposite direction, felt the connection take.

No sense looking at the new levels yet.

She reached out, disconnected the air from the other suit.

It was a suit, nothing more.

Everything she was taking were spare supplies. She needed them, and Cannon wanted her to live. Peyton wanted to cry, but would not. She *would not.*

She absently followed the instructions and connected the new air hose.

Everything complete, she glanced at the levels.

O2 level: 78.2 %

Cannon used up more air than she had before all hell broke loose. More nervous than he let on.

H2O level: 91.7 %

Not a big drinker, though.

I miss you, buddy.

She wanted to speak aloud to Cannon. He may no longer be here but talking to him was always a pleasure, a joy she wasn't ready to let go of. She would need to let it go, later, some *other* day, but for now Peyton wanted to talk.

But she remained silent. Conserve oxygen. Staying alive was the best way to honor her friend.

Peyton closed her eyes, hoping everyone outside the door were also still alive and chasing her across the universe in their rotating ring. She prayed for everyone, on both ships, for Cannon's wife, her own sister and brother-in-law, and little Ellie. For Gendrick, who had stumbled back into her life only to see her swallowed by this interstellar whale and carried away to some unreachable shore of space. Of course, she had a feeling that that distant shore was going to be Toojay. Every time she fell into prayer these past few days, her mind drifted, landing on the dead Locust in the corner of the hangar. On some distant day in the past, had it simply wandered in here, like her? She didn't think so. This was *their* ship. She'd been scanned. Now they knew about Eden.

Ships and serpents, planets and doors in space. These thoughts became images which thinned and broke apart as Peyton, eventually, returned to a uneasy, cold sleep.

54 – Benny Solomon, *Washington*, 2JSide

They had time to work out a few different options, plans put together with no clue what would happen next week when the alien ship arrived at Toojay. Time to make as elaborate a scheme as possible using only assumptions and guesswork.

Benny dug his fingers into his beard. He'd always kept it trimmed short, fighting some distant genetic trait which twisted his black hair into wild curls if left to its own devices on both his head and face. This past week, he'd let both go. His younger athletic days had instilled enough superstitious nonsense that Benny decided to let everything grow out until they'd gotten Pey, and Cannon, back in whatever state they may be in. Four days' unfettered growth would hardly register on most people. He was an exception. His hair hadn't grown much in back, but curls were already reaching out, ferns looking for the sun. Benny's beard was twice as thick already. At least he was showering. Ken offered leeway on grooming for the time being, but not hygiene. Nevertheless, after an entire week he'd look like a wild man flying his shuttle pod to rescue his friend.

Not that he would have the opportunity to be the hero when that door opened. Not an active one. The alien ship had accelerated enough to put a day's distance between them before it decelerated to match the *Washington*'s speed. Ken had been given strict orders not to travel any faster – not that this twirling ring was built to go much faster, anyway. Space was big, but there were risks even System could miss, small rocks and debris scurrying across their path. Deflector technology was still in its infancy, mostly a strong negative charge in front supported with a battery of small guns rimming the ring's edge. These could fire small-burst ammunition with directional explosive charges, blasting anything too large into smaller chunks which hopefully would then hurtle *away* from the ship. Inelegant, and with its own risks, but used to good effect in the past.

As a pilot, Benny wished the *Washington* would slow down. As Peyton's friend, he wanted the opposite.

He leaned back in his seat, suddenly wishing this whole crappy mess of a situation was over.

"I have to admit, I feel like you look, Ben." The speaker was Fawn Noble, head of security in the northeast compound on Toojay. She was younger than him, with a shock of black hair sweeping away from a dark and serious face currently sagging with exhaustion. "Let's reconvene same time tomorrow."

There were seven other faces along the edge of the conference screen, the five designated pilots from the three compounds on the planet, plus one scientist – the xenologist Ochi Miyoko from the southern location. Included with them was Seeme Kinzer, chief medical officer of the *Reach*, a Med vessel currently stationed at the mining complex on 2J4P. Benny had called him into the conference to commandeer (or try to) the man's ship. It's decompression facility was far better than the *Washington*'s, and was stationed a reasonable distance from Toojay. It could arrive the day before Pey did, provided it got moving no later than tomorrow night.

As could the Navy ship which Benny discovered was also orbiting the planet. Doctor Kinzer brought this small detail up when he'd first been invited to the meeting.

During the initial conference with ISO Command the Admiral had said flat-out there were no military vessels capable of reaching Toojay in time to help. Seems there was, and Benny's initial reaction was such a shaking rage he almost disconnected on the doctor to file a complaint. Just as quickly, he understood ... reluctantly. Whatever the military might do, there were far more lives at stake on Eden than Toojay. Benny and his new crew would have to do what they could to save Pey. Then he would see what unfolded after. But it better be good.

Opinions on the overall situation ranged from the nature of the ship and its possible association with the Locusts, to the odds of it arriving in orbit with "guns drawn." This latter possibility didn't seem likely, as it had shown no hostility to the *Washington* since the initial incident in the hangar.

Since Crew was forbidden in the current situation to leave the ship for any reason other than mandatory repairs or maintenance, Benny had gotten permission to start these meetings to work out rescue options if the hangar door opened. If nothing else, planning gave Benny a sense of control and kept his mind occupied a few hours at a time.

He wanted to argue that they had another ten minutes, but didn't have the energy. Besides, his primary goal for today – getting Doctor Kinzer to agree, in principle to sending the *Reach* to Toojay as soon as possible. Both the ISO and the military needed to approve it, but Kinzer would do his best.

Benny nodded, gave the faces on his Ep a light wave before adding, "Same time tomorrow. First up, we'll take the top two options and flesh them out more. Less than five days remaining, folks. Let's be ready. And Seeme, thank you again."

The doctor nodded but said nothing.

Benny reached up and tapped the window closed.

He left the paper propped in front of him. The background showed the up-to-date position of Toojay, the alien ship, the *Washington* and *Abad*. He would add the *Reach* as soon as everyone okayed the plan.

His cabin door opened. Zhou Lihua stood in the entrance. "System said you were in a meeting so I waited. It let me in when you were done."

Benny leaned back in his chair. He wanted to return the smile but found the expression too daunting. Instead he scratched his beard and waved her in with the other hand. "I could have been naked."

Li smiled and stepped inside. "Would have been hard to tell with all that hair." Kneeling beside his chair, she added, "How're you doing, Ben?"

"Why is everyone suddenly calling me 'Ben'?"

She shrugged, taking a hold of his arm. The gestures, kneeling beside him, holding his arm, were friendly and that was how he accepted them. He and Li had never been more than this, though both were single – the majority of deep space folks chose the single life rather than leave a family behind for months at a time. There were exceptions. Ken was one. Cannon, too.

Li said, "Benny is that goofy guy who's always cracking a joke, trying to compete with, well, with Cannon for attention. We miss him, *both* of them, but right now Ben's in charge. He's a little dour, but we love him anyway." She squeezed his arm.

Benny took in a deep breath, let it out slowly. Controlling his emotions. But this small, lithe woman touching him right now was drawing it out, deliberately or not. It wasn't time. He had to keep it together, stay sharp.

Li said, "You have a lousy poker face, buddy. Come on."

She stood, and pulled at the arm, sliding her grip down to his hand and stepping back until he was standing and she was almost to the wall. Then she led him around to the narrow bed.

"Don't get any ideas about this," she said. "Kick off your shoes." He did without argument. He hoped she wasn't going to try something. Pretty as she was, he wasn't in the mood. At least, he didn't *think* so. Tired, yes. But any time the thought occurred to him to try to sleep more than an hour at a time, the gaping hole in the middle of his body where his stomach used to be opened up. It hurt, that hole, as did the muscles in his shoulders and legs as they fought to curl up and let the empty sadness have its way inside him.

Li moved slowly but deliberately onto the bed, led him down beside her. She pressed herself against the wall to make room.

"What are you doing?" His question came out quiet, almost nervous.

"Shut up and let me comfort you. Lay on your side." He did and faced her as she lay looking at him. Too late, he realized he could have faced away from her, but that would look a bit cold if he did it now. Li smiled and lay a long-fingered hand against his face. Then she simply pulled herself into his arms, nestling her head under the rat's nest of the beard. He reached around her and pulled her closer. They adjusted for a minute, Li getting herself turned enough be able to breath away from his chest. Her arms did not reach all the way around his chest, but the sensation of them and the ease with which he enveloped her brought a blanket of calm over him. He half-expected to start bawling, but did not. Taking in a breath, letting it out, Benny felt a tentative peace for the first time since the incident. He held on to this, and her, then a moment later fell into sleep.

When he woke, they'd changed positions. Benny was on his back beside the wall, Li still sprawled across his chest with one leg dangling over the edge of the bed. He should find this way of waking up arousing, if not for the air of relaxation filling him. He had slept, really *slept*. For nine hours, according to the chron on the bedside table. At least, *he'd* slept, since at some point Li had snuck away to retrieve the plugs which now poked out of her ears.

He raised an arm and draped it gently across her shoulder. She stirred but did not wake up. He'd wait a little while before getting up to pee. She'd earned the right to sleep a little more.

They both had, he supposed.

55 – Excerpted from the series, *God's Vast Array*

by Father Gendrick Hellerton, November 2193

*A*s I write this entry, everyone on Toojay, Eden and Earth are waiting and wondering what will happen next. One of my oldest friends remains trapped in the belly of some strange beast.

She may be dead.

That sounds rather blunt, I know, but illusions of happy endings only carry one so far. She might also be surviving. The alien ship has long passed through the 3JHole into our system and most of us have no doubt it is coming here, to 2J3P. While we wait, we carry on with our daily routines and responsibilities, and do our best to deal with our own sorrow and prepare. No one knows how to stop it, given our meager tools to carry out such an endeavor, or what will happen when it arrives. In the end, whatever happens, one question hangs over us, those on the Washington and back among her family on Eden: what is the fate of our sister, Peyton Kay?

We'll know soon enough. All I can do, and those of you reading, is pray. Maybe you're not the praying type. Maybe you don't believe in God or any higher power. That's your call. The freedom to believe, or not, is the highest form of democracy. For me at least, death should not be a source of fear. We're promised a better life beyond the one we live today, and aside from some fringe groups who claim Jesus' new Covenant ended with the Final War and the desolation that ensued, most of us still believe it's firmly in force. God has not turned His back on us. He never will. Look at the doors He's opened since that terrible time, the Holes leading to new worlds and opportunities.

Interesting. Each time I reference any Hole, System insists on upper-casing the H. Mankind holds these interplanetary doorways with such reverence, our written language now reflects it. In a physical sense, they have been our salvation. I do not argue that. I've discussed who I feel is responsible for these new worlds and the next phase of our civilization. There are those among us, however, for whom science *is their only religion.*

Once upon a time, man searched for God and His purpose. We looked in our hearts, prayers, the scriptures, in stained-glass windows and the poetry of music. Now, countless funds are used to search for the next Hole and what will be revealed beyond it. That's good. It's exciting. Looking at them as anything more than celestial phenomenon, however a holy gift they might be, runs the risk of them becoming another sort of god. Idols which offer that once-elusive sense of purpose.

Be careful what you search for, in whom you lay your faith. God hasn't changed. His promise is the same. As for the Holes: after this week, one lesson we have learned is that the relatively uneventful discoveries of Eden and Toojay might be exceptions to a rule we do not yet understand. These worlds were custom-made for humankind.

Granted, there was the Eden epidemic which ravaged the first colony, but the bacteria responsible and others unique to the planet – which would have slaughtered more had they not been discovered in time – have been controlled by immunizations. They will continue to be rendered more harmless as generations are born and raised on these worlds. Epidemics of this sort are expected risks. No more than visiting another part of Earth far from your home. There are bugs for which a person has no built-up immunity. It was why the first compound was not built on Toojay until over a year after its discovery. The same will happen on 3J3P provided it, too, is habitable, and we are able to isolate its unique threats.

Now, however, we have been faced with new threats, or let's call them challenges, *because optimism is healthy. The alien ship, and the Locusts. They are more than a unique scientific discovery. They are warnings. We may be following a path laid out for us eons ago, but we do not know what is waiting (or coming) down that road. Paths travel in two directions, remember, as the movement of the derelict ship so aptly illustrates.*

We've ventured into space these past decades with relative ease, with worlds laid out for us to take at our whim. The first two, at least. What will come on 3J3P, or the world after that (if the well does not dry up) has yet to be seen. As a species and civilization, we have been given back our footing. Now on firmer ground, we need to be prepared: the human race might be allowed the privilege of earning our way into the expanded universe. *What is happening today might be the first of many tests to come.*

56 – Dwell, 2J3P

Tomorrow late morning the alien vessel would arrive in Toojay orbit. There had never been any real question about this happening, especially as the week progressed.

Every flying ship that could operate independently in orbit had been given a complete maintenance run-through, the fastest five taken *up top* for test flights. Dwell was never more happy, or terrified, to have kept his pilot's license up-to-date. The tension was cloying throughout the compound. According to his fellow pilots it was the same everywhere. More people than usual were venturing outside during the day, to get away from the tension indoors and breathe fresh air. The uncertainty of what was coming had become oppressive as a sauna. Being one of the pilots, Dwell was able to punch through the wet blanket covering everything for short bursts of time, drifting into orbit and working maneuvers with Imam Kusher. Kusher sounded as light-hearted as Dwell to be away from all the stress.

The one thorn in these moments of freedom: they had to deal with the crazy man from the *Washington* who'd been put in charge of the operation. Ben Solomon had come up with the initial rescue plans, tentative as they were, and micromanaged even the smallest changes. The guy was a modern day Captain Ahab, running his crew ragged as he waited for the whale that swallowed his friend to arrive.

Dwell understood, and assumed the others did, too. They let Solomon bark his orders, question every variation in flight patterns as a personal affront to his command and a threat to Peyton Kay's life. He chose from a pool of volunteers who would be the second on each ship, suited up for EVA should the need arise. That was fine with Dwell. Anyway, if Solomon got too annoying, he simply muted his voice over the com. Surprisingly, Kusher had the least patience with him. Their constant bickering, when Dwell had the volume turned up enough to hear, could be amusing. Two control freaks fighting and jockeying for position as everyone rolled around in low orbit. In the end, they had the same endgame – work out a plan of attack for when the hangar door opened, with nothing but guesswork to go by.

Of course, the hangar opening was a fixed assumption. There seemed no other method for the Locusts to enter the ship (if that, indeed, was their visitors' plan). Over the past week, the creatures' behavior had been validating this assumption. Before the discovery of the derelict ship, for a hundred and sixty-plus years, the Locusts followed a flight path behind the day/night terminator, their numbers stretched more than halfway to the pole in both directions. With some exceptions, the majority remained within four hundred and sixty kilometers north and south of the equator.

Because the creatures rarely fed these days, they'd been very slowly dying off, pulling their ranks together into an ever-narrowing pathway around the planet.

This past week, that adaptive concentration was accelerating. The Locusts were *all* flying within fifty kilometers of the equator. The line stretched back a third of the night's distance, blocking the stars for anyone unlucky enough to be beneath them for a few hours after sunset. They were coming together – still flying, though according to Miyoko, emitting far less Acclarin into the atmosphere than before. As if they'd finally given up on finding prey. Rightly so. Since there was very little left that hadn't adapted enough to stay inside at night, why bother farting out the drugs?

They were getting ready, packing up, moving out.

Moving *on*.

Moving on to *where*, there was little doubt. Eden was lush and full of prey. The swarm must be excited at the prospect.

Maybe not all of them. Dwell sat in the Union common room, in a comfortable chair he'd turned to face the external glass doors, and watched the one exception to the swarm's behavior staring back at him.

Loki stood on the outside balcony and opened its mandibles. The subsequent hiss carried into the room through the speakers. Somehow, perhaps because of the alien's appearance, Loki's cry seemed less menacing than usual, more tired. The Locust had broken all ties with the swarm and remained near the compound, night after night, slamming it's now-twisted and broken body against the walls as it tried in vain to find a way inside, look for a chink in the humans' armor.

Wanting only to kill and avenge its mate. That was Miyoko's theory, at least.

It wanted *him*. Dwell had been the trigger man.

Not for the first time, he wondered if it was a smart idea to be so close with nothing but electrified glass – thick as it might be – between them. He wasn't an idiot. The same gun he'd used on this thing's girlfriend was sitting on the floor beside his chair. Always, within reach.

Miyoko sat in the next chair, also too close to the doors for Dwell's comfort. He wanted to say something, but was afraid she might leave.

She was so pretty.

She sat daintily on the side of a hard-back chair and sketched on her Ep using a stylus. From brief glimpses he could catch, she was drawing Loki in pencil, or the electronic equivalent of such. Now and then she'd glance at a separate, smaller paper which flashed regular readings from the animal, caught from monitors she'd setup along the outer deck this morning. Loki had begun coming here for a couple of hours every night since the incident with Mother Doneele. When morning arrived, it would lurk around the compound for as long as it could bear the light. As far as anyone knew, daylight represented no true danger to them – Locusts weren't vampires. They'd simply fallen into a nocturnal hunting pattern which, even for the one hissing at them through the speakers, was hard to break.

Thankfully Loki was tagged. Miyoko assured Dwell it could not remove it, considering the device's depth and location between the wings. No one was allowed outside of the compound, nor were the outer walls de-charged, until System tracked Loki far enough away to warrant an *all-clear*.

Life at the compound had become a game of waiting. A mounted screen in every common area showed the unchanging path of the alien vessel and the two earth ships in far pursuit. All of them closing on Toojay.

A second window was also open on every public screen on the compound, as well as most personal Eps, showing Loki's current position and any local areas which were clear for daytime excursions.

Dwell wondered if Loki would join its kind when the ship arrived, or stay on Toojay and continue tormenting him, calling him out to fight until either succumbing to its self-inflicted injuries or the ISO gave the OK to put it out of its misery. The former seemed more likely to happen. Loki's body was bent sideways from repeated impacts against the walls. Even its face was more cockeyed than usual, one mandible partially cracked. Only its wings and tail seemed mostly uninjured.

Without looking up, Miyoko asked, "Any more test flights planned before arrival?"

He shook his head, trying to be cool while his heart began beating faster. Was she worried about him?

"Nope. Out of time. *El Capitan* wants us in orbit at least an hour before the ship gets here. No telling where it'll end up, if and when the hangar door opens, so he wants us spread out."

She smirked as his pet name for Solomon, but continued sketching. *Just ask her out, tonight. Grab a cup of coffee, something more than just hanging out like this.* These thoughts jumped around his head constantly when in the tall woman's presence. She was single, so was he. He wasn't bad looking, even if he was five inches shorter than her. They were friends. And, he might be dead tomorrow.

He hadn't really considered that possibility with any seriousness until now. "I could be dead tomorrow," he blurted out, and blushed.

She stopped drawing and looked at him sideways. He looked away. Embarrassed. *No way. Not now.* He hadn't said that for sympathy. Had he? He didn't want that.

"You think it's that dangerous?"

Something had changed in her voice. He needed to go to the bathroom. As if curious how this was going to play out, Loki stopped it's incessant pacing and stared through the glass. Dwell watched the monster rather than risk Miyoko's eyes. He was such a coward.

"No, not really. As much as *EC* wants more than anything to save Peyton, someone with more power is keeping his plans in check. Plenty of fallback if things get too dicey. The last thing anybody wants to is lose someone else."

Miyoko looked at him a moment longer. Dwell risked a glance back. Loki got fed up and began hissing again. She said, "I'll be praying."

He smiled. "Didn't know you were the religious type."

She shrugged. "Not too much. But maybe it's time I started. Be safe, Dwell. I've lost one friend already." The looked changed again, sadder, and she buried it in her drawing.

"I'll be ok. I'll come back a hero and buy you a cup of coffee to celebrate."

He said it! Sort of.

She didn't smile but her expression softened. "It's a deal."

Deal, not date. But it was a start.

Would he be a hero? The media still debated, with a passion rising to near-insulting levels as the ship approached Toojay, how Peyton Kay *could* survive. There was protocol for this situation, untried as it was, for survival when marooned in the open vacuum of space. Self-hibernation was a theory that had become more and more perfected on paper, through simulations and whatever lessons could be gleaned from the lone prior attempt — which failed.

If she was alive, and they could extricate her from the hangar, the process of drawing her out of whatever state she might be in could also kill her.

He would find out tomorrow. The *Reach* had been authorized to leave the fourth planet's small mining facility and was now in orbit around Toojay, prepping its decompression facility and whatever other tools they had at their disposal, all of which were mandatory for any mining location that did daily EVAs.

At this point, there was nothing Dwell and the others could do that they weren't already doing. Everyone was scared. He was too, but thanks to His Highness on the *Washington*, he was focused. When he wasn't looking at Miyoko.

Dwell got up from his chair, leaving her to her art, and walked away from Loki. The monster simply stared at him and hissed its eternal hatred.

57 – Oscar Capino, 1J3P Orbit

A shuttle from Eden docked with the *Martelo's* Corvette. The Rear Admiral could have easily overseen the operation from her office at Navy headquarters, but Oscar didn't question the need to be ship-side. As she floated through the lock he offered her the Conn as a matter of procedure. She'd refused. Not that it mattered. Sehrish Raad outranked him twice over, and immediately ordered his ship into high orbit. It was *very* high, eight hundred thousand kilometers, twice as far as the orbit of Earth's moon.

No reason was given. Oscar assumed they'd be the last line of defense for the planet. True to her word, the *Yamato* remained one planet over, orbiting Stain, and as far as anyone knew it was now the closest ship to the 2J Hole. In the 0J system, the *Burlington* maintained a mid-point distance between Earth and Mars. The *Far Darrig*, however, had gone dark. No communication in the last thirty-six hours. Sehrish didn't seemed concerned about this, and after their conversation a week earlier Oscar knew better than to ask anyone outranking him where it had gone. *Need to know.*

During their daily morning briefings he'd apprised the Rear Admiral of any details he thought she might care about, mostly weapons status, how many drills with the Corvette they'd done in the previous twenty-four hours and overall morale. The latter was not much of an issue. Like himself, Crew was caught in that vague state between concern over their families and excitement at doing exactly what they were out here to do, social order and peacekeeping certainly not withstanding.

Sehrish Raad was taller than Oscar, but then he was shorter than eighty percent of the Navy. He'd learned to walk quickly to keep pace with anyone, literally and figuratively. When they reached the ring the Admiral showed no unsteadiness under the unusual gravity effects. She'd come up the ranks from Seaman, after all. The fact that this woman, only ten years older than him, was now Rear Admiral with no formal education past an Associate's degree said all it needed to. She knew what she was doing.

Which made her silence and ever-present air of apprehension all the more troubling.

"We need a secure place to talk. Just the two of us and one other you trust to keep their mouth shut."

They were about twenty meters from the smallest conference room. As they approached he said, "System, direct com to Len Hatt." After a pause, "Lieutenant, conference room three. Out."

The door slid open and they entered. Four chairs around a table large enough only for each to have an open Ep in front of them and a coffee. There was no coffee today.

They sat in silence for a minute before Len Hatt stepped inside. He was a large, graying man, slightly bulging stomach more an indication of middle age than any loss of muscle strength. He nodded to Oscar and the Admiral then remembered she was in-person as the door closed behind him. He straightened and saluted.

She returned the salute in a perfunctory manner and said, "System, secure protocol 1, Raad, Sehrish X, 099561214ISM."

"Confirmed."

It was the highest possible security protocol, overriding laws requiring at least one individual not present to be able to access the System recordings. SP1 meant there would be no recordings, no record of the discussion. For the military this was unheard of.

Oscar's body tightened.

Sehrish's speech was calm as she continued, "I don't have to remind either of you what would happen if you repeat anything spoken in here without direct permission from me, or the Vice Admiral if I should not be able to give such permission?"

"No, sir," they said in unison.

"Give me your papers. Anything electronic."

After handing her their Eps, both made a show of checking pockets for anything automated. Len removed his wrist watch. She accepted it, gave each a quick look then stood and walked to the door. The Warrant Officer who'd accompanied her off the shuttle, his name evaded Oscar's memory, waited in the corridor to accept everything including a small, patterned box the Admiral removed from the inside of her jacket.

Again seated, Sehrish looked only at Oscar when she spoke. "In case you haven't figured it out, we are taking every precaution against the alien vessel tapping into our systems. We don't know the extent to which it's able to eavesdrop, but these creatures likely have skills or tech we don't yet understand. Everything about the plan I'm going to share with you is known fully to only a few individuals, and they are military."

Now his skin crawled, suddenly understanding the look which had become routine on the Admiral's face during their meetings. Being in charge of whatever this was, both she and her superiors were breaking nearly every law written since the Final War when it came to government secrecy, laws which had kept the peace on three planets.

"Aside from one medical ship we authorized last week for Toojay, all traffic has been rerouted out of the 2J system and away from the Hole." She paused for a heartbeat. "We also confiscated two local freighters. One had been returning from 2J and the other scheduled to depart Eden two days ago. All personnel aboard have been put into temporary custody with a cover story of communication issues to hopefully prevent, or delay, anyone figuring out what's going on."

Across the table, Len Hatt swallowed loudly and glanced at his Captain. Oscar felt the same apprehension. If there hadn't currently been the threat of an invasion, everything Sehrish just described could be summed up in two words: *military coup.*

She must have sensed the tension for she leaned back with a posture of false relaxation and raised one hand. "Wait for the whole story, gentlemen, before you start peeing yourselves. Because it gets worse. Just stay for the end. I promise, it'll make sense."

"Yes, sir," he whispered. Not content with only one response she looked at Len, who swallowed again and said, in a surprisingly calm voice, "Yes, sir."

"Good. Because this isn't the only big secret the Navy's been keeping from just about everyone in the universe. As you know, Stain ... " she sighed, "... *Dressel* has two moons. Ardeen is used mostly as dry-dock and Sagan, because of its point six gee, houses the miners."

Oscar nodded. So far, common knowledge.

She continued, "Every nuclear warhead on Earth was dismantled and flown into the sun as a symbolic gesture that no one," she leaned forward, "*no one* would ever blow the Earth to hell with one of them again."

Across the table Len stiffened. Maybe he'd already

figured out what was coming. He said, "Are you ..."

"Belay that and just listen."

Len nodded, eyes wide. Decorum was slipping. She must have expected it because there was no other reprimand. Oscar struggled to reach whatever conclusion his Lieutenant had, but it remained evasive. She didn't make him wait long. "In truth, we decided to store seventy warheads in the Steavin Caverns on the far side of Ardeen."

She waited. Oscar could only stare, trying to accept that a hundred years ago the Navy had stolen enough illegal weaponry to kill everyone on both planets.

"Sir," Len said, still wide eyed. "Those caverns are unstable. It's why no one uses —"

Oscar whispered, "They're not unstable; we made that story up, didn't we?"

She nodded. "None of this was a military-only decision. Before any of us were born the Senate made the choice to save a few ..."

"A few?" Oscar interrupted, then looked down, "Apologies. Sir."

She smiled. It was a sad expression, nonetheless. "That was almost my exact reaction, Captain. I learned of their existence and the reason for it a week ago. There are, above me, three Admirals and one Fleet Admiral. All learned of the weapons' existence upon their ascension. And there is also the Senate itself. Top tiers of government and military. And the three people always stationed inside the caverns who dedicate their lives to preserving this secret. And now me, and the seventeen men and women assigned to rig two warheads each onto the confiscated freighters."

She paused a moment before adding almost as an afterthought, "And the two of you."

Oscar was trying to stay calm, realizing she'd actually told them the plan, buried in the middle of all that confession. But the fact that these weapons still existed — "Permission to speak freely, sir," he finally said.

Sehrish laughed and waved at the comment like a fly. "Oh, now you ask permission? Go ahead, ask, either of you."

"Did they tell you why they kept them, and so many?"

She looked down at one hand on the table, nails tapping the lacquered surface. "No, they didn't. And to be honest I was too horror-struck to ask. But I think I know why now."

Len finally spoke again, softly. "Why?" No added *sir*. She *had* given them permission. Sehrish looked at him, and in that moment any sense of superiority, real or beaten into them, was gone. They were three people with a shared burden of knowledge.

"*This* is why, Mister Hatt. We were moving out to the stars, a Hole just discovered, new worlds, new dangers. If you've got something as frighteningly powerful as those warheads in your back pocket, you might sleep better at night."

Oscar laughed a little, though it came out more as a sudden breath of air through his nose. "Didn't know you were a poet, Sehrish."

She reached out and patted his hand. "A lot about me you don't know. *Captain*."

He got the message. "Yes, Admiral."

But her tired smile lingered.

Len looked between them, confused.

Oscar leaned back in his chair, casually slipping his hand free. "So we're going to try and ambush them."

"Yes we are."

"And the *Far Darrig*?"

"It passed through the Hole two days ago and is stationed near 2J2P."

2J2P was that system's version of Venus. "To what end?"

It was Len who answered. "I assume it's going to wait for the ship to pass through the Hole – if indeed that's what it ends up doing – then follow it through. Come up behind it in some sort of pincer movement?"

Sehrish nodded. "Correct. If that becomes necessary. And again, the less anyone knows this outside of those who *must*, the less risk of tipping our hand. In fact," here she stood, and pulled her uniform jacket tighter and made a show of fixing the already perfectly-fitted head scarf, "the only reason I'm telling you two is because your ship is serving as Command for the operation."

The two men stood. Oscar said, "The *Martelo* is at your service, Admiral."

"Thank you, Captain. As you were."

She stepped through the door. They followed until reaching the Midshipman standing a quarter circumference down the ring. He probably had no idea why there was so much secrecy. Oscar envied him for that.

58 – Peyton, 2J3P

Peyton was as close to death as her body could manage without truly, or clinically, being dead. The slow descent into simulated hibernation had begun two days ago as O2 reached the thirty percent mark. Water remained plentiful, mostly because Peyton found less and less reason to drink. Most drags on the hose by her mouth were triggered by System's incessant beeping, which did not let up until she drank enough to counteract any growing dehydration. The AI was trying to keep her alive.

Faith aside – and she had admitted this to herself even as the suit's computer kept on doing what it was programmed to do – Peyton had given up hope. She would do what was required, not give up in any physical sense, until even *that* became impossible. Her rational mind, however, understood the odds that going this long without rescue, without knowing how fast the ship might've been traveling, or to where – Toojay or Eden – she simply did not have resources between the two suits to survive. And forced hibernation simply had not worked in practical application.

There was always a chance, but to cling to that only and not prepare for death would be foolish. So she drank when System told her to, breathed slowly, and prayed that whatever waited on the other side of the veil was really there when the time came. Too many moments of fear cropped up – what if she was wrong; what if she had not done what she needed to in this life; what if there never *was* anything after; *what if, what if, what if.*

She refused to live that way in life, and would not start at the end of it. When these short bursts of uncertainty rose, she breathed a little deeper with her eyes closed, and let them go. She imagined them drifting through the frosted visor to join the dead Locust across the room. Doubt served no purpose other than push her away from whatever peace she could hold onto. A last ditch attempt by the Enemy to ruin her final days.

A day and a half ago, System's words crossed her visor. *O2 levels nearing critical. Hibernation protocol required. Do you approve?*

She had smiled, whispered, "Go for it, guy," before closing her eyes and trying to relax, knowing this was the final lap in the race. She'd let herself drift, remembered with a start, *again*, that the AI's interface was manual, and did her best to reach for the patch on her left arm to trace out a Y. It was enough.

The cold was gradual, hardly noticed in the beginning because it was already so frigid in the suit. When she fell asleep, it was a thin slumber, skittering across the icy surface of her brain. Tentative as it might be, Peyton did not wake again. Instead, the workings of her mind and body slowed, then slowed some more over the course of the day.

Now, two bulky EVA suits, joined together by a pair of fiber-wound hoses drifted seven meters from the sealed hangar door. Both were still clipped to their respective tethers. She would sleep knowing they had at least some way of carrying the both of them away. If they never came, then she would never wake up and the question was moot.

Cannon's suit was still inflated from the air pressure inside, never to be breathed again. It filled the legs and arms and chest like a human balloon. For both living and dead, legs and arms were bent in odd, frozen angles, jolted on occasion when one suit randomly bumped against the other, usually when Peyton's muscles twitched in reflex. In her suit, air was slowly taken in, like a thin tributary of water broken off from the main stream, working itself around the rocky shore, finding release farther downstream. O_2, lazily in, CO_2, lazily out. Less and less, never quite stopping. Like a bear ensconced in a cave during the winter months, the woman had fallen into a form of hibernation, taking one thin breath of oxygen every eighteen seconds, slowly letting out wisps of carbon dioxide which were sucked back into the suit's filters. Her heart beat, once, twice, then waited, then beat again twelve seconds later.

Peyton's faceplate had glazed over with frost. System did not waste power on clearing the glass since the suit's occupant had no need for visual observation. Contrary to the ice coating the faceplate, the temperature inside the suit was not *quite* freezing. It bordered two degrees Celsius to avoid frost bite, while aiding in the deep, deathly sleep of its inhabitant.

In the vacuum, all was silent. Then the walls around them shuddered to life. Long rectangular sections stretched the length of the chamber, pushing out from the inner walls. No sound in the vacuum, not that any would have been heard by Peyton in her current state. The AI noticed, and casually activated the suit's external camera. All but one of the lights had faded four days earlier, and in the near dark they were now knocked about the room as the frameworks moved outward, pushed by long, narrow pistons which had slowly, inexorably been lubricated over the past sixty-one hours while the ship approached its destination. A network of beams and pistons emerged towards the center of the room, longer ones from the inside wall covering three quarters of the distance towards Peyton. Others stretched from the outer wall, though much shorter. All, stretching fore to aft.

They resembled stadium bleachers, turned sideways and without any actual seating – only their intertwined framework. The ends turned down, facing what Peyton had once considered the "floor," then telescoped and attached somewhere unseen below, securing the overall structure.

The result was row after row after row of perches stretching floor to ceiling across the full length of the hangar. All motion stopped, save the dented and dark lights tumbling amid the latticework.

The alien vessel decelerated as it approached the planet. Its operator, living or automated, was perhaps wary of too quickly approaching any satellites or human ships. Nothing drew near to it, not at first. The orbit was high, the ship centered over the day side of Toojay.

Two small ships rose from the atmosphere near the horizon, but came no closer.

They waited. It waited. Without having to scan the ships, which would have been impossible at this distance, the intelligence controlling the vessel understood with a fairly high level of certainty what those small, nearly insignificant specks above the atmosphere represented.

It would not hinder them. Provided they did not interfere with its mission.

The massive ship changed direction, then considered the other vessels one more time before slowly, much slower than it had originally planned, headed toward the terminator of night and day on the opposite horizon.

As it did so, it opened the hangar door.

59 – Benny Solomon, *Washington*, 2JSide

"Go now, go *now!*" He screamed into the console window which showed the forward displays from both Nader Roman's and Fawn Noble's shuttles. Three other pilots from the other compounds were also in orbit, but at this point Roman and Noble were the closest. The videos revealed the same image of the massive hangar door opening as the alien craft turned about and moved away.

"Full steam, people," Ken added. "I have no idea what that ship is going to do next so get them out fast."

The readout below the windows showed the proximity of the hangar to each pod, both relatively the same. In a few seconds, Roman's numbers were closer. The shuttle being driven by the northeast compound's linguist was larger, built primarily for transport docking, whereas Noble's did mostly air travel between locations, needing to leave the atmosphere only when faster delivery was required. Her ship was built for durability, flexibility to maneuver in the atmosphere, not space. Roman's ship quickly outpaced hers. His window enlarged automatically because of this. Even so, the distance seemed too far for Benny's liking.

AV orbit diminishing.

AV had become the accepted abbreviation for *Alien Vessel* used by System.

Benny stared at the word *diminishing*. "What does that mean, System?"

"Unknown," the computer spoke aloud on the open channel, "but AV may be planning to enter the atmosphere."

"How . . ." he began, then stopped. "Position of swarm relative to everyone else."

A third window opened on Benny's console and the larger bridge display. It showed a large rectangle marked AV, approaching the night meridian with Roman's small dot catching up (the other lagging behind but still approaching). The backdrop of the planet rotated. One short line represented a Locust. Thousands and thousands of these were converging into a chaotic ball, keeping back from the sunset, but . . .

"System, has Swarm stopped?"

"Yes. Locusts have begun landing and congregating along the Cornelius Plain."

They were gathering together, waiting for their ride.

The hangar was closer in Roman's video, door still open.

Unless the Locusts could fly into space, which Benny doubted – though they hadn't ruled out that possibility – that lumbering box of a ship was going to have to somehow land and pick them up.

Why would it open the hangar doors before it entered the atmosphere?

"Oh, no," he whispered. "Roman, if the ship enters the atmosphere the inside of the hanger is going to burn. You need to get there before that happens. Faster, you need to move faster."

"Dude, I'm maxing out. Need to fire reverse thrusters in ten seconds or I'm splatting against the wall. That'll do no one any good, right?"

Benny almost replied, but pressed his lips together.

Instead he opened one window after another, flicking

each to the larger Bridge screen. Most of the crew was behind him at the Com station or spilling into the hallway. Too many per to regulations but Ken said nothing from his chair. No one spoke, leaving this moment for Benny to handle. Li sat at her station equally silent.

The main screen across the room was littered with multiple windows, showing the alien ship from the ground, visible through the late afternoon sky, passing overhead like a ghost ship, and from other cameras mounted on the shuttles, showing the full external view, filling the screen until magnification dropped back and the entire ship was visible. Cameras closest to the vast Cornelius Plain zoomed in as much as possible, showing from long range night vison the green-tinted bodies of the swarm landing, dropping in a line from the sky. They huddled close to each other, a frenzied crowd jostling for position before the big show.

Somehow, the ship was communicating with them.

The center window filled with the open hangar, growing larger.

Ken finally spoke. "I see them."

"Zoom in."

Two EVA suits, turning slightly, feet rolling over their heads, as their tethers whipped around the open hangar door. Ken said, "They're still tethered. Roman, go for the tethers, it's our best bet."

"That's the plan," came the pilot's terse reply. "Almost there. Alinn, be ready." This spoken to the woman in his own ship's airlock.

"I'm secure," she said, "opening outer door now."

"Firing reverse thrusters. In the meantime someone zoom in and be *sure* the suits are truly attached to them."

The image zoomed in.

Someone began, "Is she . . ." but stopped at another's

"shush" beside her.

They would find out soon enough.

"Crossing night line," came another voice, over the speaker so likely someone from Command.

System's passionless voice spoke up. "AV motion is slowing. Anticipate full stop in seven seconds. Altitude two hundred eleven kilometers and dropping."

Benny's voice had risen an octave higher from the stress. "What is it going to do? No way that thing is able to land. Even if it does, how would it take off again?"

Ken's hushed reply, "We have no idea what kind of technology this thing has."

Benny muttered, more to himself, "Physics is physics."

The hangar door on the video suddenly dropped away.

Everyone was talking now, speaking out of surprise.

"Roman, what just happened?"

Roman's reply, "Main hangar section has separated from the rest of the ship. It's dropping."

"Go, go, go, go, go!"

"Going . . ." came the reply, sounding both stressed and annoyed.

System announced, "AV altitude one hundred sixty-one kilometers and holding. Hangar altitude one hundred forty-nine and dropping."

Ken said, "Bring up the external view."

A large rectangular section of the ship – the bulk of the vessel – had indeed dropped away, falling towards the lower atmosphere. No sign of external heat building yet, but it was a matter of time. System highlighted the outline of two rows of five thick cables connecting the main ship to the top of the hangar.

Ken said, "Winches of some sort. The hangar's not dropping, it's being lowered."

Small bursts from the hangar roof kept the oversized

box from tilting while the thick cables unspooled from inside the upper hull.

"Zoom onto Roman's shuttle," Benny said quietly.

The shuttle was hurtling towards the open door, the image probably from Fawn Noble's ship. Thrusters suddenly fired and it swung sideways. The open door hangar dropped below it.

"Adjusting for descent." This statement was followed by a loud curse which everyone agreed with.

The two space suits had risen out of view for a moment – had in fact not moved at all but since they were no longer tethered to the door, with no air pressure they remained in place while the hangar dropped around them. The shuttle flew awkwardly into the open doorway as the two suits, having bounced off of the ceiling, hurtled in a slow spin towards it.

"Where are the stupid tethers," hissed the pilot. No one answered, everyone staring at the screen trying to see for themselves.

Li shouted, "There! One's at three o'clock from your angle," at the same instant Roman muttered, "Got it." A long arm extended from the side of the shuttle, usually used for loading and unloading cargo or managing satellites. Its three-fingered hand opened and grasped for the closest point in the wildly drifting cable.

Roman said, "One shot at this, Alinn. Once you have them, *any* part – I don't care if it's a rope or a foot – tell me."

System said, "External temperature rising. Entering mesosphere."

"Alinn . . .?" Roman screamed the name.

No reply for an eternal three seconds, then, "Have them. Go!"

"Slowly," whispered Benny, "Let the slack tighten first

or else you risk –"

"No kidding – stop talking!"

Alinn's voice added, "I've only got one tether but they're connected. Sort of. System, pull me out of here slowly. No slack but we don't want to pull out those hoses." After a pause, she added, "OK, we're out, we're out, Roman, speed up. Go higher, higher." More to herself she added, "Damn, it's hot."

The shuttle's rate of retreat increased. More than one person on the bridge gasped out loud. Alinn's EVA suit was suspended from its own tether, angled downward from the shuttle as it rose up and away from the massive form of the hanger dropping away. Benny noticed something striking in that moment but, like everyone else, said nothing.

Always wanting to be the center of attention, System said it anyway, "Hangar door closed immediately after evacuation was complete, prior to fully entering atmosphere."

"Yes, I noticed that," Benny muttered, but said nothing else, too intent on what was happening with Alinn. Both of the woman's arms were out before her, glove wrapped around one of the tethers as she was slowly pulled back towards the shuttle. Cannon and Peyton's suits spun perpendicularly a few meters below on the other end. Their spin slowed as small thrusters fired along the edges of their suits. They drifted apart, the oxygen and water hoses stretching perilously between them. Alinn began pulling on the tether, drawing them closer and whispering "Don't, don't, don't . . ."

Then she was inside the shuttle. She stopped pulling in the other cable, waited for the bodies of Peyton Kay and Cannon White to get close enough to guide them manually.

Ken suddenly cleared his throat. "Try the com."

Benny whispered, "Pey, you there? Can you hear me?"

"System," Ken said, "are you able to talk to the suit at this point? Any signs of life?"

After a heartbeat pause, System said impassively, "Peyton Kay is alive, though in a forced state of hibernation." Whispers of relief fluttered across the bridge. "I suggest she remain in vacuum in this state until the shuttle docks with the *Reach* and adequate resuscitation facilities can be utilized."

Ken leaned sideways and reached towards the Com station. With no self-consciousness, Benny gripped his captain's hand, gave it a squeeze. Then he said, "Agreed. Roman, as soon as they're secured in the airlock head for the *Reach*."

"Yes, sir."

"And thank you. Both of you. That was incredible work. You're both nuts and we're forever indebted. "

A small laugh was their only reply, though it had no humor. Benny imagined their hearts were still racing with adrenaline. "Piece of cake," came Roman's eventual reply. "You owe us big time, Solomon."

"Whatever it is, you got it."

The relief in the room was palpable, but subdued. No one dared hope for the best, not yet.

Ken said, "When will we get there?"

Li checked her screen. Benny was grateful the AI didn't barge in again with its own answer. It seemed to know when to shut up.

"*Washington* should arrive in orbit in just over two days." She looked up. "Unless we can get there sooner."

Ken shook his head. "Maintain current speed." He assumed Navigation was listening to the conversation. "If that thing moves on early enough, we can talk about pressing the gas a little."

Li looked over at Benny and smiled. Everyone was touching or hugging him in some way, at least those who could reach him. At the moment, that was all right by him.

The mood darkened a little when Ken added, "Alinn, make sure Peyton's connection to Cannon's air supply wasn't compromised in the extraction and leave them together until you get to the ship. They'll know the safest way to separate them."

Somehow, the oddness, or irony, in that statement struck him. Ken took a sudden, shuddering breath and covered his face with his free hand. The other was still tightly gripping Benny's.

No one else spoke for some time.

60 – Loki, 2J3P

Two of its right limbs were useless, having slammed into the pain-filled skin of the aliens' nest too many times. A throbbing pain radiated from three distinct cracks in the hard plating coating the damaged arms. Always, Loki would slam itself against the outer walls using this side, first out of instinct – the right side being more prominent and how it normally came in for an attack when prey was plentiful – then out of a decision to minimize serious damage elsewhere. Though also hurt, the lower arm still functioned, with only a fraction of the thumping agony of the upper. Always, Loki protected its wings, folding them tight before contact, knowing even in the rage which had consumed it for days, to lose the power of flight was to die.

They were *all* dying. A dim memory lingered throughout the swarm of other places, other worlds. But time had dragged on and this world had died – slowly, but died like all the others. Yet no one had come to take them away. They continued to fly, and weaken. Loki understood that its rage was not completely directed at the creatures who eventually *did* come to this planet. They were invaders, like its own kind, though far more docile. In the end, they offered hope of new prey. But these creatures learned quickly, communicating with each other in strange, sometimes silent ways.

And they stung, killed, when threatened. This had not happened for such a long time the Locusts had become inured to their existence. They posed no threat, and with rare exception offered no chance for food. So the Swarm had hungered, and kept searching. It took time for one of its kind to die of deprivation. They survived as long as there was air to breath and water to drink, but there were limits. Until then the swarm searched, and waited for the Others to return.

If they *ever* returned.

The Mate was now dead, stung by these newcomers, and the Follower, who for most of its life rarely left Loki's company, had rejoined the Swarm once Loki began focusing all of its frustration and anger against these aliens.

Loki did not want to hunt any longer, ignored every ingrained instinct to do so because it had finally accepted there was nothing *left* to hunt. The fat, four-legged cattle had learned to hide below the surface where the air was untainted, where Loki's kind dared not venture for no legitimate reason other than base instinct, a deep, inborn terror of anything covering them but the sky. Only when the Others came would they deign to do so. Then, they would be calmed, peace unfolding like rain, and they would enter the haven for a new world.

Now, at last, they were here. The Locusts sensed their presence days before the images began forming in their minds. These mental flashes drew the Swarm into tighter formation as they followed the night. Even Loki had been compelled to occasionally join them, falling to the surface when the pain was too much, or its rage too sharp.

They were coming.

They were *here*.

It should be joyful, crying out in celebration towards the sky like the others. It could not. Something had been lost, some dark, hidden . . . *knowledge*, had been released into its mind. What it did, what they *all* did in their lives, was pointless. Rarely did they bear young. Rarely would any but a few stop their repetitive flight to tell stories of the past. Loki was not the only Locust who found solace in these moments, but most preferred the sky, the search for food, and the occasional fight far up in the cold, starlit atmosphere. These were mere games. Loki found them as pointless as everything else. Loki wanted to stop, to draw its stories, speak color into the images it created. To watch the aliens in their protected warrens. This, it had done, for a long time, finding their behavior and tools confusing and fascinating. It feared them. Feared more, their unconcern of Loki's presence.

Finally, after they stung the Mate, it understood. Like itself, their confidence came from knowledge of their own power. The other night they had been protecting the weak one who'd wandered into Loki's reach. It understood this, but the reasoning was wrong. It had the *right* to take that weak creature, that rare meal. *They* had no right to take it back. He saw the face of the one who killed the Mate, who had taken life for no reason Loki could understand other than – it could.

What was the point of any of it? These thoughts drove it on, against the walls, against the pain they inflicted. Hate, anger, terror, pointlessness. It did not understand. When it returned to the air and considered its existence, Loki feared that perhaps it *did* understand, maybe better than anyone else.

It simply could not articulate this understanding, so foreign a source was it drawn from.

Loki hopped along the fringes of the massive crowd of Locusts. More landed amid the chaos. The clearing spread out precariously at the edge of night. All of them shoving each other, crying in joy and irritation and excitement, all calling to the Others who had begun to reach down from beyond the sky. The *haven* dropped closer. They were to go inside the artificial cave which now approached from above, painful waves of heat visible and roiling from its belly in curls of white smoke.

The Locusts were agitated, all receiving the same message. *In. Come inside.* They were aware of their numbers. The haven radiated heat a short flight above the ground, swinging heavily back and forth. It could not possibly contain them all. No one moved. Some skittered away, hissing in fear and confusion.

A sound, inaudible in the night sky but felt as a deep resonance shaking their shells and rumbling deeper into their organs, pressed against them like dust storms in the hot season. It covered them in the Others' images, insisting on peace, calm. *Safety.* It was safe. They wanted to *Come In. Come Inside. Now.*

Suddenly all of them wanted this very much.

The Swarm waited a few moments longer, feeling the message, staring with adoring understanding at the massive block above them. As one they rose towards it. Many collided with each other in their rapture, fell back or were knocked aside. Some lost use of their wings, tumbled to the planet with a cry of terror and deep, aching loss. Most of these were ignored, left behind. A few were lifted by Mates or their own Followers, aided into the waiting maw of the cave which swung above the surface of this dead world, calling to them all with such joy and welcome. The injured cried out in pain mixed with their own joy. The ones left behind wailed and thrashed and tried to rise again. Some managed to regain the Swarm, most did not.

Thousands flew into the wide opening of the hangar, mentally instructed to latch onto the extended bars with lower limbs. They folded their wings and extremities, tighter and tighter, scuttling sideways and pressing against others already mounted beside them. Harder, then harder did they press, lulled by the vibrations invading them and dancing under their skin, tickling their mind. *Peace.* They were peaceful. This was good. Even as more arrived and breathing became difficult, there was no panic. All were calm, pointed towards a purpose. The Others had come; they were going to a world filled with food and fresh growth. They would feast and grow fat and multiply. So tightly were they packed into the cavern they could not sing, only trill, a light song which moved from body to body until the walls echoed the sound back as a chorus. It resonated in constant, penetrating union with the Others' promise.

Loki had risen with them but lingered outside the entrance, perched on the edge. It heard the message, understood, saw itself feasting again, day after day. It would be fulfilled. Find a new Mate. Fly and sing and tell stories in *new* sand in a *new* world. So many stories it could tell.

Then the darkness, or this newly-discovered light, overwhelmed its thoughts. This dark-light spoke louder than the voice of the Others.

Why? Why was this good? What did it do for them?

Loki was broken, but it would heal. It could not remember any other world but this. Had it been born here? It did not remember. The vibrating song of the Others was distracting. Like other Locusts not quite ready to push away their instincts and brave the confinement of the cave, Loki squatted outside of the hangar, felt the heat of the artificial stone, like the walls of the newcomers' warrens but without their searing pain. There was *no* pain inside, only hope. Choice. The Swarm was nearly swallowed up. In fact, some were being pushed back outside. *Too* many, now. Those inside cried for patience, tried to make room. Hundreds remained trapped just beyond the door, their joy falling to a cracking and rising panic.

In. Must Come In. Wait. Slow.

They calmed. With patience, some found a way inside.

Loki watched from its perch, feeling the constant throb of its shattered arms. Many left outside were weaker than the rest, slower in flight, always trailing the Swarm. The Others would not allow them in. The weak would die. The weak *should* die.

The cave began to rise. Loki turned its head and saw the long lines connecting it to a massive shape glinting against the distant sun, its reflected light blotting out so many stars around it. It was far above. Where the lights came from.

Screams from below. Loki looked down over the edge. The cave entrance had closed. Clusters of its kind fluttered around it, slamming into it, not much different than it had been doing to the aliens' walls. Rage and panic were now dominant. The peace of the Others had left them. They clung to the sides or perched atop the cave. So many left behind, and the vessel rose still higher. Not quickly. But consistently.

The air smelled strange here. They were higher than it had ever flown before. Bodies jostled against it, shooting jolts of pain through its limbs.

The air was changing drastically now. Loki did not like this. *This* air was bad, thin. Whether it assumed this or the information was being relayed by the Others, it did not matter. It had not gone inside with the Swarm. It was outcast. Loki did not want to go any higher.

It leaped from its perch and fell towards the ground. For a few, painless moments, it chose not to fly. To simply fall, break like a clump of dirt against the hard ground.

To die.

But it could not. It had wings, so it opened them, and

flew away from the retreating hand of the Others and its own kind forever.

61 – Oscar Capino, INS *Martelo*

Once the hangar was securely docked into its belly, the alien vessel orbited Toojay a dozen times, building speed. The medical ship *Reach*, in response, altered its orbit to circle the planet pole-to-pole, keeping out of the way as much as possible.

Hundreds of Locusts had stubbornly clung to the outside of the hangar as it rose. The live feed was provided by multiple cameras videoing from various distances, first from the surface then the two other rescue ships which had remained in orbit until things played themselves out. Most of the stranded Locusts finally released their grip and fell back through the atmosphere. Many had died long before impact with the planet's surface. Others opened their wings and began to chase after the retreating night. Those who held on even in death eventually broke free of the ship and dropped through the mesosphere to be burned away in quick flashes.

Oscar stood in the back of the Mess room watching the Toojay feed, too tense to sit on the bridge. Rear Admiral Raad stood to his left. Aside from separate breaks to sleep, he'd hardly left her side. Most of Crew not currently on shift were here. Oscar understood the nervousness — and excitement — buzzing between them. Crew needed to witness this together, learn whether they were heading into a fight.

If the plan worked, there would be no need. Either way, once the Locusts were removed from the picture the next battle would begin. The human race would realize what an enormous secret had been kept from them for so long.

Reminding himself that he wasn't on the chopping block for that last point, Oscar kept his focus only on the present.

The vessel continued accelerating after it broke orbit, moving for an intercept with the Hole.

"System," Len Hatt's voice from Second Bridge, "estimate time to AV/2JH intercept."

"Assuming no change in acceleration seventeen hours, forty-one minutes."

"Notify us of any changes in acceleration then."

Since yesterday's meeting, the two men hardly spoke unless absolutely necessary. If anyone noticed the tension between them they didn't say. Both craved the chance to talk through their secret, share something so few in the universe knew. Of course, they could not without issuing the same restrictive protocol and sending a flare to their superiors that they were definitely *not* keeping their mouths shut. Best avoid each other. In another seventeen hours and forty-one minutes, there would be no more secrets.

"Captain, a word, please." This had become a common statement between him and the Admiral. He only nodded and followed her towards the conference room where she would lock out all communications and discuss plans if things failed.

These moments were hardly productive. Like him, she simply needed to talk to someone who knew what was happening. The stress of silence was overwhelming. They had time. He would let her talk, pretend this meeting was necessary. When Sehrish passed by the conference room and did not stop until reaching her personal quarters, Oscar hesitated, but only for a moment. What was one more breech of protocol at this point?

*   *   *

Nobody could sit still on First Bridge, because no one had any idea what was going on. They busied themselves typing commands into their personal screens or unconsciously swiveling back and forth in their seats. Oscar and First Sergeant Prim McGahie were the major culprits with that particular reveal. Twenty minutes until *AV Threshold,* a term coined by McGahie when the Captain and Admiral first entered the small room an hour ago.

It was almost time. McGahie finally swiveled fully in her chair and said, "Permission to speak freely, sir."

"Denied," they both said at the same time. Oscar felt an overpowering need to explain something, anything, but Sehrish's presence beside his chair was an anchor chained around his throat.

They'd all know in twenty minutes. To say *something,* he muttered, "Maintain radio silence. Let me know if anything changes." He risked a glance at his First Sergeant. She caught the look and said, "Sir," letting the look linger too long. His Coms officer did not like being left out of whatever game he might be playing. Oscar only shook his head. Hopefully all this silent non-communication was saying something. To someone.

He wanted to scream. Instead he said, "System, split main screen between the 1Jside of the Hole and estimated AV course." The leftmost window showed empty space, the view from their side of the Hole. Somewhere, likely dead center, was the entrance to (and from) the 2J system. In eighteen minutes the alien vessel should emerge. On the right, a course chart with the approaching ship demarcated as a triangle, a dotted line in yellow behind and red ahead to highlight its estimated course.

Seventeen minutes.

"Sir." McGahie again. "Picking up two broadcasts. Wide band."

"From?"

She began to speak, stopped. He turned to her. She was looking at the screen. "There," she finally said.

Oscar swiveled back towards the front. The outer edges of two rings rose into view from the lower portion of the left image.

"Play the broadcasts."

"… to our world. We are peaceful. Alien vessel, please acknowledge. We welcome you to the Eden system. We are friendly. Our arms are open…"

"What the …"

"Belay that, Sergeant."

The transmission, whether from the left or rightmost ship or perhaps both, switched to Portuguese. Likely trying to keep the alien pilots off balance, even if only a little. The rings of both vessels were now fully in view, their edges glowing from the gas giant looming off-screen to port. The transports sported massive, cylindrical hub sections which served as storage containers that could be detached much like his Corvette. Oscar wondered if they would do so now.

Eight minutes.

The two rings moved dangerously close to each other. Why were they bothering to generate spin gravity if no one was on board? Part of the charade, no doubt.

Six minutes.

The transmission, which had switched to French then Mandarin was once again Universal English. Over and over, messages of peace spoken in multiple human languages.

In a surprising gesture, the Admiral put a hand on his shoulder. She wasn't looking at him, only at the screen. Did she even realize she was touching him? The gesture was comforting but a remote part of him worried it would only fuel whatever speculation had been running through Crew about them. In front of him, Midshipman Guavera's shoulders were hunched so tightly from stress they shook. No doubt wondering what these ships were doing and why neither the Captain nor Admiral behind him were reacting. They weren't even speaking.

Oscar glanced over to McGahie. She caught his look, crunched her face in an irritated, confused stare. He only shook his head again. Her expression smoothed out. If there was fear, she wasn't showing it. Good for her. The Admiral's grip was tighter on his shoulder.

Three minutes.

The triangle on the right screen was nearly to the circle.

"... *bienvenue. Nous offrons la paix. Veuillez réagir. Prière de transmettre à ...*"

One minute.

The words wove through the silence of the Bridge, as the triangle icon disappeared into the Hole.

In sixteen seconds it would emerge in the center of the left screen.

The moment the alien vessel had entered the Hole the two transport ships fired their engines to full. A dozen cones of spent exhaust dotted along the rings; three massive cones at the rear of the hubs. They'd achieved seventy-four percent maximum velocity according the running commentary System scrolled along the bottom of the screen. The rings nearly touched but maintained enough distance to keep from tearing each other apart. All the while they transmitted words of peace and friendship. The

Locust-laden ship emerged from the Hole at the same rate it had entered.

The human transports never slowed.

Whatever navigated the emerging ship tried veering to escape collision. The leftmost transport slammed against its starboard side not far from the hangar door, the other hit head-on. Guided by the same System both impacted within a second of each other, then the front sections of both ignited with a blinding, silent explosion. Everyone on the Bridge raised their arms in response, though the conflagration extinguished immediately.

What was *not* extinguished was the force of the explosions. Four concurrent nuclear detonations, twin devices rush-fitted as close to the hubs' noses as possible and detonated by the AI.

Lord, thought Oscar, staring at the scene, *please let those ships be unmanned.*

The split screen changed to one large image from outside the Hole since there was no longer a need for the progress chart.

"System," said Sehrish, her voice a whisper, "six images, switch between whatever feeds we have. Not too fast." Her hand was still on Oscar's shoulder, digging into his shirt.

The images came from a myriad of drones likely launched before Threshold. They alternated between six slightly different perspectives. Thousands of burning and broken Locusts tumbled into the vacuum of space while their ship bent and twisted then finally tore itself apart. These scenes, Oscar learned later, were being transmitted live to the public as an unannounced break-in broadcast. A stunned audience of billions were watching everything unfold in real time. Close-ups of individual Locust bodies, hardly recognizable over debris hurtled in every direction.

Most were caught in the gas giant's gravitational pull. The twisted wreckage of all three ships spun about each other in a frenetic dance, disappearing back through the Hole or slowly, inexorably drawing down into the hurricanes of 5P's upper atmosphere. There, they would be forever lost.

Later, viewers from the three planets would learn what had caused such a complete annihilation of the three craft. From the vids it was apparent it had been more than a simple collision. Oscar wondered how long it would take for the masses to truly understand the breadth of the secrecy behind humankind's victory.

He felt his communications officer staring at him. He didn't turn around. What would be the point?

Sehrish's hand was no longer clenched, but remained on his shoulder. Oscar reached up and took her hand. She grabbed it and squeezed. Only then did he risk a look into her face. Stony, locked in desperate concentration. He suspected this lack of emotion would not last. Much as he wanted to stand up and embrace her, he could not. Aside from making her look weak (or *human* which, in the Navy, was just as bad), they needed to stay focused. He squeezed her hand again and stared hard. It had been a day of nonverbal conversations. She nodded, pulled her hand free after giving his shoulder a pat.

She'd recovered quickly. His respect for her only grew later, mentally replaying this moment and allowing a sudden truth to occur to him. Admiral Sehrish Raad was spearheading the operation, and was the one most likely to be handed over to the angry mob when its reality clarified in people's minds.

The need for secrecy, especially from the media, would have to be explained again and again. Then the bigger question would be asked: was the fear that this moment might happen truly the reason for hiding weapons from the

Final War under humanity's nose? Oscar turned back and watched the destruction of what might very well be an entire race.

These debates would come later. Angry politics would have its day, as it was wont to do. Oscar hoped that initially, the human race will do what he was doing now, and let out a collective breath at its deliverance.

62 – Gendrick, 2J3P

The *Washington* arrived two days and sixteen hours after Peyton's rescue. In that time, and the days that followed, life on Toojay had already begun to change.

According to System, eighty four Locusts had the sense to return to the surface of Toojay before the hangar rose too far. Loki had been one of them. The latter lingered, day and night, near the three boulders just outside the southern compound. The rest of the swarm's remnant followed the night for a little while longer, but did so without energy or direction. Many fell after a few days, to the ground or into the ocean. Those which could be approached lay passive as scientists, and their armed escorts, approached. The creatures ignored them. Some had already died, though no immediate cause for their death could be ascertained. Others were captured for study. If the teams could save them, they would. To Gendrick, it seemed as if the Locusts had given up, their only hope for survival having left them behind. Their salvation had come and gone. They'd fallen back to the earth, separated forever from their species.

He had written that down, of course, for a future *Vast Array*. It was too good a metaphor to lose.

The fact that they were the last of their kind, as far as anyone knew, was no incentive to keep trying to live. It was possible the Locusts did not know the fate of the swarm. Gendrick was of the other mindset – if the hive-mind theorists were correct, this very fact was what stole away the last of their reasons to live.

Vids of the Locust ship blowing apart, their bodies instantly becoming debris among so much destruction, played incessantly over every media stream. Questions as to the viability of expeditions into the neighboring gas giant's tempestuous and deadly atmosphere to recover the bulk of the ship's remains were bantered about with enthusiasm. To Gendrick, the risk and expense hardly seemed worth it. But he was not a scientist.

Besides, many viable pieces of wreckage, and a few intact Locust corpses had returned back through the 2J Hole. These were eventually gathered up and taken away for study.

Humanity was stunned, then relieved beyond words (though they managed to find words soon enough) that Eden had been saved. Lives, human and otherwise, were spared, not to mention the potential ruination of the planet.

It was a decision Gendrick did not envy anyone having to make.

As his kind often did, as the week progressed and the terror of the coming plague of Locusts had cooled to a frightening memory, accusations became more directed and vociferous.

Why – and *where* – had these nuclear warheads been hidden away from public knowledge? If those existed, where were the others? There were *certainly* more. This had become the hottest debate among commentators. How could the existence of the very weaponry which had nearly destroyed the human race be kept intact and functional? The other side of the argument, repeated *ad nasuem* by the same, exhausted-looking Navy admiral reasoned that, had they *not* been, would the Locusts have survived a simple ramming from two lumbering transports?

It was true, but beside the point, and the military and

ISO leadership knew this.

On and on, the angry (but obviously relieved) talking heads went. Much less covered, though no less heated, were other questions which slowly rose from the ashes of the week's events.

How could anyone condone the genocide of an entire species?

Had anyone thought what multiple nuclear detonations just outside the 2J Hole would have had? What if the force of the ships' destruction (the media had lately begun re-classifying the alien vessel as *derelict*, perhaps to justify the actions carried out against it) had closed the Hole forever?

Gendrick wondered this himself, not long after the events unfolded across the Union's public screens. Everyone on this side of the Hole could have been cut off from humanity.

Would that have been a bad thing, or good?

This question he noted in a sidebar then continued typing with the frenetic pace of a writer with too much to say, limited by his body's own physics. So much to say, before he forgot, and before Peyton woke up and he could begin neglecting his duties again. She was stable, the resurrection from near-death a slow, but successful endeavor. Except that she had not yet woken. No one seemed concerned about this, at least not the medical staff onboard the *Reach*, but it bothered Gendrick and her crewmates. None of them would feel she'd truly been rescued until she opened her eyes and spoke.

She was breathing on her own, at least, in a bunk onboard the medical ship. He'd managed to find transport there only once in the past week. His visit served little purpose other than to meet Ben Solomon, the pilot who'd been with her when she and Cannon were attacked, and Ken Burlov, the *Washington*'s captain. Solomon seemed to be spending most of his time at Peyton's beside. Gendrick pushed away the odd tingle of jealousy when he'd heard this from Burlov, reminding himself that his relationship with Pey was only friendship. When he asked the captain about them, Ken only shook his head and said, "He blames himself for what happened. Stupid, but that's Benny. He loves her dearly, but no, there's nothing more than that between them."

He then asked Gendrick, as they sat in the ship's Mess eating lunch and drinking coffee, if he and Peyton had anything in their past. Gendrick surprised himself by saying no, explained how they grew up together, left out the intimacy that blossomed just before moving on to different lives. No sense bringing that up with strangers – especially those who were closest to her.

He left the ship with reluctance, but Dwell was piloting the ferry and needed to get back to security duties. The man had become one of three pilots running transport from the surface to the *Washington* and *Reach* since the former vessel arrived, sharing duties with someone from each of the other compounds to balance the new work load.

No one had come to Gendrick to talk in hours. They still came, sometimes simply to rehash their old fears, other times to discuss the theological implications of all that had happened. Officially, he had very little "free" time – if people needed, or simply wanted to talk, he was available. He *wanted* to be; it was why he'd chosen this vocation in the first place. He could have been more formal with his time, and maybe later he would, but this was what he loved to do. To sit down with people, help them find their place in God's ever-expanding universe. Calling it His *Vast Array* was a more poetic viewpoint and how he managed to come out here in the first place, but God was not found only in words. He was and always would be personal, wanting more *analog* time with His people. He did that through others, and Gendrick was happy to oblige.

He stopped writing, then forced himself to re-read what he'd written over the past half hour. McCarthy had warned him, and Gendrick agreed, that his posts mustn't serve as purely historical documents, rehashing events occurring around him which every news feed had already beaten to death. Leave history for the historians. There were plenty of sometimes-conflicting versions of the *past* being broadcast already. His job, *God's Vast Array*, was to humanize everything, spiritualize the moments of mankind moving out to the stars. He liked that, wrote it down at the end of his conversation with the Prelate. It might be a good transition away from any overly-technical writings he'd released to this point.

He took a sip of cold coffee, then continued writing for the next hour. Until the panel beside his door beeped.

Gendrick blinked. "Come in?" Posed as a question. His voice was thick, too long in his own head.

The door opened. Ochi Miyoko stood in the threshold, a breathing apparatus swinging from her left hand. She was dressed for an outside jaunt, tall boots, long coat and scarf which could be pulled up over her face if the dust kicked up. More and more people were daring short jaunts outside at night. They weren't allowed to venture farther than a hundred yards from the compound, even now, since there was still one remaining Locust wandering about with any purpose – thankfully he was tagged and trackable. Soon enough, the restriction would be lifted completely. Everything at this point was just a matter of time.

"Care for a nighttime walk?"

He leaned back and rubbed his face. "No, not tonight. Taking advantage of the lull to get some writing done."

She looked at him a moment, considering, then nodded. Her reasons for asking may have been personal, she'd been dealing with Arun's death slowly, in her own, outwardly dispassionate way. They'd been close, however. Unless she said so, he'd take her at face value. Tonight at least.

The xenologist had become a regular visitor to his room since he'd returned from his stay with the cattle. Since Peyton's rescue, he'd acquiesced a few times, accompanying Miyoko out to the plain where "his herd" tended to congregate. Each time they were accompanied by either Michael Broeger or, more often, Dwell. The security men were armed and constantly scanned the skies and their Eps. Personal bodyguards, always on the lookout for a threat. Early on there had been a handful of Locusts wandering aimlessly around their stretch of the globe, but their numbers were trickling away. Loki was the sole exception most people worried about.

On their first trip out, Gendrick felt a familiar tickling fear creeping along his spine the farther they ventured from the compound. He reminded himself that aside from Loki, the Locust remnant still followed the night. After its kind began falling into death or despair, Loki had given up being migratory altogether. It had forsaken its nightly "punishment" of the buildings, at least, and spent its time skittering and drawing along the sand by the three boulders, telling stories of the past no one would ever see. Perhaps it was writing a Lamentations for its species. It drew, clicked and hissed, letting the cameras log its story only to erase and begin again. According to Miyoko, each time the symbols were different, and so likely their meaning.

Miyoko spoke of Loki with a quiet sadness. On that first trip out to Moon's herd, Gendrick understood her sorrow was for Arun, not the Locust. She'd stopped at the edge of the first herd and sat on a rock, then begun to cry in heavy, wracking sobs. Gendrick sat beside her, let her lean into him as she spoke through tears of random moments with her old friend. Michael Broeger had been with them. He held back, giving them space. This was not the first time Gendrick had consoled one of Arun's friends or lovers. In fact, people seemed to be coming to terms with his death only now that the larger threat of the alien ship had passed. The man's body had remained preserved in the adhoc morgue at the far end of the compound until things settled, but they needed to decide on an official memorial service soon. One was in the planning stages. Perhaps this had also become the catalyst for everyone to reluctantly deal with his absence.

In their time among the herds, however, Miyoko's eyes were bright, excited like a child on Christmas morning. All of the fear and pain was relegated to its proper place.

Moon had broken from the herd a few minutes after they arrived that first morning, mewling in what could only be taken as a friendly greeting.

"Hey, Moon, how're things going?"

The cow rubbed its wet snout against his arm. The gesture was one of genuine warmth, but far from submissive. Gendrick only guessed this was the case, though Miyoko later echoed the sentiment.

"He feels a certain affection for you," she'd said. "Maybe a sense of responsibility. Even now, after all this. It's amazing."

"Maybe he thinks I'm the one who slayed the dragons and rescued their planet."

She'd laughed at that, but he'd seen a sideways look in her expression, as if she were considering the idea.

Curious, a few other cows and bulls had wandered close, mewling at Moon but without the apprehension Gendrick remembered from his night in their warren. They were equally as interested in Miyoko. They knew her, or her smell, from many such visits, but their interest was far keener, now. More open.

He'd asked Moon if he could bring Miyoko into the burrow. Moon did not understand, not at first, until Gendrick walked with her to the opening leading down the same path into which he'd been dragged. Its agitation was immediate. Half the herd moved in their direction, intending to cut off their access. Cries of fear and warning rose up. Even so, Gendrick gestured with his arm into the hole in the ground.

In response Moon wandered between them and the entrance, nudging him away, back towards the spot where they'd arrived. In subsequent visits, they did not try again. Somehow, they hoped, the creatures would find a way to invite them. When the time was right.

He'd agreed to go with her again tomorrow morning, unless Loki was anywhere nearby, in which case no one would be allowed out. Especially since the creature's usual haunt – the three boulders where Mother Doneele had stumbled upon it that insane night – was directly in line with the route they took to the clearing. ISO Command seemed to be giving the last Locust on Toojay time to mourn – and hopefully die. They insisted that its writings be recorded as much as possible, so someone had installed two new cameras among the stones. So far, they hadn't been destroyed.

Tonight, he wanted to stay inside, catch up with *Vast Array*. The idea of walking outside at night still held no appeal. Maybe he hadn't been here long enough to appreciate the novelty.

She twirled her air filter in front of her, still standing in his door. She said, "Still on for the morning, though?"

"Yes, ma'am. As long as it's clear."

"OK, then. Happy writing!" Then she was gone. The door slid closed after her.

Gendrick leaned back in his chair and rubbed his face again, stifling a yawn. It would be good to see Moon again, and have some quiet time among the herd. If they were allowed. Everything depended on Loki.

63 – Dwell, 2J3P

On his way back from breakfast the next morning, Dwell ran into Miyoko and the priest crossing through the Union room on their way outside. He assumed they were heading out, based on their clothes. Miyoko carried that adorable expression of barely-contained excitement she always had when going out to visit her cows. His day became brighter with this easy excuse to spend time with her.

"You two heading out?" he called. She turned around and smiled. *What kind of smile is that*, he wondered. *Is she happy to see me or just being friendly?* He knew he was being an idiot, but he still wondered.

Father Hellerton glanced back, looking tired. He looked like that a lot lately.

Miyoko chirped, "We are!"

"Hold on, I just need to get my stuff."

"No, we're all set." She held up her Ep. Dwell kept his expression neutral, although those four words threatened to pull his face down to the carpet. "Loki is ninety clicks away, near Northeast."

"Oh, OK," he said, knowing it was time to move on gracefully. Last thing he wanted was a sympathy invite. "Well, say hi to Moon for me."

She laughed – even Father Hellerton smirked – and promised she would.

He turned his back on them and continued towards the Security wing, grateful for his Italian-German ancestry. If he'd been cursed with Broeger's Scotch genes, he'd have been blushing like someone with high blood pressure.

His day just got darker. Maybe she and the priest had something going on. He was a handsome guy. Better-looking than *he* was. Dwell unconsciously shook his head. He'd worried about the same thing with her and Arun.

He passed Crazy Woman's cell without a glance and approached the desk. Michael looked up and said, "Once and for all will you just ask her out?"

Dwell stopped and stared. "How the – "

The large man laughed, face turning red as he did. "I didn't. It was just an easy guess."

Dwell held back a few choice expletives, and dropped himself in the other cushioned seat. One advantage to being security, since they spent so much time sitting in front of monitors, they got the most comfortable chairs.

"Yea, well . . ." but he didn't finish.

Something beeped on the main monitor. As Michael reached to tap the line open, he said, "*Yea, well* hasn't been doing you any good, buddy. Time for the direct approach." He turned to the monitor. "Michael Broeger."

"Mike, hey. Wanted to give you a heads up. We're bumping up the Loki Alert."

Something tight wrapped around Dwell's chest. He sat straighter and leaned towards the monitor. Michael turned it a little so he could see the window. The *Loki Alert* was what they called any proximity warnings based on its tracker. Dwell said, "Where is he?"

"Hey, Dwell. Didn't know you were there. Thing is, we don't know. System reported his vitals flat-lining last night. Check the log, we made a note about it. We waited until this morning to collect the body. Had we known, we would have gone out sooner, but . . ."

"Known what?" Michael asked.

The man in the window shrugged, looking a little embarrassed. "He wasn't there. At some point last night – likely when the report came in – he'd managed to remove the tracker. Made a mess of his back against a sharp edge of rock. Lots of buggy blood, but he did it."

The reality of this settled on both men as they looked at each other. Dwell stood up, eyes darting back and forth as he tried to assess the situation as dispassionately as possible. Then he gave up, and kicked the chair away with the back of his legs.

"Miyoko's out there with the priest. They just left. Call them back. I'm heading out."

"Thanks, J," Michael said. "Begin visual scan. I assume System's already looking for him. We'll get back to you soon. Right now we have people outside."

Dwell opened the locker at the hallway entrance and grabbed a rifle, checked the cartridge. Full. Mostly. He wouldn't need many rounds. As he turned to leave Michael shouted, "Dwell."

He turned, bouncing on the balls of his feet. "What?"

His partner had been looking down at something, and his normally red face was drawing pale. "I just checked the monitors near Loki's favorite spot by the boulders. The camera's aren't transmitting anything. Non-functioning."

Dwell pictured the video of Loki reaching out and destroying the previous one.

"Call them back!"

He turned and ran, hoping Miyoko and Father Hellerton were slow walkers.

64 – Gendrick, 2J3P

The morning air was cool and dry. The orange tang of the Acclarin chemical was all but gone these days. Gendrick thought that was a pity. With so few other sources of aroma, Toojay smelled like dirt and cattle. He and Miyoko had come within ten meters of the boulders when the call from Michael Broeger came over both Eps. Normally calls would be preceded by three subtle beeps, no connection made unless initiated by the owner. Security, and System, had overridden the protocol.

Broeger's voice was loud from Gendrick's robes and Miyoko's hand. She was holding the Ep loosely in her right.

"Gendrick and Miyoko. This is Michael Broeger. Return to the compound immediately. This is an emergency. Loki is probably in the area. We've lost the ability to track."

They both stopped and stared at Miyoko's paper, then up at each other. The fear Gendrick had felt on his first walk with Arun returned with a vengeance. This time it was justified.

He glanced behind them. The compound was still in sight, beyond the small outcropping of boulders they'd already passed. Even so, it looked too far away. The xenologist was staring with wide eyes towards the rocks before them, and one stray ribbon of emergency tape leftover from the incident with Doneele. Her expression did not convey fear, only a growing excitement. Longing, even.

"We need to go back," he whispered. "*Back*, not forward."

She looked at him. "Yes, yes, I know."

Gendrick reached out and loosely gripped her arm. Whispering, "We're unarmed. He's a born predator who eats people. Plus," he shook her arm gently for emphasis, "he's probably crazy."

That got her attention. She nodded, but not before saying, "Technically we don't know if Loki's a 'he' or something else."

"It's just easier. We can discuss the scientific merits of pronouns later."

Both glanced one last time at the boulders in front of them, then turned to leave.

Dwell panted a few yards away, leaning forward with his hands on his knees. Gendrick was relieved to see the rifle slung askew over his shoulder. "Guys!" He was speaking a little too loudly. "We have – shoot, hold on. I'm out of breath."

Armed or not, Gendrick did not want to linger. Too many rocks and hidey holes out here. They'd have been better off in the open with the cattle. He scanned the boulders again. Nothing moved. The morning breeze carried nothing but the usual, thin air tinged with dust.

Something caught his eye as he began to look away. His goal was to lay a hand on Dwell's shoulder and turn him back towards the compound. He could catch his breath on the way home. But that motion, a dark change in the landscape at the edge of his vision froze him in place.

A long, black limb stretched over the top of the closest boulder, then another. Both were attached to something far larger that pulled itself over the top. Or tried to. The Locust's body slid sideways, almost lodging between the stone and the one beside it. Its twisted frame turned, found purchase in the sand between them. Like a monstrous spider, more appendages rose from behind and found footing on the rock.

Gendrick stepped backwards, pulling Miyoko with him.

Dwell whispered, "Oh, boy."

The creature slowly – always slowly, as if thinking these stealthy movements were going unnoticed by the humans watching it – landed on the ground in front of them. The long scorpion-like tail rose up for a moment then curled back to the ground. A couple of its right limbs began to reach out. Both were twisted oddly. With a chirp the creature pulled them back. *Damaged*, Gendrick thought. That was the sound of pain.

Loki moved sideways a half step, leaning heavily on its left limbs. It moved in slow motion into the clearing between them. The four dragonfly wings opened, prompting Dwell to step around the others and raise his weapon.

The Locust stopped, then continued moving closer in slow, deliberate movements. Gendrick and Miyoko took another step back while the security man remained motionless, rifle aimed at the center of the black mass. Gendrick was grateful for this sudden line of defense. Dwell crouched in a defensive posture. He no longer looked tired.

Loki stopped less than a meter and a half away, raising its head to consider them. Its mandibles opened with a soft hiss. A warning, or simple growl of hatred. Two black eyes scanned them, lingering longest on Dwell.

"Oh, he remembers me," he said, any levity in his voice dulled by a new timber – fear, or a readiness to fight.

"Easy," Gendrick whispered, straightening his posture. In response the Locust rose up, higher than any of them by a head. The priest raised one hand, palm open, towards it.

Miyoko whispered, "Don't shoot unless it makes a move. For all we know it's the last one left alive."

"I really like you, Mi," Dwell said over his shoulder. "But you have to understand we can't walk backwards all the way to the compound. He's itching to attack."

Loki opened its four-sectioned mandibles again and hissed with a protracted, loud breath. All of it directed at Dwell. *Posturing*, mused Gendrick. In the corner of his eye he noticed the xenologist holding forth her Ep, recording everything. With no option of retreat, she was defaulting to what she always did – study and record.

He was struck with the realization that any "conversation" that might be happening here would remain guesswork unless linguists found a way to translate. Should he try to communicate, do his *own* job as a representative of the Church? It may be the last of its kind, but that was only an assumption. How many more were out there, beyond the next Hole, or the next?

This was not the time to start writing *Vast Array* in his head. Gendrick tried to focus.

Dwell took a slow step backwards, perhaps testing the waters for the ill-advised backwards retreat. Loki did not move. Instead it crouched, ever so slightly, on its lower limbs. The head turned toward Miyoko and hissed. Inside the mouth was more hard plating, all of it pointed, jagged in places, moving and clicking against itself. Its rendition of teeth, the plates were used to quickly rend and tear prey. Efficiency was not needed. Any loose pieces were gathered up by another in the swarm. Everything was devoured in time.

Gendrick shook his head, worried any sudden motion might be misinterpreted but needing to do something physical to clear his thoughts.

"We aren't a threat," he found himself saying, raising his arms before him as if Loki had a rifle aimed at *them*. In a way it did: the long, curled tail behind it seemed menacing enough in its own right. "Please let us go. There doesn't have to be any violence."

"You don't seriously think it understands that, Father," muttered Dwell.

"No, not really. But it's worth a try."

Loki ignored him. Its black gaze lingered again on Dwell. No hiss this time. The creature only breathed out, long and slow as if it had held its breath for too long. As it did, it lowered more, folding its limbs beneath itself. The sound of exhalation continued as the hard black body dropped to the ground, legs bending at multiple joints. It looked like it was deflating.

Miyoko whispered, "What's happening? What's it doing?"

The head lowered, still turned towards Dwell but angled awkwardly, too heavy for the short neck. Finally, it stopped, a jumble of angles and hard black points sitting on the ground. A thick membrane slid across the eyes, almost closing.

Then nothing. No motion, no hiss or sound of breathing at all.

The three stood before it for a full minute, waiting, their focus only on the monster crouched motionless before them. Afraid to move.

"Is it asleep?" Gendrick asked, not knowing what else to say. It looked dead.

Maybe it was.

Still, no one moved. Another minute. In the back of his mind Gendrick thought he heard approaching footsteps. He dared not look, and prayed if they *were* steps, they were human.

After this extended silence, without the slightest twitch from the Locust, Dwell was the next to speak, and that was the moment Loki had been waiting for.

65 – Peyton, *Reach,* 2J3P Orbit

She'd been awake for a long time (she was pretty sure it was a long time) before Peyton finally opened her eyes. She wasn't dead. That much she'd gathered from the snippets of conversation floating above her earlier in the day. There'd also been other, scattered moments of consciousness when her brain rose almost to waking, only to fall back into oblivion.

Now, though, it was time. Whatever happened while she was out, she would have to deal with it. Time for sleep was done. God had decided she could stay around a little longer. Might as well see what He had planned.

She looked to her right. Benny Solomon's head was resting sideways on the mattress, using his folded arms as a pillow. His hair was longer, unkempt, and from what she could see of his face it was practically all beard. He was asleep.

"Poor guy," she said, not sure if her voice made any noise other than a thin whisper. She tried to raise her right hand. It moved a little. *I'm so weak*, she thought. Atrophied muscles. Her skin was a frightening gray color. It looked odd, as if the melanin had leeched out of her. Peyton blinked, tried to focus on the arm, willed it to move. The hand flexed. Two tubes ran from just below her knuckles, the area around them puffed and irritated. They'd had trouble finding a vein, no doubt. That was going to hurt later. Three thin wires ran from the wrist to the elbow, disappearing up the short sleeve of her gown. Electrostimulus. Shocking the muscles out of entropy. Only an assumption, but it made sense.

The hand flexed again, this time into a loose fist, then re-opened. She could lift the arm at the elbow, which itself seemed rooted to the mattress. It was enough to rotate it sideways and let the hand drop into Benny's tangled mess of hair.

He snorted once, woken by the sudden contact, then fell back asleep.

How long . . . she began to wonder, then stopped. *All in good time.* Her friend looked exhausted on his folded arms, but he'd want to know she was awake.

Someone came into the room, perhaps alerted to her movements. For the moment she ignored them. Peyton loosely grabbed a handful of Benny's hair and yanked.

He snorted again and straightened, pulling away and sitting upright in his chair. Her hand fell to the bed. On second glance, her skin was darker than she'd first thought. Maybe she just needed to get some blood moving through the muscles.

She was starting to fall back into sleep, even this small act of grabbing Benny's hair exhausted her.

Benny looked down, blinked and rubbed the sleep from his eyes.

"Hey," Peyton said, still not hearing her voice but hoping he could see her lips move. Her throat was so dry.

"Pey?" His stunned expression was wiped clear by the widest and saddest smile she'd ever seen on anyone's face. He said again, "Pey?"

She licked her lips, tongue dry like paper. "I'm OK," she tried to say. "Thirsty."

"Did you say you were thirsty?" He looked up, his entire body shaking in the seat. "She's thirsty, do we have . .

." Vague sound of another voice from the opposite side of the bed. Peyton considered turning her head to look, but it was too heavy. An arm appeared in front of her, handing a small plastic container with a long tube. Travel cup, the kind they all used around the ship. Spill-proof in case gravity cut out. Did she have the strength to pull whatever was inside it through the straw?

Benny held it to her lips. She closed her mouth, drew in the barest splash of water. Her eyes rolled back in her head from the joy of its sensation. She was a dry pile of sticks, experiencing moisture for the first time. She drew in another splash, trying to control her body which screamed for more, assuming too much too soon . . .

She swallowed, relishing it running down her throat, imagining her body a brittle, dormant plant coming back to life under new rain.

Then she was asleep again.

66 – Loki, 2J3P

It recognized the sight and smell of the creature, and the weapon raised before it. This one had the ability to inflict pain and death from the end of that extended claw. No matter. Every prey had a weakness and was susceptible to distraction. Loki remembered a story told long ago, a prey with long, armored claws which dismembered many from its protected perch on a craggy outcrop of stone. The story told of the one in the Swarm who stood to the side, waiting as others tried to take this raging prey for themselves only to be repelled again and again. The one telling the story had crept close to the creature, but never enough to be an immediate threat. It then had done exactly as Loki did now, sat motionless in a submissive pose, close to the prey but unmoving, without threat. When others moved on to easier prey, or perched on the nearby hillside to wait and plan, the creature turned to face the one which remained. The latter did not attack. In fact, it did nothing.

Nothing, except press the limb furthest from sight into the ground, bending the leg, preparing to leap. Its lack of motion confused the other creature. Had it injured its attacker, even killed it?

Loki did nothing, now. It curled itself into a common submissive pose, guessing none of these creatures understood the gesture but nevertheless relying on the fact that submission was a common trait among all life forms, even these.

It pressed its lower left limb hard against the ground, bent at both joints. Loki focused on two things only: not exposing the tension in that limb, and the prey before it. This one, who had taken the life of the Mate. The one whom Loki had been trying unsuccessfully to tear open the shell of the invaders' warren to destroy.

Now, the creature had come before it of its own free will.

Loki could die satisfied. The thing standing before it, and death itself, were all it truly had left to live for.

It closed its eyes, staring at the prey through narrow slits.

Waiting.

Tensing.

It adjusted the leg a fractional amount to optimize the leap when the time came. In contrast, the tail was draped loosely across the ground beside it. Loki did not need strength there, only flexibility and momentum. The leg would provide the latter.

When it was time.

It did not breathe. Would breathe no more until it either fell into unconsciousness or had its final, glorious kill.

One of the others spoke, its voice soft, tentative. They appeared unthreatened by the pose. That was good.

Waiting.

Watching.

Then the prey spoke. As it did the extended weapon shifted just enough from its aim towards Loki's face.

That would be enough.

The Locust shot forward with a speed none of the others anticipated. They *should* have, though the limbs on Loki's more visible right side were too damaged to be used for anything but balance. As it sprang forward so did the tail. One bent and cracked middle limb knocked the prey's weapon aside even as it fired and shattered Loki's uppermost left arm. Every other appendage grabbed the other's body at the same instant the tail slammed into – then through – its belly. Loki continued forward, opening its mandibles wide, covering the alien's head. Before it could close its jaws and tear the head free, something slammed into its side, like a hundred burning boulders collapsing on top of it. No pain. It felt nothing at all, in fact, but knew it had just been torn apart by another weapon. As it fell sideways it tried to close its mouth over the other's head, but its body did not respond. No feeling, no sensation anywhere. The tail remained thrust through the prey's body, causing both of them to collapse sideways onto the dirt in front of the boulders.

It tried again to bite down. Nothing worked.

Through half-closed lids, Loki watched helplessly as the other creature which had been there when the Mate was killed stepped closer and aimed its weapon. The tip exploded in light and sound. Then Loki was gone forever.

67 – Michael Broeger, 2J3P

Dwell was screaming, his voice strained. Broeger worked on the dead Locust's jaws, which had clamped around his friend's head. If he'd fired his rifle into the bugger's midsection a second later, Dwell would have no head to scream with.

"Dwell," he said, "I know it's bad but shut up for a second."

Thankful for the thick work gloves hooked onto his belt, the large man slid them on before prying two sections of the four-part mouth apart with a grating *crack*. Dwell was sobbing, now.

He pulled apart the rest of the thing's mouth and grabbed the back of Dwell's head. It was wet, but the Locust definitely had not bitten down before its brain caught up to the fact that the rest of its body had been shredded. Small miracles.

The tail, however, was completely through Dwell's lower midsection, had probably torn through the intestine. Michael was not a medical expert, but the fact that his partner was still alive must be a good sign. *No major organs pierced. Right? Right?*

"Mike," a voice said through his earpiece. "Do *not* pull that thing out of him. Whatever you do, do not touch it or remove it. Just try to stem the bleeding. We're almost there. The *Reach* has been notified and is getting a team of their own together."

Michael pulled his shirt over his head. The Locust's shattered body did not move, but when it had fallen it took Dwell with him, widening the gash in his gut. Blood poured out – not spraying, though. Another good sign? He put his shirt around the gash, wishing he had something to cut the jagged tail from the Locust's body so he could pull Dwell away from it.

No. Focus on what you can *do. And do it calmly. Do not move him. Just do what you're told.*

Father Hellerton knelt beside them. He'd removed his outer robes and handed them to Michael while lowering Dwell's head against his legs. Michael slowly worked the material around the wound. Mostly, they tried to keep Dwell from thrashing about too badly.

"Miyoko, talk to him," he said. "I don't care what you say but keep him focused on you. He likes you, you know."

He would have laughed at the wide-eyed look of anger on Dwell's otherwise anguished face, if his hands weren't knuckle deep in the man's blood. Miyoko spoke, thanked him for coming to her rescue, teased him for playing the knight, *blah, blah, blah*. Michael let her voice lull his own panic. Dwell's attention was riveted on her face. A sudden calm fell over him.

Michael said, "Ok, maybe that wasn't a good idea. He's getting too moon-eyed for my liking."

"He's calming down."

"Too much, though. It's scaring me."

"I'm still here, guys," Dwell whispered. This time Michael did laugh.

"Med team's almost here," Miyoko said, looking beyond the priest's shoulder.

Motion and footsteps around them on the soft ground. Michael kept his shirt and the priest's robes wrapped around the alien's tail at the entry wound. He looked into

Dwell's face. The man looked back up at him from Hellerton's lap. He was not breathing well, but calmed a little when their eyes met. Dwell whispered, "Hang in there, buddy."

Michael almost said that was *his* line, but didn't. Just like Dwell to try and comfort someone else right now.

His partner added, "He got me back. Stupid bug knew who I was."

"Dwell, please shut up. You've got a tail in your belly."

His partner tried to laugh, then his eyes rolled up into his head. Someone grabbed Michael's shoulders and pulled him away, leaving his friend in the care of the small medical team swarming around them.

68 – Peyton, *Reach*

Drinking something, anything, other than stale recycled water had not yet lost its wonder since she'd woken. She sipped her citrus drink the old fashioned way, over the lip of an open cup (a luxury she had feared might never be experienced again), and tried not to sigh in contentment each time. Maybe heaven was an eternity of slow sips of warm rum from thick, crystal glasses. Rum, because her heaven would be warm with sun and beaches. She'd been to the ocean, once, digging into the sandy shore of Eden's massive Blue Lake with her sister's family before leaving for the *Washington*. She enjoyed that, a lot.

She was still cold, every day growing more certain she'd never get completely warm again. Seeme Kinzer, the *Reach*'s senior medical officer, promised this would pass, eventually. He would not tell her his definition of *eventually*.

"In time," he'd offered. More than once.

She put the requisite cover on the cup then set it down on the table, before curling her body deeper into the long sweater.

"Still cold," Ken said as a statement. He sat across from her, drinking coffee in the ship's small Mess room. This was Peyton's first chance to leave her room outside of mandatory daily walks along the ring to get her muscles back into shape. Even this small bit of exercise sent frozen jags of pain through her legs and back, as if her blood and marrow had not quite thawed. Thankfully, the *Reach* was smaller than the *Washington*, so her laps up and down the corridor were short. Plus, the smaller ring made for slightly lower gravity. The better to walk with a busted frame.

"Being frozen like an ice cream pop will do that," she said, lifting the cover enough to welcome another sip of juice down her throat. As much as she relished the sensation, drinking anything cold still hurt a little. "In time, Seeme says. *In time*. Still thawing."

"Have more coffee."

She'd had only one cup this morning, decaffeinated but glorious. Its heat spread through every limb and she forced herself not to gulp. "Later, I promise." She raised her cup. "But I also promised to drink *this* before having a second. Need to take my vitamins like a good girl."

Ken reached out and tapped his cup lightly against hers. "To Pey's slow melting."

"Amen."

She drank the rest down.

Benny was asleep back on the *Washington*. When he wasn't on-shift, or sleeping, he was usually with her. Since the ship wasn't doing much except orbiting Toojay, Ken allowed him regular use of a shuttle pod. By now, Peyton would have begun to wonder if Benny's attention was more than simple, relieved friendship. But her conversation with Zhou Lihua two days ago put to rest any concern over the man's attention. Seemed the crisis had brought he and Li together, and rather than run from whatever might be developing, now that things had settled they were pursuing it. Good for them.

She loved Benny, but not in that way. Li always had an eye for the guy, though Peyton doubted others onboard knew it.

"So, Most High Commander, what news do you bring me this fine morning?"

Ken's visit had been the impetus to get out of bed earlier than usual. He'd walked with her, slowly, up and down the hall three times before finally taking a detour to the Mess. He hadn't given a reason for his visit, but she assumed from his fidgeting and formal air it was at least *partially* business-related. His brief moment of unprofessionalism had come on his first visit to her bedside after she'd woken three days ago. Then, he'd looked tired. If there were a few new grey hairs in his beard, she wouldn't have been surprised. He'd opened his mouth to say something that first morning, but that was as far as his composure held. His expression pulled in on itself, as if in pain, then the tears poured out. The big man sobbed like a baby, leaning over her bed as he held her in a loose, careful embrace. He muttered a few things, most of which Peyton could not understand, but their gist was apparent. She was alive; he'd done everything he could to help her, but it was next to nothing; he missed Cannon already – at least, she thought he'd mentioned Cannon. Her friend's name was spoken very little since she'd woken. Peyton had tried to return Ken's embrace, but only managed one arm raised and draped over a shoulder. Her fingers were too weak to do much but drum along his shirt. If she hadn't been so dehydrated, she would have cried, too. Of all of the people onboard, his reaction to her awakening had been the most outward, even beating Benny's by a few tears.

Ken's self-control fell that one time, but now, though still friendly, his demeanor was serious.

"Well, I mentioned the *Abad* was heading back to the Hole, to resume study of 33P."

She nodded. "He hasn't come up with a better name, yet?"

"Nope. The guy's brilliant, but lacks artistic imagination. His crew will come up with something themselves, I hope. They'll pass through the Hole this afternoon. Should be in orbit tomorrow, or the next day. Radish makes them drive slow."

She laughed. It felt good. She'd been laughing a lot lately. More and more, her good humor didn't suddenly dampen into a choking sorrow at the memory of Cannon. Even in *those* moments the misery was not as intense as she'd expected now that she was free.

Maybe she'd had time to mourn while trapped in the belly of the whale. Maybe *most* of them had. His body was down on Toojay. Ken had not requested it be brought back to the ship. Most of it was still intact, though his head had burst apart from the derelict's scan, as well as every blood vessel in his body. He would be buried, eventually, on Eden. His wife would have to wait a while for that final bit of closure, since there had been two autopsies on his body already, scientists from practically every branch except geology wanting to understand what happened to him, to try to work out the alien's scanning technology.

In the meantime, Leanne White was on a transport, coming to Toojay to claim his remains and find what closure she could. Peyton spoke to her daily, sometimes twice a day, and had done more crying and consoling with her than anyone. As much as she *could* console. Mostly, she listened, and answered Leanne's questions. That seemed to be enough.

Gendrick promised to hold a memorial service for him and the others who died these past few weeks, but not until Leanne arrived and Peyton was well enough to attend. Until then, there was plenty to do. People were studying what remained of the alien ship and the Locusts, including the remnants salvaged around 2J5P before its gravity pulled everything into oblivion.

And, of course, the resumed study of the people on

3J3P. Human, or human-*ish*. This was not public knowledge, yet, but Ken had given her a quick summary with the promise she not mention any of it to Gendrick unless she was giving her confession.

"Been looking at what you forwarded me from the *Abad*. Surprisingly little more. Are they holding out on us?"

Ken smiled. "I'm sure they are. They're entitled, but Radish thinks the probes are scaring the boogers out of the natives so he's pulled them back, reverting to high elevation observation for the time being."

Peyton toyed with her empty cup, not motivated yet to get up and grab her second coffee. "The Locusts had been there, once upon a time?"

He nodded. "Seems that way. But that's not yet a definite fact. If they were, it hasn't been for a while. The folks down there are the survivors, or the survivors' descendants." Ken's face fell a little, eyes looking away at something she couldn't see. He continued, "I try to imagine if the swarm made it to Eden. I imagine the people on 33P still have nightmares about what happened. Or at the very least, some scary stories passed down the generations."

"Winged boogeymen."

There was a light knock on the mess hall door behind her. Ken looked up. "Ah. You have a new visitor. Nice to see you again, Father."

Peyton's shoulders tensed. She knew he was coming. He'd told her last night as he was throwing some things into a bag for his trip into orbit. Still, it would be the first time she'd seen him in person for . . . how long? Twelve years?

She got up slowly from her seat, then walked toward her old friend's waiting arms.

69 – Doneele, 2J3P

Blood still coated her hands and arms. The stains reached past her elbows, lost under the sleeves of the tattered blue jumpsuit. None of it she could see. They'd cleaned her up on that first night, or more pointedly shoved her towards the sink and forced her to clean herself of Arun's blood as best she could. It was still there, however, mingling with that of her dead husband.

No one had come to visit, not since that single, awkward moment with Hellerton himself. Even the twice-daily meals the security men delivered had trickled to a single, silent deposit of stale rations. She imagined a decision was made not to waste fresh bread or produce on the bloody woman in Cell One. The rations she received were normally reserved for lean days towards the approach of new supply transports. Her transport must be closer now, that dot on the map which had slowly, painfully crawled toward Toojay and which she had so long obsessed over from her room.

She had no way of watching its progress now. No Ep, no mounted screen on the walls around her. System had turned its back on her as well. As much as God had done.

No, *she'd* turned her back on *Him* long ago. She'd danced with the demons which clawed their way into her mind and twirled her far away from His offered love. Another solar system, light years away from Eden and Earth. She should have been out of hell's reach. She should have been safe. Demons did not fly in ships across the stars. Their homes were buried in the core of the earth, chained and bound in darkness. She was too far away to be pulled down to their level of madness.

But there were worlds beyond these, not simply beyond the next Hole or the next, but other worlds unseen by the living. They were *elsewhere*. Invisible, unknowable but, apparently, always in reach of her race. She could run, *had* run, pulling Zechariah along with her. The distance was never enough.

Father Gendrick should use *that* in his ridiculous writings. Maybe *she* should write it down some day, tell the Prelate before he washed his hands of her fate and cast Doneele into the pit with the countless others who'd fallen as far as she. Prison was waiting back on Eden, or Earth itself. There would be no protection. No secret. Everyone knew. If there was consolation in any of this, the Church would have to answer for its secrecy. Vernaine McCarthy had kept silent about her confession, even tried to private her off-world with minimal ripples in the space between.

God had other plans.

Doneele rose slowly from the floor in the middle of the cell, her prayers long degraded to these long musings on her fate. Speaking to God, begging for forgiveness had long dried up and drifted into the corners of the room to be swept away by the ventilation's automated vacuum systems. Her prayers were relegated as waste along with her dead skin cells and body stink.

She crawled to the wall beside the door and used it as leverage to stand. When she did, muscles stretched and twisted painfully. Exercise. *Do something*, she told herself more than once. To what end? No one would help her nor even let her walk the halls once a day. She was fortunate they still *fed* her. She'd slaughtered a well-loved member of the team. Tried to kill their priest – obviously unsuccessfully since Hellerton had visited her after he *should* have been eaten by the Locusts. There'd been a few moments of distraction, drama outside her door since then. One of the guards had been conspicuously absent the past few days. Only Michael Broeger passed by her window, rarely looking in. From snippets of conversation in the hallway, Dwell had been hurt or was very sick. Something. This, ascertained only from overhearing occasional questions from random visitors asking after him. Not enough details for her to understand what was going on. Broeger's answers invariably followed the line of, *It's not looking good.*

Somehow, it was probably her fault.

Everything was her fault.

She wandered into the corner, sat on the exposed toilet to pee. Doneele had long forsaken embarrassment at having to do her business in full view of whoever wandered by. Mostly because no one ever did.

The transport should have arrived by now, shouldn't it? If nothing else, it would offer a change of scenery. A new cell to stare at and learn its details. Maybe they'd let her shower, give her a new set of clothes. There had to be a rule, somewhere, in the Law requiring these basic rights.

Very little pee this time. She wasn't drinking enough. They weren't giving her enough *to* drink. They wanted her dead. Dead and gone. A wart on their face needing to be scraped away and forgotten.

She remained on the toilet long after she was finished, having nothing else to do. Why did they save her? Why couldn't they let her die?

That's not what they do. Life was precious to most people. Even the life of a killer. Isn't that the way of the Church? Grace for all. Every soul needed the most time possible to reconnect with God and repent.

She could repent, turn from the path she'd walked for so long and stop listening to the voices whispering from those other worlds. Accept the gift Jesus' death represented, still offered to her even now. Forgiveness. Relationship.

All that crap.

In her case, that's what it was. She could never shut out the voices. Oh, she could pretend, like she'd done for a long time. Maybe even give in and try the medicines Zechariah had so often suggested. Pretend to turn back, walk away, recommit her life to the Creator of the universe. But it would be a lie. She would still listen to the voices and feed the images they drew in her mind and nurture the fear they cultivated. Mostly the fear, the panic of every world she ever stood upon falling apart between her fingers . . .

Everything was choice. Even deciding never to choose. Only stagnate. Die and be sucked from the corners of her cell with her prayers and dead skin.

She sat on the toilet and thought these things. Then, for a while, stopped thinking. Perhaps she fell asleep. The single meal, delivered this morning through a slot in the bottom of the door, remained untouched. One meal, waiting for her, keeping her alive enough to wake up the next day, and do it all again. Until the ship came and carried her back to the altar of humanity, upon which she would be expected to fall and beg forgiveness, or be sacrificed. If she would not ask it from God, asking it of Man was out of the question.

70 – Gendrick, *Reach*

"They would have come and taken her out long before now, but travel restrictions through the Hole had only been lifted yesterday. Too much debris. Not to mention the three Naval ships running around the area scooping up what was left of everything. The transport's on its way, now. She'll be gone or, at least off Toojay, sometime tomorrow."

"Have you seen her?"

She held his hand as they walked down the corridor. Like most ships, the main living section of the *Reach* was a constantly-rotating ring. The hall curved sharply ahead of them before disappearing above the ceiling. It made Gendrick dizzy. He'd noticed others on board walking with downcast eyes, never looking too far in front of them. He'd starting doing this himself. It helped.

"Once," he said in reply, giving her hand a squeeze. Their physical connection was not one of reunited lovers, but close friends long apart and finally come together again. She'd held his hand a lot when they were young. It felt different now. Time and experience tempered and strengthened this touch. Hers, especially. Gendrick was surprised as they began walking ('Doctors orders,' she'd explained) when her fingers immediately found his. Captain Burlov had excused himself, leaving them some privacy.

The feel of her hand in his was a marvel. He'd missed her, often, but not as much as he might have admitted to himself. When her cool hand slid into his, fingers loosely interlocked, he understood. In the age of vast distances, instant communication, touch was still the most powerful experience between two people.

When she did not reply, he continued, "We talked, a little. I think she actually admitted to killing her husband the same way she tried to off me."

Pey laughed and leaned into him for a moment. "*Off* you. That's funny."

"Only *you* would think that's funny," he said, smiling, then took in a breath. "But that was it. Too much other stuff going on that had higher priority than any return visit, even if that meant only shouting through the glass, 'Nyah, nyah, you missed me,' or some such nonsense."

Peyton's Ep beeped once. She pulled it from her bathrobe's pocket and glanced quickly, smiling as she tucked it away. "Benny, checking in on me. I'll reply later."

A twinge of jealousy ran through him, but Gendrick simply acknowledged it and let it go. He had nothing to be jealous of. They had two different lives, which had simply come crashing together lately. Simple enough. They weren't about to start anything at this juncture.

Their steps slowed along the corridor. Then they stopped. "They're not letting me back aboard the *Washington* just yet." She nodded towards the Med door. "Come inside. I'll show you my etchings."

He smiled, followed her into a stark white lab. Uncluttered, their contents locked away in cabinets faced with clear plastic windows. Everything onboard battened down. Any moment they may have to stop the ship's spin, and as such its gravity. On a medical transport some pretty bad things could start floating around.

Pey was moving slower. Tired. The pallor of her skin was much healthier than the first time he'd seen her laying in a near-coma on this bed. Her grey complexion was gone. His old friend was as dark and beautiful as he remembered. Except her hair. She pulled herself onto the mattress.

"I assume this is permanent," he said, running one finger across her close-cut curls. Like him, the once-black hair, short as it was, was peppered in grey. *More* than peppered, in her case. At least half was streaked along the top and back. "Unless this was a deliberate coloring style. Some new fashion I missed."

She smiled, albeit sadly, and ran the palm of her left hand along her scalp. "Nope. My time as Frozen Girl apparently did a number on the follicles. It's been getting lighter by the day. I'll look like Gram before the week's out."

He sat on the bed beside her and leaned in, kissed her forehead. "You'll never look like Gram, trust me."

Pey wrapped both of her arms around his left and pulled herself close, leaned her head against his shoulder. "How long are you here for?"

He tilted his head until one cheek rested on the top of her head. "Shuttle's heading back in three hours. I'm supposed to see Doneele off when the transport arrives and security comes to get her."

"Well," she said, then let loose a long, silent yawn, "you'll have your chance to yell at her then."

He nodded, relishing the feel of her bristly curls on his cheek. "More than that." He paused, swallowed, afraid to say the next thing because then it would become real. "They let me know that Dwell died this morning."

"He's the one who got attacked by the Locust?" The news about Dwell had already spread. News always did, and Toojay had been producing more than its share lately.

"Yes. It was touch and go for a while, really bad sepsis, but not anything they couldn't handle in the end.

Thankfully no organs, and the med team managed to stabilize him and things looked promising. But a weird infection set in. Some kind of bacteria on Loki's skin, maybe."

Pey tried to stifle a yawn but failed, then leaned away, laid on her side on the bed. Gendrick stood and pulled up her feet then made her scurry under the tightly-made sheets. She said, "It's not your fault, you know."

He did know that, but also knew that Arun and Dwell had both died trying to save him. "Miyoko, the xenologist, is taking this pretty hard. She and Dwell were close. And she'd already lost one friend."

"The man Mother Doneele killed." Another question posed as a statement, though partially mumbled against the pillow.

"Yea." He tucked the thin sheet up to her chin. She still wore her robe but it looked comfortable enough. "Sleep," he said.

She nodded, muttered, "Come see me again before you leave." Her eyes were already closed. He said he would, and leaned down to kiss her on the cheek. She made a happy noise in her throat when he did, but she'd fallen asleep by the time he'd straightened.

She was still sleeping two hours later when Gendrick looked in on her. He didn't wake her.

71 – Gendrick and Peyton, 2J3P

The day was dry and warm. There'd been little wind to whip up the loose sand in the clearing, where an adhoc staging had been rigged by the maintenance crew using plastic crates. Because the deceased Toojay personnel had been stationed in the southern compound, the memorial service was held there. The platform didn't need to be big, only enough to raise any speaker above those sitting in chairs carried outside from the Union and Mess hall. Anyone wanting to sit carried their own.

Dozens of scientists and crew from the north and eastern stations arrived earlier in the morning. A reunion of sorts, everyone bringing food and extra chairs from their locations to supplement what was available here.

The *Washington* had very little in the way of portable furniture, but Ken Burlov and his people brought a few meals thrown together the night before from their newly-restocked shelves. All but four of their crew had come, those absent watching a live feed of the ceremony.

No caskets were displayed. Arun Renault had revised his will eighteen months earlier, stipulating upon his death that he should be buried on Toojay – providing it posed no risk of contamination to existing, or future, research. There *had* been such a restriction on the books, but in light of his request ISO leadership lifted it to allow a square of land east of each compound for such a purpose. His body would be interred tomorrow, after today's memorial. This morning, his body remained preserved in storage.

Cannon White's body had already been loaded onboard the *Horizon*. The transport arrived two days ago with his wife Leanne. He would be buried and mourned again after his return to Eden.

Dwell would also return home, someday, stopping at Eden long enough to be loaded onto the first available Earth-bound ship for burial in the cemetery of his parents and sister. For now his body was in official quarantine in a hastily-constructed annex off the Medical wing. The first of the autopsies would commence later today. Three high-level medical personnel from Eden had boarded the *Horizon* last minute, in order to decide if Dwell's fatal infection posed risk of contamination outside of Toojay.

Mother Doneele O'Coin was already in custody onboard the *Horizon*. Security had been the first to disembark the shuttle and went directly to her wing. Once the remaining inbound passengers had left, Doneele was ferried through a side exit and aboard the ship.

Gendrick *had* planned to talk with her one final time. When he'd arrived at the security wing, only fifteen minutes after System informed him of security's arrival, she was gone. He returned to his room and watched the recorded footage of an emaciated and pale woman walking slowly between two burly men in reinforced black combat gear. Had they expected a struggle? If not from her, maybe the community? Gendrick audibly gasped when he'd seen her physical state.

He hadn't checked on her, nor ever inquired of System if he might be allowed a glimpse of the video feed from her cell. Anything to show he had some concern for the woman. She was sick. That was an obvious answer to any weak protests he might make. Now he could add frail, even sickly, to her adjectives.

She had attacked him. Nearly killed him. But Doneele was a part of his congregation, and a peer.

What kind of a priest had *he* become?

He'd left the Order for a woman, then ran to the end of civilization because that same woman subsequently broke his heart. He recently reunited with an old girlfriend. In the meantime, he turned his back, rather than his other cheek, on someone who was in need of serious, loving attention. Nothing he'd done had been motivated by holy intentions.

Even so, he now stepped onto the makeshift podium to speak to a hundred-plus people mourning the loss of their friends. He would beat himself up more later. Right now, he had a job to do.

*   *   *

"Thank you all for coming."

Peyton thought Gendrick looked a little uncomfortable up there. When she'd asked him this morning how he was feeling, he'd only shook his head and said, 'Tired.' There was more, of course, not the least of which was the murderous Mother Doneele. He'd talk about it when he was ready.

As she watched him speak about the victims of the sudden breakdown in the universe's calm these past few weeks (his words), she wondered if they could ever be more than friends again. Everything about her life insisted she could never love him in that way. Not outwardly. She had too many other plans, other directions in which to move. Each time they talked, however, she knew it was possible even under such impossible circumstances. The single thread of truth running through her was that it *would* be nice to settle down and marry her best friend.

But that was not supposed to happen.

Too many worlds for her to find and conquer. For Gendrick, too many souls in need of a shepherd. They had found each other again after all these years and that was enough. And they were together now, until the *Washington* left, hopefully with her. No reason it shouldn't. She was fine. Mostly.

Gendrick was fine, too, and still would be when she was gone. Whatever time they could squeeze in together, they would. Maybe he'd keep discovering ways to follow her around the galaxy (or galaxies, funny how no one really knew where any of these planetary systems were).

She almost smiled. Gendrick mentioned Cannon, and her expression flattened. The look came too easily these days. A neutral stare. No longer miserable, but hard to enjoy being happy for too long.

"He died," Gendrick said, looking directly at her, "doing what he loved to do, and with people he loved doing it with." He looked away at the rest of the adhoc congregation and shrugged. His robes drifted as a breeze found its way around the compound's walls. "I know, the expression sounds trite, but I've spent the last couple of weeks speaking with some of the *Washington* crew and more recently Cannon's amazing wife Leanne." He looked down at Can's wife sitting beside her. He wore such a warm, loving expression Pey almost questioned if she really wanted to leave when the *Washington* broke orbit. *Almost.*

Leanne White lowered her head and wrapped an arm around Peyton's, leaning in. It was one of many such affectations Leanne made towards her since landing. Peyton had gotten permission from Ken, who was now sitting stoically on her right, to meet Can's wife when she stepped off the shuttle and to stay with her until she left.

Peyton still wondered what the woman truly thought of her. Was there jealousy? Leanne knew how close they'd been, and *should* know they had never pushed the envelope of their friendship. But a wife's protectiveness had sharp edges. At least, Peyton assumed so. She'd never had a chance to see for herself and at the rate she was going, she may never.

In truth, nothing felt uncomfortable between them. Even when Leanne made Peyton tell her, in person, everything she remembered of how he died, Peyton simply told her. No hesitation. The woman needed to know, needed to be *there* with him in those last moments, regardless of the fact that all of humankind had watched the horror unfold in real time.

Now, sitting in her chair not listening to Gendrick, feeling Leanne's slight weight against her, Peyton thought she finally understood their connection. She'd been the closest person to her husband on their missions. Leanne had not been able to physically touch Can for months. Now, she never would. Peyton had become his surrogate. Leanne needed to cling to and cry against someone, a hand to hold, an arm to lean on while she grappled with the reality that he was truly, forever gone.

Gendrick was talking about the security guard now. Someone behind her, a man from the timber of his voice, began crying. Peyton did not look. He had a right to privacy. So little of that was available today.

Instead, she watched her old friend do what he did so well, and let herself love him more than ever. She would miss him when she left. Either they would write, or repeat history and drift apart again. The latter was a choice she would not make. But distance does funny things to people.

She raised her free hand and laid it over Leanne's, which was still wrapped around her arm. She gave it a squeeze, then did her best to stop thinking and listen.

*   *   *

Six days later the *Horizon* broke orbit, carrying Mother Doneele, Leanne White and the body of her late husband back to Eden. Cannon would be buried as a hero. A martyr for the grand expanse of mankind across the stars.

That was how one news commentator put it. Gendrick thought it was a bit much, even if it was true. Peyton thought it was sweet. Leanne had stayed glued to Peyton's side for her too few days here. She'd been given a tour of the *Washington*, and there they'd remained for the majority of her stay. She saw what Cannon saw, smelled the scent of his room, ate meals in the Mess hall. Benny Solomon had taken her out for a short excursion in one of the pods. Always, Peyton was by her side, wanting to do what she could for her friend's widow, to offer whatever closure she could. Leanne was usually silent, taking it all in, knowing these moments were fleeting and soon to pass away.

Of course, the woman wasn't blind. More than once she tried to send Peyton away to spend time with Gendrick. Peyton agreed only in allowing herself an hour here and there to talk over the com. When they were on Toojay, however, Gendrick was always with them.

Yesterday Leanne said goodbye and offered too many thank-you's, to both of them, before pulling herself from a final embrace and walking down the well-worn path towards the landing platform.

Only then, finally, did Gendrick and Peyton take a step towards each other, hooking their arms together. Side by side they watched Leanne pull her travel case towards the waiting shuttle. They stood like that a few minutes after the shuttle was no more than a distant dot above them.

Then they walked back to the compound, talking quietly, got some dinner, always touching each other in some way. They eventually found their way to his room.

This, then, was their final opportunity to rekindle the intimacy they'd shared during that final year of high school, before each moved on to separate lives.

They did not take advantage of it. Crossing that line would imply something permanent. As much as both yearned for a more physical connection, it would make the inevitable separation too painful. Instead they sat on the edge of his bed, arms interlocked and leaning slightly against each other, and talked. Whenever the conversation lagged and their attraction began to pull them a little too close, one or the other would snicker, or outright laugh at the absurdity of it all: two grown adults with an overinflated moral compass trying to stay chaste.

It worked, though, and knowing they could trust the other not to tip the balance, they eventually lay back on Gendrick's narrow bed. The forced closeness on the mattress was comfortable, if not more intimate than they would have chosen. Peyton's head nestled in the hollow of her friend's shoulder like a lover, and they talked some more.

She mostly spoke of other times, with Cannon and Benny and Ken. Everyone on the ship had become her family. Gendrick told her a few scattered details about the woman who'd broken his heart, and other uneventful moments in the cloister before that. With his free arm he reached for his Ep and showed his notes for *God's Vast Array*, wondering aloud how many people read it on a regular basis. He could ask System, but didn't want to know. She was going to check when she was back on the *Washington*. He made her promise not to tell him.

Their words slipped with exhaustion, drifting to the future and random tidbits of plans and dreams. Eventually, fully clothed, they fell asleep.

*   *   *

When they awoke, staring at the ceiling, both tried not to break this final, fragile moment of peace.

Gendrick finally turned his head and noted the time. "You need to go soon."

She turned herself to lay on his chest again and nodded. "I know. Do we have time for breakfast?"

He turned his head to kiss her thin curls of hair. Her fear of going *completely* grey had been unfounded, though the light streaks were more prominent than the black. "Actually, no, based on your schedule. Besides, they stopped serving breakfast an hour ago."

She lifted herself from his chest and gasped at the time displayed on his folded Ep. Early afternoon. "I have to go."

Slowly, she reached up to touch his face. She said again, "I have to go."

He smiled in reply, though it did not reach his eyes.

They were still wearing the same clothes as yesterday. Peyton had no other outfit so Gendrick didn't bother changing. They stopped at Mess to grab a quick bite of lunch, then he accompanied her, hand in hand, back to the landing site.

The shuttle was already ramping up its engines, the sound of its drive a low-running hum. Someone at the door pointed to Peyton and waved. She raised her finger in the universal *Be right there* gesture.

"Stay in touch, my friend," Gendrick said.

She kissed him quickly. "You, too. Promise?"

"Promise."

They stayed together for a heartbeat more, then Peyton Kay ran along the path and into the shuttle, never looking back. When the ship lifted off, he turned around and walked back to the compound.

Neither had said "I love you," in that final moment nor any time they'd been together. They didn't feel the need. It was there, and always would be. Gendrick walked back into his life on Toojay, imagining the shuttle far above him, gliding silently towards the massive ring of the *Washington* and delivering Peyton to *her* own life. They would be fine. What would happen, would happen. There were many more doors to pass through. With luck, or Grace, they would see each other again.

About the Author

Daniel G. Keohane is the Bram Stoker-nominated author of *Solomon's Grave*, *Margaret's Ark* and *Plague of Darkness*. His short fiction has been published in dozens of magazines and anthologies over the years, including *On Spec*, *Cemetery Dance*, *Borderlands 6*, *Apex Digest* and many more. You can visit Dan and keep up-to-date with prior and future work at www.dankeohane.com